Praise for

The School for German Brides

"In *The School for German Brides*, Aimie Runyan has penned the thoughtful and original story of an SS officer's bride and a young Jewish mother, whose lives collide in unexpected ways in World War II Germany. This is a moving and memorable tale of sisterhood, strength, and survival, which will resonate deeply with readers of historical fiction."

—Pam Jenoff, *New York Times* bestselling author of
The Woman with the Blue Star

"*The Stepford Wives* meets *The Alice Network* in *The School for German Brides*. Aimie Runyan brilliantly evokes the sinister, gilded world of 1930s Berlin—a world where young women are forcibly groomed to become perfect mates to men who hide their brutality behind toothy grins and perfectly pressed uniforms. It's also a world where secret acts of feminine resistance flare beneath the surface, along with heart-tugging compassion and daring bravery. You won't be able to put this one down."

—Kris Waldherr, author of *The Lost History of Dreams*
and *Unnatural Creatures*

"Equal parts fascinating and horrifying, *The School for German Brides* is a riveting tale of love, loss, and survival, not only of life but of the human spirit. Readers are dipped into a genteel world of young ladies, wooing suitors, satin dresses, and proper etiquette, but this world is a thin veneer for hatred and intolerance for anything less than perfect. Compelling from start to finish, this is Runyan's finest work yet."

—J'nell Ciesielski, author of *The Ice Swan*

"*The School for German Brides* is intriguing and often heartbreaking, yet the lovely connections between these women—and their determination to hold onto family and self in the midst of the darkest time—kept me cheering them on in the face of incredible danger. It's a touching story that fans of women's historical fiction won't want to miss."

—Libbie Grant, author of *The Prophet's Wife*

"A stunningly singular book experience, *The School for German Brides* is a study in the nuance and complexities afforded us from the privilege of historical hindsight. Runyan paints in the grey areas where women were victim not only to the rising atrocity of power and depravity but also to the social constructs of yet another time period demanding they bend to a patriarchal norm. Runyan's evocative and unsettling tale excels at exhuming the hauntingly real corner of elegant barbarism. A bravely examined and deeply important book destined to elevate the discourse central to historical fiction."

—Rachel McMillan, author of *The Mozart Code*

THE SCHOOL FOR
GERMAN
BRIDES

THE SCHOOL FOR
GERMAN BRIDES

A Novel of
WORLD WAR II

AIMIE K. RUNYAN

WILLIAM MORROW
An Imprint of HarperCollinsPublishers

P.S™ is a trademark of HarperCollins Publishers.

THE SCHOOL FOR GERMAN BRIDES Copyright © 2022 by Aimie K. Runyan. All rights reserved. Printed in the United States of America. No part of this book may be used or reproduced in any manner whatsoever without written permission except in the case of brief quotations embodied in critical articles and reviews. For information, address HarperCollins Publishers, 195 Broadway, New York, NY 10007.

HarperCollins books may be purchased for educational, business, or sales promotional use. For information, please email the Special Markets Department at SPsales@harpercollins.com.

FIRST EDITION

Designed by Diahann Sturge

Title page photo © Derek Adams/Arcangel.com

Library of Congress Cataloging-in-Publication Data has been applied for.

ISBN 978-0-06-309420-8
ISBN 978-0-06-323873-2 (international edition)

22 23 24 25 26   LSC   10 9 8 7 6 5 4 3 2 1

For Stephanie.
With gratitude for the years of friendship
we've shared, and those yet to come.
You are the sort of woman my heroines would
admire for your strength, courage, and grace.
I know I do.

THE SCHOOL FOR
GERMAN
BRIDES

CHAPTER ONE

Hanna

August 1938

*D*on't worry about the future. It will be no match for you." Mama's words echoed in my ears as the vast thickets of trees gave way to a forest of cement, stone, steel, and brick as the train entered Berlin and I left all trace of her behind. It was hard to heed her advice just then, but she'd never led me astray.

I pulled my worry stone from the secret pocket I had furtively sewn in my new brown traveling dress. I held the rock in the palm of my left hand and rubbed it with my right thumb.

Twelve years earlier, Mama took me to the bank of the stream that ran by our house. She took a stone from the bed of the stream and another from dry land beside it. *"Liebchen, do you see how the water has made the stone smooth? The water has washed over it until the rough edges had no choice but to yield. You carry the same power within you."* She tossed the smooth stone back into the stream and handed me the small hunk of pinkish-white quartz that she had picked up from the muddy bank. *"When your stomach begins to tighten, your shoulders begin to seize up, or when you can't seem to fit air in your lungs no matter how hard you try, take this in your hand, concentrate on rubbing the stone, and let it take your troubles away like the stream rushing over the stone. It won't happen in a day, but you'll learn to smooth the jagged edges of worry that pierce your gut."*

That Mama's suggestion worked didn't surprise me at all. Mama knew how to fix every ailment that ever presented itself to her. That she knew exactly how it felt when my nervousness overcame me was what stole my breath. Some of the children in Teisendorf said Mama was a witch. I wasn't sure they were entirely wrong. But if it were true, she had been a kind and benevolent one, so I didn't much care if she was.

I didn't care if she was a witch, a goblin, or Father Christmas. I wanted her back.

But she was gone, and I was on my way to live with Uncle Otto and Aunt Charlotte.

I also understood Papa's reasoning for sending me to Uncle Otto and Aunt Charlotte to finish up my last year of schooling. They lived in the city and would be able to give me opportunities that he living in a small town could not. I understood why Papa wanted to send Pieter and Helmut to boarding school. He was too busy with his work at the shop to give two young boys the attention they needed. But just because I could make sense of it didn't make it hurt any less.

Mama had been my monolith. Unmovable and constant like a star in the night sky to help me find my way. I kissed her cheek on the way out the door to school two weeks ago and came home to an ashen-faced Papa announcing that she'd been killed by a careless driver. There would be no funeral. No memorial. No viewing.

With all that was going on in the country, Papa thought such things were an extravagance. I got no chance to say goodbye.

And now it seemed the Führer would get the war he'd been begging for, and I was headed away from my beloved green hills right to the center of the hornet's nest. Exactly where I had no desire to be. The train groaned to a stop in the Berlin Hauptbahnhof and I wanted nothing more than to stay in my place until the train returned to Teisendorf. But I stood, shaking as I grabbed my valise, and walked down the aisle.

"My goodness, this young woman cannot be little Hannchen," Aunt Charlotte said as I stepped onto the platform. She was as tall and reedy as my father's brother was short and stocky. She had long, glistening honey-blond hair that was coiffed to perfection while he covered his bald pate with a brown porkpie hat. The contrast between them had always struck me, but it seemed even more distinct now as she greeted me with an ebullient smile and he with a silent scowl. She kissed my cheeks and Uncle Otto took my one suitcase wordlessly.

"I was expecting a girl, but your father sent us a young woman!" Aunt Charlotte breathed as she held me at arm's length to look at me. "Isn't that right, Otto?"

"Quite the grown lady," he agreed, his eyes scanning me from head to foot. For a fleeting moment I felt like a promising cow at a livestock auction. I rubbed my stone discreetly in my palm behind my back as he looked me over.

I hadn't seen my aunt and uncle in more than six years. I'd been barely approaching the threshold to adolescence then and more than likely had been covered from head to toe in dirt from scouring the woods for wild herbs and mushrooms to use in Mama's medicines. Today, I was scrubbed fresh, my hair neatly styled, and was wearing one of two new dresses Papa had bought for me so I'd have something decent to wear in the big city. I feared I looked like the poor country relation, and rumpled to boot, after the better part of the day cooped up on the train, but I hoped to at least meet with their approval on first impression.

"You must be exhausted, my dear. Let's get you home so you can rest and eat, shall we?"

I nodded my approval and they escorted me to Uncle Otto's shining gleaming black Mercedes-Benz. It probably cost twice what our home in Teisendorf did, and I was afraid I'd somehow spoil it just by looking at it. It was a half-hour ride from the center of town to the villa where they lived in the Grunewald district. I felt a frisson of relief as the trees became denser and the houses much larger and more dispersed. These mansions seemed too vast for single families. Manicured lawns and pristine gardens weren't the same as the rambling woods but at least there was the comfort that their neighborhood wasn't as cold and foreign as the heart of the city.

Uncle Otto pulled up the curved drive in front of the house where a uniformed man took his place behind the wheel, presumably to park the car in a garage. I looked up at the sprawling villa and wished I could vanish on the spot. I'd need breadcrumbs to find my way from my bedroom to the dining room if I didn't want to starve. I tried not to appear overawed but was sure I was failing in the attempt.

Inside, Aunt Charlotte showed me to an impressive suite of rooms down the corridor from their own. "This is where you will stay while you're with us," she said. The bedroom was the size of the kitchen and parlor of my parents' house combined and had deep crimson damask wallpaper and heavy oaken furniture with stark white linens to lighten the room. There was a sitting room with a freshly polished desk and an adjacent bathroom with a cavernous claw-footed tub as well. It was elegant and tasteful, and seemed more suited to an important guest and not a visiting niece.

"I really don't need anything this grand," I said. "Please don't go to any trouble on my account."

"Nonsense, darling. You're the daughter of the house as far as your uncle and I are concerned. We're determined to see your education finished and send you off into adulthood properly. It's the least we could do for your poor mother."

"You're very kind," I said, bowing my head, now worried I'd offended her somehow.

"You've had a few hard weeks, my dear, but I know you're the clever sort. You're going to make good use of your time here. And if you can enjoy yourself in the meantime, all the better. I've taken the liberty of buying you a few personal things. Nightgowns and such. I think I've done all right for size, but if there's anything amiss, just let me know and we'll set it right."

I opened my mouth to protest that I had plenty of clothes but thought it might be unkind. Aunt Charlotte was childless, after all, and perhaps had always longed for a daughter to dress and fuss over. Mama would want me to accept her generosity with grace, though it felt disloyal to get motherly affection from anyone else.

She left me to rest until supper. Though I was bone-weary, I knew that if I laid my head on the decadent goose-down pillows I'd not wake until morning unless roused with a bucket of ice water. The process of unpacking took only minutes, though I agonized over where to put my one photo of Mama. My belongings probably made the room look shabbier, but at least it felt somewhat more familiar. I looked in the drawers to find starched white nightgowns with the hem and cuffs trimmed in tatted lace and silky underthings finer than I'd ever owned. I opened my case and wondered why I'd bothered to pack. As I placed them away, I knew my own clothes would look grungy in comparison to all the lovely things Aunt Charlotte had procured. Silly as it was, I began to almost feel sorry for them and the months they would likely spend relegated to the back of the drawer.

From the bottom of my case, I removed the small mortar and pestle that had been Mama's, some of her dried herbs, and a few of the medicines she'd made before she died. I would never be as proficient as she was, but I knew enough to make a simple pain reliever or fever reducer. Papa had ordered me to throw out all her medicines, knowing that they weren't fully in line with the law, but I couldn't bear to throw away something that had been so dear to her. I'd hidden the most precious items where he wouldn't find them and then smuggled them here. I tucked them away in the deepest recesses of the bottom drawer of my armoire under a few of my old nightgowns. It would be foolish to risk tinkering with medicines, but it was a comfort to know they were there.

The room was so large that I took up very little space, which left me feeling unsheltered and exposed like a woodland creature in a vast meadow. I longed for the snug solitude of my attic room back at home. I should have been grateful for such a lovely space to call my own, but I didn't feel myself in such grand surroundings.

A half hour later a soft knocking at the door stirred me from my putterings about the room. I opened the door to find a young woman, perhaps five years older than myself. She had her dark hair pulled back in a tight knot at the nape of her neck and wore a black dress with an apron starched so severely, it didn't seem to need the wearer to lend it any shape.

"I am Mila, Miss Hanna. I came to help you prepare for dinner."

"Oh," I said, taking a step back as though she'd brandished a dagger. "Oh—do come in. I think I can manage, though."

"All the same, Herr Rombauer likes things done properly. It's best to do as he asks."

"It seems that's a prudent course of action in all things," I observed.

"You're a quick study, Miss Hanna. You'll do well here. If you like, I can offer you advice on things. How the house is run and such."

"That would be so wonderful," I said, wondering if it would be unseemly to hug her. Though she didn't seem like the type who would welcome such familiarity.

She moved with practiced efficiency as she began preparing my evening toilette. Given that I'd only brought the brown dress I'd traveled in and another in robin's-egg blue that was a degree or two nicer, selecting an outfit for the evening wasn't a time-consuming task. We opted for the blue dress and a simple milkmaid-style braid wrapped like a crown encircling my head with a few loose tendrils to soften the effect.

"There. You will please him just as you are," she declared. "Herr Rombauer does not believe in rouge or perfume and other such frivolities. He prefers a healthy, natural glow."

"Well then, I suppose it's just as well I don't have any of those . . . frivolities," I said, though I wasn't sure how I felt at the prospect. He seemed to have so many opinions, I was sure to come out on the wrong side of one of them before long. When Mila pronounced me suitable, I walked to the dining room, miraculously finding it without a map or trail guide.

"A quiet girl. This is good," I heard Aunt Charlotte say to Uncle Otto in a low voice as I approached the door. "She seems respectful. And pretty, too. As beautiful as poor Elke was."

"Better than I hoped for," Uncle Otto agreed. "She's come along well despite any . . . disadvantages. She still seems shy, but nothing like when she was a girl."

Disadvantages? Papa was hardly wealthy—being a shopkeeper in a small town would never earn more than a modest living—but I would hardly consider myself disadvantaged. Of course, there was much to learn from life in a big city like Berlin, but I hoped my education there would be of short duration.

"No, her quietness is an asset. There will be plenty who prefer her reserve. I don't consider it a fault now. It's tedious in a child, but more becoming in a young lady."

I waited another moment before entering so they wouldn't think I'd overheard their commentary. Though perhaps they thought I'd do well to hear it.

"Good evening, Aunt Charlotte and Uncle Otto," I said, not quite raising my eyes to theirs.

"I trust you're comfortably settled," Aunt Charlotte said, gesturing for me to take a seat to her left at the foot of the table.

"Extremely," I said. "Your home is lovely."

"I hope you will come to think of it as your own, my dear."

I couldn't think of a suitable reply, so I muttered a "thank you" as she passed the platter of roasted lamb. I took a small portion before passing it on to Uncle Otto.

"We don't stand for daintiness here, Hanna," Uncle Otto said. "Take a decent piece and eat well. Weak women only serve to look pretty on movie screens. Strong women are useful."

"Yes, Uncle."

Aunt Charlotte turned to me. "If you've recovered from your travels, tomorrow I'd like to take you into the city to get you the rest of the things you'll need for school. If you need anything altered, it will take some time these days."

"That's very kind of you, Aunt Charlotte, but I have clothes enough to suit, I'm sure."

"Nonsense, every girl needs some pretty new things when she starts a new school. Isn't that right, Otto?"

"Her economy is admirable, Charlotte," Uncle Otto said. "But if I've learned anything in twenty-odd years of marriage, it's that contradicting you can never arrive at any good outcome. You'll go into the city with your aunt tomorrow and have a jolly time of it, too." His words were kind, but they were a commandment.

"Yes, Uncle Otto."

"That's a good girl. Now tell me, how are things in Teisendorf these days? It's been ages since I've been back."

"Quiet as always," I said. "Farming and shopkeeping and such."

"Is there much fervor for the cause?"

"You mean Hitler's plans?" I asked. I'd heard Papa muttering over his newspaper about it and it was all anyone in town could speak of.

"What else could I mean, girl?" he asked with a chuckle.

"Oh, well, yes, Uncle. I would say there is."

More and more men were in uniform and the boys had all enthusiastically joined the Hitler Youth. The zeal for Hitler was rising steadily as farmers, laborers, and shopkeepers struggled to rebuild the country after the Great War and longed for the glory of the days before the defeat. They looked to him to deliver a prosperous new Germany, and more, to restore the pride of Germany. Mama was dubious of Hitler's motives, but was always careful never to speak against him, even in front of Papa and the boys. With me she was more open.

"That's good to hear. Mark my words, Hanna. He will set Germany on the path to glory again and your children will praise his name. I hope you see how worthy the cause is. Or will before long."

Aunt Charlotte beamed at him and then to me. Silently, I reached inside the secret pocket on the side of my dress and found my worry stone.

CHAPTER TWO

Tilde

August 1938

T*he law is not truth, Tilde. It's only a glimpse into the values of man at any given point in history. Don't confuse the laws of men with the word of God.*" My grandfather's words rang in my ears as though he'd spoken them yesterday. I thought of him more and more these days as the regime squeezed the life from our people like a boa with his prey. I'd longed to follow in my grandfather's footsteps, and my father's, but that dream was dead now.

"Good afternoon, Frau Fischer," I said, the tinkle of the shop bell stirring me from the courtroom back to the fabric shop. "I trust you're well."

She was a tall, imposing sort of woman with a pinched face that looked perpetually disappointed with everyone and everything. "Fine, fine, thank you. Have you got any more of that nice white calico with the pink flowers that I bought last month? I'd like to make a dress for my granddaughter."

"I don't believe we do, Frau Fischer. That particular floral was quite popular. But we've had a few new prints come in, several of which would do quite nicely for a young girl."

"Very well," she said with a sigh so deep one would think I'd asked her to swim the Atlantic to claim her fabric. I pulled several bolts of the floral calico that was becoming more and more popular as the magazines steered away from the high fashion of Paris and toward a more "wholesome" traditional aesthetic. Plain dresses with high necks made of sturdy fabrics. Sensible, feminine, and utterly boring. I held in a sigh of my own as I set the fabric on the cutting table for her to examine. A floral print was fine from time to time, but I'd seen enough in the past two years that I swore I'd never wear a dress made of the stuff again in my life. I personally favored the clean lines and bold colors that were gaining in popularity elsewhere. I longed for a tube of red lipstick like the American actresses wore, but Mama would have killed me for wearing something so daring.

I showed Frau Fischer a soft periwinkle blue with white poppies, a pretty lavender with yellow daisies, and a green with peonies. Nothing was quite right, but she settled for a pink-and-cream print with roses that was close enough to her original that she gave in. She selected some thread, buttons, and trim to complete the job.

"I'm sure she'll be the prettiest girl in her class," I said as I cut the yardage for her and wrapped the purchases into a parcel.

"Yes, yes," she said. "It's a shame she has to attend public school at all, but her father insists. So many undesirables these days. I taught my girls at home, and I'd hoped my daughter would do the same. But I suppose there's only so much a grandmother can do."

Undesirables. She didn't have to say what she meant. Foreigners. Gypsies. Jews like me. I forced a smile as I accepted her payment and let it sink into a scowl as she left.

I was a *Mischling*, of mixed blood. My mother was Jewish, and my father was a Gentile. He abandoned us as soon as it became clear that Jews would be facing persecution when the Nuremberg Laws were passed three years earlier. Papa insisted on a divorce, and my mother and I had no choice but to move from Papa's beautiful Charlottenburg town house to the ancient apartment above a yardage shop. Mama had come up with just enough savings to buy the apartment and the shop and had used her ingenuity and sweat to turn the rickety building into a home worth living in and a shop worth patronizing. We were left to run this modest fabric shop and scrape together our living selling yardage, doing odd tailoring jobs, and occasionally giving sewing lessons to girls from families who could afford such little luxuries. Thankfully Mama's skill with a needle soon became renowned in the neighborhood and she took the time to teach me what she knew. It had taken us three years, but we finally had a loyal clientele.

I switched the sign from OPEN to CLOSED and locked the door for a few moments so I could go check on Mama. Spending the bulk of her life upstairs took its toll and the more I looked in on her, the less isolated she felt.

"Ah, sweetheart. Look at how the dress for the Vogel woman is coming along. Good work, though I run the risk of being boastful by saying so."

A lovely day dress in dove-gray wool graced the mannequin. It only needed hemming and a few finishing touches, but even the uninitiated could see that this was the work of a master craftswoman.

"It's not boastful if it's true, Mama. It's gorgeous work. I couldn't in a million years finish a seam as beautifully as you do. It's far too lovely for the likes of that cow."

"You shouldn't say such things. Especially about a good client. Even if you're right." She snorted at her own jibe. Frau Vogel had been the most demanding woman we'd met in our years of running the shop. No matter what lengths we went to, there was no pleasing her.

Mama did most of the tailoring upstairs and I was the face of the shop. She looked "too Jewish" for the neighborhood and would be a liability for our safety and finances. My mother's absence was the main reason we were able to stay in business. Because of my father, my hair was a soft caramel brown and I had hazel-green eyes. Altman wasn't a surname that attracted suspicion as it was a "good German name." Mama and I didn't belong to a congregation, choosing to pray in the safety of our own home.

I denied my heritage to save my neck. And, necessary as it was, there wasn't a day I didn't hate myself for it.

"I'll make dresses like this for you to wear under your judge's robes," Mama said. She had never thought my hopes to enter the law were silly or unrealistic. My father always thought my passion for his profession was both quaint and flattering, but never a realistic prospect. My grandfather—my mother's father—was a different matter entirely. He'd made no attempts to hide the fact that the road to a legal career was a slog for a woman, but rather than discourage me from the pursuit, he endeavored to show me I was equal to it.

He'd been a preeminent lawyer and a senior partner in one of the largest law firms in Berlin. When my father entered the firm as a promising young attorney, it was my grandfather who mentored him, and later introduced him to his precious daughter. Mama claimed it was love at first sight, but that changed when having a Jewish wife and a *Mischling* daughter became tantamount to professional suicide. He claimed the divorce was just a formality, that he would be with us much the same as he had been, but he remarried to a blond, doe-eyed woman from the "right" family barely three months after we moved out.

Grandfather refused to work with him after that and had been applying pressure for the other partners to force Father out. But then the laws came down that disqualified Jews from practicing law and his battle was left unfinished. What was worse, Father was promoted to Grandfather's position as senior partner. It was too much for Grandfather's heart to bear and he died not six months after the goons made him pack his desk. I only wish he'd lived to see how well we'd rebounded after Father left us behind.

"I have another party dress for Frau Becker to start on, too. Emerald satin. It would look far better on you, but so would most everything."

I bent down and kissed Mama on the cheek. For all the ways my father had failed me, Mama was parent enough for both of them.

THERE WAS A small cluster of people waiting for me to reopen, some looking rather impatient, though none could have been waiting for more than a few minutes. I swallowed a sigh, for too many customers was far less grave a concern than the inverse. Three women pushed in right away. They were the ones armed with a lifetime of experience tending families and came with fabrics already in mind and a list of notions at the ready. They were rarely friendly but were efficient as customers, which was of far more importance.

After the gaggle of housewives cleared out, I noticed in their wake a tall, pale young man with a mane of curly black hair stuffed under a dark cap. While we did have the occasional male customer, he didn't seem like our usual confirmed bachelor sort who were determined to learn how to do a bit of mending. He looked vaguely frightened to be in such a feminine domain and seemed relieved when the other customers left.

"You're lucky you survived. They've been known to trample a man if the notion takes them," I said, replacing fabric on the shelves.

"Thank you for the warning. I'm glad I made it out with my life." He spoke with a slight accent, and I realized his mother was one of the Polish immigrants who frequented the store. She was a sweet woman, and I could see that same kindness in her son.

"It's your lucky day, it would seem. And a fortuitous day for buying fabric. What can I get for you?"

"Well, it's a gift for my sister. My mother wants to make her a dress for her birthday."

"Ah, is it a special birthday?" I asked.

"She'll be twelve," he said. He cast his eyes downward for a moment as though he were betraying a secret. It was possibly the most significant birthday his sister would have, and this was meant to be no ordinary dress. She was coming of age, according to our laws. If she had been born a boy, she would have become a bar mitzvah at thirteen and read from the Torah before the congregation. As she was a girl, she would take those first steps into adulthood a year earlier. There wouldn't be the same ceremonies, but she would most likely have a special meal and hearty congratulations from her congregation. And a new dress.

"Ah, becoming a young lady. Nothing too babyish, then."

"Exactly right," he said. "I thought sixteen was traditionally the significant birthday among—" He stopped himself short.

"It is, among the Gentiles," I said.

"But you're not?" he asked.

I shook my head.

"I thought I sensed something of the kindred in you," he said. "But you don't . . ."

"My father isn't," I said simply.

"Ah."

I turned my attention back to the task at hand. I found a pattern that I knew would suit her well. It was still demure enough for someone so young but acknowledged the transition to womanhood with subtle nips and tucks in the right places.

"That should do well," he said, not paying much attention to the details of the design. I stood, arms akimbo, considering a few fabric choices.

"Is she dark haired like you?" I asked.

"Yes," he said. "Though her skin is a bit fairer."

"She would do well in a nice plum color. Perhaps a nice rayon crepe? It's light but a bit more durable than chiffon. It should last her a few seasons at the least. If you're looking for something more durable, I'm sure we can find some nice calico."

"I think the rayon would do well," he said. "Since it's meant to be a treat."

"Very well," I said. Mama had stocked the rayon on a higher shelf because winter wools and tweeds would soon come in and most people had already done their summer sewing. I glanced up at the stacked bolts of fabric and decided climbing up the shelves like a monkey wouldn't be exactly professional. "I just need to get the stepladder."

"Let me help," he said. "I can reach it for you."

He came to my side, reached the fabric I pointed to, and placed it in my arms. I felt pinpricks of electricity on my skin when he looked at me, rooted in place. Never before had a man's proximity registered with me in such a way, and it was all I could do not to stammer like a fool.

"You smell like lilac and vanilla," he said, breathing deeply. He shook his head and took a step back. "I'm sorry, that was rude of me."

"N-no," I said. "It's fine." It was more than fine. I'd had a few crushes in school so I wasn't completely inexperienced with the sensation of flutters in the stomach and sweaty palms, but those seemed trifling compared to the sensation I felt now. I hadn't considered taking in his scent, but now that I did it was a pleasant combination of freshly laundered cotton and linseed oil. I supposed he worked as a carpenter or in some other line of work that required him to finish furniture.

I went about cutting the fabric and gathering the notions his mother would need to complete the dress. When I presented him with the parcel, he looked reluctant to leave.

"I hope your sister will enjoy the dress. Every girl needs something pretty to wear on such an important birthday." His eyes flashed upward and he smiled. She was important to him.

"It was a pleasure to meet you, Miss . . ."

"Altman," I said. "Mathilde Altman. Everyone calls me Tilde."

"I'm Samuel Eisenberg," he said. "I hope I have the chance to see you again soon."

I nodded and felt the warmth of a genuine smile spread across my face. The occasions for smiling were rare enough now that the sensation seemed foreign. He took my hand in his ever so briefly before he left, and at once all the evil that surrounded us seemed blissfully unimportant and distant, even though neither was true.

CHAPTER THREE

Hanna

September 1938

I felt as stiff as my starched collar as I entered the classroom and shielded myself with my notebook. The school Aunt Charlotte enrolled me in was one of the most elite in town. It was for girls only and housed in what once was a grand old home. These girls came from elite families—all party members, all wealthy. I knew I'd stick out like a cabbage in a rose garden and would have given anything to vanish. I didn't dare remove my worry stone from my skirt pocket but concentrated on feeling its weight at my right side. Just knowing it was there helped. I wondered how far behind the other girls I was in my schooling.

"Come in, girl. No one is going to eat you alive." The science teacher, Fräulein Meyer, was a tall mountain of a woman and looked like the sort who was perpetually annoyed. And from the looks on the faces of the other girls, I wasn't convinced she spoke the truth. There was one open seat toward the middle left of the room. I slid into it with silent thanks that I wasn't front and center where I would be never free from Fräulein Meyer's gaze. The other mercy was not being made to introduce myself to the class. She didn't seem the sort to abide by such rituals, and so far, it was her chief quality.

"Don't worry, Meyer is that way with everyone, you'll get used to it," the girl next to me whispered. She had lovely dark curls, striking gray eyes, and a sweet smile. I returned the smile gratefully, glad that there was one welcoming face in the room. The rest of the girls seemed as friendly as lionesses at feeding time.

I mouthed a thank-you as I removed my notebook from my bag and began taking careful notes. It was meant to be a biology class, which had piqued my interest because of Mama's past as a doctor. She'd been a prominent physician in Teisendorf before Hitler's decree barred women from practicing medicine outside of midwifery. She enjoyed delivering babies and helping women transition into motherhood, but her skills had stretched far beyond that one narrow focus. She still helped the people in town who could not afford a proper doctor, though she was gravely limited by not being able to prescribe medications or perform operations. She concocted her own medicines when she could but always knew when to send a patient for care with a licensed doctor who could do more for them within the scope of the law. Papa fought with her, worried that the authorities would punish us all if they learned what she was doing, but she never yielded to his pleas.

I wanted to learn about biology and chemistry to follow in her footsteps, but the information Fräulein Meyer was presenting would be of little use. It had more to do with the superiority of the German race than with human anatomy, cellular development, or anything that might be practical in the medical field. I was disappointed but hoped the course would move on once the Führer's point had been made.

"I'm Klara Schmidt," the girl next to me said as we packed up our things to head to the next class.

"Hanna Rombauer," I said, extending a hand, which she accepted enthusiastically.

"I thought you must be. I hear you're staying with Herr and Frau Rombauer?" Klara asked as we walked down the corridor to literature class.

"Yes, they're my aunt and uncle," I said.

"They're great friends with my parents. I was so glad to hear they had a girl my age coming to stay. I'll beg Mama and Papa to have you all to dinner soon."

"That would be lovely," I said, thinking that it would be less tedious than the dinner parties Aunt Charlotte had hinted they would be hosting soon.

"Will you be coming to the BDM meeting after school tomorrow?" she asked.

The Bund Deutscher Mädel was growing in popularity in Teisendorf. Mama had her doubts about the BDM, so she always found an excuse for me to avoid going to meetings. Emergencies at home and such. I'd once heard Mama and Papa disagreeing about this as well, but in most things, Papa had left the raising of me to Mama. Of course, things were different now, and I sensed Uncle Otto and Aunt Charlotte would be enthusiastic about my involvement. Given how kind they'd been, it seemed like a small gesture to please them.

"I suppose so, yes," I answered. "I'll have to ask my aunt and uncle first."

"Oh, they won't stop you. But of course, you should ask."

"I haven't been to one, so you'll have to be my guide if you don't mind."

"Glad to," she said. "Some of the girls are a bit snobbish, but it's really a fun time. No one will mind if you don't have a uniform by the next meeting. The Rombauers will get you one, I'm sure."

I nodded, having no doubt on that score. Aunt Charlotte had gone positively mad while we were in the department store a few days earlier and I felt like my wardrobe was now sufficient for four girls to have more than they needed.

Upon returning home from school, it was apparent that Aunt Charlotte hadn't finished with her mission, either. She greeted me at the door and whooshed me to my bedroom where a woman with a pinched face, a tape measure, and a pin cushion was waiting.

"We'll need three dinner dresses and one for dancing for now," Aunt Charlotte proclaimed. "Colorful, too."

"This young lady needs a pink gown. All pretty girls should have one," the seamstress declared.

"Then that's what she shall have," Aunt Charlotte said, then looked to me as if suddenly remembering that I was in the room. "You're very lucky, darling. Frau Himmel is a very busy woman and her services are much in demand of late. Her dresses are some of the finest in Berlin."

"That's wonderful," I said, trying to hold still as Frau Himmel draped fabrics over my shoulders, presumably to assess how the colors and textures would complement my complexion.

"How was school?" Aunt Charlotte asked, not looking at me, but rather watching the dressmaker's practiced movements.

"Not bad," I answered. "I made friends with a girl named Klara Schmidt. She says you're friends with her parents."

Her eyes flashed upward to me at last. "Indeed, we are. Oh, Hanna, I'm so pleased to hear that you're making friends with the right sort of people. Your uncle will be thrilled."

"She wants me to go to the BDM meeting tomorrow," I said. "Would that be all right?"

"I have your uniform all ready, dear. I was going to speak with you after dinner about it. Your uncle and I feel it's an important part of your education. That you've decided to go on your own is truly wonderful."

She pulled a plain blue skirt and white blouse from the closet along with a blue sort of necktie that matched the skirt, and a pair of sturdy shoes. "Not fashionable, but serviceable," she said. "And there are exercise clothes as well. They'll be putting you through your paces, make no mistake about that."

"Thank you," I said as she placed the garments back.

"I was hopeful that you would be smart and amenable to good training," Aunt Charlotte said. "But I see now that you need precious little of it. Your uncle and I will be here to make sure you stay true to the good instincts you've shown and secure a good place for yourself in the world."

I smiled, though I felt a cold prickling in my spine. Aunt Charlotte spoke of good instincts, but I wondered if Mama would fully agree.

"You don't seem pleased, darling," Aunt Charlotte said as I stood stock still for the dressmaker. "Don't you like the dresses?"

I looked at the length of pink taffeta draped over me and couldn't possibly envision the finished product. It was impossible to render any sort of opinion aside from that I'd never owned a formal dress in my life. But perhaps this was what a girl my age should want. Maybe Mama had missed a few important lessons along the way. I mustered a smile.

"Oh, Aunt Charlotte, you and Uncle Otto have been wonderful. So incredibly generous. It just feels like nothing is as it was."

"Nor is it, my poor dear," she said. "But as sad as it is, it's up to you either to accept it or to wallow in it. I know which one I'd choose."

"You're right, Aunt Charlotte. I'll try."

"Like I said, you're a smart girl. And a pretty one. The future holds nothing but promise for you."

Her words sounded so much like Mama's that I felt the clenching in my stomach loosen ever so slightly. She wasn't Mama, but she was trying to fill her shoes the best she could.

THE SUN WAS relentless as we hiked in the woods outside of Berlin, but I welcomed the rays, feeling nourished by them after too many hours trapped in the classroom or under Aunt Charlotte's watchful eye. While I was able to keep pace, Klara was drenched from the exertion and most of the other girls were faring worse than she, so unused to the heat they all were. A few had fallen behind and our group leaders were lecturing them sternly. Saturdays were reserved for extended outdoor activities with the BDM, each outing meant to test our stamina and fortitude.

"Have some of my water," I said, offering Klara my canteen. She accepted it gratefully.

"We've hiked plenty of times before, but nothing like this," she panted.

"It's the heat. They should have us going slower," I said. "And they should have told everyone to bring water."

"They want to toughen us up," she said, shrugging her shoulders as she huffed.

"Giving us all sunstroke won't make us stronger," I said. "They ought to know better."

"Shhhh," she warned. "If they catch you saying things like that, you'll have trouble."

"I can't speak the truth?" I asked. "Are they so afraid to hear it?"

Klara gave me a warning look that betrayed the answer.

"Why aren't you struggling?" she asked. "As much as I like you, I think I hate you a bit right now."

She shot me a martyred look and I laughed, truly laughed, for the first time in weeks. "I spent most of my waking hours walking the hills with my mother when I wasn't in school. She was quite an outdoorswoman. All the meandering gave me stamina."

I stopped under a particularly fine spruce tree, took out my pocketknife, and used it to take a cutting from a low-hanging branch. I placed the cutting in my pack and continued on before people noticed we'd stopped.

"What's that for?" Klara asked.

"Spruce can be dead useful if you infuse it into an oil. You can use it in all sorts of medicine from a cough syrup to helping with rheumatism. Mama showed me how."

"I have to tell you, I heard your aunt tell my parents that your mother was a bit . . . eccentric," she said slowly, looking over to see how I reacted.

"I can see why some would think so," I said. "She cared a lot about treating people. It broke her heart when they told her she couldn't be a doctor."

"She must have been wonderful," Klara said, wrapping an arm around my shoulder. I felt my throat constrict and my eyes sting. In the six weeks since Mama died, no one had made that simple gesture. Not Papa. Not my brothers. Not Aunt Charlotte or Uncle Otto. I took a deep breath to quell my tears. Something told me that the organizers of the hike wouldn't take too kindly to such displays.

"She really was," I said, once I'd mastered myself. "She knew people. She understood them. Not just what made them ill, but what made them well. What made them whole. If I am half the woman she was, I'll be pleased with how I spent my life."

"Well, she did a good deed by getting you outside so much. It's given you an advantage over the rest of us who were trapped inside with knitting and needlework."

"I'm awful at those things," I admitted. "I'll have my reckoning when we start working on housewifely stuff."

"Bah, you'll have an easier time learning how to darn socks than any of us will keeping up with the group leaders on these hikes. Though it's better than all the 'housewifely stuff,' as you put it." She glanced around again, checking to see if any ears had been listening.

"You don't like it?" I asked.

"They're obsessed with us being good mothers and we're not even fully grown yet," she admitted. "Never breathe a word that I said this, but their constant harping on the subject gets tedious."

"I'm sure it does," I agreed. "So why do you come?"

"My parents want me to. And it's not like any of us can join up with other groups."

It was true. Hitler's edicts had even reached as far as football clubs and choirs. No youth groups were permitted beyond those created by the party.

"We have time to worry about families and the like, don't we? We're not even out of school."

"Ah, if they catch us while we're young we won't get too enchanted with our independence. Not me. If I got to design clothes for one of the big houses in Paris, there wouldn't be a man alive who could get me down the aisle. Who'd want to leave a posh job in a big city to go change diapers?"

I laughed. "You paint a rosy picture."

"I think that's it, though. They want us making babies before we know what we're missing out on."

"I don't want to settle down right away, either. I'd like to see the world and accomplish a few things first. Establish a career," I said. I always pictured a small brood of children, but when I was closer to thirty than twenty. "My mother was able to manage a career and a family rather admirably."

"I wouldn't talk too much about your aspirations in front of anyone else," she said. "Not even your aunt and uncle. Perhaps especially not them."

I glanced over at her. "You're probably right," I said.

She knew my aunt and uncle better than I did, and I knew I'd be a fool not to heed her warning.

"I hope you don't think I'm being too forward," she said. "I just want you to feel welcome here."

"You've been nothing but kind, Klara. I appreciate your advice."

"If that's true, then promise to be my hiking buddy from now on. You make me look good."

I laughed again. "You have a deal."

We arrived back at the school, drenched in sweat and many looking severely dehydrated. It took everything in me not to tell the group leaders they were being completely irresponsible. Mama would have done, but I wasn't as brave as she was.

"Hanna Rombauer, I'd like to speak with you," one of the group leaders called out before we dispersed to go home.

I walked over to where the group leaders were circled up. They watched me as I approached.

"You were quite impressive out there today," one said by way of greeting.

"Thank you," I said. I maintained eye contact, though I wanted to bow my head. It was a habit of mine from childhood that Papa had despised and insisted that I correct.

"If you show such skill in other areas, there will be a lot of opportunity for you to move up in the BDM. We'll be keeping a close eye on you."

"I-I'll do my best," I said, and scurried back over to Klara to walk home. I thought of my helplessness when it came to knitting and sincerely hoped they weren't counting on me.

"I told you that you make me look good," Klara said with a laugh when I related what they said on the way home. "Don't be surprised if the girls are friendlier on Monday. These things get around."

"And more of the girls will want to be friends because I've impressed the BDM leaders on a hike?"

"Yes. And that's why they've been standoffish. They didn't want to risk looking friendly before they knew what you were made of."

"That seems rather calculating, doesn't it?" I wasn't used to the social machinations of girls. I saw them from afar in Teisendorf, but preferred my mother's company to their petty squabbles. Papa said I was too aloof, but Mama said it made me serious. From her there rarely was higher praise.

"It's just the way things are nowadays. It doesn't do to make friends with the wrong sort."

"No, I suppose you're right," I said. Uncle Otto made muttering sounds every morning as he read the papers at breakfast. There were political stirrings, but I didn't dare inquire what made him upset. "Why did you take a risk, then?"

"You were too interesting not to take a chance," she said. "Mother gone, tragic orphan and all that. I'm a sucker for a sob story."

I punched her arm playfully, but was glad she'd taken the risk.

Klara was right about news traveling quickly. By the time I reached home, the group leaders had called Aunt Charlotte. She had the cook prepare a magnificent spread for lunch that was served as soon as I washed up and changed into one of my new dresses.

"Eat well, darling. You've had a vigorous morning. We'll make this our little tradition after such strenuous exercise on Saturday mornings, shall we? You'll have to tell me all your favorite things so that Cook can put them on rotation."

"Quite right. Such good work should be rewarded," Uncle Otto proclaimed. "Charlotte, make sure the girl has a pretty necklace to wear. Nothing gaudy, mind. Something dainty and feminine."

"I know just the thing," Aunt Charlotte said. "I saw something lovely in the window downtown just last week that will suit our Hanna perfectly."

"Just the ticket. See to it, dear," Uncle Otto said to Aunt Charlotte. He then turned to me. "We're having a dinner here next Wednesday and I want you at your best."

"Yes, Uncle Otto."

"I expect nothing less than perfection, my dear. In looks, manner, and deed. Sparkling conversation, too, if you can manage it. Respectful and attentive silence if you cannot. Follow your aunt's directives precisely and observe her in society and you'll do well."

Aunt Charlotte couldn't hide a small, prideful smile at Uncle Otto's praise. He wasn't lavish with compliments, and his vote of confidence was as close to a glowing endorsement as she would ever get from him. I wondered how it was for her, such a vivacious person living with such a stern man.

I retired to my room and was grateful when Mila finished our evening ritual of helping me change for the night and brushing out my hair. She was a nice enough woman, but it was a night for quiet.

I took out Mama's mortar and pestle and pulled out the spruce cutting from that morning. I thought of infusing it in oil for medicines, but I knew I'd face questions if anyone found it. Instead, I set the branch aside, took out one of my old petticoats and a needle and thread, cut a few squares of fabric, and sewed little pouches. I then put the spruce needles in the mortar and swirled the pestle about until they released their scent. I worked slowly and methodically, like Mama had done, careful to treat the plant with respect as she taught me. I took the thick, sticky paste from the mortar and sealed it in the pouches, which I then placed in each of my drawers.

If I couldn't have home, at least I could have its wholesome scent and remember.

CHAPTER FOUR

Tilde

September 1938

Y ou!" A deep voice boomed behind me. "Where are you going?"

I froze as churning, molten bile rose from my gut to my throat.

*Stand still. Be polite. Answer their questions as briefly as you can. Do
not smile, but do not scowl.*

Mama's rules were as ingrained as scripture in my brain. We did
our best to blend in, but we couldn't afford to just "do our best."
We had to be flawless if we wanted to remain safe.

The booming voice belonged to an appropriately hulking man
in a brown shirt and black gleaming jackboots. One of *them*.

I recalled all too clearly my first encounter with these thugs who
patrolled the streets. I was twelve. I was wearing a Star of David
necklace. It glinted in the light at just the wrong moment and caught
the eye of one of the patrolmen.

"What is a dirty little Jew girl doing in this neighborhood?" he
sneered.

"I live here, sir." I remembered Mama's edict to be polite. One could never go overboard with politeness.

"Doubtful," he said, and his massive hand came down across my cheek. I thought certainly the bone had cracked from the blow. That I'd bear a black eye for weeks—months—was a certainty.

"I swear, sir."

"Don't lie to me, little bitch." He slapped me again. There was a high-pitched whistle perhaps a block north and he turned his head. His entire body was tensed, torn between teaching me a lesson and going to investigate the blow of the whistle, a signal from one of his comrades in arms. In a moment he took off, running faster than I thought possible for a man of his size. I lost no time and ran in the opposite direction. I never wore the necklace again. Mama wept for two days over the incident. Papa told her not to overreact to an overeager policeman trying to do his job.

Now, I waited for the crushing grip of gloved hands on my shoulder, but the uniformed man passed me and began chasing after a man in front of me who broke into a dead run when he heard the unmistakable *thud-thud-thud* of boots against pavement. The pair continued their flight and pursuit around the corner, and it was all I could do not to collapse on the sidewalk in relief.

And I hated myself for it.

Another man—a Jewish man—was being chased down and there was nothing I could do about it. Even if I tried, it would just mean two of us would lose our freedom instead of one.

I could do nothing but offer a prayer of thanksgiving for my own safety and continue on to Klara's house. In all things, I tried to emulate the way the Gentiles acted. The self-assured way of walking and talking that demonstrated that there wasn't a single place they didn't belong. God, how I envied that confidence. What a joy it must be to feel well and truly welcomed in a place.

Klara's home was large and decorated like a French chateau. Mini-Versailles, Klara called it. She always stood out there, a modern thing in a home that tried so desperately to cling to past grandeur. Of all the girls I taught to sew, Klara was the cleverest and most talented. In a better world, we might have been friends, but I didn't dare indulge in that level of intimacy with anyone besides my mother. People couldn't be trusted. Most especially the daughters of up-and-coming party members, no matter how approachable and friendly she seemed. It just served to make her all the more dangerous.

"Assume every question is a trap. Assume they suspect the truth about your identity and are just looking for enough proof to report you."

I knocked at Klara's door and, as was the weekly custom, I was shown to the back room where Klara's mother had fashioned a little studio for her.

"I finished the blouse," she greeted me, barely looking up from the machine where she worked hemming a skirt and gesturing to the plain white silk blouse. "I thought you could help me with a dress for dinner next week."

"Well, let's see," I said, examining the blouse that hung on a dress form. White silk blouses were a true test of a tailor's skill. There was no hiding a puckered seam with a bold print or relying on forgiving fabric for poor technique. Many of my students balked at this test, but she was one of the precious few who understood the challenge and the point of the exercise. Klara's blouse didn't have much in the way of style, but the lines were true, and her technical skill was without fault. We'd worked on pleats, darts, buttons, and all manner of rules for choosing fabrics for a specific pattern. What Klara needed was to learn to work without one.

"Yes, I think you're ready," I assessed. "What did you have in mind?"

"Nothing too complicated just yet," she said, trimming the thread from the finished hem and placing the skirt with the blouse on the dress form. The navy blue of the skirt made the white look all the crisper and more polished. She had an eye for these things, there was no denying it. She showed me a pattern for a fairly standard dinner dress. Long skirt with a draped V neckline. Fashionable, but not flashy. Respectable, but not dowdy.

"A good choice," I said. "What did you have in mind for the fabric?"

"I have some silk Father bought when he went to Paris on business," she said, opening one of the drawers of the massive table we used for cutting and pinning. She pulled out a length of lavender silk as lovely as I'd ever seen. Finer than anything we managed to source for our shop. The color would make her complexion look even more brilliant and would be a lovely contrast with her dark hair.

"Gorgeous fabric, but it will be a test of your skills," I said, running a finger along the edge. Smoother than any silk I'd ever touched. It was enchanting stuff to work with. Durable as iron but easy to fray and snag. Remarkably strong, yet so easy to spoil. "But you showed your mettle with the blouse."

"I thought so," she said, her chin jutting forward a bit. She was never one for false modesty and I liked that in her.

"Are you making the dress for an occasion?" I asked. She pulled the thin pattern tissue from the envelope and began to cut it to size.

"An important dinner," she replied. "They're hoping Friedrich will finally propose. It's seemed like he's been on the verge for weeks now but hasn't brought himself to ask. Mama thinks a dashing new dress will help, though I'm convinced he's not one to notice such things."

"The silk wasn't just a father's gift to his beloved daughter?" I asked, smoothing out the fabric for her to cut when she finished the pattern.

"Ha," she said, a little more rancor in her voice than I was accustomed to. "In Papa's world, there's no such thing as gifts. Only investments. The length of fabric you see is an investment in me securing the good Captain Schroeder in a walk down the aisle and nothing else."

"I'm sure he just wants what's best for you," I said. *Captain. Military. One of the jackbooted goons patrolling the city. No. More clout than that if Klara Schmidt's parents want him for her. Worse.*

I knew now that this house was a dangerous one. Each lesson I offered Klara was a risk not only to myself, but to my mother. But we needed the money and there were few options for me. I couldn't get so much as a secretarial job without having to prove ancestry. I'd need to find other students, but I was beginning to fear that fewer and fewer families were "safe" for girls like me.

Klara worked in silence for more than an hour. I only had to interject very occasionally with a pointer or suggestion. I'd be able to tell her mother, in truth, that she'd soon be beyond my range of ability. More to the point, if she married this officer, Klara would be able to buy tailored clothes and would largely give up sewing altogether. She'd probably mend her husband's things to give the appearance of being a doting wife, but she wouldn't *have* to. People would think the gesture all the sweeter because it wouldn't be required of her. I saw her hands move expertly, and thought it was a shame that her skills would be wasted.

I was glad she needed little of my help, for I had no great wish to help her create a gown for wooing German thugs. I could see rough, uncaring hands marring the delicate fabric as they danced after supper. I could see appraising eyes sizing up a woman like a brood mare, unaffected by her intellect or spirit. I wanted no part of it.

I thought of Samuel from the shop. His kind brown eyes that had the haunted spark of one who had seen too much in too few years. They would never seek to reduce a woman to her simplest functions. I thought of the brush of the rough skin of his fingertips against the back of my hand. They were made rough by honest work. Not by strong-arming the country into submission. So much could be learned from one sweet-natured man. I grieved for the world that could be if more people followed his example of decency and integrity.

But I watched attentively as Klara worked on the lavender gown, precisely because the world was not yet that place.

"Tilde, I need you to go to the registry office this afternoon. We'll close the shop. Everyone is scrambling for help these days, no one will think anything of it."

My pale skin, light brown hair, and hazel-green eyes meant that I stood a chance of being heard when we asked for emigration visas. They were becoming harder and harder to obtain and Mama lamented more than once that she hadn't decided to leave when Hitler began his ascent to power. Of course, he'd won office by blaming the Jews for all the ills of the country, but so many clung to the idea that it was idle campaign bluster to get himself elected. And at first they felt vindicated. Hitler didn't seize our businesses overnight. He didn't take away our travel papers the day he took office. He issued one small indignity at a time, like placing a series of small pebbles on our chests as we lay prone. Each pebble was endurable, but as the number increased week by week, we recognized that our people were going to be crushed to death under the weight of them.

"Again, Mama? Do you think the result will be any different?"

"Possibly not, but we have to try," she said, heaving a sigh as she dried a plate from breakfast. "They got two more families last night."

"How do you know this, Mama?" I asked.

"I have my ways. It's just as well you don't know. Though if anything happens to me, I may regret not telling you."

"Nothing is going to happen to you, Mama."

"Don't speak a wish as if it were a certainty," she chided. "It's bad enough in good times and downright foolhardy now. I've been told we have a chance to get a visa to go to America if we're lucky enough. We just need an affidavit from your great-uncle. If we can get the application started, we'll be ahead when his forms come back."

It was my mother's turn for relentless optimism. She had been trying for the past eighteen months to persuade her uncle to vouch for us. We'd not heard a whisper of a reply. Uncle Ezra had to be in his eighties by now—well entrenched in them. We had an address for him in Brooklyn, but it was ten years old. Mama couldn't accept the likely reality that he was dead, and perhaps had been for years. No one else in his family had ever laid eyes on us; no one else would be able to sponsor us. But he was Mama's best lead, and she was clinging to it as fiercely as a life preserver in the North Atlantic. And at this point, she'd probably be willing to float to America on that life preserver if it got her out of Germany.

She had more plans in her back pocket if this failed. England. Palestine. Even Singapore. Each seemed more unlikely than the last, but she was determined. She wrote dozens of letters, made calls, and filled out more bureaucratic forms than I ever thought possible. When she wasn't doing that she was learning languages, studying up on local customs, anything she could to prepare herself for a complete uprooting.

I promised I would go, but I knew the outcome would be the same. More paperwork.

More vague answers. More disappointment. She held steadfast to her hope, though, and smiled as she sat down with the English textbooks that she'd been studying faithfully for two years. She worked hard, but still wasn't really proficient in the language. She preferred her native German and peppered it generously through-out her attempts at English. I helped her when I could, but it was a rare evening when I had the energy after dinner to do anything but collapse in bed with one of my grandfather's old legal texts.

I knew the trip would lead to nothing, but I had to try, for Mama's sake.

Later that afternoon as I crossed town to the registry office, on foot because public transport might have caused problems, anger rose in my chest. People milled about as though nothing was different. They shopped and gossiped and dined with friends as though their neighbors weren't living in fear. If they had acquaintances among those who were rounded up, it was unfortunate, of course. But by and large, it seemed people thought the new edicts were in the best interest of the country.

There was a line of women at the registry office. I knew their stories all had to be in the same vein as ours: Wives who wanted their husbands released from prison. Mothers who wanted papers to emigrate with their children. Daughters seeking the whereabouts of their parents.

We had to be the voice of our men because the government didn't fear us as much as they did our male counterparts. They didn't think we were able to organize and rebel against the system the way our men did. And in one respect, they were right. We didn't try to take the system head-on. We tried to circumvent it by getting passage to any place that would have us. We let them think we were lesser, so that we could escape with our lives.

"Name?" an old man with a permanent frown asked as I finally reached the front of the line.

"Altman, Mathilde," I replied automatically. He looked up from the form he'd begun to fill out. It wasn't an overtly Jewish name, but it didn't exclude the possibility. He paused at my face. I launched into my well-rehearsed request for an application for visas for myself and my mother. I'd made it often enough I ought to have had it memorized.

"And why is it your family wishes to leave Germany?" he asked. This question was a trap, and he was well aware of it.

"We have family in America. Beloved family that we've been

separated from for too long. My mother has been despondent without them since her mother passed a few years back and it seems the only thing that might restore her spirits."

"I see," he said, though his tone didn't indicate any real understanding. "And do you have the affidavit?"

"It's coming in due course. You know how these things are. They always take longer than one expects. The American authorities aren't as efficient as ours here," I added for good measure.

"Quite right," he agreed. "It's a wonder anyone would want to live in such a lawless place."

Another test.

"I agree with you, sir, but I cannot refuse my mother anything. Her happiness must come before my own."

"She's lucky to have such a dutiful daughter. There are many girls of your age who could stand to take a page from your book."

"I'm flattered you think so, sir."

"We'll get your application started, but these things take time. No promises of a successful outcome, of course, but I'll do what I can to make sure your application is seen by the right people."

"Thank you, sir," I said, daring to offer him the smallest of smiles. It was the closest thing we'd had to progress in a long while. It would be foolish to cling to it like a certainty, but I would at least enjoy the fleeting sensation of hope.

CHAPTER FIVE

Hanna

October 1938

I t fits perfectly," Aunt Charlotte breathed. "You're a vision, my dear."

"It's lovely," Klara agreed. She was already dressed for the evening in a lavender silk dress several degrees more fashionable than my own. "You'll be a sensation tonight."

Frau Himmel bustled about making sure the fabric on my new dinner dress lay properly against my curves. It was a pink confection of a thing, just as she promised. Flowing layers of chiffon with a modest sweetheart neckline. It made my skin look rosy and healthy and caught the spark in the blue of my eyes. Frau Himmel wasn't a particularly friendly woman, but she did know her trade.

When the dressmaker was satisfied, Aunt Charlotte summoned Mila to do my hair. While we waited for the maid to emerge from the kitchens, Aunt Charlotte produced a little velvet box in which a small pearl pendant on a gold chain was nestled.

"Delicate and feminine," she pronounced when she clasped it around my neck "The perfect finishing touch."

She kissed my cheek, and I returned the gesture, reaching my hand to my neck to touch the necklace as I looked in the mirror. I had to admit, I felt pretty. I'd never paid my looks too much heed, as Mama never had time for such trivial things, but there as Mila put my hair into an elegant braid across the top of my head and curls down my back, I felt worth looking at. Aunt Charlotte permitted the barest hint of rouge on my cheeks and lips for the occasion, though Uncle Otto had forbidden the use of perfume, deeming it "too French" for a respectable German girl.

Aunt Charlotte went on to prepare for the arrival of the guests, leaving Klara and me behind for a few minutes before we'd be expected to join them.

Klara took her turn going over my dress and hair. "You look wonderful," she said again. "You'll have a throng of young men after you before the evening is through."

"You're far too optimistic," I said. "I'm an awkward country girl who wants nothing more than to hide away with her book for the night."

"Just try to relax and act like none of it matters. The less you care, the better it will be."

I nodded at the sage advice. "What about you? You must have an entourage of admirers by now."

"Oh, perhaps. But I've set my sights on one. Mother and Father are eager that he'll propose soon. He's a promising match."

"He's a fool if he doesn't sweep you off your feet," I said. "You look beautiful tonight, and that's not even toward the top of the reasons why he'd be lucky to have you."

She kissed my cheek and we walked downstairs side by side. I longed for the worry stone I'd left hidden in a drawer upstairs. I remembered its cool smooth surface, worn down by my fingers over the past twelve years. I pictured my fingers like water slowly polishing the stone one worry at a time. I found myself able to take a proper breath and walk forward. Klara was whisked away by her parents almost as soon as we reached the bottom of the stairs, and Uncle Otto and Aunt Charlotte swooped down on me.

"There she is," Uncle Otto said, a rare smile gracing his lips. "Friedrich Schroeder, I want you to meet my niece, Hanna. Hanna, may I introduce Friedrich Schroeder, captain in the Führer's Schutzstaffel."

"Pleased to meet you, Fräulein Rombauer," he said with a formal bow. He wore the black uniform of the SS, pristine from the crisp shoulders to the gleaming boots. He was a good-looking man, perhaps thirty-five years old, tall and muscled like the men in the recruitment posters. He embodied the blond-haired and blue-eyed look that the party seemed to prize.

"Likewise, Hauptsturmführer Schroeder." I returned his bow with a shallow curtsey. Aunt Charlotte winked her approval when the captain wasn't looking. There were several other couples, both closer to Uncle Otto and Aunt Charlotte's age. Most men wore more decorations on their chests than the captain, but they seemed to treat him with deference.

The dinner was far beyond anything I'd ever experienced, even during the most lavish holiday meals of my childhood. Goose, fish, braised carrots, whipped potatoes, sautéed green beans in butter sauce, several kinds of bread. The butler stood in the corner of the room, prepared to fill any glass that looked scant with one of Uncle

Otto's best wines. Though I was seventeen, Mama had never allowed me to drink, so I only took sips to look polite. The red liquid
was bitter on my tongue, but the others seemed to enjoy it heartily.
Klara was at the opposite end of the table, which I lamented. She
shot me a look that implied the same.

"You are enjoying your time with your aunt and uncle, Fräulein
Rombauer?" the captain asked as he sipped from his glass. He was
seated directly across from me, and from the glint in Aunt Charlotte's eye, I knew it wasn't a mistake. In contrast to Aunt Charlotte,
Klara's mother shot me withering looks, though I couldn't imagine
what my offense had been.

"Very much so, Captain Schroeder," I said. "They are very welcoming."

"Who could be otherwise when such a sweet little bird has come
to roost?" Aunt Charlotte purred.

"It pleases me to see families working together in trying times,"
the captain responded. "It reinforces in our youth a spirit of community that will build strong character and further the cause."

"Hear, hear," one of the older men said, raising his glass. The
rest of the table followed suit.

The remainder of the dinner discussion revolved around the
growing troubles in the east and the Führer's plans. There was
much excitement over the agreement Hitler had signed with Britain
and France that gave Germany control over the Sudetenland. The
crux of the agreement was that Hitler wouldn't be able to invade
any other countries in exchange for this concession, but I couldn't
imagine him keeping his word. Hitler's zeal for Lebensraum seemed
insatiable. I tried to follow along but found their fervor tedious. I
didn't turn too much attention to the array of food, not wanting to

appear piggish, so I tried to count the number of times the intricate wallpaper pattern repeated on the wall behind Captain Schroeder's chair. I was able to give the appearance of paying rapt attention but was actually staring off behind his right ear.

"I'm glad you agree, Fräulein Rombauer," Captain Schroeder said after a while. I thought the ruse would prove more effective if I occasionally nodded in agreement when someone was speaking particularly forcefully.

"Of course," I said, wondering what I'd agreed with.

"It's wonderful to see young women taking an interest in political matters, within reason," he said, offering a smile.

"Yes, an interest is a positive thing, but involvement is another," Uncle Otto said. "The Führer has time and time again spoken on the importance of women staying home and raising strong families. We need our young women to escape the monotony of office work and return home."

"Quite right," Captain Schroeder said with a nod to Uncle Otto. "Beyond politics, what subjects interest you, Fräulein?"

"Science," I replied. "Biology and medicine mostly."

Uncle Otto's face drained.

"Serious subjects for a young woman," the captain said. "How very surprising."

I glanced over at the head of the table. Uncle Otto's face had grown somber and his color high. I was on dangerous ground and had to keep the appearance of ambition in check or I'd risk embarrassing him. "Oh, I think it's rather useful for a woman to have some knowledge of such things," I said, deliberately taking my voice a few notes higher than usual. "It's easier to treat little maladies at home than to keep running children to the doctor for every little sniffle, isn't it? Our medical personnel seem stretched so thin these days." I wanted to insert a jab about how removing women and Jews from the practice of medicine had depleted the field, but such a comment would see me dragged to my room by the hair by Uncle Otto himself. I couldn't dare, but the temptation was sweet as honeyed wine on my tongue.

"How very clever," Captain Schroeder said. Aunt Charlotte's resultant smile illuminated the room.

"Perhaps we can adjourn to the hall for some music?" Aunt Charlotte suggested. She hadn't gone to the extravagance of hiring a band for an intimate dinner but had one of the maids poised by a large phonograph machine and a stack of records.

"Dance with me, Fräulein?" the captain asked, extending a hand as a waltz began to soar above the room.

I accepted his hand and allowed him to take me in his arms. He moved gracefully, leading me deftly across the floor in the familiar *one-two-three, one-two-three* rhythm I'd learned in my living room as Mama instructed me and my brothers. His hand felt too warm at my waist and his carriage was rigid, but he was skilled enough.

"You dance beautifully," he said, his tone just above a whisper.

"You're kind," I said, casting my eyes downward.

"I speak as I find," he said. "And I've rarely met a girl as lovely as you."

I could find no words that felt equal to a response, so I simply followed his lead in first one dance, then three others. By the time the group began to disperse, I was grateful for the reprieve. Captain Schroeder was the last to depart, leaving a lingering kiss on my hand as he bowed his farewell. Klara had gone already, and I was sorry to have missed her. I wondered why she hadn't taken a moment to say goodbye, and hoped it was merely because her father was impatient for the comfort of his bed or her mother had come down with a slight headache.

"Well done, my dear. You charmed the captain," Aunt Charlotte said as the staff scurried to erase the signs that we'd had visitors.

"I don't see how I was very charming," I said. "I barely spoke two words together."

"You settled upon it from the first, my dear. Most men don't care for chatty women," Uncle Otto pontificated as he walked over to the sideboard to pour himself a measure of brandy.

"You were demure and feminine," Aunt Charlotte said. "And he was besotted. I can see it as plain as the nose on your lovely face."

"He's rather too old to be interested in me, isn't he?" I asked.

"Stuff and nonsense. Age doesn't matter. He's a good solid young man with one of the most promising futures in the SS. If he takes an interest in you, you're a lucky girl." Uncle Otto took a large draught from his glass. "We'll have him over again soon so you can continue to get acquainted."

I opened my mouth to protest. I wanted to tell him I had no interest in pursuing a man for many years yet. Mama had married at nineteen and always said that her contentedness in marriage was the happiest accident of her life. All the same, contradicting Uncle Otto would achieve nothing.

"I know it seems like you have your whole life in front of you yet, but time marches more quickly than you realize," Aunt Charlotte said. "A smart girl knows to snap up an opportunity when she has the chance. And you're a smart girl, aren't you?"

"I hope so, Aunt Charlotte."

"So do I, my dear. Now hurry along to bed. You did marvelously tonight, dear. I'm going to go into town to get you a bracelet to match the necklace. You earned it."

"YOUR CLOTHES ARE divine," Klara breathed as she inspected each of the dresses that had been delivered from Frau Himmel. It was a rainbow of chiffon, organza, linen, and silk all custom-tailored for me under Aunt Charlotte's careful direction. What had been two dinner dresses soon became a full wardrobe of evening attire since the captain's visit.

"They're nice," I agreed. Klara was allowed to visit whenever I liked because Aunt Charlotte approved wildly of her family. The friendship was an unexpected advantage of my move to Berlin. I'd rarely had friends my own age back at home and depended upon Mama for companionship. I'd never felt like I was missing anything before, but now that Mama was gone, I felt that absent element in my life more keenly.

"Nice? They're masterpieces," Klara rebuked. "The styles may be a little outdated, but I've not seen such fine fabric in ages. And her machine makes stitches so perfectly. Mine is an antique and needs to be sent to a museum. I've been begging for a new one for ages."

"I didn't know you sewed," I said. "My mother never taught me much. She said she was a miserable failure when my oma tried to teach her, and she accepted her shortcomings with a fair amount of glee."

I was able to figure out enough sewing by hand for a few basic things, but anything by machine was beyond me.

"That's a shame," she said. "It's rather fun. Dead useful, too. I can teach you a few things if you like. Mending and such at the least."

"I'd like that," I said. "I wonder if Aunt Charlotte has a machine I can use."

"If she doesn't, she'll probably rush out and buy you three new ones tomorrow. They rave about you to Mama."

"They're so kind," I said. "More than I deserve, I think."

"They're proud of you. You caught the eye of Captain Schroeder. He's a favorite of the Führer himself at rather a young age and he's got his sights set on you." She held a turquoise silk dancing dress up to her reflection and twirled a bit before tossing it on the bed. "Every party member's dream for their daughter."

"He may be young for the army but he's almost twenty years older than me. He can't possibly be 'interested' other than out of sheer politeness to Aunt Charlotte and Uncle Otto."

"He's not one to lavish attentions carelessly," she said. Her face grew a few shades paler, and I saw her stiffen in a way I never had before. "He's usually far more reserved than he was last night."

"You know him well?" I asked. "Is he a nice sort of man?"

"I've known the captain for a year or two now," she said. "He's got wonderful prospects."

"Prospects are fine, but is he kind?" I placed the turquoise dress that Klara had flung on the bed back in the closet.

"I don't see what difference that makes. Kind or not, he's got position and clout. That's what matters."

"Affection doesn't?"

"Only in American movies. They won't give you a choice anyway."

"I see," I said, picking at a nonexistent speck on my comforter. "I thought you said it was ridiculous, the BDM all encouraging early marriages and such."

"It is," she said. "But fighting it is useless. They have plans for us."

"I don't see why it's useless. It's our lives, after all," I said. "What happened to *our* plans? University? Careers? A choice to do something else?"

"Those are options for girls who can't find husbands. You're not going to fall in with those girls." She spoke with a confidence I found unnerving.

I said nothing, but she read the silence well.

"Listen, I know it seems unfair. I had my own dreams. Paris, fashion . . . something better than domestic life and being charming at parties. I don't particularly like children, and don't much look forward to having a brood of them. But it's what's expected of us. My best hope for happiness is to marry a man well-off enough that I can hire help and not be too bogged down with the daily unpleasantness of keeping a house."

"I thought you wanted more than that," I said. "To make a life of your own. You've been saying that since I met you."

"Why hope for the impossible?" she retorted. "I'd just be miserable wishing for what I can't have. The captain would provide well for you. It would leave you some freedom to do as you please. Not a lot, but some."

A few hours to go to the salon. To have lunch with girlfriends. To shop for the latest fashions so I could look good on his arm. The picture of that life was clear, pleasant, and uninteresting.

"Don't blame me," she said, as though reading my thoughts. "I didn't make it this way. I'm just being realistic about my future. If you want to be happy, I suggest you do the same."

"I suppose," I said. "It's a lot to think about."

"Or you could just accept it and move forward," she said. "You'll end up in the same place for all of your thinking."

I felt the truth of her words weigh on my gut. I wanted to double over around it, but I didn't give in.

"Don't be so glum," Klara said as she twirled again with my pink dress. "It's not like your options are terrible ones. If you have to be a brood mare, at least the stallion they chose for you is a nice one to look at."

I felt the bile rise in my stomach at the analogy. It was crude. It was far too accurate to accept without revulsion.

"It was never what I wanted," said Klara. "But it's the box they'll nail us into."

"You make it sound like a coffin," I said, giving up my attempts at cleaning up after Klara. I'd enlist Mila's help after Klara went home.

"That's not a mistake," she said.

"But you have your own aspirations," I said. "You've told me about them."

"Sure, I wanted to be a fashion designer. I wanted to travel the world and make gowns for movie stars and politicians' wives and all the fancy people that only seem to live in magazines."

"So what happened?" I asked.

"I grew up," she replied. "Those are the pipe dreams of children. I'll just marry the highest-ranking man that will have me and amuse myself making clothes for the children. I'll have them in taffeta and silk at the park. I'll be the most ridiculous mother in Berlin. It's enough."

But there was a wistful quality in her voice that betrayed that this was not just some childhood phase. She'd studied as seriously as her situation would have allowed. She'd not just dreamed idly about creating dresses out of thin air, but actively sought to learn the skills she needed to master the craft. She hadn't dismissed her dreams as the idle fancy of youth.

She let them die. And recently, too. Something had happened to Klara since the night of the dinner party, but she didn't seem willing to talk about it. I hoped in time she would be.

Like so much else, Klara's change of heart made me think of Mama. Mama had been forced to—at least officially—abandon her career when the Führer no longer allowed women to practice medicine, but at least she hadn't snuffed them out willingly.

What made me even sadder was that Klara and Mama had at least figured out what they wanted from life. I hadn't even been given the opportunity to figure that out for myself, and it seemed I wouldn't have the chance.

CHAPTER SIX

Tilde

October 1938

It was silly to keep the shop open as late as I did—no one came shopping for fabric and patterns after dinnertime—but I kept it open anyway. It gave me the feeling of doing something when I felt like there was so little I could actually do to change our situation. I couldn't persuade officials to give us papers. I couldn't convince the Nazis to give up their bloodlust. So at night I pored over the account books and organized the fabric and notions to the point of obsession with the light on and the door unlocked in the idle hopes that I might be of service to a late customer.

The tinkling of the shop bell caused my head to rise automatically from the account books.

It was Samuel. Since the last time he was in the shop, I looked over our records to jog my memory of his mother's visits to the shop. She never bought very much, but I remembered her as a slight woman with a shy smile who looked as though she was always just a bit nervous. Though I supposed many of us looked that way these days.

"How did the dress turn out?" I asked by way of greeting. "Did the fabric suit?"

"She hasn't seen it yet, but my mother raved about your choices. She said she's always admired your taste. From what I've seen of the work in progress, I have to agree."

"She must be as kind as I remember," I said.

"Indeed, she is," he said, the corners of his lips curling up as if he were recalling a fond memory.

"Did your mother need anything else to complete the dress?" I asked. "Thread? Buttons?"

"No," he said. "She's got it all well in hand."

"Oh, does she have another project in mind?"

Samuel began fumbling with the hem of his jacket for just a moment, then smoothed it flat when he realized what he was doing. "Actually, I was hoping you might be willing to take a stroll about the neighborhood. I've noticed the long hours you put in and thought some fresh air might do you some good."

"You did?" I asked, amazed that he'd paid such close attention to my habits.

"Yes. I pass by here to make deliveries for my father rather often, and no matter how late it is, your light is always on," he said. "I know it's bold of me, but it's still light after dinner, and it seemed like a nice evening for it."

He looked as though asking me for a simple stroll was the hardest act of his life to date and his expression was so hopeful, I couldn't have found it within myself to deny him. Moreover, I didn't wish to.

"You realize the quandary you've put yourself in, don't you? Every time you've spotted me working late, you were working, too," I said, shutting the account book. "So you're just as guilty of overwork as I am. But you're not wrong. Sometimes it feels like I'm going to go stale from sitting indoors too long. Like a potato forgotten in the back of the pantry."

"Well, we'd better get you out of doors before you sprout," he said, his smile widening. His jaw seemed to loosen, and his breath deepen as his nerves lessened.

I called up to my mother that I was going out for some air and locked the door behind me. She didn't need to know I was with a boy. She'd come down and make a fuss as if I were a sixteen-year-old girl in her first bloom of romance. Samuel offered me his arm, and we walked into the comfortably brisk fall evening.

"I'm glad you didn't think I was too forward, asking you for a walk, since we've only just met," Samuel said. "It took me some time to work up the courage, I confess."

"I might think you're forward," I said with a chuckle. "But lucky for you I don't mind it in this instance."

"My lucky day," said Samuel, gently squeezing my arm with a mischievous glint in his eye. "Though not quite as lucky as the day my mother decided to send me for fabric and thread. To think I considered begging off to work on a viola for an impatient client. The very idea haunts me. If I'd known someone like you was running the yardage shop, I'd have started running her errands long ago."

I laughed at the obvious hyperbole.

"See, young men should always do as their mother asks. There are rewards for being a good son," I chided. "But what's this about a viola? Are you a musician of some sort?"

"An instrument maker," he said. "As is my father. The family trade, so to speak. Has your family always been in the clothing business?"

"Not at all," I said. My tongue was burning with questions about his work, but he turned the conversation before I had the chance. "Just the past few years, to make ends meet."

"I see. Your father passed?"

"No," I said, unable to keep the gloom from my voice. "He divorced my mother when he began to see his career affected by the new decrees against Jews. We were a liability."

"What a coward," he spat. "I'm sorry, I shouldn't have spoken against your father, no matter how I feel about him."

"You're not wrong, but sadly, neither was he," I said, somehow wishing that there was still a spark of loyalty left in my soul with which to defend my father. I lowered my voice. "After we left, his star went into ascendancy. Not only was he willing to forsake his wife and daughter in the name of political expediency, but he's also willing to work with the thugs that passed the laws to make us second-class citizens in the first place."

Samuel looked around, presumably to make sure no one had overheard my rant, despite my whispered tones. A new habit we'd all acquired.

"Worse than a coward," he said. "A monster."

I nodded my head. "If only I could disagree."

"I wish you'd been born in kinder times," he said. "Someone as beautiful and sweet as you are deserves better."

"I think we all do," I said. "I don't think anyone deserves to live in hard times, but we have to keep going all the same."

"So very true," he said. "Though I can't say things are totally bleak in this exact moment."

"I'm sure you've said that to a hundred girls," I said, laughing despite myself. "You're a practiced flatterer."

"Not one, and I'm not, I assure you. I'm shocked that I'm not stuttering over every syllable. I usually am whenever I try to speak to a girl."

"Perhaps the other girls made your heart flutter more than I do."

"Perhaps you're the first girl who was worth being brave for," he said.

He turned his head to look at me.

"It would mean a lot to me if you'd come to my sister's birthday," he said. "My mother said she'd love to have you, and Lilla would be happy for guests. Anything to make it feel like a real party. We can't make a fuss like in old times, but we want to make it fun for her. Please say you'll come."

"Of course," I said. "I'd love to meet her. And see the dress your mother made, too."

"You'll make them all very happy," he said. "Don't expect anything too grand, but we'll do our best to have a merry evening all the same."

"I'm sure we will. It was kind of your mother to extend the invitation to me. She barely knows me."

"Well, I may have persuaded her," he said, looking a tad sheepish. "But it didn't take much. She's fond of you. And sometimes being a good son has its rewards.

"I should get you back home," he said, noticing some guards walking on the street. We hurried our pace back to the shop and felt relief when it came into view. They had to ruin everything, including this.

"Thank you for taking a turn with me," he said, hesitating to release my arm.

"It was a pleasure," I said, unable to hide a smile.

"One I hope will be repeated," he said. He made no attempt to linger at the door but turned around and gave a parting wave when he was half a block away. I'd stayed rooted to the spot watching him leave. The flutter in my stomach seemed a juxtaposition with the terror that usually lived there of late, but I found delight in knowing I could feel anything else.

"I AM SO bored with these peasant dresses they keep trying to foist on us," Klara exclaimed, tossing a copy of *NS Frauen Warte* in a dustbin in her sewing room. She pulled a matronly yellow dress with pink flowers from a hanger and draped it against herself. "My mother actually bought me one and wants me to wear it. In public. This is Berlin, not some Bavarian backwater."

"They're dreadful," I agreed. "I don't understand it myself."

"My father says the party is hoping to get women to focus on the home and family. They think some appeal to tradition will make that happen. As if dressing like milkmaids will make us better wives."

"It does seem far-fetched," I said. "Particularly in the cities."

"Let's get out of here," she said. "I have just the antidote to this calico nightmare." She tossed the dress aside and pulled me from my seat.

"Where are we going?" I asked. She'd never pulled me from a lesson like this for an impromptu outing. I wasn't sure if I ought to be flattered or scared.

She whisked me outside before her parents could ask questions and had us walking at a quick pace. We ended up on a picturesque street in the heart of Charlottenburg, the most fashionable neighborhood in the city. At first, I worried that someone would notice that I didn't belong in this neighborhood and would call attention to it. Then I realized that being with Klara was the best sort of protection I could hope for. Not only would she make my appearance look legitimate, but if I were seen in her company, it might lessen suspicion about me in general. I hated that things were this way, but if my association with Klara could keep my mother and me safe, then any number of harebrained errands were worth it.

"Now don't you dare tell my father where we're going," she said as we turned down a wide avenue.

"Easy enough, since I don't know myself," I said with a roll of my eyes.

"We're going to a French bookshop," she said. "To get proper magazines."

"Why would your father object to that so very much? Fashion magazines aren't all that scandalous."

"No. So long as I don't leave them lying about, they really don't care," she said. "But the woman who owns this shop is Jewish and Father would have an apoplexy if he knew that I was giving her business. I tell him they're passed on to me from friends and he's happy to believe that lie."

I looked at her, blinking. They'd never registered that I was Jewish. I supposed I should have felt relieved.

"Now don't be tiresome and tell me it bothers you?" she said.

"Oh, not at all. I was just surprised is all."

"Good. I get so tired of that trope at dinner parties. How the Jews have ruined everything and how we've got to reclaim our country for 'good Germans.' From what I can see they're just going about their lives the same as the rest of us. If anyone's to blame, it's the warmongering old Kaiser who got us into wars we didn't need to be fighting and we're still paying for a generation later."

"How enlightened of you," I said.

"Oh, I know. There are a few more things rattling on up here aside from French seams and box pleats," she said, tapping her head. "But enough of all that."

She opened the door to the little shop that was as welcoming as a well-appointed parlor. There were a crowd of women, all impeccably dressed and from the upper echelon of Berlin society, waiting in a queue and chatting merrily. Most in German, though a few practiced their French with varying levels of success.

"Magazine day always brings a crowd," Klara explained. "Madame Frankel can only get a small shipment across the border. No one wants to miss out."

A short woman with dark brown curly hair stood behind the counter, cheerfully attending to the women who wanted nothing more than to get their hands on the photos of fashion that was becoming more and more unobtainable. The more we distanced ourselves from Paris and New York, the more fashion would suffer. It was a small concern to most, but these women clung to the elegance that was being ripped away from them by each decree. They recognized the genius of these foreign designers, so many of whom were Jewish like me, but they stood either in support of, or complicit with, a government that seemed more and more determined to have them eradicated.

The women were thrilled with their vibrantly hued copies of *Vogue Paris* and *Marie Claire*. A blond woman smiled in a red-and-white bathing costume on the cover of *Marie Claire*, looking ready for a summer at a resort on the Côte d'Azur where her only care would be running out of suntan oil. There was still some joy in the world somewhere, at least.

"Ah, my dear Klara. I knew you'd be here today," Madame Frankel said as we approached the front of the line. "I've set aside your copies."

"You're a lamb, Madame," Klara said, beaming a smile. "This is my friend Tilde. She's an amazing seamstress. She'll be just as glad to pore over these pages as I am."

"What a treat," Madame Frankel said, assessing me. She paused at my eyes and turned back to Klara. "You must tell me whose collections will sweep the runway, won't you? I trust your judgment more than anyone's."

"You can count on me," Klara said, handing over her money.

I found myself wanting to lose hours in the bookshop, though there were other, larger establishments in the city. There was something unique about this place, as though we had been invited into her private library rather than a public shop. Each volume had been chosen lovingly. Some of the patrons seemed as comfortable in this place as they would their own homes. I didn't read French as well as I would have liked, but there was a charm here that made me want to stay for hours.

A uniformed man entered the shop, his expression completely devoid of humor. Madame Frankel's face fell for a split second, but she recovered her composure with an alacrity that only extended time in Paris could achieve. I envied her self-mastery as my heart raced and I fought to keep my breathing even.

"Frau Frankel, have you received copies of *L'Humanité* in your shipments?" I was no expert in French newspapers, but knew that it skewed far to the left of the party's ideology. And to be honest,

I doubted there was a foreign paper that would meet with their approval.

"Why yes, sir. I have. As I have for the past eighteen years."

"It is now on the forbidden list. I will need you to hand over your copies."

"Of course," she said, without hesitation. She bent down and reached for the stack of papers and set them on the counter. She didn't dare question him or his mandates. She would have to accept the loss of revenue with a smile like so many others.

The man took the papers with a salute and walked out.

She was lucky. She caught my eye again and we realized we both were.

It would only take one sour word from a neighbor to change our lives irrevocably, and living on that tightrope was exhausting.

Klara seemed unfazed by the proceedings and looped her arm in mine to escort me out of the shop. She thumbed through the magazines with a childlike enthusiasm as she showed me the designs that she wished to emulate. Most were in her skill set, others would take months of practice to be able to master. She seemed to have the good sense to know which was which.

"So you never told me how your dinner went," I said as she continued flipping through the pages. "You worked hard on that dress."

"He spoke precisely three words to me," she said. "The Rombauers' niece commanded his attention all night. She's from some far-flung town in the middle of nowhere. I didn't think he'd fall for some bumpkin, but apparently she's more his type than I am."

"Then more fool he," I said. "Are you very disappointed?"

"Not really," she said, though there was a lack of sincerity in her tone. "He's handsome enough, to be sure. And well connected. I thought he was interested for a time, but apparently he was looking for someone better to come along. It's Mother and Father who are truly disappointed." Her words seemed hollow to me, somehow. She'd mentioned the promising young captain enough that it couldn't possibly be just her parents who were disappointed. Klara was putting on an act to save face—and protect her own heart.

"Well, they can set their sights on someone else. Someone who will appreciate you."

"And no doubt they will," she said. "What about you? Do you have a string of suitors mad with love and ready to throw themselves into the Rhine for your sake?"

"Ha!" I exclaimed. "I'm too often locked in a shop frequented by women for any young man to know I'm alive." I could have told her about Samuel, but he was a secret too delicious to share just yet.

"A shame. We should invite you to dinner and introduce you to some men from good families."

Good families. The sort that wouldn't approve of mine.

"You're kind, but I know your parents wouldn't truly want a seamstress at their dinner table. It would be awkward for them."

"It might be good for them," she said. "They need to be shaken up a bit."

"Maybe so, but I don't think I want to do the shaking," I said. "The seamstress often doesn't fare well against the financier in matters like these."

"You're probably right," she said. "But how boring it is to be constrained to the same circles."

"It must be," I said.

Klara looked so intently at the restaurant across the street, I couldn't help but turn my head to see what had her transfixed. The best I could tell, she was staring at a couple—a lovely blond woman and a tall man in an officer's uniform. Klara could hardly blink, she was so transfixed.

"What's the matter?" I asked. "What's got you so fascinated?"

"You don't think I'm plain, do you?" she asked with a quick-fire subject change.

"Not in the slightest," I said. Indeed, with her chestnut hair against her alabaster skin and rose-hued cheeks, she was more than pretty. She clearly hadn't noticed the number of men who had looked up to admire her and the women to envy her. I looked back at the woman in the restaurant a second time. She was gorgeous, to be sure, but not in a way that ought to induce jealousy in Klara. "Why would you ask such a silly thing? I've never pegged you as one for false modesty before. You know perfectly well you're lovely."

Klara's glance hadn't wavered, and I realized the pair across the street wasn't some mere example of a happy couple she wished she were a part of. It was her captain and her friend.

"Klara?" I prodded.

"Oh, just something I overheard my parents saying after the party. 'Perhaps we should have Cook make fewer desserts. More greens,' Father had said. Mama wondered if the color of my dress was flattering enough. That sort of thing."

"They're being foolish," I said, surprised at my own fervor. "Making problems where none exist. That shade of lavender was made for you, and you haven't an ounce of flesh too much for any man's liking. And from what all your magazines say, good German men are supposed to want sturdy wives. If anything, perhaps he thought you were too waifish."

"Men are such contrary beasts," she said. "Maybe you're right."

"I know I am. Maybe his vision needs to be checked."

She laughed out loud.

"No, no. Captain Schroeder is the finest marksman in the Reich," she said, clearly quoting her father.

"You know what? My grandfather couldn't abide my grandmother's ginger crumb cake. My mother and I loved it. Oma made a finer crumb cake than any French pâtissier could possibly ever concoct. But if you gave him a good Sachertorte, he was in heaven. It's most likely that you are a superlative ginger crumb cake, but he is still looking for his slice of Sachertorte."

She threw her head back and laughed at the ridiculous analogy, her mood lifted instantly.

"Cake and coffee for both of us," she announced, and she pulled me inside the nearest Konditorei.

We both ordered ginger crumb cake and coffee—each a pale imitation of what my mother made in our humble kitchen, but thoroughly enjoyable.

"Not much of a sewing lesson today," I said, sipping from the potent brew that helped cut the sweetness of the cake.

"A day off is good for the soul," she proclaimed.

"Bad for the pocketbook, though," I chided.

"Well, this is on me," she said. "No need to worry."

"Very kind of you," I said.

She waved her hand dismissively. "Don't mention it. You're a good friend to me."

I bowed my head for a moment, humbled that she considered me such. Though I was sure her parents considered me their paid employee and likely wouldn't think well of their daughter being so

familiar with me. But that I was in their employ seemed a minor offense compared to what they didn't know about my heritage. It was
clear she'd picked up her gracious nature somewhere outside the
walls of her own home.

"Klara, I want you to know that whatever your parents say,
you're a remarkable person. You ought to be studying fashion in
Paris with the masters. You have a lot to learn, but you have a rare
natural talent."

"Oh, I'm giving it all up," she said, her eyes not fixing on mine
but focused on the wall behind me. "My parents are right about one
thing. Men aren't looking for accomplished women. They're looking for mothers for their children. They're looking for a woman
to tend the house and keep order. A real career is of no interest to
them."

"I won't contradict you, but I do hope you're wrong," I said.

"So do I," she replied. "I'll continue my lessons for the time being, though. It's useful in any case."

"Useful or not, you shouldn't give up something you love to
become the person others want you to be."

Her eyes met mine, and for just a fleeting moment I saw a pain
reflected in them I hadn't noticed before. She might claim disinter-
est in this Captain Schroeder, but his rebuff had hurt her more than
she would ever admit.

"How I wish I lived in your world, Tilde."

I said nothing, but I wished I knew the safety of hers.

CHAPTER SEVEN

Hanna

October 1938

Klara had become more and more distant at school to the point where I dreaded the invitation to Klara's house like I would dread my own hanging, but Aunt Charlotte said we couldn't escape the luncheon. Aunt Charlotte had me wear a wispy afternoon dress with caplet sleeves in periwinkle crepe that seemed far too elegant for a small luncheon among friends, but she wouldn't be swayed on the subject. I was only mollified that her own dress was even finer and might succeed in taking some attention off me.

The entryway had two massive paintings of a foxhunt and a gilded mirror as well as a small fountain. The butler had us wait in a sitting room that was no less ornate.

"Hildi Schmidt is the most pretentious woman in all of Berlin," Aunt Charlotte whispered. I giggled as softly as I could, but the sound still echoed off the cavernous walls. It helped explain the formality of the clothes, and when Frau Schmidt and Klara emerged, they looked just as smartly dressed as we were.

Frau Schmidt showed us to a large formal dining room dominated by a hulking oaken table that was stained a ruddy deep brown. The lights were dim, but the table was polished so it gleamed brightly enough we could see our faces reflected back. The ivory china and silver candelabra made it feel more like a formal dinner than a midday meal, but it seemed to be exactly what Aunt Charlotte expected.

Platters of roasted quail in a cherry wine sauce, braised leeks, sautéed potatoes, and a host of other dishes spread over the table. Aunt Charlotte only took minuscule helpings, and Frau Schmidt followed suit. Uncle Otto wasn't here to insist on "healthy helpings" of food, so we weren't obliged to stuff ourselves to please him. At least in that it was a pleasant change.

"We're so glad you've come to stay with your aunt and uncle, Hanna," Frau Schmidt purred. "Klara has hardly spoken of anything else since you came to town."

"Klara has been a good friend to me. My first days at school would have been miserable without her," I said. Klara smiled at me, though it wasn't the warmest I'd seen.

"Well, you've certainly brightened our little circle," she said, sipping from her glass of claret. "First in your subjects, pride of the BDM, and now that you've caught the eye of Captain Schroeder, it seems like your time here has already been productively spent. Perhaps you can coach Klara in a few things."

Klara stared at her mother, and it was only because of Aunt Charlotte that there weren't daggers in her eyes. Friedrich. Klara's parents had hoped for a match between the pair of them and I'd ruined things. The realization weighed like a stone in my gut and the meal became as appetizing as soot.

"Klara is wonderfully accomplished. I doubt I have much of anything I can teach her," I said, unable to look up from my hands.

"Oh, Klara does her best," Frau Schmidt said. "But often falls short of her goals despite our best efforts."

"Mother, really," Klara said. "Must you?"

"What, dearest. I only speak the truth. It's a shame. You really do try. Not too much of the potatoes, dear. You know they go right to your hips."

"Hanna tells me that Klara has been indispensable to her in the BDM," Aunt Charlotte said. It was a classic move to defuse awkward situations, and I envied her skill at it.

"Oh, I'm sure you're doing well enough on your own. But it's nice of you to say."

"I mean it," I said. "Truly."

"It's fine, Hanna. Just leave it. She won't believe it no matter what you say. Just save your breath."

Klara tossed her thick linen napkin onto the table and scurried off in the direction of her room.

"Oh, you'll have to excuse her. She's been moody since, well. Never mind. She's just in one of her moods. It'll pass."

"I think I'll go check on her," I said, rising without waiting for a response. I followed the echo of Klara's footsteps down the corridor and finally caught up with her. I moved to embrace her, but she just waved me away.

"I'm sorry. I just can't handle her sometimes. She's always like that." Klara's face was white with the effort of restraining her tears. She leaned on the door to her room for a moment before opening it.

I'd not had the chance to visit Klara's room before and discovered it was a complete opposite to the room I'd imagined. I'd envisioned a messy, artistic space filled with her sketches, swatches of fabric, and clandestine fashion magazines. Something a bit on the dark and moody side. In reality, the room was airy and bright and looked rather like a picture from a catalog. The bed was covered with pink floral linens and the whole space smelled of rosewater and freesia. Not an item out of place, nor a single scrap of personality to be found.

She observed me assessing the space and said, "Mother has her ideas about home décor. It's easier to go along with her."

"It often is," I said, thinking of Aunt Charlotte and her way of steamrolling everyone who got in her path.

"Since Mother so tactfully brought up a certain elephant in the room, how is Friedrich?" Klara asked, sitting down in her chair with her sketchpad. She never showed me her work, but I'd seen a few of her casual doodles on paper. They were always sketches of women's clothes. Everything from simple blouses to elaborate gowns. They looked like something out of a French magazine and would have been stunning if realized in fabric.

"Oh, it's hard to tell really. He speaks of the looming war and the party and the Führer until I'm ready to run from the room."

"So he hasn't changed much," she said. "It was always impossible to get him to speak of anything else."

"Do you hate me?" I asked. "You know it was never my intent . . ."

"No, it wasn't. But it was your aunt's. She had no qualms about setting me aside."

"No, that doesn't surprise me, but I am sorry."

"I believe you," she said. "It doesn't help much, but I do believe you. My parents act like I lost his attentions out of negligence. That's a delight, I assure you."

"I'm amazed they allow me here," I said. "They must be furious."

"Are you kidding? They thought you were well positioned as your aunt and uncle's ward before. Now that Friedrich has cast his eye at you, they know how much influence you might have. They wouldn't chase you from this house if you stole a thousand suitors from me."

"Is there any way I can make this right with you?" I asked. "If I spoke to Friedrich maybe he'd see reason. He'd see how much better off with you he is."

"God, anything but that. It would make me look like the most pathetic girl in Berlin. There's nothing for you to do, really. Just let me be seen with you, I suppose."

"What does that mean?" I asked.

"It means, my dear, that your star is in its ascendency. If I'm to make a match even a fraction as good as the one I thought I had, I will need to play all the cards in my hand. Being seen with you will help me appear to be well connected and interesting. I promise I won't be a nuisance."

"A nuisance?"

"I know you'll be busy with your life. Finishing school and waiting for Friedrich to propose. Which he will. I'm just hoping you'll spare some of your precious time for me."

"Klara, you're my friend. I can't believe you'd think that I'd ever think that about you."

"Not now, but when you get swept up in that world, you will.

Don't worry. I won't take it personally. If the situation were reversed, I'd be much the same."

"That's not how things are at all," I said. I felt the tears sting-
ing at my eyes and I wanted to scream in frustration. Every time I
wanted to assert myself, the damned tears threatened to leak.

"Listen, I know you can't help it, but it's just the way life is. We
don't live in a fair world or a kind one. We just have to do our best
with what we have. You have Friedrich, so make the best of it. I'll
find someone else. My parents will always compare whoever it is to
Friedrich, and he'll likely come up wanting, but so it is."

"I never asked for this. I don't want to lose your friendship over
him."

"Oh, don't be daft. You don't let friends get in the way of a match
like that. It's foolish to trade a lifetime of comfort and position for
the benefit of hanging on to a school chum. I thought you were
more cunning than that." She stood up and held open the door to
her room and looked out to the hall expectantly. An invitation to
leave.

"And I didn't think you were that conniving," I said. I was able
to leave the room with my dignity intact, but the tears spilled over
as soon as I was halfway down the hallway. Aunt Charlotte was
still in conversation with Frau Schmidt, so I slipped out a side door.
I'd have to apologize later, but it would be easier than facing anyone now.

I tried not to run on the way back to Aunt Charlotte's but found it
hard not to burst into a sprint when the foot traffic on the sidewalks
permitted it. As soon as I reached home I shut myself in my room
and locked the door, despite Aunt Charlotte's dislike of the practice.

Perhaps a quarter of an hour later, a knock sounded at the door.

I wiped my face and unlocked the door expecting Aunt Charlotte on the other side. I felt my shoulders drop with relief to see Mila instead.

"You'll forgive me, but it seemed like you were upset, Fräulein Hanna. I thought I'd take the liberty of looking in on you. I brought you some coffee and pastries."

"I'm fine, Mila," I said.

"It may be bold of me to say it, but you don't seem fine to me." She set the tray on my bedside table, and while the Mohnstückchen, my favorite poppy-seed pastry, looked as appealing as sawdust, the smell of the coffee was enticing enough that I sat on the edge of the bed and took the cup. In a breach of protocol, I gestured for Mila to take a seat on the bedside chair.

"You're right. I'm not fine. I've lost the first friend I've ever had. I never intended to steal her beau, but she blames me all the same."

"Girlfriends are a dime a dozen. A good man with a good position is hard to find. Especially in this day and age. If she's a true friend, she'll understand."

"If you were in her position, would you?"

She hesitated. "Perhaps not. You're insightful. It comes from not being born rich. If you were Herr and Frau Rombauer's daughter instead of their niece, you'd not spare a second thought for Fräulein Schmidt. You'd have been trained from the time you could walk that nothing matters more than getting ahead. I'd say the Rombauers are worried you're too old to learn that lesson properly."

"I don't think I want to learn it," I said. "Friedrich may be a good catch, but I don't want to get him by taking him from a friend."

"Well, your scruples will do you credit at the pearly gates. I'm just not sure if they'll serve you all that well here on earth."

"She was my friend. I feel awful."

"No worse than she does. Just take comfort in that."

"How on earth would that be comforting?" I asked.

"Because you were lucky this time. You won the prize. And if the situation were reversed, she'd have no compunction about claiming him for herself."

CHAPTER EIGHT

Tilde

October 1938

I knocked at the door, trying to quiet my nerves. I'd lied to Mama and would have to make amends later. I told her I was giving sewing lessons at the Schmidt house, but had come to Samuel's sister's party instead. She wouldn't want me visiting a Jewish family for their safety as well as ours. But it had been so long since we'd been able to spend time with our friends. So long since anything felt normal. I felt like one afternoon celebrating something as innocent as a girl's birthday could come to little harm. I'd been careful about the route I took, trying to avoid the busiest areas where the police were ever-present, but neither did I want to sneak along the deserted alleyways where anything might happen. These measures were probably extreme, but the police had become a law unto themselves and I didn't want to risk any sort of interaction with them.

The door was flung open, and I was immediately grabbed into Samuel's mother's fervent embrace. We'd never met beyond a few exchanges at the store, but she ushered me in like a member of the family. Clearly Samuel had spoken of me frequently since we began taking walks together. She knew how smitten her son had become in such a short time, and she clearly seemed in favor of the match.

"Welcome, sweet Tilde," she said, kissing my cheek and holding me at arm's length to get a better look at me. "Such a lovely girl. I now understand why my Samuel offers to run errands for me. The world being what it is, I forgot that my son is growing into a man."

Heat pricked at my cheeks, but I managed to stammer my thanks. She ushered me into the parlor and had me sit. The room was small, but impeccably clean. The furniture wasn't abundant, but what they had was built to last for generations. The Eisenberg home was a proud one. These were the sort of people of whom Mama approved enthusiastically. While she wouldn't want me here while things were so dangerous, she wouldn't have objected to the company in normal times.

Aside from the decadent aromas wafting in from the kitchen, there were a number of instruments hanging from the wall, which were better described as works of art than musical instruments. The intricacy of the woodwork was beyond anything I'd ever seen before, even in the finest furniture in the poshest Charlottenburg homes where we used to socialize before Papa had us leave. There were two cellos, four violas, and a number of violins, each more exquisite than the last.

"Samuel's work," she said, noticing where my gaze had drifted. Her face glowed with pride as she joined me in admiring their artistry. "And his father's. They sell most of their work, of course, but occasionally there are pieces too special to part with."

"I had no idea Samuel made such beautiful instruments," I confessed.

"He's modest," Mrs. Eisenberg said. "Too modest. He's surpassed his father and grandfather already. His father would be the first to tell you."

"I assume they play very well," I said.

"You should hear Samuel. He's a wonder. Though it's true many instrument makers don't play much. The crafting and the playing of an instrument are two different trades. Samuel is a rare talent at both. He begged us for lessons from the time he could hold a bow. We decided that it would only serve to increase his interest in the family business, so we found him a tutor. I think it's why he's come so far at such a young age."

"I felt it was important to learn if I wanted to make them. I had to know the soul of a cello if I wanted to capture it in the instrument," Samuel said, entering the room. His lips turned up in a shy smile at the sight of me in his parlor.

"Play for us," a voice said from behind him. A lovely young woman, presumably the guest of honor, stood at Samuel's shoulder. She was wearing the dress her mother had made from our fabric and pattern, and I congratulated myself on my suggestions. She still looked young and modest, but less like a child. The rich plum color of the fabric was just vibrant enough to spark color in her face and to complement her lovely black curls.

"It's Lilla's day, after all," his mother prodded. "Indulge us."

Samuel took one of the violas from the wall. It was finished in a gleaming chestnut varnish and shone like a mirror. Though I'd had no lessons, even I could tell the instrument was masterfully crafted.

I wasn't familiar with viola music, not having grown up in a musical family, but I found it enchanting. The viola was lighter and less morose than a cello, less plaintive than the violin. The short melody he played was haunting. He played with technical skill that even the uninitiated could recognize, but also with an emotional resonance that was impossible to ignore.

Even to a novice ear, I could tell he was a virtuoso and should have been on the great stages of Berlin, Milan, Paris, and New York.

I joined Lilla in clapping when he finished, and I smiled at the tinge of red on his cheeks as he placed the viola back on the wall.

The front door opened without a knock, and a tall man who looked like Samuel's twin, though thirty years older, entered, his face ashen.

"Papa, what's wrong?" Lilla asked.

"On the day of my daughter's twelfth birthday? Not a thing, *zeeskeit*. Why don't you fetch your old papa his slippers? My feet are sore." His face brightened for his daughter's sake, though the underlying crease of concern remained on his brow.

"Of course," she said, kissing his cheek and bobbing toward the back bedrooms.

When she was out of earshot he turned to his wife and Samuel. "The Birnbaums have gone missing and it seems the Tuchmans and Ochses are looking for passage to America. Three families this week and four the last. Pretty soon there won't be any of us left."

"Precisely what they have in mind," Mrs. Eisenberg said. "Thugs and brutes the lot of them."

"We simply cannot allow it," Samuel said. "We can't let them scare us from our homes. We have as much right to be here as any-one."

"You're right, Samuel. Of course you're right, but let's drop the subject for today, shall we? Let's not spoil Lilla's day. It's already not what it should be."

"Right as usual, my love," Mr. Eisenberg said, kissing his wife on the cheek. "Let's do what we can to make the day as cheerful as possible for her."

"It's awful, isn't it?" I whispered to Samuel as his parents re-treated to the kitchen to tend to the final preparations for dinner.

"Abominable," he agreed. "I think Mama wants to leave like the others."

"My mama does, too," I said.

The color drained from his face, but Lilla then reemerged with her father's slippers. Mrs. Eisenberg served a hearty meal that was as fine as they'd have for a great holiday. There were chicken dump-lings, potatoes, Brussels sprouts, and freshly made bread. It wasn't grand cuisine, but ample and enticing. The aromas caused my stom-ach to churn in anticipation. Lilla was allowed to serve herself first and did so with an enthusiasm that made her mother smile. The rest of us were more reserved, thinking of the three families who wouldn't be having dinner in their homes that night. Who would likely never rejoin the neighborhood. The Tuchmans and Ochses would know happier times, but who knew what fate had befallen the Birnbaums.

Everyone tried for Lilla's sake to be cheerful, and the effort was largely successful. As she spoke, it was clear she was a smart girl with a creative mind. She hadn't grown into her brother's quiet re-serve, but was maturing into a charming woman, though the last vestiges of childhood were still with her. She didn't notice her father's stony expression when she wasn't looking, nor her brother's stoic resolve. I was glad for that small mercy.

In addition to the dress, her parents gifted her a heart-shaped gold locket that sent her into raptures. I had made her a handbag to match her purse from the same fabric her brother and I had chosen at the shop. Samuel produced the largest box, meticulously wrapped, and placed it before her. She opened the box gingerly, trying to show the restraint of her years. Inside was a violin, no doubt crafted by Samuel himself. It wasn't just a finely made violin varnished in a handsome shade of brown. There were intricate wooden inlays that must have taken him months to create. It was finer than any of the specimens on the wall. She knew enough of her father and brother's craft to be rendered speechless.

"You've shown a lot of talent," Samuel said. "I want you to have lessons like I did. Just promise me you'll practice."

She nodded, her eyes full of tears, and wrapped her arms around his waist.

"You know how I feel about girls learning such things, but I can see it makes her happy," Mrs. Eisenberg said with a sigh of one who knew she was defeated.

"She'll be the best advertisement the business ever had," Mr. Eisenberg promised.

As the evening drew dark, Samuel offered to walk me home. Mr. and Mrs. Eisenberg kissed my cheeks and said they hoped for my speedy return. Lilla hugged me and made me swear to teach her how to sew on a machine.

"They like you," Samuel said as we crossed the threshold of his home into the cool night air.

"And I them," I said. "You have a lovely family."

"I'm fortunate in more ways than I can count," he said. "I can think of precious few things to ask for in this world."

"Oh? I'm glad you have a few things left to hope for at least. Tell me one."

"I'd like to hold your hand," he said.

I offered it to him and felt a thrill when he laced his fingers through mine. His hands were strong but hadn't been made rough by his daily toils. I found myself wishing we lived farther apart so that the walk could go on longer. As it was, I made him stop before we reached the storefront. Mama didn't know who I was with, and I didn't want to end the evening with a scolding. I didn't want to mar its perfection. I could make my peace in the morning. And I would, because I wanted her to know about Samuel.

"Thank you for coming tonight. It made Lilla's night to have a guest. She's already keen on you."

"She's lovely," I said. "I enjoyed myself more than I have in ages."

"I'm so glad," Samuel said. "Do you think you'd like to go walking again tomorrow?"

"I'd like that," I said, still holding his hand. "I love walking with you."

His eyes glistened at the word *love*. He looked at me, his eyes forming an unspoken question. I nodded and he lowered his lips to mine. Cautiously, then enthusiastically as we explored this new sensation.

Timidly, we tore apart and spoke our goodbyes. I walked into the shop knowing my life was forever changed.

CHAPTER NINE

Hanna

October 1938

"What shall we do with your hair?" Mila asked after she'd brushed it until it shone.

"Whatever you think best," I said, without much conviction.

Klara remained friendly at school, acting as though nothing had changed whenever anyone was in earshot. But she never came over to the house unless it was a formal visit with her mother, nor did we walk home together. It wasn't the same as losing my mother, but the pain was all too familiar. I missed the idle chats about clothes and Paris and the possibilities life would hold after school was out. I'd had a brief taste of what it was like to have a sister, and though Klara and I had only been friends a short while, the loss was acute.

"You've been downtrodden for days, Hanna. Chin up, or the captain will think you're given to melancholy."

"Heaven forbid we upset the captain," I said, fiddling with the earrings she'd set aside for me to wear with my navy wool dress. It looked more like a BDM uniform than not, and I wondered if Aunt Charlotte hadn't suggested it for that reason.

"That's right," she said. "Once you're married, you can be as dreary as you choose. Though I don't think it's a happy way to go about life, myself."

"You're right, Mila. I ought to cheer up," I said. Mama was never one to expect me or my brothers to constantly be in good moods, but when she could see we were downcast, she always found a way to remind us of our blessings. She couldn't do that now, so I just took stock of the roof over my head, the clothes on my back, and the opportunities Aunt Charlotte worked so hard to give me. I didn't feel cheerful, but it helped somewhat.

"That's just the thing. Remember a smile, sincere or not, covers a thousand flaws. You have so few, one quick smirk will make you breathtaking."

"Thank you, Mila," I said as she tucked the last strands of my hair into the braided coronet atop my head. "I don't suppose I could have a few minutes alone?"

"Of course, but don't dally. You're expected in the parlor in ten minutes."

I felt myself exhale as I heard the click of the door and the soft padding of Mila's footsteps down the hallway.

I pulled my worry stone from its hidey-hole, closed my eyes, and pictured the water rushing over it just as Mama had instructed. I'd taken to hiding the stone in the back of my vanity drawer as my wardrobe had grown far too extensive and my schedule too full to allow me to sew hidden pockets in the garments. I couldn't count the number of times I'd reached for it in the course of a normal day, only to be thwarted in my attempt. I'd taken to rubbing a thumb in my palm and remembering the cool, smooth stone I'd left behind. It wasn't as soothing as holding the stone in my hand, but even visualizing the weight in my hand helped my heartbeat to slow and my breath to even out.

I looked at the ornate little clock Aunt Charlotte had procured for me, and realized I'd lingered too long over my stone. I dashed to the parlor just in time to see Aunt Charlotte and Uncle Otto welcoming Friedrich like the son they'd never had.

"If your aunt and uncle don't mind, I thought we'd go for a drive today. A day off is such a rare treat for me, I thought we could enjoy some time out of doors before winter truly sets in."

"Hanna would be delighted," Aunt Charlotte said before I could speak a word. I nodded my agreement, however. If I preferred to do otherwise, that was immaterial.

Aunt Charlotte thrust a sheer scarf in my hand as Friedrich whisked me off to his car. I understood why when I saw the silver convertible BMW idling in the driveway. The chauffeur relinquished his spot in the driver's seat and held the door open first for Friedrich, then for me. I hastily tied the scarf around my head, hoping I'd come back with hair that didn't resemble a three-year-old bird's nest.

"I thought this might be more fun than another stodgy luncheon or dinner party. Don't you agree?"

"Certainly," I said, thinking of the hours I'd already spent feigning interest in any number of conversations that didn't remotely approach my bailiwick. I'd likely still have to do plenty of that on this excursion without the benefit of other guests to divert Friedrich's attention, but at least the scenery in the woods outside of Berlin would be more interesting than the wallpaper in the dining room.

Friedrich kept one hand on the steering wheel and the other draped over my shoulder as he drove. He made idle chatter, probably thinking he gave off the appearance of nonchalance, but his driving wasn't as smooth and practiced as he thought it was. I found myself gripping the door handle and wishing he would remove his hand from my shoulder and put it on the wheel where it belonged. He didn't notice my stiff carriage or my terse replies, or simply didn't care.

We finally came to a clearing and he pulled the car to a stop. I exited the car with knees wobbling. He fetched a basket and blanket from the backseat and spread the blanket on the grass. Never mind that it was fifteen degrees too cold to picnic on the ground and that Aunt Charlotte had insisted I wear a thin crepe dress that was perfectly well suited for the dining room, but not the outdoors in fall. He was dressed in wool from head to foot and would probably be fine. By the time I made it to the blanket, the ridiculous heels Aunt Charlotte had bought for me were caked in mud. I sat gingerly so I could keep my feet from sullying the blanket.

Friedrich joined me on the blanket, and I tried not to shiver. I pulled my jacket tighter and curled my legs up underneath me. He opened the basket and began foraging. "I'm glad your aunt and uncle allowed you to come alone. It may not be exactly proper, but it's hard to truly get to know someone when there are a dozen eyes peering all the time, isn't it?" He emerged from the basket with two cups and handed me one. I endeavored not to shake as he offered it.

"I suppose so," I said, hoping the thermos he produced was brimming with hot coffee, tea, or chocolate. As he poured, I heard the rattle of ice. Lemonade. The man clearly had no patience for weather or seasons that didn't coincide with his plans.

"Is there anything you want to know about me?" he asked. "You're not the most talkative girl. I don't want you to feel bashful around me."

I cocked my head. "If you want me to speak, wouldn't it make more sense for you to ask about me?"

"I see your point," he said, taking a bite of a sandwich. He'd offered me one, but it sat untouched. "Very well, what would you like *me* to know about *you*?"

"I don't know," I said. "I don't know what you want to learn about me. It's a vague question."

"Are you usually so exacting?" he asked. "I know some women take these approaches to be charming, but I find it rather tedious."

"Perhaps I am," I said. "But I hate to bore anyone with unnecessary information. If you want to know about my thoughts on the best areas in Teisendorf for snowshoeing, I don't want to prattle on with an anecdote about my childhood."

"Something tells me you could blend the two beautifully. Come on, then, a childhood anecdote about snowshoeing. Anything less and I'll be heartily disappointed."

"Very well. When I was twelve years old, my mother had me go with her to check on a woman who was about to have her third baby." I made sure my version of the story didn't reveal the true scope of her practice, which extended far beyond midwifery. I imagined Aunt Charlotte sitting ramrod straight in her chair at the dining table, praying with every syllable that I wouldn't reveal anything scandalous. "It was only early November, but the snows came hard and furious that year and we had to snowshoe through snow that would have been up to my thighs without them. I was so bitterly cold that I was worried I was going to get frostbite, but I didn't dare say anything to Mama. I wanted to help her so much. By the time we got to the cabin out in the woods I was so cold that I shook every time I passed Mama a clean cloth or an instrument from her bag. She thought I was nervous at the sight of blood, but I was just chilled to the bone. I didn't feel properly warm for a week."

Friedrich gave a genuine laugh at the anecdote. "You loved your mother very much," he said. He spoke with the certainty of observation, rather than posing it as a question.

"Yes," I said. "She was remarkable. She had a talent for healing that was astounding to watch. She'd been a good student, but what she did you can't learn in medical school. She had an instinct. She could walk into the room and sometimes *smell* what was wrong with the patient. She could diagnose a dozen different maladies by the color of your cheeks. She dealt in miracles as much as she did in medicine."

I ducked my head and fiddled with a blade of grass, realizing I'd spoken too much. They expected me to acknowledge her as a capable midwife and nothing more.

"It's good for you to be proud of her," he said. I looked down and blinked in surprise. "Of course, a woman's most important duty is to raise her family, but it doesn't mean that she can't have other talents. Indeed, it's rather tiresome if she doesn't."

"Like Klara. She's remarkably talented as a dress designer. Her designs could grace the great runways of the world if she were given the right training."

He sat up a bit at the mention of her name, I hoped in remembrance of the feelings he'd once led her to believe that he shared with her.

"Really? I never knew that. How clever of her."

"She's a lovely girl. I think she's rather sorry to not be here in my place." I saw no trace of regret in his face and felt my heart fall on her behalf.

"She *is* a lovely girl. And someday the right chap will come along and make her very happy."

"But not you?"

He shook his head. "Alas, my eye has been caught by another. One with charming anecdotes about mad snowshoeing expeditions with her mother and who has the loveliest blue eyes I've ever seen."

"I wish you wouldn't say things like that."

"Really? Most girls prefer a man to coo sweet nothings in their ear."

"That's just the problem. They usually are 'nothings.' I'd rather you speak the blunt truth."

"You are a different one, aren't you? A wood nymph who has bewitched me, I'd swear it."

"I'm not sure if you mean that as a compliment or censure," I rebuked.

"No more do I," he said, stone-faced. Then at once, he erupted in a gale of laughter and pinned me playfully to the blanket. "Now, you little wood nymph, I have you where I want you. I can gaze into those eyes as long as I choose."

And gaze he did for some time, until he lowered his lips to mine. It was a curious sensation at first, but the warmth in my core soon made me oblivious to my inhibitions. I felt my unease slip away in his gentle caresses and felt the prickle of guilt I'd harbored out of loyalty to Klara fade away.

CHAPTER TEN

Tilde

October 1938

Samuel and I walked hand in hand through the streets of Berlin, completely oblivious to the crowds of people that surrounded us. I loved the feel of his fingers laced in mine. I loved the warmth of his body just a few inches from mine, so close I was able to breathe in the scent of him. He always smelled of good castile soap tinged with the linseed oil he used for finishing his violins. It was clean and wholesome and so unmistakably Samuel. I wanted nothing more than to enshroud myself in his perfume and luxuriate in it for the rest of my days. We'd gone walking together a dozen times. He'd grown bold enough to steal kisses when we could. It seemed impossible to be doing something as decadent as falling in love as so much discord brewed all around us, but even flowers occasionally managed to bloom through the cracks in the sidewalk.

I was yearning for a quiet backstreet where he would feel comfortable enough to lower his lips to mine, but before I suggested a change of direction, I noticed Samuel's expression had gone from carefree to deep in thought.

"Your face looks cloudier than the sky. What's the matter?" I asked, clutching his hand tighter.

"Another block warden came to the workshop yesterday. He didn't cause any real trouble, but he wanted to." Though he was naturally pale, he became almost ghostly as the memories of the encounter played through his mind. I could imagine all too well the things that were said and the threats that were made. These block wardens were the lifeline between the party and the people, and all of them were puffed up with notions of their own power to terrorize their neighbors.

"Monsters, the lot of them," I said. "Why can't they leave people alone?"

"Because they thrive on making life miserable for anyone who isn't like them," he said. "That's their entire purpose. They want to provoke us into fleeing."

"Which makes no sense because they make fleeing almost impossible." Mama's quest for travel papers had become her full-time employment. "They're chasing us with a broom as though we're mice. But not out the door. Into a musty old corner."

"Where the cat is waiting for his supper, I assure you," he said.

"I fear you're right. I hate all of this. We've never done a thing to anyone, and they act like we're all criminals who threaten their way of life. I'm a burden on society—except when I can find five yards of the calico they so desperately needed or can manage to tailor a suit in a week. Then I'm useful for a few moments. It just isn't fair."

"It's no way to live," Samuel agreed. "It's not what I would wish for either of us. Especially you."

"Well, it isn't our choice. I suppose we have to do what's best with the circumstances we're given."

"That's just it. You have options, Tilde. I hope your mother is successful in getting you passage to America or somewhere else where you can be safe. But even if her efforts fail, you can pass as one of them. If you're seen with me, people will begin to know that you're one of us. Either way, you're far better off without me. It's hard enough to be Jewish here, but to be an immigrant . . . every moment we spend together puts you at risk."

"Nonsense," I said. "I won't let some mustachioed gargoyle in a stodgy uniform keep us apart. We can't let them win."

"We can't even risk playing the game," Samuel said, brushing a lock of hair from my face. "Not when your life is at stake."

"Yours is, too," I said.

"It would be regardless. But you stand a chance of surviving this. That's the material point. You've been cut off from our kind, but the rumors are horrifying. And they're getting worse and more consistent. You need to forget about me."

"You're asking the impossible. I could never forget about you. This is the first time I've ever felt—" I began.

"Me too. And it's for that reason I won't put your life in danger even though it means denying myself the one thing I've ever hoped for. I want you to go to America with your mother and lead a happy life. I have been foolish in indulging my feelings for you, cruel to both of us. You need to go and make a life for yourself."

I dropped his hand and looked down at the expanse of gray concrete before me. I wished I could disappear into it. I'd only known Samuel for a couple of months, but the pain enveloped me. I found myself swallowing against the lump in my throat. I hadn't entertained the thought of *not* going with my mother, but I also hadn't processed that it would mean leaving Samuel behind.

"We can get papers for you, too," I managed to say between ragged breaths. "I can't leave you here."

"Getting papers for yourselves is hard enough, let alone trying to get papers for me. And it's not just three of us; it's six of us, really. I can't run off and save my neck and leave my parents and sister behind. Getting papers for four Polish immigrants would be asking for the moon."

"We'll get the papers. I swear it," I said, praying I wasn't making a promise I couldn't keep.

"Tilde, I don't want you to delay leaving. Not for one moment. I can feel in the marrow of my bones that things will get worse for us before they get better. I have to know you'll be safe."

I pulled him to my chest and let loose a torrent of tears I hadn't known I'd been holding back. I hadn't had the time to consider a future, but every iteration of one that appealed to me had him in it. But there was no convincing him that we had a way forward together.

CHAPTER ELEVEN

Hanna

October 1938

W here is it, Mila?" I screeched as I fumbled around moving the contents of my dressing table for the tenth time.

"Quiet, Fräulein Hanna, or you'll alert the mistress of the house. Tell me what's gone missing."

"My worry stone. It would look like an ordinary piece of rose quartz to you."

"The pebble on your vanity? I thought it was just something you'd found in your shoe and I tossed it in the bin."

"Oh, Mila, you couldn't have," I said, furious at the tears pricking my eyes. Now was not the time for blubbering. She was apt to tell Aunt Charlotte I was mad for this anyway.

"Why all this fuss over a rock?" she asked. "We have a yard full of them, not to mention a whole countryside at easy distance if you can't find another to suit."

"You don't understand. I've had it since I was a girl. It was from my mother."

"If you don't mind me saying so, it might be just as well that it's gone. I hear your aunt and uncle speak of her sometimes at night and it's not with fond regret. The more you distance yourself from her the better off you'll be."

A variation on the same advice Klara had offered when we first met.

"Your mother wasn't like other mothers. She was different. You need to conform even more to overcome that stigma, or you'll be cast out like she was."

"I do mind you saying so," I countered. "And I expect you to not be so cavalier with my things in the future. If something is meant to be tossed in the bin, I'll do it myself."

"But the mistress . . ."

"Is your boss and the head of housekeeping around here, I know. And you don't want to lose your job. I can't order you to do anything. I'm not your employer. I'm asking you to let me have the sanctity of one room in this house. It's not my home, but I need to feel like this corner of it is mine."

"I understand, Fräulein. But understand that respecting privacy is not something your aunt and uncle are terribly worried about where you're concerned."

"What do you mean, Mila?"

"They inspect your room while you're gone, and they'd be right to dismiss me for telling you that. If you see something out of place by my hand, it's because I don't want your aunt and uncle to find anything untoward. I've never mentioned to them the kit you have with all the herbs and goodness knows what. I like you and I don't want them to send you away."

"Thank you, Mila. I owe you my gratitude," I said, lowering my head. She was risking everything for my benefit.

"Don't think on it a moment," she said. "I'm only sorry I tossed away such an important keepsake. I'll be more careful in the future."

"As will I," I said, thinking of the kit in the back of the armoire. Of course it had seemed like such an out-of-the-way place when I first arrived. But now that the room no longer seemed the size of a gothic cathedral to my provincial eyes, that corner was a painfully obvious place to tuck something away that one didn't want noticed. I'd have to seek out a better spot and pray that Mila was telling me the truth about keeping my confidences.

But this was the world we lived in, where I couldn't rely on the solemn promise of a young woman in the service of my nearest relations. The rewards for turning people in to the authorities—for offenses both real and conjured up out of malice—were all too enticing. Informing on other people was a good trade for those who were down on their luck, and a juicy temptation for those of reduced or even middling means.

I wanted to launch myself into the massive waste bin in the kitchen where Mila and the rest of the staff consolidated the contents of the bins from throughout the house, but I couldn't soil my dress or end up smelling like refuse before the BDM meeting I was to attend with Aunt Charlotte. She'd taken a more active role in the Women's League—since I came into the house, and they occasionally did joint activities.

Of course, Klara and her mother would be there as well, and she and I would be forced to be friendly. She'd eye my clothes—almost always new—with envy and well-concealed disdain. I'd see her eyes flit to the ring finger on my left hand, looking to see if Friedrich had made his intentions clear. As ardent a suitor as he was, he'd not yet broached the topic of marriage. He was too keen to discuss the war and all of Hitler's strategies in mind-numbing detail. As painful as it was to listen to, it was preferable to any awkward attempt at romance. Battle plans and troop movements were bad enough but listening to him try to wax on about the shade of my eyes or the curl of my hair would have been downright insufferable.

Aunt Charlotte had sent word that I was to dress in my smartest day dress, an elegant thing made of maroon wool that was a favorite of mine.

She surveyed me with satisfaction when I met up with her in the foyer. Of course, her brown tweed ensemble looked a million times more chic than mine, but I didn't have the years or the gravitas to pull off most of her looks.

"Good, good," she said, examining her watch and seeing that I was a few minutes early in joining her. I'd learned quickly that punctuality was a key factor in domestic harmony in this house.

The car took us a few blocks away to a house even grander than Uncle Otto's. Impressive as it was, the lady of the house lacked Aunt Charlotte's taste and scrupulous attention to detail. Had my aunt been in charge of the gathering, no one would have had to wait in the foyer to hand their coat to staff, there would have been a maid at the ready—even if she were merely brought in as help for the day. The hostess, whom we'd yet to see, had a plentiful display of finger foods with a few drab flower arrangements to fill the bare surfaces. There was no art or style to either. After a few months in Aunt Charlotte's shadow, I knew what the event was lacking, and it surprised me that I was calculating how to improve things, despite myself.

Klara nodded to me from across the room, but she did not approach me. Nor did I expect her to unless her mother made the overture first.

The crowd was directed to a room where a lectern stood before ten large round tables encircled by chairs. The ballroom had been converted into stations where we would sort cast-off clothes for the less fortunate, but there was no doubt we'd be enthralled by a lecture while we worked. No matter the purpose of the event, it seemed there was always a lecture. Whether it was a knitting bee or a lavish charity dinner, there always had to be a speech about the Reich, the Führer, the efforts to expand Germany's borders—usually all three. And they were never brief. If one did not wax poetic about the heroes fighting for the great causes dear to the Fatherland or our noble leader, the depth of one's devotion might come into question.

Aunt Charlotte led us to one of the tables, calculated carefully to ensure we'd sit with the right people.

"What luck. Frau Schroeder, I'd like you to meet my niece, Hanna. No doubt your Friedrich has spoken of her frequently."

Friedrich's mother. I felt the heat rise in my cheeks, but tried with some success to keep mastery of myself.

Frau Schroeder was a tall, thin woman who resembled her son more than a little. She was a handsome woman, in her way, but she didn't have any of Friedrich's charisma to enhance her looks. "Yes," she said, looking me over, as if to discern why I'd captured his interest. The answer wasn't readily apparent, it seemed. "Several times. Quite the most talked about girl in Berlin."

"I'm not sure if I ought to consider that distinction much of a compliment," I said.

"I'm not sure I meant it that way, dear," she retorted. "The old adage that any press is good press doesn't always hold true, I find."

She was sharp, I had to admit. I'd have to be careful with her, as it seemed that barbed tongue of hers was quite capable of leaving scars.

"Oh, quite right. No girl wants the stain of notoriety attached to her name," Aunt Charlotte cooed. "And there's nothing more tiresome than attention seeking."

Frau Schroeder nodded her agreement and turned back to focus on me. "You're rather fortunate that your aunt and uncle have taken a shine to you, it would seem," she said, taking a sip from the coffee a waiter had just placed before her.

"Indeed, I am," I agreed. "They've been wonderful to me since I arrived."

"Just a lucky thing for you they're such generous people. My parents took in a cousin of mine when I was a girl. A proper nightmare that was. It wasn't six months before my father sent her packing. My mother took to her bedroom for two weeks to recover after she'd gone. I never knew what happened to her, but I can't say I wish her well after what she put my parents through."

"And it's lucky for us, too. Our Hanna is the sweetest girl to ever draw breath," Aunt Charlotte said, patting my back. "She's been a joy since the day she crossed the threshold."

"Well, see that you stay that way, girl. Your aunt and uncle are good people and don't deserve trouble."

"Of course," I said, unsure how else to respond.

"I'm sure Friedrich has told you how sweet our Hanna is. Smart as a whip, too."

"She'd have to be to interest Friedrich. He took highest honors in mathematics. He was on his way to a brilliant career before he was called to join the cause."

"No doubt of it," I said, knowing what a mother would want to hear. "A man would have to be of keen intellect to advance as far as he has at such a young age."

"Well said," Frau Schroeder said, setting her coffee cup down with a *clink* on the table. "You do have some sense, don't you?"

"That's for others to judge, ma'am, but I certainly hope so."

She cocked her head to one side, appraising. "You must come with your aunt to the house before too long. I should like to get better acquainted with you."

"We'd be delighted," Aunt Charlotte answered for me. "You've only to name the date."

Frau Schroeder looked satisfied and turned her conversation to a rather stern-looking old woman next to her who seemed keen on discussing various charity efforts for the cause.

Aunt Charlotte squeezed my knee, and I knew it was her silent signal of approval. I'd not only caught the eye of the most eligible bachelor in Berlin, but seemed to be on my way to earning the favor of his mother.

Another bauble would appear in my jewelry box in a day or two, and I'd wear it. I'd muster enthusiasm for the trinket and plaster on a smile.

I was ready to fall into bed when we returned home after nearly two hours of speeches and several hours of rolling bandages and small talk.

But on my vanity, the little pink stone had returned. Mila had scoured the bins to find it for me. I'd have to find some way to repay her, though I wasn't sure what gesture would be large enough. Beneath it was a note that read "Be careful with your treasures." *Especially when they resemble another man's trash*, I thought.

I turned the stone over between my thumb and forefinger a few times, but then quickly placed it in the corner of a drawer where it wouldn't run the risk of being taken again. It would have to serve as my talisman from afar, though I missed the weight of it more each day, rather than less.

CHAPTER TWELVE

Tilde

November 1938

My hands were busy stocking a shipment of fabric, but my brain had been let loose to remember that final afternoon with Samuel. If I thought hard enough, I could almost smell the linseed oil, and it flooded me with the joy and bitterness of remembrance. My reverie was shattered by the sound of sobs coming from the apartment above. I bounded up the stairs two at a time and flung open the door to see Mama weeping at the kitchen table.

"Mama, what's wrong?" I asked, going to her side and taking her in my arms.

"I've gotten a call. My uncle was able to sort things out with the authorities to get papers," she said.

"That's wonderful, Mama. I know you'll miss Berlin, but you should be overjoyed. You've been waiting for this day for so long. Why are you crying?"

"Because, darling, I can't go. My uncle didn't include you in his affidavit. He's old and easily confused and the lawyers bungled everything as they usually do." A hint of irony laced with her bitter words. My father wasn't far from her thoughts in moments like these.

"Go without me," I said. "You can work to get me papers from America more easily than you can from here. It doesn't make any sense for you to stay if you can get out."

"I will not leave you behind, Tilde. I've been forced to do things I never thought possible in the last five years, but you cannot ask that of me. I won't leave you alone."

"I'll manage fine on my own. I'll run the shop as I've been doing and will do just fine."

"But you'll be on your own. An unmarried girl in a big city. It's not right."

"You'd be silly not to go. It's safer for me here than it is for you. I'm *Mischling*. With an Aryan surname, too. And I look the part. You have to spend your days trapped in this apartment without a soul for company. It's no way to live."

"Tilde, it isn't right for a mother to leave her daughter behind. I'd never be able to live with myself. I can't do what your father did."

Her face tightened as she mentioned him. I understood her anger; I was rarely able to control mine when it came to him as well.

"Mama, this is nothing like what Papa did. You aren't abandoning me."

"I'd like to know what else you could call leaving your daughter behind in a country ruled by brainless thugs."

"Mama, please be reasonable. If you have the chance to leave, you should take it."

"No, Tilde."

I wanted to shake her shoulders. To scream. To drag her onto the boat myself. But she was a proud and stubborn woman and any of those tactics would have just strengthened her resolve to stay behind.

"What if I were married?" I asked. "Would that change things?"

Mama paused. "What do you mean?"

I had told Mama about Samuel weeks ago. I found it hard to keep even small secrets from her, so to keep something this dear to my heart from her for long was unthinkable. She didn't know the depths of my feelings for him, but she was intuitive enough to know they went further than I had let on.

"Samuel has asked me. And I accepted. With everything going on, I wasn't sure how to tell you. I wouldn't be able to go without papers for him anyway. So you need to go to America for my sake as well as my husband's." The lie burned like acid in my mouth, but I had to make her believe it.

"His family are immigrants," Mama said, running her long fingers through her hair. "If you marry him, you'll be in greater danger than you are now."

"So we won't register the marriage," I said. "We'll be blessed by a rabbi and be married in the only way that matters. Who cares what this government says about anything, anyway?"

"I can't argue *that* point, my darling. But are you sure?"

"More sure than I've ever been, Mama."

She wiped her eyes with the back of her sleeve, an action that would have seen me sternly rebuked when I was a child. She took a few breaths to regain her composure.

"My little girl is getting married?"

"I am, Mama. And I'll be fine as long as you go to New York and get us papers. You can do this for us."

"I can do this," she agreed. "If you promise me you will stay safe. No heroics. Nothing foolish."

"I swear it, Mama."

"And he'll watch over you, this Samuel?"

"He'd protect me with his life," I said, confident that at least in this I was telling the truth.

"Let's pray it doesn't come to that," she said. "But it would be foolish to think the chances of that are remote. At least you can continue to run the shop to have some income."

"You won't have to worry about us, Mama. Even in such dire times, people need to clothe themselves."

"True enough. If you're sure about this boy, I give you my blessing. Not that it seems like you need it. But you must answer me one thing."

"What's that, Mama?"

"Do you love him?" she asked.

"With all my heart."

"Well, I don't know him well, but I'm certain you've chosen better than I did."

"He's a good man, Mama. Now please promise me you'll leave on the next boat," I pleaded.

"No. I won't leave until I see you married and settled. I can leave you with a husband and a family-in-law, but I can't abide leaving you until things are certain. I want to hear his intention to marry you from his own lips."

I sucked in a breath and squared my shoulders with resolve. I hurried back downstairs and grabbed my coat on the way out the door as I flung the sign to CLOSED. Samuel was going to have to agree to marry me, even if I had to get down on one knee and propose myself.

MRS. EISENBERG LOOKED surprised to see me as she opened the door. No doubt Samuel had told her that he'd cut me loose to save our future heartbreak. She looked both pleased and sad to see me, which meant she'd been disappointed by the breakup. The thought cheered me momentarily until I remembered the task at hand.

"I'm so sorry to disturb you, but I was hoping I could have a moment or two alone with Samuel."

"Of course, my dear. Wait here in the parlor and I'll get him. Lilla and I were just going to do some marketing and their father is at the workshop a bit late."

Within moments, she whisked Lilla off in her hastily donned winter coat and left Samuel to emerge from his room, walking slowly, as though to a bitter fate.

"I—what are you doing here, Tilde? I mean . . . hello."

"I'm sorry to come unannounced," I said. "I wouldn't have if it wasn't important."

He took the space next to me on the sofa, carefully keeping his distance at first, but inching closer as I told him about Mama and her papers.

"I didn't know what else to tell her. She has to go, Samuel. There is no sense in her staying behind if she can save herself. I'm sorry I lied."

He wrapped his arms around me and kissed me slowly. It was

the first time we had the luxury of kissing where it was truly private and we lost ourselves in the moment. He broke away and planted another kiss on my forehead.

"I'm sorry you had to speak an untruth. I've wanted to ask you practically from the moment I saw you in the shop for the first time. The only reason I didn't ask you before now was because I didn't want to give you a reason to stay behind."

"But now—if you marry me, it could save my mother's life."

"To marry the woman I love and save a life in the process . . . I've never had a simpler decision put before me."

He knelt before me and placed his lips on my hand before looking up into my eyes.

"Tilde Altman, will you do me the honor of becoming my wife?"

I spoke no words, but fell into his arms, nodding my answer into his neck and dampening his shirt with my tears.

Samuel and Mama got along famously, just as I knew they would. He was polite, deferential even, and made all the promises she wanted to hear. Though I wished she'd had more time to get to know him, he'd made a good enough impression on her that she'd not made a single quip about our rapid courtship or the brief acquaintance with his family. The day after the three of us shared coffee and cake in Mama's kitchen, she began packing and making her arrangements to leave for America.

Mama went to the bureau, opened the middle left drawer, set the contents on her bed, and removed the bottom. I had no idea she'd crafted a false bottom, but it was utterly convincing.

In her secret compartment were jewelry and a considerable

amount of money in gold coin. No paper money at all. She was planning for an end to the Reich and the fall of our economy.

"I know that this Hitler and his men aren't to be trusted. I've been hiding things for years. I saw my father lose everything after the last war. I know another is coming and I was ready for hard times. I just never thought I'd be forced out of my home."

"I'm so sorry, Mama. Someday it will be safe to return. You don't have to leave forever."

"I wish I could take comfort in that, but I confess I can't."

"I know, Mama."

"I won't come back to this place," she said. "I feel it in my bones. There is nothing for me here any longer."

"You have a fortune, Mama," I said, looking at the gleaming pile of coins.

"Not enough to buy our freedom, but it's something to keep you going. I want you to keep it hidden. Don't even tell your Samuel. If he wonders how you're able to afford things, tell him the shop is doing well. Tell him you took on extra mending. Promise me you'll keep it safe and only spend what you need in order to be comfortable."

"Mama, you will need it in America."

"I've got enough to get my start. Now listen to me. Every single coin in there came from the sweat of my brow alone and it's the last gift I can give you to keep you safe. You won't begrudge me this."

"No, Mama."

"And if I can't be here for your wedding, you'll have something of me with you." She walked to the closet and pulled out a large garment bag. She unzipped it to reveal a wedding dress made of the nicest oyster-white silk we had ever carried in the store. It was simple, but every stitch was that of a master craftswoman. It was flowing and modest, exactly right for a synagogue wedding. She'd made a veil as well that would cascade behind me on the way down the aisle. "I started making it two months ago when I heard you and Samuel talking down in the shop."

"You knew?"

"Of course I did, Tilde. I always thought he was a nice boy. I wanted to get to know his family better. He's exactly the sort of boy I wanted for you. I know you'll be happy together. The dress may be a bit much for a quiet wedding in his parents' parlor, but at least you'll look like a bride."

"Mama, it's absolutely breathtaking."

"I'm glad you approve, darling girl. Just one last touch." She reached into the secret compartment and handed me a small jewelry case. Inside were a heavy emerald necklace, bracelet, and earrings. I remembered seeing them in my mother's own wedding photograph. "They belonged to my mother and her mother before her. I hope someday you'll be able to pass them on to your daughter."

"I'll keep them safe, Mama," I promised.

Mama took my face in her hands and kissed my cheeks. "You know, I'm glad I let your father have his way about something."

I cocked my head sideways. "What on earth could that be?"

"I wanted to name you Rachel or Esther. A good Jewish name. Your father thought a German name would make things easier for you. I agreed to Mathilde and I'm glad I did. It means 'strength in battle.' I don't think there is a more fitting sentiment for what you'll need in the months ahead."

"I'll try to be equal to it," I said.

"I know you will, my darling. I know you will."

She looked down at the drawer and took a ragged breath. "Even with all this, I feel like I'm abandoning you. I've never felt like such a poor excuse for a mother in my whole life."

"Mama, I'll follow as soon as I can. I promise."

"You're a good girl. You've always kept your promises. I know I can trust you to keep this one."

Mama kissed my cheek as tears streamed down hers. I clutched her to my chest and held in the screams that beat against it, yearning to be set free. I wanted to rage against the injustice of my loving mother being chased from her home. I wanted to rail against the forces that would keep my parents from walking me down the aisle.

But my mother needed me to show strength enough so she could leave me behind.

I wondered how much bile and anger I could swallow before it would make me a hardened and cynical woman, and I spoke a silent prayer that I'd never find out.

CHAPTER THIRTEEN

Tilde

November 9, 1938

I stood in the parlor of Samuel's parents' apartment dressed in the gown my mother made for me. I wore my great-grandmother's emeralds. Mama Eisenberg had fashioned a chuppah along the side of the room and crammed in chairs for the few guests we'd dared to invite. The guests had come in intervals so as not to attract attention. Most came on foot so their cars wouldn't be noticed. So many measures taken so that we could celebrate a wedding in safety. A wedding that would never be registered with authorities because it would risk far too much.

I walked into the room, feeling an ache on my right where my father should have been and on the left where my mother should have been. It was a blur from the moment Samuel lifted my veil and we approached the chuppah. I walked around Samuel seven times. The rabbi said the blessing over the wine. The guests recited prayers. Samuel gave me a golden wedding band. As Samuel broke the glass to symbolize the fall of the temples in Jerusalem, a piece of my heart shattered with it amid the hushed chorus of "mazel tov" from the guests.

Papa Eisenberg did his best to enliven the guests with his buoyant nature. Where Samuel was quiet and serious, his father was outgoing and effusive. Samuel played for the guests, Lilla joining in on occasion, too. She'd only been taking lessons for a few months now, but showed her brother's same talent for music and drive for study. Music wouldn't have attracted the attention of any of the neighbors as they were used to Samuel's practice sessions. Anyone in the building wouldn't have suspected anything more than an extra few guests for dinner, which was, at least for now, still legal.

We shared a meal and danced. For a few moments we forgot the bleak realities of the world outside. Samuel held my hand in his most of the evening. It was warm and reassuring—something tenable where so little else was. And while nothing at all seemed right in the world, I felt I wouldn't be facing it alone.

The guests dispersed as slowly as they'd arrived so their leaving wouldn't be noticed. I had to change from my gown, as the last thing I wanted was to attract attention. Mama Eisenberg took me back to the room that had been Samuel's to help me change.

"I'm so glad you've joined our family, my dear. A whirlwind romance, to be sure. But who's to say that isn't exactly what we need in such troubled times."

"You've made me feel so welcome. I feel so blessed to be with you all. You've raised Samuel to be such a fine man."

She laughed as she helped me with my buttons. "He didn't take much raising. One moment he was a baby, the next he was a young man fully formed in a child's body. I think I've learned more from him than I ever taught him. I hope you will be just as blessed, my darling girl."

"I hope you're right. When I dream about babies, they're all miniature versions of Samuel."

"They would be lucky to have a bit of you in them as well. Though I do have a request for you that's a bit odd coming from a mother to her daughter-in-law."

"What's that?"

"Take care of Samuel. And I don't mean cooking meals and mending his shirts. He's not like other men. He feels the world so keenly. With all the terrible things happening, it's bound to be too much for him to bear on his shoulders alone. You're a strong girl and I know you can help him bear it."

"I'll do my best for him, Mama. He deserves a better world than this."

"Don't we all, but him more than most," she said. "You know I always dreaded his wedding day. I worried that no woman would ever understand him. Not really. But you see him. You see him well and truly for the incredible person he is. It makes it easier to part with him." I was now free from my gown and slipped into the green dress I'd made for the occasion. We weren't flitting away on a honeymoon or to a fancy hotel. We would be going to live in my mother's home as she left the apartment for us to keep and the shop for us to run. All the same, it seemed fitting for a bride to have something pretty to change into from her wedding dress.

"You don't have to part with him, Mama. We're all part of the same family. And we'll need each other now more than ever."

"So many daughters-in-law say this, but in my heart, I know you mean it. I will pray for you every night for the rest of my days, my darling girl."

I embraced her and kissed her cheek. Lilla came in to say the rabbi had taken his leave as well. Samuel and I would be next.

We didn't own a car, so there wouldn't have been a grand farewell with people waving and wishing us well, but it seemed even more fitting for us to leave the warmth of his parents' apartment and descend into the darkness of the cold November night. We would have to find our path in the dark and make a light of our own.

I tucked my arm in Samuel's and breathed in deeply, letting the brisk autumn air chill my lungs. The smell of fading leaves mingled with the smell of cinnamon and nutmeg from the spice of our wedding cake.

"You're content, my Tilde," said Samuel.

"How could I not be?" I asked. "We were married on this beautiful day and are going home to *our* home."

"All good things," he said.

"It's almost like being happy," I said. I paused, realizing what I'd said.

"Don't fret, my love. I know what you mean. They ration happiness like butter, and some of us must make do with margarine. Right now, everything is a pale imitation of what it should be."

"Our parents had such joyous weddings. Our aunts and uncles. Grandparents. It's as though the happiness ration card skipped over this generation."

"Maybe for now," he said. "But I know in my bones this cannot last forever. People must wake up and come to their senses sooner or later."

"You speak the words of my daily prayers," I said.

"You will know happiness in our lives, my love. True happiness. I'll make it my life's work."

"And what of you?"

"If there is better happiness than knowing you're my wife, I don't think my mortal form will know it. I have enough."

He bent down and kissed my forehead and we walked in silence to the apartment. Our home.

I'd spent the last lonely two weeks scrubbing the few rooms and moving furniture, making the apartment as different from the home I'd considered to be my mother's as I could. It might have been tempting to dip into the secret stash of coins from the hidden drawer in Mama's dresser to buy some new furniture and to freshen the space as so many new brides were able to do, but I had to obey my conscience and only spend when it was absolutely necessary. My only indulgence was to use some of the best damask fabric from the shop to make new curtains for the parlor and the largest bedroom. The room I'd share with Samuel. I'd kept the tradition of sleeping in my own room until tonight. Now that I was married it would become my sewing room. Mama's little sitting room would become Samuel's workshop and practice room. It would be cramped, but he would be able to continue crafting his beautiful instruments.

We crossed the threshold into the bedroom, and we fell into each other's arms, finally giving into the desire we'd been feeling for months. Samuel cradled me in his arms, and we cooed loving words to each other until we drifted off into a sleep more peaceful than any I'd known since my girlhood.

Until the sounds of breaking glass and the screams of our neighbors robbed us of a peace we would never know again.

CHAPTER FOURTEEN

Hanna

November 9, 1938

We assembled at Frau Schroeder's home at the appointed hour. A butler saw us to the drawing room, where we waited for our hostess to join us. It was truly Friedrich's home now that his father was gone, but his mother stayed on and kept house for him, and she took the duty as seriously as a dowager countess on some great estate in England. While her tastes were not as stylish as Aunt Charlotte's, there was a timeless grace about the way she managed things. I recognized this effortless elegance in Friedrich, but knew I was hopeless to emulate it. Uncle Otto looked the picture of boredom, pacing the floor as we waited, but Aunt Charlotte was taking in the space and calculating each of Frau Schroeder's meticulous choices in décor, staff management, and any other detail that might tell her more about our hostess and the way she conducted her son's home.

"You'll have your hands full with her until she dies, I'm afraid," Aunt Charlotte warned me under her breath as she assessed the room. "She won't like stepping down for a mere slip of a girl, but she'll have to."

Aunt Charlotte spoke as though the engagement was a done thing, and I felt as though I'd been doused by a bucket of ice water. It was clear she expected me to accept him without question and she was already envisioning my life as mistress of this household and having to manage an overbearing mother-in-law.

"Perhaps Friedrich would do well to choose a woman nearer his age that might be better equipped to keep his mother in her place."

"I rather think he'd prefer a younger wife that he can mold to his liking. And to be frank with you, my dear, I'm not sure there's a woman alive who can put Adelheid Schroeder in her place."

"You make this marriage seem less and less appealing by the moment, Aunt Charlotte."

"Best to go into things with your eyes open. I could pretend that life will be all champagne and roses for you, but I'd be cruel to deceive you."

It was the closest thing she'd ever said to mirroring my own mother's advice. Mama had always been truthful—relentlessly so—and it was one of the things I loved most about her. At least I always did in retrospect, after the sting of the truth gave way to the wisdom of it.

Frau Schroeder marched into the room, clad in a steel-gray evening dress that complemented, rather than attempted to distract from, the strands of silver in her dark brown hair. Though we were the only guests that night, she was dressed as though she were welcoming foreign dignitaries. It was likely how she viewed us: as a friendly, adjoining nation that might prove useful in forming an alliance. I silently thanked Aunt Charlotte for insisting I wear one of my nicest gowns in peacock blue with several pieces of the jewelry she and Uncle Otto had purchased for me since my arrival. My aunt was dressed in a fetching amethyst-hued gown that I'd thought a bit too extravagant for an intimate dinner at home, but clearly her instincts were finer than mine.

"You'll have to forgive my son. He's going to be quite late in joining us this evening. His duties are terribly important, you understand. I'm hoping he'll be able to join us after supper with any luck." Frau Schroeder spoke as though his profession in the SS were more of a religious vocation, and I suppose to her it was every bit as sacred as if he'd taken the cloth.

"Naturally," Aunt Charlotte said. "I hope there isn't any serious trouble."

"Well, even if there is, Friedrich and his men will root it out quickly. Restoring law and order after far too long in chaos, if you ask me."

"Hear, hear," affirmed Uncle Otto.

Frau Schroeder ushered us into a posh dining room where we were served little plates of smoked trout that we ate slowly, waiting for Friedrich to join us. Uncle Otto and Frau Schroeder dominated the conversation, prattling endlessly about the buildup to the inevitable war, Otto proselytizing about the triumphs of the Führer and Frau Schroeder taking every opportunity to boast about Friedrich. Aunt Charlotte interjected the occasional witty commentary or charming remark, while I remained silent. No one seemed to mind my absence from the conversation, which was just as well. I studied the room, which was lined with a half dozen somber portraits of long-dead men and their families. Each of them had Friedrich's proud nose and serious blue eyes, and many wore military uniforms. There was a family resemblance in more than one regard.

As I stared at the portraits, I wondered whether, if Aunt Charlotte's plan worked and I ended up yoked to Friedrich, our children would have anything of me in them. The children in the portraits all seemed to strongly favor their fathers, while the mothers faded into obscurity. Perhaps our daughter might inherit the shape of my mouth or the point of my chin . . . or would my features and characteristics be swept away by the Schroeder genes, never to resurface again? There were probably some dutiful girls out in the world who would find it an honor, in some strange way, to have her children be mirror images of their father, but I did not want to lose all of myself. I wanted something of me to live on after I was gone.

Frau Schroeder kept looking at the clock as the courses were served and cleared. She lamented Friedrich's absence about once every ten minutes. She heaved a great sigh when the last of the dessert plates was cleared and there was no sign of him. She had us adjourn back to the parlor where Uncle Otto enjoyed brandy and a cigar and the women sipped coffee or blackberry liqueur. The conversation continued for what felt like hours, though the clock betrayed the hour was only eleven.

Friedrich interrupted the animated chatter of his mother's friends by bursting into the dining room. His usually impeccable uniform was muddy and torn. There was even a gash on his head near his left temple. Clearly there *had* been trouble and it had taken some doing for Friedrich to escape it.

"*Gott im Himmel*," Frau Schroeder breathed as she took in the sight of her son. "Neumann, get some help for the captain for his injury."

"No need, Neumann." Friedrich waved dismissively at the butler, who had already taken several steps toward the doorway in search of a medical kit or to phone a physician. "It's nothing but a few scratches."

Friedrich took one of the starched white serviettes from the table and held it to the bleeding area on his forehead. His mother blanched at the sight of him ruining her linens but did not raise her voice in a rebuke.

"Really, Friedrich. It looks like you've been in a tavern brawl. Are you sure you aren't in need of some help?" his mother pressed.

"And so I have, Mother. Several. Not just taverns, but shops, restaurants, and synagogues, too."

"What on earth is going on, my boy?" Uncle Otto asked.

"Come to the window and see," he said. We joined him at the large window in the adjoining drawing room that pointed toward the heart of the city. There was an orange haze on the horizon that slowly melded into one giant blaze. The longer we watched, the more fires we could see pop up across the skyline.

Berlin was burning.

Friedrich placed his hand on my shoulder, his chest puffed up with pride. "This, my dearest friends, is the realization of the Führer's dream, and the night is just beginning."

CHAPTER FIFTEEN

Tilde

November 10, 1938

We trembled on the floor of the closet, holding each other and wordlessly lifting up prayers to anyone who would listen.

I offered prayers to keep us safe.

I offered prayers to the disembodied voices whose screams pierced the still of night.

I offered prayers of thanksgiving that my mother was safely on her way to New York.

I prayed this was all some horrid dream from which the whole country would soon wake.

My back was pressed against the cold plaster of the closet wall, Samuel's arms encircling me. We both shivered despite the linens I'd stripped from the bed and pulled over us. Samuel had positioned himself as a shield against anyone who might invade the sanctity of our home. The gesture was kind, but we both knew it was useless. If what we could hear was any indication of the forces at work that night, Samuel's sacrifice would only buy me a few extra seconds of terror.

I waited for the thunder of boots coming up the stairs and the splintering of wood as they kicked down the doors. If they came, our only hope was that they would see the stripped bed and almost-empty drawers and assume the residents of the apartment had fled. If they asked our Gentile neighbors, that's the story they would get. There was no smell of a recently cooked meal lingering in the air. Thanks to my weeks of cleaning, there were no telltale signs of recent habitation. I sent up another prayer—that it would be enough for them to pass us over.

I had no idea how many hours we stayed huddled in the closet, clinging to each other and wondering if our first night of married life would be our last. I wasn't sure what time it was when we realized the horrifying sounds in the distance had faded and light began to creep in around the edges of the closet door. Slowly, the demands of my body made themselves known, but I was terrified to move, let alone speak.

Samuel sensed my subtle shift and tightened his embrace.

"Do you think it's safe?" I asked in the barest hint of a whisper.

"We can't stay in here forever," he said, but he remained still. He finally heaved a sigh and rolled to his side to open the closet door.

The light was blinding, and my muscles screamed against the movement after so long lying in one place. My legs quivered as I attempted to stand. I steadied myself by holding one of the bedposts until the blood flowed normally back to my extremities. Samuel pressed a finger to his lips and opened the door to the bedroom. He gave me one pleading glance and shut the door behind him. *Stay put. Stay safe.* I didn't know what he was planning, only hoped it didn't involve heroics. I stepped to the window but did not move the drapes aside. I carefully peered from the edge and hoped no one would notice the gentle ruffling of the fabric. It seemed everyone nowadays noticed everything. Some Gentiles noticed every move of their Jewish neighbors so they might report it. We who were Jewish noticed every move of our Gentile neighbors in hopes of staying alive. Of course, there were those in the middle. Those who weren't Jewish or out of favor, but who didn't support the regime. They were our greatest hope, and so very often our biggest disappointment.

From what I could see of the Berlin skyline, there were plumes of smoke coming from various points in the city. I couldn't tell where they came from, only that the damage was not limited to our neighborhood, and it was extensive. I couldn't begin to calculate the homes destroyed, the livelihoods ruined, the families pulled apart.

A few moments later, Samuel returned.

"The apartment is empty, and the shop was untouched," he said, the relief plain on his face.

"Many were not so lucky," I said, gesturing for him to look from the window. His face turned ashen as he stole a glance at the smoldering city.

"Oh, Tilde," was all he could say. He crossed his arms over his chest and exhaled.

"We should eat," I said. I knew neither of us would be able to stomach much, but would be able to face the day more easily if we had some fuel.

We dressed in our sturdiest clothes, and I took care to hide our nightclothes under the bed linens. It might be completely unnecessary to hide our presence in the apartment from Hitler's goons, but it was an advantage I didn't want to lose.

We ate a simple breakfast of toast and eggs. It should have been a joyous occasion—the first meal I'd made for Samuel. The first meal we'd shared as man and wife in our own home. We picked wordlessly at our food, unable to speak about the horrors that had encircled us that night. I knew the same questions circled in his head as did in mine. Why had this happened? What was left of the city? Who among our neighbors had been left alone and who had gone missing?

After twenty minutes of trying to eat, Samuel pushed away his plate of cold eggs and half-eaten toast.

"I must go check on my family."

I felt a lump of iron form in the pit of my stomach. They were immigrants. They had made no attempt to hide their identities. If the party had been targeting Jews, and it seems they always were, the Eisenbergs would have been prime targets.

But there would be no persuading Samuel to stay home. Nor would I want to have married a man who was willing to when he thought his family was in danger. We had no way of knowing what danger lay beyond our front door, but it was my sacred duty to follow him as we crossed the threshold.

SAMUEL TOOK MY hand as we walked the streets of Berlin toward his family home. We didn't dare speak. We didn't make eye contact with anyone, nor did they with us. The smoke burned our nostrils and scratched at our lungs. Books, clothing, and household goods were strewn among the shards of glass. Scattered like ashes over the cobblestones. I thought back to all the arguments between Mama and me about when it would become too dangerous to stay in Berlin. It was clear that we had crossed that threshold just that night. I had argued that when that moment came it would be impossible to leave. For perhaps the first time, I hoped I was wrong.

As we approached the Eisenbergs' neighborhood, I realized the mistake we were making could be fatal. If people saw us anywhere in the vicinity of the Eisenberg apartment, they would recognize Samuel. They would connect him with me. Our best hope was that the chaos surrounding us would be enough to distract people from paying too much attention.

We didn't need to enter the building to know that the instrument shop had been pillaged. Perhaps a dozen instruments— cellos, violins, violas—lay in splinters on the sidewalk. Countless hours of work destroyed for nothing. The building and the apartment above it still stood, but the contents had all been ransacked by expert looters.

The blood drained from Samuel's face as he crossed into the shop, the door of which now lay in pieces by the entrance. His eyes were wild as they scanned for any sign of his parents or sister.

He bounded up the stairs, me a half pace behind him. The door was splintered and the apartment was as disheveled as the shop. China and glass everywhere.

"Mama! Papa! Lilla!" Samuel called once we shut the apartment door behind us. There was no answer.

Samuel knelt. Lilla's violin lay on the parlor floor, pulverized by the heel of a jackboot.

Lilla. She would never have willingly left behind this treasure.

"Maybe they've hidden somewhere," I said, knowing we ought to be doing the same.

Samuel cast his eyes up to me. He was clinging to that glimmer of hope.

"Samuel!" An unfamiliar voice called up the stairs. We rushed down to answer it.

The old man who'd lived in the building next door for more than half a century was doing his best to climb the stairs despite arthritic knees.

"Get out of here, boy!" he warned. "It isn't safe."

"Herr Vogt, what happened here?" Samuel asked.

"The same thing that has happened everywhere. They're punishing the Jews for the assassination of some German secretary in Paris. Looting. Imprisonment. Burning synagogues. I've never been more ashamed to call myself a German."

"But what of my family?" Samuel pressed. "Where have they gone?"

"I didn't see for myself, but one of the neighbors said they saw them loaded up in a truck. Foreign-born Jews. More trouble with their passports, or some such foolishness."

Samuel slumped onto the step and buried his head in his hands.

"Son, you can't help them by getting caught. Get out of here and stay hidden the best you can. If I hear anything, I'll find a way to send word."

"You can find me—"

"Hush, boy. I know where to find you. I've known your parents since the day they arrived in this city and have always kept an eye on things. Go home. Don't go the way you came. Have your wife run your errands and don't do anything to attract attention to yourselves." He turned to me. "Tilde, open your shop this afternoon as though it were any normal day. Do everything as you normally would and pretend all this is just 'unfortunate business that happened to others.' If you want to keep Samuel safe tell everyone who will listen that you are a German-born Aryan and do anything you can to keep that story alive."

I nodded and pulled Samuel to his feet and back onto the street, leaving Herr Vogt to hobble back to his own apartment alone. I'd never met the man, never even been properly introduced, but it was the only advice we'd been given, and it seemed like the best we could ask for.

My mother's apartment—our apartment—seemed colder and more unwelcoming than I'd ever felt it. Samuel's face was gaunt, and I couldn't tell if he needed a hearty meal, a week of sleep, or both. If he was anything like me, he wouldn't be equal to food, so I made up the bed and ordered him to rest in it while I carried out Herr Vogt's orders and opened the shop. According to my watch, I was only a quarter of an hour behind schedule, which could easily be explained by all the "unfortunate business" that had happened in the neighborhood.

Klara bounded in not long after I'd flipped the sign from CLOSED to OPEN.

"I'm so glad you're okay," she said, panting to catch her breath. "My father says the damage is everywhere. I had to lie to get out of the house."

"I saw some of it," I admitted. The worry for my parents-in-law and sister-in-law had to be plain in my voice, but I tried to master it. Klara might be sweet enough, but her parents were party members and their loyalty to the Nazi cause was sacrosanct. "Are you well? I wonder that you didn't spend the day at home with all the chaos in town."

"Oh, I'm fine. Listen, my father seems to think things are going to get worse before they get better. Are you going to be okay?"

"Of course," I said. I'd never admitted to her that I was Jewish. And I never would. I wondered if her concern now wasn't just a ploy to get me to confess my vulnerability. "Why wouldn't I be?"

"You're alone," she said. "It's uncertain times. If you want to stay with us, I'm sure I can get my parents to agree."

She didn't know about Samuel. This was good. Or claimed not to. I wouldn't enlighten her.

"You're so sweet, Klara. I confess I was worried. I had no idea what was going on. I spent the night under my bed fearing that the world was coming to an end. But clearly it was just some . . . unpleasantness."

"That's one way to put it," she said wryly. "But truthfully, if you don't want to be alone, you needn't be."

"You're after free lessons," I said with a wink.

"You've spotted me in my own con," she said. "My very own live-in tutor."

"You can't afford me full-time," I said with a flippant chuckle. I walked over to some new claret-red wool we'd had in a few weeks prior. I cut six yards and wrapped it for her, along with a pattern for a flattering suit with a particularly fussy lapel. The color would complement her complexion and the heavier fabric would be practical with the coming winter. "I want you to work on this suit before I come see you next. You need a challenge to take your mind off all this," I said, gesturing to the world outside.

"If only things were solved so easily," she said, accepting the parcel. "I'm not doing much sewing these days, but it'll do more good than harm to have a project."

"Well said." I opened the door to the shop and watched as she merged with the ever-increasing foot traffic outside and went back to the outskirts of the city.

And for a moment, I envied her hours of oblivion as she sat at her machine and lost herself in her craft for a few days. She didn't have to worry about her family disappearing. She didn't have to worry about thugs breaking down her door as she slept. She would sleep soundly and wake untroubled—a luxury I hadn't known in years and wondered if I would ever know again.

And for hours I would have to keep at my station while my husband worried over what had happened to his family. It was true that we all might be in the same ocean, but some were sailing on very different vessels.

CHAPTER SIXTEEN

Hanna

December 1938

One morning, early in the Christmas holidays, a faint knocking sounded at the door of my room and Aunt Charlotte entered a few seconds later. Long enough to acknowledge that I was a young lady in need of privacy, but not long enough for me to give her leave to enter. In all things, she carried herself as the lady of the house, and I found I envied her poise. She always looked and acted as though she belonged precisely where she was. There wasn't a place in the world where I felt that way.

"You've been working so hard, darling. I thought you and I could go out. Have some lunch and gad about town a bit?"

"Of course," I said. "I could use your help finding a gift for Uncle Otto." I'd already purchased a lovely pair of kid gloves for Aunt Charlotte with my modest savings and had just a bit left to find something for Uncle Otto. Aunt Charlotte had provided me with more spending money than I usually saw in a year, but I wanted to buy their gifts with my own money. There was no way it could repay their generosity, but it would be better than leaving the occasion unmarked.

"Oh, he doesn't expect anything, dear. The party doesn't like to make a fuss over the holiday. But there will be parties and things. It's important to keep spirits up in winter, especially now."

Uncle Otto had taken to wearing an SS uniform like Friedrich's. He'd accepted some position in their ranks, though in some sort of advisory role. He wouldn't be sent into battle when the time came, but he was working longer and longer hours. Aunt Charlotte didn't have to worry about his safety, but I feared his absences left her lonely.

"It is," I agreed.

"What fun," she said, turning on her company smile for just a moment. We walked to the hallway, and I saw just a flash of what might have been sadness or regret as I closed my bedroom door behind me. "I'd always hoped to have a daughter to do these sorts of things with."

"Why didn't you?" I asked, instantly regretting that I couldn't pull the words back into my mouth. "I mean . . . it's not my place to ask. It just seems like you're such a natural mother."

"It wasn't what was meant for us," she said simply as we walked down the corridor. "The doctors were never able to find anything wrong with me, but there isn't any other logical explanation. My mother would have said it was God's will. Of course, we know there must be some scientific reason for these things."

"Did Uncle Otto ever go to the doctor?" I asked, thinking of Mama's line of questioning when these matters came up.

"No, darling. It's almost always the woman, isn't it? Much more to go wrong."

Mama might have disagreed with that. I'd heard her giving instructions to hopeful fathers almost as often as their wives. I wondered if they'd ever consulted with her on the matter, but then they had a city full of specialists. They probably dismissed her as a country midwife with little expertise beyond seeing a baby safely delivered to its mother's arms.

"Now, my dear. I know these questions might seem interesting to you, but dwelling on the past is a waste of energy. And besides, if I'd had my own brood of children, you and I might not be so free to have our fun today, would we?"

"I suppose not," I said, trying to emulate her smile. She caressed my chin with her thumb and forefinger before ducking into the backseat of Uncle Otto's gleaming black Mercedes while the chauffeur held the door for us.

Aunt Charlotte prattled on about her work with the Women's League, and I sensed she was happy to have more to accomplish in a day than ordering about the staff. Bandage rolling, sock knitting, canvassing funds. She had her fingers in all of it. And from the veiled note of pride in her voice, she was good at it, too. But there was a sadness in her, perhaps born from her not having children, that was present in all she did. Given the number of men who had died in the previous war, there were plenty of childless women in Teisendorf. Many accepted their childless state happily, but I didn't think Aunt Charlotte was one of them.

The chauffeur dropped us off in Charlottenburg, the smartest part of town, where the shops weren't crowded with harried housewives. There were doormen and attentive clerks who followed Aunt Charlotte and attended to her whims as though she were royalty. It was a world Mama had never introduced me to, but one Aunt Charlotte was firmly entrenched in.

"What do you think of this hat for Uncle Otto?" I asked, looking at a display. There was a rather fine brown fedora that I thought might be a bit more fashionable than the porkpie hat he usually wore.

"He'll be in uniform so often it won't get much use," she said. "Better to save it for another time."

I exhaled. I remember agonizing over gifts for Papa and my brothers earlier in the month, and I had the advantage there of having known them my whole life.

"Is there anything he could use?" I asked. "Perhaps a good book?"

"Let's not worry about your uncle just now, darling," she said, taking my arm. "I thought you might find a small token of esteem for Captain Schroeder."

Suddenly the scheme made sense. Aunt Charlotte hadn't wanted to spend time with me for my own sake; it was all to encourage the captain. I shook the thought from my head and tried to smile. She thought she was doing what was best and was acting out of concern—if not love.

"What about a nice cigarette case?" Aunt Charlotte suggested, leading me to the case. "We can have it engraved just in time."

I'd always been repulsed by the smell of smoke and had begged Papa to take his cigarettes to the great outdoors. I hoped Friedrich was one of the few men who abstained from the habit. "I've not seen him smoke," I said. "He seems like the sort that wouldn't abide such a French habit."

"You may be right," she said. "But don't let your uncle catch you saying that. He's grumpier than a bear coming out of hibernation if he goes too long without a cigarette. If he decided to give it up, I'm not sure any of us under that roof would survive longer than three days."

It was true I'd rarely seen Uncle Otto without a cigarette between his lips, and I'd had to stifle a gag at the stench of the smoke more than once since I'd moved in.

"How about some handkerchiefs?" I suggested. I'd have just enough money for them and could perhaps learn to embroider something simple before the week was out.

"Oh, he isn't your grandfather, dear. Let's find something a little more romantic. But something he would carry with him as a reminder of you would be a smart choice. You're right in that."

We ended up in front of a case with cuff links that varied from simple silver studs to ornate golden pieces with mother-of-pearl and precious gemstones. Aunt Charlotte rejected the simple silver pair I suggested that still would have been far beyond my budget.

"Those would be appropriate for a clerk or a shopkeeper. Not a man of Captain Schroeder's station."

"My father is a shopkeeper," I reminded her. "I thought they were nice."

"My dear, your tastes will elevate to the rank you attain. You want better than the life your father gave your mother, don't you? Your mother worked tirelessly her whole life."

"She loved her work," I countered. I wanted to protest further, but this wasn't about Mama. It was about Friedrich and his gift. "What about those?" I motioned to a slightly more elaborate silver pair with lapis inlay that didn't seem too garish or expensive.

"Much nicer," she agreed. "I predict he'll wear them often and think of you."

I remembered the way he held me as we danced, the feeling his kisses gave me, and part of me hoped she was right. The more reasoned side of me was loath to consider being ensnared by anyone just yet.

"Let's get you some earrings while we're at it," she said, eyeing my expression. "Nothing like a little sparkle next to the face, is there?"

She selected a pair of diamond studs that were small enough to be dainty but large enough to have a staggering price tag. I didn't mention to her that my ears weren't pierced. It wasn't a detail that would have escaped her notice and was a situation she'd have rectified before long.

"Just don't mention the cost to your uncle," she said with a wink. "He's happier not knowing."

She then proceeded to select a pair for herself that were three times as large as the ones she'd selected for me. "One of the few advantages of age, my dear, is the gravitas to pull off real jewels. Enjoy your delicacy while you can, though."

She waved away my purse when I offered to pay for the cuff links, though she did allow me to buy a handsome green woolen scarf for Uncle Otto. It wasn't extravagant, but I felt better knowing there would be something under the tree for him from me.

"You look somber. Tell me what your troubles are," Aunt Charlotte said as we sat down to lunch in a lavish restaurant. I glanced around at others to take my cues for decorum. Napkin on lap, order of forks. This was precisely the sort of thing Mama had no time for, and I now wondered if my education had been lacking for it.

"It's nothing, I'm well," I said.

"Of course it's not nothing," she said. "It's your first Christmas without your mother. Not to mention your brothers and father. It must be very hard."

"It is," I agreed, though Mama's absence for the holiday had barely registered with me. Finding my place in this new society into which I'd been flung seemed of far more immediate concern.

"Just try to enjoy the celebrations," she said. "They won't be what you're used to, but you'll have fun if you can keep your spirits up."

"I'm sure you're right," I said. "I'll do my best."

"That's a good girl. And you'll have the captain for company."

"I know Uncle Otto and you are convinced of his attraction, but don't you think his attentions are mere politeness?"

"Nonsense, my dear. I've heard from several reliable sources that he's besotted with you. Half mad with distraction, I hear."

"That seems dangerous with everything going on," I commented.

"Oh, you'll come to understand how men are. They can focus when they need to. I imagine we scarcely exist for them once they get inside a war room and start strategizing."

I doubted either the captain or Uncle Otto was high enough in the echelon to merit a place in one of the war rooms when decisions were being made. I hoped not.

"Come now, after lunch we'll get you something spectacular to wear for the parties. A new dress is a cure for most ills."

I chuckled at her little personal proverb but wondered if it didn't explain why she had a wardrobe to rival Greta Garbo's.

AUNT CHARLOTTE MADE good on her promise to find me something spectacular to wear for the Christmas parties. We found a red

velvet dress that was nothing like the pink and periwinkle confec-
tions that Frau Himmel had concocted. Aunt Charlotte took me to
have my ears pierced and lent me rubies to wear in my ears and at
my throat for the occasion. Mila was charged with styling my hair
in an elaborate updo and the end result was that I looked and felt ten
years older than I was.

We were at the home of one of the higher-ups in the party. There
were evergreen boughs and a Christmas tree, but no sign of a manger or baby Jesus. The party preferred to take the celebration back
to its pagan roots and remove all Christian sentimentality. Aunt
Charlotte stood beside me until Captain Schroeder came into view.
As soon as she saw the crowd part for his tall form, she discreetly
ducked away to chat with a friend a few yards behind me. He looked
at me in my red dress and made no attempt to conceal his appraisal
of me in my new finery.

He closed the space between us in a few long strides and took
my hand in his.

"Dearest Fräulein, I was hoping I'd have the pleasure of seeing
you again." He bowed and pressed his lips to my hand, lingering
just a moment longer than he needed to.

"Good evening, Captain," I said. "I trust you're well?"

"As well as can be expected in such busy times," he said.

"Of course," I said.

"You are ravishing tonight. I hope you don't mind me taking the
liberty to say so."

"No, I don't mind," I said. I felt as though a smarter girl would
rebuff his advances, but I found his words alluring in a way I'd
never experienced.

"Come, there are people I want you to meet. Important people who may prove useful to you. To both of us."

I cocked my head, wondering what he might mean by this, but thought better of asking. I accepted his proffered arm and allowed him to escort me around the room to meet various party players—major and minor—and the wives that accompanied them.

The men seemed to speak of nothing but the Führer's plans for expansion. Boasting about gains, projecting victories, and touting their own strategies for the days ahead. Their wives stood at their sides, rapt. They were marvelous at their work. I could not discern whether they truly were absorbed in their husbands' pontificating or if they were quietly making shopping lists in their heads.

Friedrich escorted me about the room, my hand pinned between his arm and his side. He paraded me like a prize show pony, which made the color rise in my cheeks. As we walked, I felt the heat of envious glances from the other women burning into my flesh from each direction. Being envied was a new sensation, and one I wasn't convinced that I enjoyed overmuch.

"You are resplendent," he whispered in my ear as discreetly as he could manage.

I said nothing but cast my eyes downward for a moment. He rubbed the hand he held prisoner with his free hand. I saw Aunt Charlotte chatting with someone I didn't recognize, but her eyes flitted to me as inconspicuously as they could to check my progress. She smiled in my direction once when the person she was speaking with was distracted for a moment. I was doing well, and she was pleased.

I remained silent through dinner, interjecting only to show I was paying attention to the conversation. The captain was attentive throughout the meal and seemed charmed by my quiet reserve. I wondered how he would feel if I gave my true opinions or prattled on about high school. Likely not favorably, but it was tempting to find out.

When dinner came to an end, the dancing began in the other room. The captain led me to the dance floor without bothering to ask my feelings on the subject, but it somehow felt good to be dancing instead of talking.

"My god, you're going to drive me mad in that dress," he whispered in my ear, his tone urgent like a plea for help.

"I-I'm sorry?" I stammered.

"Don't be," he said with a low laugh. "I've never seen a creature like you."

He pulled me closer and I felt his hands creep lower until the one at the small of my back grazed the top of my buttocks. I wanted to pull away, but Aunt Charlotte was at the side of the room, her eyes screaming their approval.

"I want to show you something," he whispered when the dance was finished.

"Oh . . . um, of, of course," I stuttered my agreement, though he'd already pulled me from the dance floor. We climbed a flight of stairs, Friedrich fairly dragging me behind him.

"Where are we going? I don't know if they want us here," I said as we entered a corridor full of private rooms.

"No one will question me," he said, the confidence radiating from him like heat from flames. In that moment I knew it was the truth. He opened the door to a bedroom.

"Perfect," he assessed. It was spacious and pleasant but lacked anything in the way of personal mementos. A guest room.

"What—" I began to ask, but he silenced me with a finger against my lips. He pulled me close and began kissing me, softly at first, but then with an urgency that was infectious.

His hands began to fumble with the zipper at the back of my dress and he lowered his mouth to kiss down the length of my neck.

I pushed back against him.

"We shouldn't," I said. I knew what he wanted. Mama had explained things to me, and I knew the end result could be a child.

"Then you shouldn't have come to this party dressed like a French harlot," he said.

"I didn't . . ." I began. He lowered my dress so that it lay in a crimson pool on the floor at my feet. Encircling me like flames. I instinctively covered myself with my arms.

"Your aunt dressed you, did she?" he asked. "Shrewd. Well, her plan was effective."

He pulled my hands from my chest and removed the rest of my clothes. I trembled as he pushed me to the bed and removed his own.

I wasn't sure if I should fight back, but I knew that trying to escape him would be futile. What would I do? Try to grab my clothes on the way out the door? Run naked into the ballroom? Each scenario seemed less plausible than the last. I simply lay back and let him claim what he desired. It was painful, as Mama explained it might be the first few times, but not overly so. I just prayed it would be over soon so I could go home.

But he took his time. It felt interminable, but I refused to cry in his presence. I wouldn't look weak by begging him to stop. I clenched my eyes shut and thought about my lessons. About hiking with Klara. About anything but what he was doing to me in that moment.

At long last he emitted a groan and rolled off to the side. He looked at the blood pooling where he had been.

"Ah, Frau Müller will be needing a new bedspread. I will have to have one sent to her," he said, unfazed by the damage he'd done to me. "Tidy yourself, my dear, and we'll go back downstairs."

I rose from the bed, shaking. I did my best to dress and straighten my hair but knew I must look a fright. The truth of what had happened would be broadcast on my face, betraying me to the whole crowd.

I looked at myself in the mirror and found myself less disheveled than I'd feared. The captain came behind me, placed his hands on my hips, and once again kissed the contour of my neck. It took all I had to not shudder in response to his caresses.

"You were an innocent. This pleases me," he said.

The look in his eye was triumphant. He had claimed me and was reveling in his prize.

He escorted me back downstairs and fetched me a glass of wine. A stout French red that was strong enough to take my mind off the events of the evening. I usually didn't care for wine all that much apart from a sweet Riesling with dessert, but was grateful for the aromatic potency of the Bordeaux. I drained the glass a little more quickly than was decorous but found I didn't much care. The captain paraded me around to chat with various people of impressive rank, but my input in the conversation was rarely needed. I accepted another glass from a waiter who circulated with a tray and wasn't too concerned if anyone thought I was overindulging.

Finally, I spotted Aunt Charlotte and gave her my best *please get me out of here* face. She looked loath to comply, but I saw her walk over to Uncle Otto's side and whisper in his ear.

"I'm sorry to claim your charming companion, Captain Schroeder, but it's getting rather late. We hope to see you again soon."

"You may depend upon it, Frau Rombauer," he said with a bow. He kissed my hand, formally as when we'd first been introduced, and bade me farewell.

I felt relief as the cold night air lashed at my face while we waited for the chauffeur to bring the car around.

"The captain is simply smitten," Aunt Charlotte purred. "Another excellent performance."

Performance. Like an actress. Well, it certainly felt more like I was playing a part than living my own life.

"You should be proud," Uncle Otto said. "To interest such a promising man so soon. I never dreamed it."

I nodded but said nothing.

It was all I could do not to run to my room in tears when the car pulled to the front of the house at last. Mila was there waiting, and I gratefully let her help me undress. I wanted nothing more than for the satin dressing gown to swallow me whole.

"I need to wash," I said. She saw the state of my underthings and understood.

"Of course. Are you feeling unwell?" She thought my cycle had come unexpectedly, and it was just as well. She brushed my hair and put it back in a simple braid.

"Not especially," I said. And physically it was true. My body would heal from what he did to me. My heart would take longer.

"I'll bring you some good herbal tea," she said. "It'll soothe you."

I patted her hand in appreciation. She poured a hot bath and cleared away my clothes before laying out one of my nightgowns. When she exited the room, I slipped off the dressing gown and dipped into the warm, perfumed water Mila had prepared for me.

"Is there anything else I can bring you?" she asked from outside as I slid into the tub.

"Perhaps wait fifteen minutes and ask Aunt Charlotte to come see me if she hasn't already retired for the evening."

She left with a little curtsey, and I let the warmth of the bath wash over me. Exactly fifteen minutes later, I heard a rapping at the door, so I quickly dried off and slipped on the nightdress and dressing gown Mila had left out for me. I was washed clean of Friedrich's— surely, I could use his given name now—advances and felt a little more human for it.

Aunt Charlotte, still dressed for the party, looked surprised to see that I had changed so quickly. She produced a small box and placed it in my hands.

"A little token of esteem for you from your uncle and me," she said.

I opened the red velvet box and inside was a diamond pendant on a thick gold chain. It was likely worth more than my father earned in a year. Even in the dim firelight of my room it glinted brilliant beams of light on the darkened walls. I could have stared, trans- fixed, at its frozen beauty for hours, but snapped the box shut to regain a measure of courage.

"Aunt Charlotte, I wanted to tell you something about the cap- tain," I said, rushing my words into a jumble.

"He took you upstairs to one of the guest rooms," she said.

"You knew?" I asked. The air seemed trapped in my chest like a scream I couldn't release. It strained against my ribs, and I was helpless against it.

"Of course. You were never out of my sight the whole night, dear. Except, well, you know. Do you have any questions, dear? Did your mother explain how it all works? I hope you weren't too frightened."

I had been, but not of the act itself.

"But you didn't try to stop him . . ." I stammered.

"Why would I, dear? Now that he's . . . enjoyed your company . . . and learned that you were innocent, he'll be even more entranced by you than ever."

"But shouldn't we have waited? What if there's a child? What if he loses interest in me and no one will want me because of what we did?" The questions sprang from me like a torrent.

"He's not a cad. If there's a child, he'll marry you. It's what your uncle and I would hope for above all things. To see you married and settled with a family of your own. It's what we promised your father, after all."

She invoked my father, the cruelest thing she could have done aside from invoking my mother.

"Listen, darling. I know it wasn't perhaps the most . . . gallant way things could have gone. But fairy tales are for children. You're a young woman living in challenging times. You have to be practical. Don't fret. Your uncle and I won't let any harm come to you."

I nodded and held my tears at bay until she turned and left the room.

As soon as I heard the door click and her steps pad down the hallway, I let them loose, standing in the middle of this massive room, swaying on the point of collapse. My humiliation wasn't just an unfortunate turn of events—it was orchestrated by my own blood. Nothing, from the events we attended to the dresses I wore, had been left to chance by Aunt Charlotte.

Mila entered with a knock perhaps five minutes later, carrying the promised tea. She set it on my bedside table, then took me by the elbow and sat me on the edge of the bed.

"Drink this," she said, brushing a loose tendril from my forehead in a gesture that felt quite maternal coming from one only a few years older than I.

Obediently, I sipped from the odiferous cup. It tasted as vile as it smelled and burned its way to my stomach. I couldn't help but wince at the taste.

"I think the tea has gone off," I managed to gag.

"Black cohosh root, among other things. And you'll drink it all if you know what's good for you. Your aunt and uncle may trust the captain with your future, but I don't think so well of men as they do. Don't get yourself in the family way until you have a ring on your finger, if you want my advice."

"You overheard everything?" I asked.

"Not everything. But enough. And I guessed what had happened from your knickers. I know your aunt is keen on this man, but she's taking a foolhardy gamble with your future."

"And this will . . ."

"Protect your future, if we're lucky," she said. "It's never foolproof, but it's safer than other methods. If you find you've missed your courses, we may have to do something more drastic if you're willing."

I knew Mama had performed this service when people pled their cases to her. In the end, she always believed the patient knew her own mind and heart better than she ever could. But as understanding as Mama was of these women, she never let me watch or help when a woman wished to be relieved of an inopportune pregnancy. I'd never been allowed behind the veil of this aspect of Mama's work, and now I wished I knew what advice she'd offered to women in such a predicament. I was now at the mercy of Mila's folk medicines or Friedrich's honor.

Both prospects made me feel like I was standing on the edge of a melting ice sheet.

I finished the tea and Mila took the cup without our usual exchange of pleasantries.

I thought about reaching for my worry stone, but instead grabbed the framed photo of Mama from my bedside table. I clutched it to my heart and fell asleep with the small remembrance of her in my arms. I would have traded all the riches in the world to have her back in flesh and bone to hold me in my sleep one last time.

CHAPTER SEVENTEEN

Tilde

December 1938

I'd never been overly enamored of my light brown hair and alabaster skin, nor of the fact that I'd inherited my father's classic German bone structure. My appearance made my mother's people treat me like an outsider, and my father had made sure that I was never truly welcomed among his. But my looks allowed me to keep my shop open and my husband fed.

The world kept turning, and most of Berlin acted as though the horrible night we experienced was just an unfortunate disruption to their routines. To them, I supposed that's all it was. To the rest of us, it was Kristallnacht, the night of broken glass. The sound of each shattered pane forever etched in our memories.

The neighbor who ran the cheese shop next door, a plump woman named Frau Heinrich, made a habit of frequenting our shop as often as she could justify a new dress. Mama and I always made sure to give her shop our custom in repayment for that loyalty.

"My dear, I'm so glad to see you well after all the terrible business last month. I've been so worried for you here all alone. I hope you won't think me overstepping the mark, but it wasn't right for your mother to leave you here alone. Who knows what might happen to you without someone looking after you?" She spoke with the genuine concern of a grandmother, not the condescension of a meddlesome crone who has no affairs of her own, so must enmesh herself in those of her acquaintance.

"Frau Heinrich, aren't you a widow? And your children left home quite some time ago, didn't they?" I reminded her gently. She had, more than once, crowed to my mother about the joys of living alone and how she was enjoying the peace of her golden years.

"That is a very different thing, my dear. I'm old. Even if trouble comes for me, it's of little consequence. But you have your whole life ahead of you."

"Well, Mama didn't have much choice. Travel is a perilous thing these days and she was lucky to get an exit visa." I restrained myself from saying more. Frau Heinrich wasn't Jewish and might not be sympathetic to our plight. For all I knew, she thought Hitler's goons had the right idea, though I wanted to think better of her.

"I've heard tell of that, to be sure," she said with a tut-tut and a shake of her head. "Such odd times we're living in. But I suppose we've all got to soldier on, haven't we."

"Quite right," I assured her. "Can I get you anything?"

"Oh, a couple of yards of some sturdy broadcloth for a new apron would do the trick," she said, idly milling through the calicos and muslins. I sensed she wasn't in need of a new apron but had been looking for an excuse to check on me. It was either a very kind gesture or one born of a more sinister impulse. She'd never been blessed with great wealth, and if the Nazis were offering rewards for outing Jews who had gone into hiding, I wouldn't have put it past her to turn me in. Though perhaps it was a poor investment on the part of the Nazis. There were more than enough people in Berlin willing to betray us for free; Hitler's government didn't have to offer a payout to get the citizens to comply.

I retrieved some of my best broadcloth in a nice navy blue and cut the length for her, adding the bias tape and thread she would need to the pile.

"Thank you ever so much, my dear. By the by, I've noticed you've taken up the violin."

"Why do you say that, Frau Heinrich?"

"I could hear you through the walls last evening. So proficient so early in your studies. It seems we have a Fräulein Mozart in our midst."

Samuel had been playing last night. I hadn't dreamed anyone would notice.

"Oh, I was listening to a record. I'll be sure to keep the volume down. I do apologize."

"Really. Your phonograph must be of the first quality. The sound was as clear as if I were sitting in a concert hall."

"How remarkably sound can carry. I'll be sure to keep it down."

"I rather enjoyed it, my dear. I lament that I never learned to play an instrument. I spent much of my girlhood behind a sewing machine, anxious to have the prettiest dresses in school. I confess sewing is becoming more of a chore in my old age than the joy it was in my youth. Cling fast to those sweet pastimes, my dear, for they won't always give you the pleasure they once did."

"Perhaps I could do some sewing for you when the need arises,

Frau Heinrich. I'm sure you have plenty of other things to occupy your time."

"You really are a sweet girl, aren't you?" she said. "Of course, you must put everything on my account."

"Naturally," I said. I could see in her probing eyes that she was looking for any sign of discomfort with the arrangement. If I voiced any, I was sure she'd have a troop of guards at my door before the day was out. For years, I'd thought she was a kind old woman, but now I realized she was using the situation to extort me for all she could.

I'd claim to add it to the ledger but would never ask her to settle her account. And I knew that the moment I asked her to pay up or if I refused her anything from the shop, there would be more "unpleasantness" of the sort we'd just experienced, only right under our noses.

I sensed she'd need more than an apron or two in the near future in exchange for her silence, but it was a small price to pay to keep her quiet.

"Why don't you leave these with me, and I'll have the apron ready for you in the next three days or so? Would that suit?"

"Beautifully, my dear," she said. "And I'll have a lovely morsel of Bergkäse for you. Our last delivery was some of the best I've tasted in years."

"My favorite," I said. She was trying to convince herself she wasn't blackmailing me, but it was plain that she was.

I ascended the stairs after she left, turning the sign to CLOSED for the evening.

"A busy day for you, my angel," Samuel said. He sat at the

kitchen table, where he was sanding one of the violins that we'd managed to salvage from the shop. It would be a magnificent piece.

"Quite," I said. "And thank heaven for it."

I was true to the promise I made my mother and didn't tell Samuel about the money I had hidden in the dresser. There was a good chance we'd need every last dime and more to escape. Showing concern for our finances would mean he'd be less apt to suspect Mama had left us with a small fortune that had to remain a secret. Spending much would attract unwanted attention anyway, so I pretended it didn't exist for both our sakes.

"I wish I could produce instruments like I used to. Give lessons. Contribute to the household."

"But you are," I said. "You manage the house while I tend the shop. It's a weight off my shoulders."

"That isn't real work."

"I assure you that every housewife in Berlin disagrees with you," I said, deliberately taking a harsh tone. A good argument was one of the few things that roused him out of his fits of melancholy. "It's damned hard work, yet husbands think the fairies come in the middle of the night and clean and mend and cook. More men ought to be put in your shoes and be made to keep house for a while. It would do them good."

"I'm sorry, darling. It was a thoughtless comment."

I eyed him. "It was indeed. My mother worked herself into a stupor keeping house for my father. Your mother worked hard to give you a happy home when you were a boy. That position deserves better than your condescension. I want you to know I value the work you do here, and even if it isn't your preference to spend your time keeping house, it's honest and necessary work."

Samuel, looking thoroughly chastised, turned his attention back to his instrument rather than say anything more to incite my ire.

"I'm sorry to say this, my love, but we need to be on our guard," I said, changing the subject. "Frau Heinrich heard you playing the violin last night. She knows I've never studied. If it continues, she'll have cause to send someone around looking. She won't buy my story about the phonograph a second time."

"So they're to steal my music from me as well?" he asked. "I'm beginning to wonder what's left for me in this world."

"Your family, for one. We don't know where your parents and sister are, and we owe it to them to find them. And you do have a wife that needs you."

I tried to wrap my arms around him, to stop this torrent of self-pity, but he was determined to languish in it.

"For what? An extra mouth to feed? An extra burden on your shoulders?"

I felt my stomach sink to hear him speak so lowly of himself; but like so many other men in his position, the lack of occupation was making him feel useless. "Stop talking nonsense, Samuel. I'm sorry about the violin, I truly am. But if Frau Heinrich talks, we're both in danger. Our lives depend on you staying hidden and safe."

"Do you really think they're still alive? My family?"

"I know it, Samuel. I'd feel it in my gut if they weren't." I spoke with more certainty than I truly felt. The stories my patrons in the shop were telling had become more and more grim as the days went on. People disappearing, people increasingly desperate to flee. But if it meant sparing Samuel from slipping into the abyss of his despair, I'd cling to hope until we had reason to believe it wasn't true.

CHAPTER EIGHTEEN

Hanna

December 1938

Christmas—or *Julfest*, as Uncle Otto insisted we call it—wasn't strange that year because of how different it was, but rather, how similar it tried to be. We had so many of the usual holiday trappings: a massive fir tree in the drawing room was meticulously decorated by the staff. From afar it looked like a typical Christmas tree from any other year. But when I approached, I noticed that between the painted glass bulbs of red, gold, and silver were miniature busts of the Führer. In place of the usual angel or Star of Bethlehem, the topper was a blown-glass spire that otherwise looked normal, save for the black swastika emblazoned in the middle. The pile of gifts underneath was far more abundant than I'd ever experienced even in the most prosperous years with my parents. I hoped the package I'd sent to Teisendorf with new boots for Papa and toy cars for the boys had arrived, but I had received no call or note to confirm it.

There were, however, no trips to church in our finest clothes.

Aunt Charlotte didn't put out a miniature wooden manger with the Holy Family and the Three Wise Men, but rather a miniature garden with wooden animals. Deer, rabbits, and other forest animals surrounded a figure of a blond woman and baby boy. She was to represent the virtues of German motherhood and the baby was to represent the constant renewal of the German race.

I looked at the faces of the figurines. The mother looked smug, knowing she was doing her duty to her country. The baby's expression was eerily blank. He was a tabula rasa waiting to be taught about the regime and his place in it. His birth wasn't the product of a miracle. He was as human as the child I had been praying would never come for the past week. Just two days before the holiday, my prayers were answered in the form of my monthly courses. Mila gave me a hug in celebration, breaking the unspoken rule of quiet reserve demonstrated between employers and staff. Though I wasn't really Mila's boss, there was enough of a disparity in our situations that she was usually on her guard with me.

"Merry Christmas, my dear," Aunt Charlotte said as I entered the drawing room on Christmas Eve. Both she and Uncle Otto were dressed in smart evening wear, though we weren't expecting company. I'd wondered why Mila had laid out one of my nicer dresses in a deep forest green, despite Aunt Charlotte's assurances we were having a quiet holiday with just the family. The reason made itself apparent when Friedrich appeared in the drawing room, escorted by the butler, just a few minutes later.

I shot Aunt Charlotte a pleading look she pretended not to notice. For the first time since we met, Friedrich was not in uniform. He wore a dark gray suit with fine pinstripes with a coordinating solid gray tie. His shirt was starched impeccably. Though it wasn't leisure wear, the effect still softened his appearance when contrasted with the utter rigidity of his uniform. His blue eyes looked less steely. There was something more like humor in his expression.

"I'd call you beautiful, but the word doesn't do you justice," he said, accepting a glass of brandy from Uncle Otto.

"You flatter me," I said, not breaking eye contact. The time for well-bred coyness seemed long behind us.

"I speak only the unvarnished truth," he said. I rolled my eyes as I accepted a brandy of my own.

Aunt Charlotte noticed the rude gesture and returned a glare. "You haven't slept well, have you dear? What a shame. I hope the festive spirit of the evening will catch up with you soon enough." A warning.

"Of course, Aunt Charlotte," I said, forcing my expression to soften.

The evening meal was served, a veritable feast with roasted goose, glazed pork tenderloin, freshly baked breads, perfectly sautéed carrots, and a half dozen other dishes I didn't even bother to register.

Uncle Otto and Friedrich kept up a steady flow of conversation in which Aunt Charlotte occasionally interjected something clever or endearing. She'd mastered the art of charming companionship. The BDM would do well to have her teach courses on the subject to young women in the throes of courtship. Sadly, they likely wouldn't appoint a childless woman to such a post, no matter how qualified. They'd worry she'd be a bad influence on the girls, somehow. As though childlessness were somehow catching. I didn't bother interjecting, and mercifully no one prodded me.

We gathered in the drawing room after a decadent dessert of

chocolate torte with brandied cherries and took turns opening gifts. Aunt Charlotte accepted the gloves with pleasure, and even Uncle Otto seemed pleased with the scarf. I received a silver tray for my vanity and a lovely brown cashmere coat from my aunt and uncle. I handed Friedrich the cuff links I'd selected with Aunt Charlotte.

"I hadn't expected a gift when you yourself are such a treasure, my dear." He proceeded to open the package and immediately replaced the cuff links he was wearing with the ones we'd selected. "Exquisite taste, but I'd have expected nothing less. I only hope my offering is acceptable."

He pulled a red velvet box from his pocket and knelt before me, opening the lid to reveal a glittering emerald-cut diamond set in a thick gold band. Timeless, classic. It was lovely, but in the moment I failed to understand the significance of the gift.

"Dearest Hanna, would you do me the honor of becoming my wife?"

I opened my mouth and stared like a simpleton. It couldn't possibly mean what I thought.

"Hanna, answer the man," Uncle Otto said at last.

"You've stunned her," Aunt Charlotte said. "It's not every day a girl gets engaged."

I could only concentrate on the air forcing itself into my lungs as though the passageways were blocked with sludge. *Get engaged.* Aunt Charlotte made her expectations clear.

I instinctively reached for my worry stone, but had left it upstairs, as this dress, like so many of my other new acquisitions, was without pockets. *What do I do, Mama?* I wanted to scream. To run.

Friedrich's face was taut with anticipation. It was the first time I'd seen anything other than unflappable confidence in his eyes. I found I liked him better for it. Perhaps he realized how brutish he'd been. Perhaps he meant to be kinder in the future.

"I-I I'm still in high school," I stammered. "I can't get married."

"You've only a few months left! What difference does it make?" Uncle Otto interjected.

"I want to finish my studies. It's what my mother would have wanted."

Uncle Otto scoffed and turned his back, retreating to the sideboard for another brandy.

"It's not as though the wedding would be tomorrow, dear. I'm sure Friedrich can be persuaded to wait until summer," Aunt Charlotte said gently.

"Quite right," he agreed, rising from his knee to sit beside me on the couch. "A wedding takes time to prepare, after all. And I know your aunt likes to see things done properly."

"Indeed, I do," confirmed Aunt Charlotte. "A real wedding is precisely what we all need to cast off the gloom, isn't it?"

"Just what I think," said Friedrich. "But Hanna would have to say yes."

I glanced over to Aunt Charlotte and Uncle Otto, both of whom gave me expectant looks. There was only one answer they would accept. Aunt Charlotte touched her neck and glanced to mine. Suddenly the necklace they'd given me seemed to become a millstone around my neck. A reminder of all they'd done for me, all they'd given me, and all they'd promised my father.

I nodded, unable to speak the word aloud. He slipped the ring on my finger, and in moments I was awhirl in congratulations and champagne.

"I'm so proud of you, my dear," Aunt Charlotte cooed. "You'll be so happy."

She meant to speak with confidence, but it felt more like an order. If only she could command such a thing.

In a way, perhaps she was. She was commanding me to make the world *think* I was happy. To give Friedrich's social circles the illusion of happiness. That's all it was.

Friedrich was beaming, and kept his arm draped possessively over my shoulder. As he held me close, the scent of cedar and oakmoss drifted from his skin. The honest scents of good working men seemed incongruous with his polished exterior and ruthless resolve.

I think I smiled as Otto and Friedrich spoke of the future of our now intertwined families, the party, and the country. It was as though this marriage represented a victory for the Reich, and indeed it was a coup for Friedrich. A wife—and the niece of staunch party supporters—was a necessary step on his way up the party ladder. I was an asset.

I was grateful when Friedrich took his leave. I'd been worried he was going to ask for an invitation to stay and there was nothing my aunt and uncle would have refused him. But perhaps the ring on my finger changed things and he would give me a reprieve. I was to be his wife, and that position, at least, commanded some respect.

When I retired to my room, Mila was adding a few new items to one of my drawers.

"Some new night things from Frau Rombauer," she explained, noticing my confusion. It wasn't laundry day, and it was unusual to see her at the task otherwise. "She didn't want to embarrass you by

having you open them in front of Herr Rombauer and the captain."
She held up one of the gowns. It was pink and completely sheer. The
sort of thing that women wore for their husbands.

Aunt Charlotte had been hoping he would ask for an invitation,
too. She would have given him a guest room, of course, for appear-
ances. Near mine but not too close. She was confident that when
the house was asleep, he would come to my room and take what
he'd laid claim to.

And it was my duty, even more so now, to oblige him.

CHAPTER NINETEEN

Tilde

January 1939

I have a job for you, if you're interested," Klara said without preamble as she walked into the shop. "A friend of mine is engaged to be married and needs quite a few new things. It'll pay well, believe me."

Part of me yearned to tell Klara my own joyous news, but given that she was without a serious prospect, I didn't want to make her feel any worse than she might already with her friend's announcement. And, of course, there was the lingering fear of sharing news with anyone these days.

"Why hello, stranger. I'd be interested, especially since my best student has given up lessons," I said. The shop did well, but the truth was that I couldn't afford to turn down work, especially if it promised to pay well and had the prospect of repeat business. "What is she looking for?"

"Some suits and dresses. Possibly a few evening pieces. I'm not sure exactly. She's marrying a bigwig, so nothing's too good for her."

"I hope my skills will meet her expectations, in that case."

"Oh, she's not all that fancy herself. Rather down-to-earth. She's just got connections and had some good luck. Hanna will be pleasant enough to work with."

"What sort of a 'bigwig' is she marrying?" I asked.

"A captain in the SS," she replied.

"Your captain," I said.

"He was never mine, but yes, the very same."

"I'm sorry," I said, knowing that she was burying pain behind her indifferent façade.

"Don't be. I wasn't what he wanted. I'm better off finding someone who thinks I'm worth spending time with. And Hanna is a sweet girl. She'll be a good wife to him and make pretty babies. They'll be happy."

"You're a good friend," I said. "She's lucky to have you."

"You give me too much credit. Besides, if her wedding means throwing you some business, it's cause for cheer, no?"

"True enough."

"I'll arrange it all. I'll pop back in when I have it all settled."

She bounded off as though we hadn't gone two months without seeing each other and as though her visit was as expected as the rising of the sun.

She proved good to her word and returned a week later with an address and appointment time. After a bit of pleading, she promised to accompany me to the first appointment. Whether it would make her uneasy to see another woman being outfitted for a wedding to the man she'd set her cap at, I didn't know, but her presence would make working for a complete stranger far easier for me.

We approached the sprawling villa in the Grunewald district, and I struggled to keep my composure at the sight of the massive swastika on the flag that hung over the front door. Another reason to have Klara with me: my presence with an Aryan girl would make them look less closely at me.

We were ushered inside by a harried butler. Two blond women were waiting for us in a lavish bedroom. The elder looked like she was used to commanding a room, but the younger—presumably the bride-to-be—seemed like she'd prefer to be hiding under a rock. She looked the part of the sweet Aryan bride, but there was an intelligence and wit about her that I sensed would give her trouble.

"This is Tilde," Klara said grandly. "I promise you she'll suit far better than your previous seamstress. Hanna can't be wearing the girlish frocks that Frau Himmel is so fond of. The captain needs to see her as a woman grown."

"I hope you're right. Frau Himmel has left us in quite a lurch," the older woman, Frau Rombauer, said, looking dubiously at me. On her face, I could see her concern over my youth and likely inexperience warring with my poised appearance and well-made clothes.

"We'll be needing three suits and two evening dresses. Fairly heavy fabric for winter, I should think. And we don't have much time."

"We have some lovely wool suiting that will do just the trick. One in a brighter shade of navy will be stunning with her blue eyes, and maybe an overcoat in a thick saffron wool. It will be a striking contrast," I said, addressing the elder. She was clearly the decision maker, and that sort would always prefer to be spoken to directly. "Perhaps the other two suits in a dark charcoal and a nice hunter green? And I think your daughter's figure would do well with a fuller skirt to accentuate her waist."

"Niece," she corrected, though without any apparent rancor. "You seem to know what you're talking about. If this goes well, we'll have more work for you."

"I hope my work will be up to your standard, then," I said.

"I'll leave you to take your measurements. I'm sure the girls can show you out when you're finished." She left with a kiss to her niece's cheek and a nod to Klara. "And not too dowdy with the evening dresses, no matter what the current trends are. She needs to keep his attention."

She exchanged a charged glance with Hanna, whose even composure faltered for just a moment.

"So, when's your big day?" I asked, gesturing for her to raise her arms and taking the tape measure around her bust. "Take notes, will you, Klara?"

Klara poised herself with a pen and paper. She may have given up the trade, but she missed it.

"Oh, I'm sure they'll tell me at some point. If Aunt Charlotte had her way, it would be tomorrow."

"And what about you? Holding out for a spring wedding?"

"Spring five years from now, perhaps. Maybe ten."

Klara did an enviable job of keeping quiet, but I was certain I could hear her teeth grinding. It was one thing to lose a man to a girl who was madly in love with him and would try to make him happy. It was quite another to lose him to an indifferent bride.

"Is there anything in particular you'd like?" I asked. "Colors? Fabrics? I'm sure I can make something to please both you and your aunt."

"Whatever you think is suitable will be fine with me," she said, her eyes cast downward for a few moments before fixing on me again.

"Certainly you have some thoughts on your own clothing," I prodded.

"Truly I don't. If Aunt Charlotte trusts your judgment, so do I. Do you have all you need?"

"If you want to stay behind, Klara, I'm happy to see myself out," I said, taking the paper from Klara's proffered hand.

"I need to head home anyway," she said, snapping her notebook back in her handbag. "I'll see you back to the shop."

She and Hanna exchanged stiff embraces in farewell and Klara screwed on a smile until we exited the front door. I could hear her exhale a breath I hadn't realized she'd kept within.

"That wasn't easy for you," I said. I didn't need to ask; it was plain on her face.

"No, but it doesn't really matter, does it? He chose her."

"And she doesn't love him,"

"No, she doesn't. Then again, neither did I. But she's a smart girl. She'll realize what a catch he is before too long and act accordingly."

"You're awfully magnanimous for a friend. There are plenty of those who wouldn't do as much for a sister, let alone a school chum."

"She's a special case, I think. She took the loss of her mother deeply to heart, and she doesn't know her aunt and uncle particularly well. It's been difficult for her. She's actually rather sweet and a darn sight more interesting than most of the BDM girls. All the same, it's hard not to resent her luck."

I felt the blood drain from my face at the mention of the BDM. I'd been asked to join when I was in school, and even attended a few meetings until people realized who my mother was. When I learned what they stood for, I was terrified, but even more scared to leave. The girls who didn't participate were shunned and bullied. I'd liked the idea of running around the woods and learning a few new skills, but it didn't take long to understand that this wasn't just another scouting group. But of course Klara was a member. All girls were now. She was probably a de facto part of the Women's League already, accompanying her mother to all manner of meetings even before she was out of high school. I could well imagine her idly sketching dresses and longing to be elsewhere. But perhaps I was wishing for her to be something she wasn't. As sweet as she was, it was possible—maybe even likely—that she would cheerfully turn me in to the authorities if she knew who and what I was.

We turned down the busy street toward my shop, though Klara didn't seem to be in any sort of hurry to return home.

"And what of you?" she asked suddenly. "Why do I never hear about the dashing young men throwing themselves at your feet? You may work hard, but you don't live under a rock. Certainly someone interesting has noticed you by now."

"Oh, not really," I said. "The shop isn't a place where men come in any real numbers."

I wanted to tell her more. I was bursting to wax poetic about the husband who had so thoroughly captured my heart. Klara was the closest thing I had to a real friend, and I wanted so much to confide in her. But trusting her would be more than foolish.

"I suppose that's true," she said. "Still, there's hope for girls like you and me yet, isn't there? We're not old spinsters yet."

"Not yet," I said with a laugh. "We have a solid six months before we're past our prime."

"Thank heaven for the gift of time," she said, tossing her arm around me. I squeezed her hand for just a brief fraction of a second, so eternally grateful for a moment of levity. I couldn't imagine her vivacity tempered by the bonds of marriage. Anything that would suck the color from her cheeks and the spark from her eyes could never be a force for good in my book.

"None of them deserves you, you know that?" I asked her.

"And there isn't one alive that would ever be worthy to scrub your boots, let alone share . . . everything with."

I thought of Samuel, the warmth filling my chest with the knowledge that he was, exceptionally, a man worth getting to know. I hoped Klara's parents would be insightful enough to pick a man who would appreciate her as she was, but knew their considerations would be far different from my own.

CHAPTER TWENTY

Hanna

January 1939

ovely, dear," Aunt Charlotte pronounced as I joined her in the
foyer. I wore a dinner dress of periwinkle blue, courtesy of Frau
Himmel, and made my obligatory twirl for her to inspect me.
The dinner party was set to begin in fifteen minutes, and I was expected to be there to greet the guests like the daughter of the house.

"Thank you," I said, wishing I were clever enough to come up
with an excuse to stay in my room with a good book.

"Don't forget to smile. You have a tendency to look a bit sullen at
the table on occasion."

"It happens when I get lost in thought," I said.

"Stay in the moment," she said. "No man likes a silly day-
dreamer. You can indulge your idle thoughts when you're alone, if
you must, but be present in the room."

"Yes, Aunt Charlotte," I said, swallowing a sigh. I made sure my
mask rarely slipped for these people, but Aunt Charlotte insisted I

be flawless. To the point where I couldn't even be the sovereign over my own thoughts.

As usual, the most elite members of Aunt Charlotte and Uncle Otto's social circles were in attendance. Klara's parents entered the room, with her a pace behind them, looking flawless in an evening dress in a shade of Bordeaux red that was exquisite with her dark hair and milky complexion. She looked thinner than the last time I saw her, especially in her face, and her gait implied that, despite the weight loss, she was wearing a girdle tight enough to crush all her internal organs from the waist down. I cast a side eye at Frau Schmidt when she wasn't looking. It had to be her doing.

We sat down to the meal, elegant as always, and I smiled and made idle conversation with those around me. I smiled between bites of meticulously prepared food and made sure to keep my conversation light. Friedrich was seated to my left, and I wanted to remind Aunt Charlotte about what she'd said about seating couples together at dinner parties being a tedious practice. But, of course, that had a lot more to do with her enjoying as much time away from Uncle Otto as she could manufacture and was at odds with her desire to see me married off. The meal seemed to last an eternity, but I endeavored to be charming for the duration of it. When the waitstaff came around with the dessert trays, I had to stifle an audible sigh of relief.

"Klara, I think you can skip dessert," Frau Schmidt chided loud enough for the whole table to hear as the staff was offering slices of cakes and pies for the guests to select from. I'd tried not to pay Klara too much attention during the meal, but she'd taken minuscule portions of each course.

Klara flashed a weak smile and waved away the uniformed footman, who scurried on to the next guest.

"Klara should have some of the chocolate marzipan cake," I interjected, addressing the footman. "It's her favorite. I asked Cook to make it especially for her."

"How very thoughtful of you," her mother said before Klara could respond. "But Klara is watching her figure at the moment."

"How interesting," I said. I turned to my left. "Captain Schroeder, isn't it true that the Führer has discouraged women from the wasteful pursuit of waifish figures? Seems rather French to me."

"Well," he began. "I suppose that's true."

"I should think young women like Klara and myself, on the verge of family life, ought to be focused on building strength for the upcoming challenges of motherhood and running a household. I believe, Uncle Otto, you reminded me of this on my first night here when my appetite wasn't what it should be."

"Just so," Uncle Otto said.

"Let the girl have some cake, Hildegarde," Klara's father piped in. "For God's sake, it's a party."

The footman, looking as though he wanted to disappear into the blue-and-silver dining room wallpaper, placed a delicate china plate with a sliver of cake in front of Klara before moving on. Klara's mother flashed me a challenging look but softened her expression just as quickly.

"You've been taking the BDM teachings to heart," she said. "How clever of you."

"Why else would I attend if that weren't my intention," I said. "If indeed the goal of the BDM is to prepare women to establish healthy

German homes for a stronger Germany, it seems to do otherwise would be foolhardy."

"Especially for one engaged to the captain," Frau Schmidt said. It sounded more like a threat than a simple statement of fact.

"Hanna understands her upcoming role in society, Hildi," Aunt Charlotte said, her face cool and expressionless, but I knew her well enough to know she was seething under that calm façade. "And takes it seriously. She'll be a leader in society and a role model to the women of her acquaintance."

"Quite so," Frau Schmidt replied. She turned to the person to her left, a lieutenant of some description, and began chatting. Anything to change the subject.

As soon as dessert was ended, we retired to the parlor for coffee and conversation.

"Without caffeine," I assured Friedrich as I handed him a cup. The party discouraged the overconsumption of caffeine, and coffee, being imported, was especially suspect. Decaffeinated coffee was an acceptable indulgence, especially as it was a German coffee merchant who invented the process for removing the caffeine from the coffee beans.

"You made rather a spectacle at dinner, didn't you?" he said, his tone biting but his face placid. I half wondered if he'd been studying Aunt Charlotte's technique.

"I was simply sticking up for Klara," I said. I felt a pang in my chest when I realized I almost said "my friend." I didn't want to impose my friendship on her if it wasn't wanted, and it was clear it wasn't.

"You should learn to mind your own business and let families deal with their own matters," he growled in low tones. "I was mortified. I'm sure Klara's mother knows what's best for her."

"Hildegarde Schmidt is a beast," I countered. "It looks like she's starving Klara. I've heard the way she speaks to her daughter in public and don't even want to consider what she says in private."

"I'm telling you now, don't concern yourself in the affairs of others. I won't have it."

"Even if someone I care about is being mistreated?" I hissed. "I'm just supposed to ignore it?"

"Precisely, if you wish to have a peaceful life," he sneered. "I won't have a meddlesome crone for a wife."

"I thought I was meant to take my place as a 'leader in our community and a role model for other women of my acquaintance.' Isn't it my duty to point out when a mother is mistreating her child? And not adhering to the teachings we're supposed to espouse?"

"Your duty, first and foremost, is to be charming and hold your tongue. And not to embarrass me. Is that understood?"

"Well and truly," I said.

And it was clear I was not meant to have any role of significance at all, other than as a cloak of respectability for Friedrich to wear.

MY SUITCASE WAS open on the bed and my belongings were strewn about in a maelstrom. I packed my best blue dress and was wearing the brown one I'd worn on the trip to Berlin. I wrapped Mama's picture carefully in some underthings. Of all the items Aunt Charlotte had purchased for me, I only took a few basics, some nightgowns and a couple of sturdy skirts and blouses that she'd be unlikely to begrudge me. I didn't want to be accused of theft, nor did I want to give the impression I was coming back. If I only took what I'd brought with me, I figured the message would get through.

The engagement ring from Friedrich lay in the wood-and-tooled-leather jewelry box I'd been given shortly after my arrival. It was accompanied by the rest of the jewelry "rewards" from Aunt Charlotte and Uncle Otto and a note containing instructions to return the ring to him with my fervent hope that he'd find someone better suited to his needs. Someone like Klara.

A knock sounded at the door, and I redoubled my efforts. I ignored the knocking and kept packing. Aunt Charlotte would stop me, and any of the staff would betray me to her. A more insistent knock followed, with Klara entering soon after.

"Your aunt said you'd be in here. Mama left her cloak last night and asked me to come fetch it." She rolled her eyes dramatically. "She thought I ought to pay you a visit while I'm here. I don't mean to intrude, but if your aunt were to tell my mother I hadn't come when I promised I would . . . well, you understand."

"Yes, I can imagine. It's fine. I never said you couldn't come. Though you won't have much call to be vexed with me for long. I'm leaving."

Klara eyed the tattered old bag and the clothes strewn all about the bed. "What? Are you eloping with a dashing chauffeur? That would sort things for me, wouldn't it?"

"Hardly, Klara. But I hope the end result will be the same for you. I'm going home," I said, snapping my grubby bag shut. "On the seven-o'clock train if I can hurry. And I'll be gone, and Friedrich will be yours."

"You clearly don't understand men like Friedrich. They don't go back to their castoffs. They're too proud."

"Well, that I can't help," I said, flinging more clothes in my bag. "But none of it matters to me. I'm going home."

"What are you talking about? You *are* home."

"No, I'm not. Teisendorf is home. This isn't my home and never will be."

"Have you thought this through?" Klara asked. "Your father wouldn't have sent you here if he thought your prospects were good at home."

"He sent me here to get me out of his hair. So he could grieve for my mother in peace. I'll simply show him that I can be of more help than he realizes. I'll do my lessons by correspondence at night and help at the shop during the day."

"So you're going to trade the most eligible bachelor in all of Berlin and a life of comfort to help run a dry goods store with your father?"

"You got the measure of it in one try. Well done." I didn't bother concealing the rancor in my voice. She wasn't a friend any longer, so she didn't expect any of the kindness that went along with such an attachment.

"Are you mad? Why would you sacrifice all this?" She stood, mouth agape, as if I'd suggested the sea were a violent shade of green.

"Because this isn't me." I gestured my hands at our grand surroundings. "It isn't my life. It's not what I want, nor what my mother would have wanted for me, no matter what everyone says. I knew her best. Even better than Papa, I think. She wanted me to be happy and to have choices. Marrying Friedrich would determine the course of the rest of my life, and I'm not ready for that. Not by half."

"Don't do anything rash," she said, her tone softer. "Tell your aunt and uncle you're homesick. Once you're there you can decide for sure what it is you want."

I looked at Klara, who, for the first time in ages, looked completely sincere. The advice was being given in earnest, and it would be ungenerous not to take it. Besides, options were what I was after.

"You might be right about that," I said. I eyed the letter I'd left and collected it. I considered tossing it in the bin but didn't want to risk anyone reading it. I'd rip it to shreds and toss it at the train station. Part of me wanted to leave it behind. To burn this bridge and forge something different. But I knew in my heart that Klara was right.

"What about the ring?" she asked. "Leaving it behind might be suspicious."

"I'm a young woman traveling alone. If they ask, I'll just say it was safer to leave valuables behind," I said.

"Smart," she said. "I still think you're foolhardy, but at least this way you have an out. Or, a way back in, more precisely."

"Options are good," I said, remembering Mama's words. But I was fairly certain that, as the miles separated me from Berlin, I would strengthen my resolve to stay in Teisendorf. Uncle Otto and Aunt Charlotte had been kind, but their sort of life was not for me.

"Well, I showed my face here. I don't see any point in staying long enough to see your aunt Charlotte in high dudgeon. Good luck, I suppose." She turned at the door. "But thank you for last night. You embarrassed my mother and it made me happier than I've been in ages."

I paused and cracked a genuine smile. "I assure you it was my distinct pleasure."

I collected the last of my things and tidied what I was leaving behind. I inhaled sharply and walked to the foyer, bracing myself for the worst of Aunt Charlotte's temper.

"Why are you wearing that old thing?" Aunt Charlotte said as she saw me in the entryway. She was removing her coat and passed off a stack of parcels to one of the maids. More shopping to compensate for her loveless marriage. It seemed cold comfort to me, but I hoped it gave her some joy.

"It's only a few months old," I reminded her.

"Well, nevertheless, dear, you have so many prettier things to wear now. This isn't Teisendorf, after all."

"That's just it, Aunt. I'm terribly anxious to see Papa again. With the holiday and all it's made me homesick. I hope you won't mind terribly my going back home for a while." I didn't state a specific time so that I wouldn't be telling a lie.

"My dear, what about your studies? You made it clear you're so very keen to finish them. Why keep Friedrich waiting if you're really so cavalier?"

"I've arranged it so the teachers can give me some work so I don't fall behind."

"I don't think it's wise to leave when you just got engaged. Men can be so fickle."

"Absence makes the heart grow fonder," I said. "It will make him all the happier for my return."

I feared that was true.

"Well, very well. I just don't think it's all that prudent a move. But perhaps a short trip home will remind you of what you have here."

"Just so, Aunt Charlotte."

Surprisingly, Uncle Otto offered to accompany me to the train station and was perfectly jovial as we took the ride into the city. He kissed my cheek before I hopped onto the train and waved from the platform. He smiled.

A pang of doubt surged in my gut. Maybe they did care. Maybe they did just want what was best for me and my future. They were convinced that Friedrich was just that. Even if they were wrong, they were trying to do what they thought was right. They could hardly be faulted for that.

I spent the ride to Teisendorf wondering if I was making a grave error. Perhaps I *was* foolish to leave Berlin and all the opportunities it afforded. Maybe I could grow to love Friedrich. In time I might come to see what everyone else seemed to see in him.

By the time I arrived in Teisendorf, I was twisted in knots and felt like I'd worn my worry stone down several centimeters over the course of the trip. I was clutching it in one hand and my valise in the other when I stepped off the train. I saw a familiar face waiting for me in the crowd. His arms were crossed, and he looked put out.

"Papa!" I exclaimed, tossing myself at him. "I didn't expect to see you here. I was going to walk home."

"Your aunt and uncle called to tell me you were coming back. I had to leave Felix in charge of the store." Papa never liked leaving the store in anyone's charge. Even his most trusted clerk, Felix, was rarely given the honor.

"You didn't have to go to such trouble, Papa. I know my way."

He said nothing, but then looked me up and down, pausing at my left hand where I held my worry stone.

"For God's sake, put that pebble away, girl. Your mother never should have given you such a crutch."

I stowed the stone in my secret pocket before he got a notion to toss it out. He'd done that once before and it had taken Mama and me hours to find it.

He rolled his eyes but looked mollified. "Let's continue this discussion at home, shall we?"

We rode in his old pickup truck in silence. As we entered the house, I was greeted not with the rush of familiarity I'd expected, but with the pang of something that was so close to right that it just felt off. A middle-aged woman with a lumpy figure in a stained dress stood at the sink peeling potatoes. In the same spot my mother had stood countless times when she prepared our meals, usually with me at her side. I arched a brow at Papa.

"Greta, I have an extra for dinner tonight. This is my daughter, Hanna. Hanna, this is my housekeeper, Greta."

She gave me a courteous nod and went back to her labors without giving me more than a cursory glance. Of course Papa had hired a housekeeper. It made more sense than him learning how to manage on his own. But it would reduce his need for me considerably.

Greta served us a hearty meal of chicken stew and crusty bread and left us to enjoy it in peace. She didn't live with Papa, and this pleased me. In that moment it occurred to me that the next time I saw a woman at the sink, she likely wouldn't be a simple housekeeper. He would want to remarry and move on. He probably saw me as an impediment to that process.

"Your aunt and uncle tell me you've become engaged to a rather promising young man."

"Well . . . yes. It's all been so sudden."

"And you wanted to come back here because it scared you. I

warn you, Hanna. I won't coddle your nonsense like your mother did. I want you back on the train tomorrow so you can face your duties."

"But I don't love him, Papa. He's a brute."

"Most men are, Hanna. And your mother would have done well to prepare you for that. Life will have to teach you that lesson now. Your aunt and uncle have done a tremendous amount for you, and coming here is poor repayment for that generosity. I sent you to the city to give you a chance at a real future."

"Papa, I don't like the city. I'd prefer a simple life here in Teisendorf like you and Mama had. I can be useful to you, Papa. I can help run the store. I can cook and clean for you. Wouldn't it be better to have me here taking care of you than some stranger? You could bring the boys back and we'd be a proper family again."

"The only house I want you keeping is your own, Hanna. I don't want you wasting your youth taking care of your brothers and me. This Friedrich your uncle tells me about will be a good husband to you. Don't throw a good proposal away on a girlish whim."

"How could you possibly know? You haven't met him. You want me to run off and marry a man you haven't even taken the time to know yourself."

"I trust my brother and his judgment. If he says this young man is a good match, then I believe him. You should, too."

"I trust my own heart, Papa."

"The most sentimental nonsense I ever heard. Many a time I've kicked myself for giving your mother free reign over the raising of you, but never more than today. She mollycoddled you instead of teaching you the ways of the world. But I won't have it, Hanna. It's long past time that you give up these childish ideas your mother stuffed in your head and face reality. You're nearly a woman and you need to settle your future."

"I just wish you, Aunt Charlotte, and Uncle Otto would give me some say in it."

"You've shown by your visit here that you're not grown up enough for such a responsibility. These decisions will be left to me now. And my brother. And if you have any sense, you'll recognize what we're trying to do for you."

"Yes, Papa." I pushed my bowl, still mostly full, to the side.

"Good. I know you miss your mother, Hanna. You were as close as a mother and daughter could be. But you'll see, by and by, that we know what's best for you. You were left too long under some dangerous influences, and I won't have you succumb to them. I blame myself for it, but I can rectify my mistakes now."

I bowed my head. "So I'm to leave tomorrow, then? I won't even be able to have a proper visit with you or see anyone at all?"

Papa sighed. "You may stay a week. You can get some rest from the city. I know how tiring it can be."

"Thank you," I said, my voice little more than a whisper. He'd always hated trips into the city and ensured that they were few. At least in that, we could agree.

THE HILLS OF Teisendorf were enchanting, even in the shroud of winter. I ambled aimlessly in them during the day, perhaps hoping to see Mama around the next bend. Papa refused my help at the store, mostly because he didn't want to have to admit how much help I could be to him. He couldn't bear to be proven wrong, so he didn't give me the opportunity. On the Wednesday of my trip, with only three days left in my reprieve, my wanderings took me to a lonely cabin on the edge of the forest. There was a Romani family that Mama checked in on frequently, and I was sure she would have wanted me to carry on when I could.

The eldest daughter, Kezia, was a bright girl of about fifteen who spoke German better than the rest of her family. She had the most arresting hazel-green eyes I'd ever seen. If she'd been free to socialize in town, I was certain that the boys and young men would have been half-mad for her. Her lovely face lit up as she recognized me, and she called to the rest of her family in their native tongue. I could hear the commotion inside as she rushed over to embrace me.

"I am so sorry about your mother. I wondered what happened to you."

"I've been in Berlin. I'm only here for a visit."

"He sent you away?" She cocked her head to the side. The whole idea was anathema to her.

"He sent me to be with family. It's complicated."

She shrugged as if our ways were incomprehensible to her. I scarcely understood them myself, so I could hardly blame her for her confusion.

"Do you think you could come look in on Vano? He's been unwell and Mama is worried."

"Of course," I said, wishing I'd thought to bring Mama's kit along. I'd left it hidden in the darkest recesses of my case in my bedroom. I didn't dare leave it unattended in Berlin but didn't want to risk Papa seeing it, either.

Her brow was furrowed as we entered the little cabin. She was an unflappable girl, so even this minor show of concern gave me pause. Vano was only about five years old, the youngest of the children, and the beloved baby of the family.

The one-room cabin was kept cozy warm against the chill of winter. It was tidy and cheerful, though their mother made her living off the land and hardly had two pennies to rub together. Kezia spoke to her mother in Romani, and the woman lifted the boy from the bed and brought him over to me. I sat in the chair in the corner of the room and let her place him in my lap, where he immediately went limp. He had a high fever and was a listless imitation of the vibrant boy I knew.

"How long has he been like this?"

"Two days," Kezia replied. "Mama has tried everything she knows."

"And she hasn't taken him to a doctor?"

"How can we?" she asked. It was a fair point. We'd all heard about the party's absolute hatred of the Romani. They were disappearing in greater numbers with each passing year, either because they fled Germany or because they were rounded up. The only way Kezia and her family were able to stay safe was because they were hidden in these remote woods. There were no Romani left in our cities to speak of, and I'd heard Friedrich speak of this with pride on more than one occasion. These were people my mother had cared for and considered her friends. To the Nazis, they were vermin.

I racked my brain to think of any fever remedies that Mama used that Kezia's mother wouldn't have already tried. I wished more than anything that Mama were here to treat the boy herself and give him a better chance at survival. I'd been a fair apprentice, but I wasn't ready to treat people on my own.

"Have you tried yarrow or elderflower tea? Bone broth?"

"Yes. None of it did much."

"He needs real medicine," I said, knowing I might as well have been asking to borrow the Queen of England's favorite tiara.

"We know this, but there must be something else we can do."

"Give him cool baths to lower his temperature, but don't let him get chilled. And all the water he can drink." I rattled off the list of remedies Mama used before seeking out a licensed doctor. "Keep up with the yarrow tea. It will help him sweat it out."

She looked panicked. She knew these efforts weren't enough.

"Can he keep anything down?" I dreaded the answer but knew it all the same.

She knew the significance of the question, too, and looked pained. "He hasn't purged in a while, but I'm not sure he has anything left to get up."

"If he can't keep anything down, even the best medicines won't work. The best we can do is try. You do what you can here, and I'll see what I can do about getting him some medicine."

"Please hurry," she said. "Please."

"Just hold tight." I bounded out the door and found myself running back toward the house. The boy needed a sulfonamide or he'd be gone within a day, provided he was lucky. Asking a doctor for a prescription when I was well would raise dangerous questions. But Pieter had been ill last winter and Mama had to break down and take him to the physician. She'd gotten a second dose of the medicine in case of a relapse, but he'd pulled through with just one round. Mama was certain to have kept the rest on hand. I just had to pray Papa's new housekeeper wasn't overly efficient at her job.

To my dismay, Greta was there preparing dinner when I burst through the front door.

"What has you in such an all-fired hurry?" she asked, looking up from the stove.

"Never you mind," I said, not bothering with pleasantries. Chances were my visits to Teisendorf would be few if any once I married Friedrich, so there was no sense in pretending I had any feelings for this interloper in my mother's home.

I ran down to my father's bedroom, crossed over to the small private bathroom he'd shared with Mama and flung open the door to the medicine cabinet.

Greta followed me down the hall and stood at the doorway to the bathroom. "This is your father's private room. You don't belong in here."

"Mind your own business. This is my home and I'll go where I please."

"I'll tell him you've been meddling."

I looked over the bottles of pills and nearly cried for joy when I found the bottle of sulfonamide. I grabbed it and slammed the cabinet shut.

"You do just that," I said, turning to face her. She looked like she wanted to challenge me, but stepped aside reflexively. Perhaps my time at Uncle Otto and Aunt Charlotte's was proving to be of some use after all.

I dashed past her and ran back to Kezia's cabin at full tilt. Little Vano looked just as ill, but had managed to keep some yarrow tea down. There was at least a shred of hope.

"Give him one pill morning and night," I instructed. "And pray he keeps them down. I won't be here to get you more."

Kezia nodded and relayed the information to her mother. Both offered me their thanks and I hugged them both with prayers for

Vano's recovery in my heart. If he'd been in Mama's care she would have returned twice a day to check on the boy until she was convinced he was well. She would have brought salves and restorative broths even after he began to improve. But I could not fill her shoes. It pained me with every step I took toward the house. I didn't run this time but walked slowly. Greta would have told my father everything by now and I would have some somber music to face.

True to my premonition, my father was waiting at the dinner table, his arms crossed, when I got home.

"What have you been up to?" he asked. "Greta says you were rummaging in my room."

"I was not rummaging in your room," I said. I did not raise my voice or give in to my anger. I would meet him rationally. "I went to find medicine Mama left in your cabinet."

"She said you ran in and out of here like a possessed banshee. What was the matter?"

"I came upon some old friends. Their son was sick. I gave them some of Pieter's old medicine. It wouldn't have been good for much longer anyway."

"Precisely what I was worried about. You know you're not supposed to prance around acting like a doctor. Your mother did and it caused more trouble than you've been made privy to."

I took a breath to steady the rapid beating of my heart. I would not let him see my rage. I was on the point of marriage and yet I was still a child to him. To be dictated to and ordered around. "My mother didn't act like a doctor. She was one."

"They took her license. She wasn't permitted to practice medicine. She did so against the wishes of the country and my own as well."

"She did what she thought was right, and so did I."

"You went off to see that gypsy family in the woods, didn't you?"

"How could you possibly know?" I asked. "Are you having me watched?"

"I don't have to, Hanna. People are watching anyway. I knew what you were up to before the boy swallowed his first pill. At least you owned up to it, but you shouldn't have gone. I was foolish to let you stay even a week."

"If I hadn't, he would have died."

"That's their own affair," Papa said. "And you going to their shack won't be doing the rest of them any favors, whether the boy lives or not. You were foolish today in ways you don't understand. And not just to yourself, but to your brothers and me. People are watching. Your mother never believed that. She never cared for our safety like she should have."

Papa's face wasn't filled with rage. It was filled with resignation and fear. He was right in one thing. If my going to their home brought attention to them, I'd exposed them to danger.

"I promise I won't go back," I said. "I didn't know I was being watched."

"If you're smart, you'll assume you are at every moment from here on out. Every move you make is seen. Every word you speak is heard. Every word you write is read. And no, you won't go back to the gypsy family. You're going back to your aunt and uncle's on the morning train. You'll pack your things after dinner and be ready to go at first light. This foolishness has gone on long enough."

"Yes, Papa," I said. I took my place at the table. Greta put a plate of sausage and potatoes before me while shooting me a triumphant expression. I returned a glower that seemed to scare her back into submission. I'd find a way to convince Papa to replace her. I wasn't too childish to think that I'd approve of anyone taking my mother's role in the home, but Papa could certainly find better than this nasty old crone.

I ate enough of my meal to satisfy my father and my own conscience and put the rest of my belongings back in my valise. And just like the night a few months earlier, before I embarked on my trip to Berlin, I cried myself to sleep wishing that my mother could somehow return and make things all right in a way they never would be again.

CHAPTER TWENTY-ONE

Hanna

January 1939

Aunt Charlotte, to her credit, didn't gloat when she picked me up from the train station. She looked as though my return was just on schedule and nothing was amiss. I wondered if Papa told her what I'd been up to with the Romani family in Teisendorf, but decided he would have probably kept the information to himself. He wouldn't want to further jeopardize my chances with Friedrich. He wouldn't risk Uncle Otto and Aunt Charlotte refusing any further hospitality because of what he considered to be my foolish devotion to my mother's calling.

I had no idea how Vano was faring, nor if I would ever find out. I could only hope that he would pull through with the help of Pieter's medicine and the loving attentions of his mother and sister. I couldn't ask Papa or anyone else in town to check on them. It was becoming clearer to me that no one could be trusted. Aunt Charlotte embraced me like the prodigal, but as the driver sped through town and she chatted to me merrily in the backseat, I had never felt more alone in my life.

"I'll let you lie down, dear. We have company coming later this evening," Aunt Charlotte said as we walked into the cavernous entryway.

"Would you mind too much if I just took a tray in my room?" I asked. "I really don't feel equal to company."

"Friedrich is coming especially to see you. I'll send Mila to you at seven. Dinner is promptly at eight."

There was no gentle suggestion in her tone. No sugarcoated coercion. It was a command.

"I trust you got your wanderlust out of your system, dear. We're all going through hard times, but we mustn't make things worse for ourselves. And don't wear that dress again unless you're called on to scrub some floors."

She left me no time to respond to her orders. She spun on the ball of her foot and walked off toward her quadrant of the house with her heels making a businesslike *click-clack click-clack* across the marble floor of the foyer as she went off to her private rooms.

Going to see Papa had been a mistake. I gained nothing apart from the knowledge that I was well and truly without allies. Mila and Klara were wonderful girls, but would they truly protect my confidences if the need ever arose? Mila's loyalty, ultimately, had to lie with Uncle Otto and Aunt Charlotte. They paid her wages and gave her lodging. She couldn't afford to cross them. Klara would never cross her parents—who would never cross my aunt and uncle.

I wanted to hurl myself on the bed and cry as I'd done upon my arrival and so many times since. But that time had passed. I had to come up with a plan to evade Friedrich long enough to strike out on my own. If I had to serve in a beer hall or make beds in a hotel, so be it. It didn't seem too far-fetched to think I could find work as a secretary in some humble office somewhere. I paced and paced the room until the grooves in the carpet might never rebound. I began to notice subtle differences in the room. Mila had certainly been in to clean, which wasn't unexpected, but all my personal effects were shifted slightly. Aunt Charlotte was the likeliest culprit as Uncle Otto wouldn't involve himself in the nitty-gritty of the handling of me. I'd taken Mama's medicine bag with me to Teisendorf, knowing it was the most damning thing I owned. I couldn't trust she'd think it was just an old piece of luggage and not worth her notice. But she'd probably rifled through every drawer, every nook, to see if there was any correspondence or anything that would indicate something untoward. Most noticeably, my engagement ring was no longer in the jewelry box, but beside it. A reminder.

Mila arrived promptly at seven, precisely as I expected. I had actually laid out a dress for the occasion. Powder blue and modest. It made me look young for my years and I hoped I could turn that to my advantage. "You've kicked a hornet's nest," Mila said as she finished the long row of buttons up my back.

"That bad?" I asked.

"Your uncle cursed a blue streak when he heard you'd gone. It took your aunt an hour to calm him down. And though she's as composed as they come, I could see her seething. They're worried the captain will think you're flighty and too attached to your parents."

"He needn't worry about that. Papa made it quite clear I'm not welcome back any time soon. I have nowhere to go but here."

"Well, if you want my advice, such as it is, you'd act penitent. As though you didn't realize the inconvenience you'd caused. You're young and they can overlook a bit of selfishness, I suppose."

I contemplated her words. "Penitent? I'm not so sure. Perhaps I should act as though it were preposterous that my going back home for four days would even really be noticed. I can't be the only newly engaged girl who takes a short holiday to see her family."

Mila cocked her head to the side in a way that seemed to convey, *Give it a shot if you like. I've heard of worse ideas. Just not many. I hope you live; I'm rather used to you by now.*

It was a gamble, but one I had to take. If I came off as meek and repentant, I'd never be able to wield any power on my own. What I needed was time. Before leaving the room, I slid my engagement ring back on my left hand. I refused to look down at it.

I looked very much my age, if not younger, when I greeted Friedrich, Aunt Charlotte, and Uncle Otto in the dining room. It was the opposite strategy to what Aunt Charlotte had done at the Christmas party, deliberately choosing clothes that made me look like a woman well into her twenties.

"I trust you had a good holiday?" Friedrich said, placing a kiss on my cheek.

"Oh, yes. So good to see Papa. I worry about him there all by himself, you know. He's not used to it."

"He's hired a woman, hasn't he?" Uncle Otto interjected.

"Well yes, but that's hardly the same as family, is it?" I said. "And it seemed like a good time to go. I wouldn't want to get too far behind in my studies."

"Our Hanna is such a diligent student," Aunt Charlotte said, motioning for us to sit down. "Always so concerned. And to think she'll be free of it all in just a few short months."

"Frau Hoffman thinks I should sit for entrance exams to the university," I said, playing a card I knew she would dislike.

"University?" Aunt Charlotte asked. "I don't think there's any need for that."

"Really? When I'll be expected to entertain and charm so many important people at Friedrich's side? There are only so many ways to make a conversation about the weather all that interesting. I assumed the good captain would want a wife who could be a true conversationalist."

"There is truth in that," Friedrich said. "But I'm not sure a formal university education is called for."

"Quite right. Why take a place that could go to a man if you're going to be married so soon after?" Uncle Otto said. "Much better to be settled and learn as you go."

"Of course, it's as you wish," I demurred. "But I'd hate to be thought of as the young, stupid wife when so many of the other women in your circles are so much older and more accomplished."

A hush fell over the table. "She makes a point," Friedrich said. "And some of them can be rather merciless to those they consider to be their inferiors. It's something to consider."

Aunt Charlotte's expression fell, but she recovered it quickly.

Not a word was said about my willful departure to Teisendorf, but there would be no earrings or bracelets to reward my "performance" at this dinner. And I could do without them.

Aunt Charlotte and Uncle Otto left Friedrich and me alone in the drawing room once dessert was concluded. The privilege of engagement, I supposed.

"Your trip was unexpected," he said after a long pause. "I wasn't sure what to make of it."

"What was there to make of it?" I asked. "I wanted to tell my father the news of my engagement personally. To see how he's faring. As I said."

"In the future, you will talk to me before making such plans," he said.

I said nothing, but my gaze never wavered from his face.

"You think I'm a brute, don't you?" he said.

"I think you're very used to having your own way. I also think you make little attempt to see things from my point of view."

"I want you to be happy, Hanna. Truly." His face radiated sincerity. For all his brash behavior, I think he meant it.

"Friedrich, I'm eighteen years old. I can't possibly know what would make me happy."

The truth.

"I wanted to . . . well, apologize for the way things happened at the party. I indulged in too much champagne and let my baser instincts take over."

I raised my brows. I had not expected such an admission from him. He seemed the sort that was too proud for anything like an apology.

"I never imagined that moment to be . . . quite so . . ."

"I know. It was beastly of me. I've chastised myself at every moment since that night. In truth, I was worried you'd gone to Teisendorf to escape me."

He was canny, I had to acknowledge.

"Perhaps you do need some time. The university might not be such a bad idea. You're smart and would make good use of your time there. It could be a good investment of time and resources."

"I think it is," I said. "I don't want to be an ornament on your arm, Friedrich. I want you to be proud of me."

It was true as well. I couldn't bear to be a decoration to be paraded around. And I hoped Friedrich had enough substance within him to want more as well.

"We can discuss it further," he said. "I think I'll leave you to rest after your day of travels."

"Thank you, Friedrich."

He leaned in to kiss me and I found myself responding more enthusiastically than I had in the past. Not because I wanted Friedrich, but because I'd bought myself the gift of time to find a way out.

For once, I felt a glimmer of hope.

CHAPTER TWENTY-TWO

Tilde

April 1939

Y ou should have gone with your mother," Samuel said for perhaps the hundredth time in the months since the violence broke out.

"I wouldn't leave you behind then, I won't do it now." He picked at his dinner but couldn't bring himself to eat. I myself could hardly face the plate of food before me, but for more reasons than the constant worry that weighed us down. We spoke in whispers at our own dining table, hoping the neighbors continued to believe that I was alone in the apartment. The ruse wouldn't last forever. We would have to hide elsewhere but the quieter we were, the more time we had to devise a plan. I'd already gone to the registry office to enquire about papers for Samuel and to ask where his family had been taken, but neither query met with any satisfactory outcome.

"I was wrong to help you stay behind. If you end up dead because of it, I'll answer for your death in heaven just as sure as if I'd pulled the trigger myself."

"Nonsense," I said. "You're not responsible for their behavior any more than I am. The only people to blame are those committing these horrible acts and those who are allowing it to happen. Don't shoulder any of their guilt—they deserve it all."

Samuel didn't speak but forced a bite of potato into his mouth.

"We'll find a way out of this," I said. "Mama will get papers for us. Now that she's reconnected with the family in America, she'll have more resources to help us leave."

"I've heard such things cost a fantastic sum of money," Samuel said. "How will we ever be able to find the money for illicit papers? If they find me, they'll deport me to a ghetto like they've done with all the other Polish-born Jews."

He'd had one postcard from his mother a few weeks after Kristallnacht. They were in a ghetto, but we didn't know where. They were alive, or had been. It wasn't certain how long they would stay that way—if indeed they still were.

I'd still not told him about the money Mama had left, nor would I. It could be seized for any reason and the fewer people who knew about it, the safer it would remain.

"We'll find a way, Samuel. The store turns a profit. We're not paupers."

"I hate having to depend on you for everything. I don't feel like a real man, hiding away like this."

"Well, then you should never have gotten married, Samuel Eisenberg. Marriage means depending on each other. Even when it's uncomfortable."

The words tasted bitter in my mouth, knowing this wasn't the lesson I'd learned from my parents' marriage. My father should have stood by us, in this hour of our gravest need, but after twenty-five years of marriage and twenty-two years of fatherhood, he abandoned his duty to us to save his hide and his pocketbook. I wondered when my journey to forgiving him would start, but I knew it wouldn't be until Samuel and I were on safe ground.

"I will spend the rest of my life making this up to you, Tilde. I promise you."

"And I promise to do all I can to ensure that you have years and years left to keep your word."

"When we're free from this place, I'll compose a symphony for you. When I can play and make instruments again."

The sight of his life's work destroyed weighed almost as heavily on him as the disappearance of his parents and sister. He wasn't able to practice or to craft his beautiful instruments. I could see in his face that a world where he couldn't make music didn't make sense to him.

"Your music will play in the great halls of New York, London, Paris . . . even Berlin."

"Never Berlin," he said. "I won't allow it."

"Why?"

"This is no longer the country that gave the world Beethoven and Brahms. If I am not welcome here. If my parents are not welcome here. If my darling sister, who has done nothing but bring light and joy to this world, is not welcome here, then neither will my music be welcome. As soon as we have our papers, we'll leave Germany and never cross over its borders again."

I reached my hand out to hold his, but it was a cold comfort. Nothing soothed an ache like this. The only thing that might come close would be if his parents and Lilla came crashing through the door at that moment and threw themselves in his arms.

"I'll go to the registry in the morning," I said. "I'll try again."

"You're wasting your time," he said. "Nothing ever comes of these pleas."

"Nothing ever happens until suddenly, it does. Try to keep some faith, my love."

"I may have to settle with admiring yours from afar this time," he said. "I'm afraid my supply is low."

"We'll have to find a way to replenish that well in due time."

I cleared the dishes and washed up while Samuel tried to read, but most of his time was spent staring off into space. He could focus on nothing and that only added further to his frustrations. I worried that if we lived like this for much longer, he would run mad and there would be nothing left of the man I married.

Samuel wasn't wrong that papers would be expensive . . . but he didn't know that since the violence broke out travel papers had become even harder to attain, even for a prince's ransom. One needed more than money. One needed connections. I had one, but I had been loath to use it. But for Samuel, I would go to this man on bended knee and beg if it meant securing our passage.

And it wasn't just for him that I would fight. I had managed to hide my morning nausea from Samuel and he'd yet to realize I'd missed my monthly courses . Our one solace was the few quiet hours in the night when we found a small measure of safety in each other's arms. I shouldn't have been shocked that our embraces had led to their natural conclusion, given that we were young and healthy, but the possibility of bringing a baby into this mess of a world had never crossed my mind.

But there would be a baby, of this I was more and more certain each day. And though how we would care for a child in the midst of the maelstrom of our lives was still an enigma to me, I could feel nothing but joy at the prospect. With all the hate that was being spewed in the streets, this child would be born of love and would be loved completely.

And for this, I would break the vow I'd held sacred for years.

I would go to my father.

CHAPTER TWENTY-THREE

Hanna

April 1939

There were only two months left in the school year and I felt them speeding by as though the earth spun twice as fast with each succeeding day. I clung to each one, as I hadn't yet been successful at keeping the grains of sand from trickling down the glass. I was fervently devoted to my studies, locking myself in my room with my books at every opportunity. Of course, Aunt Charlotte and Uncle Otto insisted I join them whenever Friedrich came calling, which was becoming more and more frequent. And though I wanted nothing more than to hole away from the world, I did attend the BDM functions at Aunt Charlotte's insistence. And she was right in that. If I were to go missing, I would have been noticed. By the other girls, by our district leaders, and eventually by someone who would have passed word to Friedrich.

Aunt Charlotte might try to claim that he was kind and gentle in his heart, but I had more trouble accepting this truth. As in so many things, she was convinced her fervent hope would translate into reality, simply by wishing it so. To risk igniting his temper would lead to disastrous outcomes, and I would not be persuaded otherwise.

Because of this, I had to endure Klara from afar. I thought things might improve between us after she'd advised me before my retreat to Teisendorf, but she seemed keenly disappointed by my return. At first, when her anger was still fresh, she wasn't able to control her countenance well enough to keep from shooting daggers at me whenever her gray eyes scanned the room and saw me there. I was a reminder of what she'd aspired to and lost, and she made no attempt to hide that she felt my arrival in Berlin had been the largest obstacle to attaining those dreams. Over time, her daggers grew smaller in number and rather less sharp, but I still saw the fire behind her eyes from time to time. Then after more time had elapsed, she grew indifferent. Her eyes did not stop when she saw me in a crowd. She only spoke to me when her mother pressed the issue. She did not acknowledge me in the halls at school. It was infinitely easier to bear when she openly despised me.

We were old enough now to be part of the voluntary Belief and Beauty group that served as a bridge between the BDM for the girls and Nationalsozialistische Frauenschaft for the grown women. And so it felt. Lingering between the innocence of girlhood and the responsibilities of womanhood. Our meeting today was precisely the sort that Klara liked. We were working on painting simple still-life scenes—a bouquet of roses on a sparsely set dinner table—with which to beautify our homes and impress our suitors.

Klara's easel was set next to mine, and I dutifully kept my eyes pinned to the subject or my canvas to the point where I was sure I'd be able to recall the exact curl of each pink petal and the brown spot on one of the leaves. While Klara had exceptional talent for anything artistic, owing to her hours and hours of sketching fashions, I was helplessly mediocre. The curve of the vase was wrong, the shadows on the table were laughable, and though I endeavored to mix the proper shade of pink from the paints provided, I produced a puce color that was so vile that I was certain it didn't exist in nature.

"Well, not every meeting can be a hike," Klara finally said, breaking the silence.

"Nor should they be," I replied, not meeting her gaze. "But I'd look less pathetic than I do now."

"Let's hope Captain Schroeder didn't have his heart set on an artistic wife. I think he'll be rather disappointed in his choice if so."

"Oh, I'll disappoint him, no doubt," I said. "The only question is how long I'll be able to delay that unfortunate day and how spectacularly I'll mortify myself."

Klara snorted. "Your aunt has you well trained. I'm sure you'll make him the perfect wife."

"It's not what I wanted," I said. "Though I could say it until I'm blue in the face, you won't see the truth of it. I tried more than once to convince him he'd be better off with someone like you. Someone who'd be a far more charming hostess than I'll ever be. Someone who only cares about rank and prestige rather than actual people."

Klara looked at me, her mouth agape. It was a cutting remark, but no less than she deserved. I left my canvas behind and fled to find the washroom.

I washed the paint from my hands and took even breaths in and out, trying not to let my anger seize me. I wanted to lash out at Klara for being so deliberately cruel, but knew no good would come of losing my composure. I watched the red splotches of paint dissolve into crimson-stained water and swirl down the sink. I scrubbed until my hands were bright pink, then splashed my face with the cold water. As if I might somehow awaken from my own life.

I was, rather, summoned back to the stark realities of it by Aunt Charlotte barging into the washroom, the color high on her cheeks.

"What are you playing at?" she demanded.

"Leonardo I am not," I said, opening the door and starting out of the room. "Sorry to disappoint."

"That's not what I mean, and you know it. What were you thinking, storming off like that?" Aunt Charlotte said, cornering me out in the hallway. "Frau Schroeder is watching, you know."

"I had to use the washroom, obviously," I said. I didn't have the energy to control my tongue.

"You don't have to make a scene to use the loo. There's something else going on."

"Klara—" I began.

"Klara Schmidt doesn't matter," she interjected. "She's a jealous little chit and not worth your concern. But your leaving attracted attention. People will think you don't take the mission of this group seriously. Do you know what the consequences of that might be?"

"Friedrich would lose interest," I said, my tone dry.

"That would only be the beginning. It would be ruinous, not only to you, but to your uncle and me by association. You cannot afford to take any of this lightly."

"I'm sorry, Aunt Charlotte. I didn't realize anyone would construe my behavior as anything more than a spat between two teenage girls. I assure you that's all it was."

Aunt Charlotte seemed to lower her shoulders by a fraction of an inch, but she was right. "One more petty outburst and this little pipe dream of yours about going to university will be just that—a dream."

"I'm sorry, Aunt Charlotte, I didn't realize that anyone would pay attention to anything so insignificant."

"Well, there's your first lesson about Berlin society, my dear. Everything you do is seen, scrutinized, and usually painted in the worst possible light. Don't expect charitable interpretations of your behavior from anyone. Most people are happy to believe the worst about you and will use that to their advantage in whatever way they can."

"What a dreadful, cold world," I said.

"Darling, it's the one you were born into. There's no sense in lamenting it."

I nodded and followed her back to my sorry attempt at artwork, picked up my palette, and tried to paint something discernible on the splotched canvas.

"I'm sorry," Klara whispered after some time.

I kept my eyes focused on my canvas and didn't respond.

"Listen, you don't have to forgive me or anything, but I've been a brute. It's just that Mother and Father have been so beastly about Friedrich—you know how it is."

"All too well," I said. "Any step I take that they think might set him off is censured before my foot hits the pavement."

"And I've been living with constant analysis of every move I made that turned him off to me. Every minute detail from my clothes and hair to my very personality."

"My god, if only mothers would put such pressure on their sons to meet with *our* approval, we'd be happy wives, to be sure."

Klara snorted with derision, causing a stern look from the woman conducting the class. We fought valiantly to control our giggles, and were largely successful.

"Listen, Hanna, I'm sorry," she said. "I haven't been fair to you."

"And I'm sorry it happened at all, Klara," I said earnestly. "All of it."

"I'm sure you are," she said. "But that doesn't make it any easier."

"I know," I said, turning back to my canvas.

I knew our friendship wouldn't be as it had been—perhaps ever—but maybe we could rekindle some cordiality. It wasn't what I hoped for, but it was at least a small measure better than solitude.

As we left, Frau Schmidt smiled at Aunt Charlotte and me. I looked at the paintings our Belief and Beauty members had produced. A few were even worse than my own, but my attempt was among the feeblest in the group. It would seem that being seen socializing with the right people was far more important than creating anything of worth.

CHAPTER TWENTY-FOUR

Tilde

April 1939

I'd visited my father's law offices more times than I'd been able to count in my formative years. His secretaries had sweets for me in their desks, his partners were always ready with a smile and a pat on the head. When I was small, half the men in his office were Jewish. My father had always respected his Jewish colleagues, saying they had quick wits. One by one, they left. In a trickle at first and then in a torrent. I'd once dreamed of joining my father there. There had been one or two women attorneys in the office over the years. They were the least likely to show an interest in me, perhaps not wanting to appear too maternal before their male colleagues. But I watched them. I wanted to emulate them more than I could express.

The last one, Ursula, caught me spying on her, no doubt owing to my poor skills in subterfuge. She looked like she should have been friendly. She had bouncy dark-blond curls and a round, sweet face. But I don't think she spoke more than a dozen words to me in the three years she worked in my father's office. Still, she didn't turn her back on the pest of a child who wanted to live in her shadow; instead, she surreptitiously left books by my chair when I went to the restroom or to help with some task. They were advanced for my age, as most legal texts would be, but I could parse out the majority of the material. As time went on, she left more complex offerings. She was my favorite of all my father's colleagues and I cried bitterly when I found out she had moved to Düsseldorf.

At one point, I thought my father had taken a shine to the idea of me following him into the profession. He encouraged my studies and when I went to the office, he delighted in telling his colleagues how bright I was. But as Hitler's star went into its ascendency, that talk slowed. Then disappeared completely. Then came the day four years ago when Papa declared to Mama that they needed to divorce for safety's sake. Laws were making things very difficult for Jews, and particularly difficult for those in "mixed" marriages. Aryans married to Jews could face jail time and were losing their jobs all over the country. Father was too prominent a lawyer for his marriage to go unnoticed for long.

"Darling, you know this kills me," he said on bended knee as Mama sat on the sofa with her head buried in her hands, her shoulders racked with sobs. "I love you. I love Tilde. I can't stand that our marriage has been disrupted by this silly question of politics. But providing for you two is my sacred duty. If I can't do that, then our marriage is a sham anyway."

I watched, my parents unaware, as my father swore that the divorce was just a formality. That as soon as the tides turned back in our favor—and they would—he would marry her again in a lavish ceremony and take her on a second honeymoon that would make a Rockefeller envious.

She believed him. I believed him.

They were divorced a month later. He remarried three months after the divorce was final.

Every word he'd said to both of us was a lie. He thought Hitler would be successful in expelling the Jews from Germany and he was determined not to go down with us.

I'd despised my father every day for the past four years. He'd discarded us and started over; he already had two babies with his beautiful blond-haired, blue-eyed wife. He didn't care if we'd lived or died, as long as we got out of his way.

He was the worst sort of coward, and there was not a fiber of my being that didn't want to spit in the man's face rather than ask him for help. But Samuel was the only thing on this earth that could make me debase myself like this.

I waited in the lobby, grateful that the secretary was new and didn't recognize me. I couldn't see the whole of the office, but there were only one or two familiar faces. I was glad no one called out my name in gleeful recognition or even came to offer me a hand-shake. I was fairly certain my success depended on this.

"Frau Eisenberg, Herr Altman will see you now," the secretary said. She looked at me, assessing. My clothes were smart for a young matron. My caramel-brown hair shone, and I wore only the barest hint of pink lipstick. Acceptable. She glanced at my eyes and hesi-tated. Was there something foreign in them? My new surname was enough to raise her suspicion, but she seemed to keep her doubts in check for the moment.

I walked back to my father's office, as familiar as my own little apartment, and knocked on the open door before crossing into his domain. It was an oppressive room with heavy oaken furniture—

"Solid, German-built stuff," as he'd said—meant to intimidate his enemies and impress his allies. At least I had the advantage of knowing this particular strategy, so I would not fall victim to it.

He glanced up at me, opened his mouth to speak, but then clenched it shut just as quickly.

I snapped the door closed and sat in the chair opposite his desk without waiting for an invitation.

"You shouldn't have come here," he said by way of greeting.

"And hello to you, too, Papa dear," I said in a low tone. "So wonderful to see you after all this time."

"Tilde, do you know what could happen to my career if—"

"Your career? Spare me. What are you going to do? Stop paying Mama her alimony? It seems we're several years past all that."

"Fine. You had no business giving a fraudulent name to my secretary and sneaking in here under false pretenses."

"I didn't give a false name. I'm married. I'll accept your felicitations later, though. I didn't come about that."

"Married? What sort of man is he? What are his prospects?"

"You can stop with the concerned father routine. I'm not buying tickets to that farce. But Samuel is a good man and a wonderful husband. Something you could learn a thing or two about. It's because of him that I've come."

"What do you mean?"

"I need travel papers. For both of us. I can pay. In fact, I insist on it. I won't be accused of asking you for a handout." I'd brought along some of the money Mama had left behind and was ready to toss it across his desk. It was the only thing he cared about, really. He could have emigrated with us and started anew in New York or anywhere else when he realized the implications of the laws that

kept stripping us of our rights. But it was the love of his practice—
and the vast sums of money he made from it—that caused him to
forsake us.

"You might as well ask me for the holy grail, Tilde. They're re-
scinding passports as fast as they can run the paper shredders. Why
do you need to leave? Is he in trouble?"

"We don't know. They took his family."

On our wedding night. But I wouldn't share that detail with him.
I didn't want anything like sympathy from him.

"Do you have any information on where they were taken or why?"

"I've been to the registry office three times and haven't been able
to find out a thing. They're quiet, decent people. The authorities
can't have had a real reason for taking them."

"They don't need one. Not anymore. Were they foreign?"

"They *are*, yes," I said, insisting on the present tense. "They
emigrated from Poland when Samuel was just a boy. His younger
sister, Lilla, was born here, though."

"Eisenberg? They're foreign Jews? God knows where they've
been taken. Why on earth would you cast your lot in with such a
family? You're a first-degree *Mischling*. If you married a privileged
second-degree *Mischling* with the right ties, you'd have been much
safer."

First degree, Jewish parent. Second degree, Jewish grandparent.
The Nazis loved their organization and hierarchies. The more complicated and maddening, the better.

"Well, I met Samuel instead," I said. "And I don't want either of
us to meet the same fate his family has met. Or may have met. Can
you help?"

"Tilde, if anyone found out, it wouldn't just be *my* life at risk."

"I know. You have a family that you seem far more invested in keeping safe than you were your first."

"Things have changed, Tilde. You're a smart girl. I thought you of all people would understand."

"I'm sorry to disappoint you, but no, I don't understand your decision to abandon us. But none of that matters anymore."

"I'm glad of that at least," he said.

"It's not that I've forgiven you. It's that I don't have time to spare you any thought. I need to get my husband and myself to safety."

"I don't know what you expect me to do."

"Don't pretend you don't have connections. You used to brag about them at every cocktail party to anyone who would listen. Certainly you have a favor you could call in somewhere."

"You overestimate my influence. I could make some calls, but the chances of me being able to procure papers would be next to none."

"Next to none is not none. I've never asked you for anything since you went away. I left you in peace to be with your new family because I knew it was what you wanted. But I'm still your daughter and I'm asking you for help."

"I wish there were something I could do, but even if I tried, I'd just end up under even more surveillance and no closer to getting you papers."

"Try. If not for Samuel and me, for your grandchild."

He looked at me, his eyes sparkling with recognition. My stomach churned at the manipulation I was using, but if it meant saving Samuel and the baby I was fairly certain would be joining us sometime in the fall, it was worthwhile. I hadn't even told Samuel. The knowledge that he was going to be a father would have been enough to send him into a spiral of despair. It felt wrong that the only person on earth who knew my secret was a man who had left me and my mother defenseless.

"I'm sorry, Tilde. If I go around asking for papers, people will get suspicious. I barely kept my job as it is. If that happens, then my sacrifices will have meant nothing."

"*Your* sacrifices," I repeated. "Really and truly, your selfishness is almost awe-inspiring. Mama is well rid of you. She's well, by the way. Not that you asked. And safe in America."

"She got papers?"

"Yes, though we couldn't manage them for me. And I wouldn't have gone without Samuel in any case."

"Why on earth not, child?"

"Loyalty, Papa. I don't expect you to understand."

"I wish we lived in a different world, Tilde. Truly. I'm sorry I can't do more for you."

"I knew you'd be a disappointment. I'm just sorry I let myself have the slightest hope you'd act decently. I won't make that mistake again."

"You're a clever girl, Tilde. You'll find a way to get to New York. And when you do, pass on my regards to your mother. You may think I'm a monster, but I do miss both of you."

"I won't dishonor her by mentioning your name in her presence. She deserves to forget you. I only hope I'm able to in time."

I left the office without taking a glance back at the man who, of all people on this earth, should have been willing to risk his life for mine. I wanted to feel grief for the loss of the man who had lavished me with dolls and taken me to the circus as a child, but all I could feel was rage. It would temper in time, I knew, and I hoped one day I'd be strong enough to mourn.

CHAPTER TWENTY-FIVE

Tilde

April 1939

I rocked back and forth in my place in line at the registry office like so many other women in my position. Waiting for papers and trying to find loved ones. We got on intimate terms with waiting. I'd waited weeks to see if my application for an exit visa would be accepted. We waited for weeks to learn more about the fate of Samuel's parents. Each time we thought we'd gotten a step closer to making real progress, there was more waiting to be done. In a way, it became comforting. *No* could come in a hurry, but *yes* took time.

I prayed silently that today would be a step forward, even a small one. Our contact at the local registry office rang the shop to let me know I should come around in the afternoon to collect information. There was no use going early, so I waited on customers and forced a smile, but all the while I wanted nothing more than to bar the door and rush to the office to learn what was in store for us.

I was finally summoned to Herr Hase's desk. His face was grim, but that was no matter. They all made the same faces whether they were imparting good news or bad. I secretly wondered if it wasn't part of their training.

"Good afternoon," I said, giving him a smile that was friendly, but not overeager. If I anticipated he had good news for me, he might be put off by my presumptuousness. "I hope you're well." I didn't much care if he was, but the niceties had to be observed.

"Fine, fine, thank you," he said. "I know you're anxious to hear more about your travel papers, yes?"

"Quite," I said. "I've missed my mother quite a lot, as you might expect."

"Indeed. I wish I had more news on that front for you. These matters are becoming increasingly difficult."

"Naturally," I said, plastering the smile back on again. *Cruel bastard, why call me here if you don't have news!*

"I asked you here today because I managed to track down the persons that you were concerned about. The Eisenberg family?"

"Yes?" I said. "Can you tell me how to find them?"

"The older gentleman was taken to the concentration camp at Sachsenhausen. His wife and daughter to a women's camp nearby."

"For what possible reason? I can't imagine they've done anything wrong."

"You'd be shocked at how many people are hiding secrets. May I ask why you're asking after these people, Fräulein? I must caution you that it's highly irregular for a young lady of your sort to take an interest in people like these. Questions get asked and it can become awkward, you understand."

People like these. He meant Jews. He was trying to warn me away before the wrong people took notice. "Oh, they were old friends of the family. Before she left, my mother was concerned and wanted me to send a telegram with news if ever I was able to find any. Clearly she wasn't wrong to let the acquaintance fade."

"Quite right. It must be quite serious if the women were taken away. From what I understand, the vast majority of those taken during the unfortunate events of November were men. Were I you, I'd tell your mother to sever the relationship and not enquire further."

"Naturally. I'll send her a wire as soon as possible. I do appreciate your time."

"Always a pleasure, Fräulein Altman."

I shook all the way back to the shop but took care not to look too downcast as I went. I tried to walk not too fast nor too slow, as either would attract unwanted eyes.

Back in the apartment, Samuel sat at the kitchen table, reading his book, but not making much progress. He saw the truth in my face before I was able to say a word.

"They're gone?" he asked. "All of them?"

I related the sparse information that Herr Klaus had provided, knowing it didn't provide answers to the most essential questions.

"But are they alive?" he asked. "Can we know?"

"He didn't say one way or the other, but as he didn't say they were counted among the casualties of the violence, it may not be beyond hope that they're still alive."

"Alive and languishing in some filthy camp."

He threw the book across the room, where it bounced off a cabinet door and onto the tile floor. He buried his head in his hands.

"We don't know anything yet. Not really."

"Tilde, they wouldn't have taken my mother and Lilla if they ever planned on letting them live. I know I won't see them again."

I wanted to tell him not to despair. I wanted to assure him all would be well, but I could not bring myself to offer platitudes when his premonition was the most likely outcome.

"I can't bear this," he barely managed to wheeze out in between silent gasps for air. I could well imagine the flashes of his memory running through his mind. His father, a master craftsman that Samuel had idolized his whole life. His mother in all her earnest affection who cared for everyone in her sphere as though they were family. Lilla was the cruelest blow of all. She was just getting started in life and had only just begun to show the glimmer of her brilliance.

I held him in my arms, knowing no words would be able to soothe him. He folded in half, his head buried in my lap. I stroked his hair and prayed that I'd be inspired to do something that would be of help.

No tears came, and it was this that frightened me. He was beyond grief. He shook in place, struggling for each new breath. I felt helpless as an infant and wanted to wail as though I were one. I wanted someone to rush to my side and make it all better. But no one was coming. Not for me. Not for Samuel. Not for his family.

I had no idea how long we sat at the table. I was only faintly aware of a few knocks at the shop door. They would have to come back another time.

"I can't believe you didn't tell me," he said after a long pause.

"About what?" I said. "I came straight from the registry office to tell you what I learned about your family."

"Not that. The baby," he said.

I gasped. "What do you mean?" I asked.

"You haven't had your courses in at least two months. Perhaps longer. We're living in an apartment the size of a shoebox and I never leave. You haven't used your supplies, nor refused my attentions during your courses. I may be useless, but I'm not stupid."

"You're neither stupid nor useless," I countered.

"Then why wouldn't you tell me?" he pressed.

"At first because I wanted to be sure. Later because I felt you had enough to be getting on with."

"You tell me I'm not useless, yet you treat me like a child. What am I supposed to believe, Tilde?"

"The truth. That I love you and we're going to have a baby. And despite everything, I'm thrilled about it."

He turned his face and buried it in the soft flesh of my midsection, breathing deeply and whispering things I couldn't fully hear. After a few minutes he rolled to his back and stared up at the ceiling. His eyes bore an expression of utter defeat.

"You'd both be better off without me," he said.

"We both need you," I said, running my fingers through his hair. "Don't say such things."

"You blend in. You have a good German surname. Even if the baby looks like my spitting image, no one will notice until he's older. If I stay, you'll never get out of this damned city."

"Don't say such things," I said. "I won't leave Berlin without you."

He pulled his head up from my lap with a jerk and left the sofa. He rummaged in the bedroom for a while and emerged carrying a small suitcase and dressed for travel.

"What are you doing?" I asked, folding my arms over my chest. "It will be dark soon."

"I won't see you and the baby tossed in some camp on my account. I'm leaving."

"I'll go with you," I said automatically. "We can find a way out of Germany."

"I'm not leaving Germany. I need answers about my family," he proclaimed.

"Answers from whom? I've told you all I know. I don't think the man at the registry office knew anything that he didn't tell me already."

"Maybe he doesn't. But the guards at the camp do. I'll go myself and ask to see my mother and sister. Beg for their release. Whatever it takes."

"Don't be foolish, my love. You'd be walking straight into the lion's den. You won't be of any use to them if you get yourself arrested in the process."

"I'm of no use to them here, either."

"You're of use to me. Of use to our child."

"Sitting up here while you work? Unable to do anything to care for you and the baby? I don't see how you find me anything other than a burden."

"Samuel, you're alive and well. That's as much as I need from you right now. It's enough for now."

"I cannot live with myself, Tilde. Not now that I know where they are. Not knowing there's a minuscule chance I might be able to save them. And I can't stay and put you at risk."

"There's a far better chance you'll end up in a camp yourself. Or worse. You're not being rational."

"I'm not a lawyer at heart like you are. Being rational means nothing right now. I have to do something to save them."

I knew the desperation in those eyes. I'd seen it the day my father asked my mother for a divorce to save his own hide.

"You made a vow to my mother you'd protect me. You swore to her you would. Did that mean nothing to you? We'll get some help. Lawyers. Officials of some kind. We'll find someone to help us."

"Tilde, they might still be alive. Who knows how long that will be true. Lawyers take time. I have to do this now."

"Then think of your child, Samuel." I held my hand to my belly, which was now just visibly swollen in fitted clothes. I'd have to re-sort to ruffled smocks and bold prints before long. "Do we mean nothing to you?"

"I couldn't look my own child in the face if I didn't try to right this. I wish you understood, Tilde." He stood as if daring me to contradict him.

I wish you understood, Tilde. The very same sentiment my father had used. I gritted my teeth. I found it scarcely less infuriating com-ing from Samuel. At the root of it, they were both selfish. Samuel loved me. He would love the baby. But not so much that he would swallow his grief and stay alive for our sake.

"You made a vow before God you wouldn't abandon me and that's exactly what you're doing. You told both our families a bald-faced lie. I thought you were better than that."

He dropped his head under the weight of my words. "I hope, in time, you'll come to forgive me."

"If you come back alive, perhaps. If you don't, I'll spend the rest of my life angry with you for being so selfish. If you go now, what good will you be able to bring about? Hitler and his goons are too big for one man to take on. What is it you plan to do? March into the concentration camp screaming? Barge into the Führer's very office and demand answers?"

"If I must," he said. "I need to know what happened to them."

"No one knows yet, Samuel. But you know in your heart the news can't be good. If they're alive and in a camp, you attracting attention to them will not do them any favors. If they're gone, this is all in vain. They wouldn't want you to do this."

"I have to, Tilde," he said, turning to the rack to fetch his hat and coat. "I wish it could be different."

"It can be, but you won't let it. You're leaving me alone so you can go off and die to no purpose. You're leaving our baby without a father. You're leaving me to live the rest of life alone."

"Then may it be long and full of happiness and health, my darling. And trust that I will love you until my last breath." He leaned in to kiss me, and all of me wanted to melt into him as I usually did. To lose myself in him as we'd done so often in the past months to help ease the pain we felt from the world around us. As much as I wanted to return the kiss, I pushed him back.

"And how many hours from now will that be? I never pegged you as a fool, Samuel."

"Go to your mother's and live a happy life. Spare a kind word about me to the baby if you can manage it."

I grabbed him by the shoulders as if to shake some sense into him. But I just held on to him. I clenched my fingers around his arms, wishing I were strong enough to hold him there forever. Wishing that he could see the folly of what he was about to do. Barring that, I wished I could see some purpose for his sacrifice.

But I could not.

The sobs and the screams were trapped in my chest. I just stood there, holding him. Silently imploring him to see reason. After what might have been a few moments, or perhaps full minutes, he broke free. He kissed my cheek, opened the apartment door, and descended to the shop without another word. I listened for the bell to ring as he exited onto the street below. I walked over to the sink to wash the dishes, but slid to the floor, pulling my knees to my chest and letting the pain wash over me like the relentless licking of flames at my feet. He'd chosen the ghost of his childhood family over the certainty of a future with the baby and me.

Certainty was the wrong word. But at least there was *possibility.*

It seemed like something to live for. Wasn't it?

And I knew in my heart that our baby would never have the chance to know for himself how wonderful a man his father had been. Finally, the sobs broke free from my breast and as I lay on the floor, I let them have me.

CHAPTER TWENTY-SIX

Hanna

August 1939

Klara sprawled on my bed with a French fashion magazine as I organized the new clothes Aunt Charlotte had bought me to wear to university. My aunt wasn't pleased that I was going, but she was determined I would be the best-dressed girl on campus. Where Klara had gotten the magazine, I didn't know. It was becoming harder and harder to access any foreign press. But Klara's father had connections and was high enough in the party's hierarchy that no one would question his daughter having access to a few French magazines. The same leniency wasn't afforded to the rest of the rest of the country, but Klara didn't seem too fussed by the ethical inconsistencies as long as she got her copies of *Vogue*.

We weren't as friendly as we'd been, but her mother was keen on the connection between our families, and I couldn't say I minded the company.

"Your aunt has good taste," Klara said, looking up at the piles of wool and tweed I was transferring to the closet. I'd rather have been packing them into a suitcase to study in Frankfurt or Freiburg, but that had been asking too much. I would study in Berlin and stay with my aunt and uncle, or I wouldn't study at all. It seemed like a compromise worth making. "My mother would have picked the dowdiest things in the shop. She's impossible."

"Well, soon you'll be able to dress as you please, won't you? This new beau of yours is sure to propose and buy you anything you set your heart on. Not to mention you can make your own things." Klara didn't seem particularly keen on the new young officer that had shown interest, but she welcomed his advances. I gathered she thought she would be a more enticing catch to someone more appealing if there were other men in pursuit.

"That does help," she admitted. "But who knows. This one may turn out to be a dud, and I may yet get stuck with one of the men who actually *likes* the flowered peasant look that's being pushed." She waved my own copy of *NS Frauen Warte* in the air. The pages were filled with articles on how to keep husbands happy, how to rear healthy children, and how to maintain a perfectly ordered home. The women were, almost as a rule, tall, blond, without a trace of makeup, and in the dowdiest clothing I'd ever seen in print. I'd been given a copy each week and Aunt Charlotte tried to stealthily ask questions about its contents to see if I'd been reading. I made at least an attempt to glance at the articles so I'd be prepared for those little sessions, but I was never very interested in articles about keeping house and serving Germany.

"I doubt it. Any man who takes a fancy to you would have better sense."

"We can hope."

"What will you be doing now that school's out?" I asked. She'd spoken about the end of her studies as if it were a liberation, but had yet to mention any real plans.

"I'm helping my mother with her duties at the Women's League. Being charming for male dinner guests until one asks for me . . . you know."

"I'm sorry you can't come to the university with me," I said. "We'd have so much more fun together."

"I never even bothered asking," she said. "I've heard the word *no* before."

"They might have surprised you," I said.

"Not all of us are as used to getting our own way as you are, Hanna." She sat up on the bed. "I know you'll do well at university. You'll earn top marks and make loads of interesting friends. Just remember that it means far more to you than it does to your aunt or uncle or Friedrich. If they think it's turning your head or that you're losing sight of what they think is important, you'll be yanked out of classes before you know what's happened."

"I'll toe the line," I said. "I already agreed to the course of study Friedrich preferred. I wanted to work toward my degree in biology. He insisted on German literature."

"He'll never give you the chance to be a doctor anyway. Might as well give the spot up to a man who will use it."

I bit my tongue, but hated that she was right. And Germany needed all the doctors it could get. They would never let me be one of them.

"Just promise me you'll be smart. And safe. I can't say more, but just know that there will be trouble if you cross the wrong line."

She embraced me and left, citing a need to help her mother with some urgent task pertaining to a Women's League fund-raiser. Aunt Charlotte would surely be involved, and I was grateful that preparing for my studies was giving me a reprieve.

I heard a knock at the door as I finished putting the last of my new clothes away and was surprised to see Friedrich on the other side when I opened it.

"Your uncle said you were home," he said, kissing my cheek. "I thought it might be a good time to bring these by."

He presented me with a stack of books written by the German masters with two wrapped parcels on top. He gestured for me to open them. One was a sturdy cordovan leather portfolio for note-taking, the other a sterling silver fountain pen with gold accents. My name was skillfully embossed on the portfolio and engraved on the pen.

"Those books were some of my favorites. I look forward to discussing them with you. And I thought every serious student needed the proper tools for note-taking."

"Thank you, Friedrich," I said, clutching the portfolio to my chest. Of all the gifts I'd received since I'd arrived in Berlin, these were the only ones that touched me. "They're lovely."

"I'm glad you like them, darling," he said. He slipped the portfolio from my hands and pulled me to him. He'd learned to temper his advances in the months since Christmas. He wasn't insistent, but gentle and tentative. He'd refrained from taking full liberties since then, and it made things a little more bearable.

"You know how sorry I am about how I behaved at the party all those months ago?" he whispered in my ear. His fingertips glided down my spine, causing my whole body to tingle as he caressed me.

I couldn't speak, but nodded. He cupped my face in his hands and kissed me with the eagerness of a man denied for many months. He'd not accepted Aunt Charlotte's veiled hints for him to spend the night and see the negligees she'd bought me.

"I want you to be happy, Hanna. Truly. I want you to learn and understand the works of the great men who came before us. To understand why we fight for the Fatherland. I want to build something great with you. A family that will be the pride of Germany. That can't happen if you're miserable."

"Thank you, Friedrich," I said, returning his kiss. "I just need time."

"Then time is what you'll have," he said. He pulled me taut against his body and laced his fingers in my hair before lowering his lips to mine once more.

I felt him unzip the back of my dress, but this time, there was no brutish force. There was no hurried rending of fabric. He caressed me slowly until I wanted his caresses as dearly as I wanted the very air in my lungs.

He stepped back and removed my clothes as gently as if I were made of porcelain. Unable to resist the pull of his desire, I removed his clothes as well.

His movements were slow and deliberate, taking his time as he savored me. I was able to relax in the moment and enjoy his embraces, though the worry of conceiving a child still nagged in the back of my head. For all of Friedrich's promises, a child would force him to break them all.

We lay entwined for what seemed like hours. His breathing was deep and contented as he drifted in and out of sleep. In this moment of peace, I was able to admire the beauty of his chiseled features.

The curl of his lashes. The boyish pout of his bottom lip when he slept. He truly was a thing of beauty. And that he desired me should have filled me with delight.

At least in that moment, it didn't fill me with dread. And for that evening, it was enough.

CHAPTER TWENTY-SEVEN

Tilde

August 1939

I'd flipped the sign to CLOSED for the evening and set to organizing the new bolts of fabric for the shop that had arrived that afternoon. I was annoyed as my hands shook with nervous energy, as if I'd had too much afternoon coffee, though I'd given up the stuff weeks before due to heartburn. That was perhaps the cruelest deprivation of my pregnancy so far. My back ached and my feet were swollen as my body reacted to the changes within, and there was no getting used to the ever-present shaking of my hands, no matter how I tried to master myself.

The days were tolerable. I kept busy tending to clients and threw myself into the day-to-day bustle that came with running the shop. It kept my hands busy and took up just enough space in my head to keep me from running mad. The nights were torture. I couldn't lose myself in Grandfather's legal texts like I had in the past. I couldn't find the focus to take in the words, and it was too dangerous to let my mind wander. It always ended at the same place: Samuel. I woke up each morning covered in tears and clutching the pillow that had been his. Parched for water but loath to replenish myself only to expend the water again the following night.

I wanted to let the tears flow so long, so fervently that I would simply dry up and float away on the breeze like a crumpled, brown autumn leaf. I thought longingly of disappearing. Floating away from the realities that faced me as a widowed soon-to-be mother. To exhale one last time and let the pain wash away. But I would not be the coward my baby's father had been. I would not be the coward my own father had been.

I would keep my head down and I would survive. For the baby's sake if nothing else.

I'd managed to keep my condition well hidden for months, though I'd noticed a few more glances at my midsection as the weeks passed. I wore loose clothes to minimize my growing abdomen and was lucky that my bulge wasn't yet that noticeable. But my time wasn't far off—only three months left until the baby would make his way into the world and I'd have a fresh new set of worries on my shoulders. Soon, no dress in creation would be able to conceal what Samuel had left behind. I wished I could will the baby to stay as it was for another year. To wait until I could devise a real plan for us. But, like all mothers before me, the timing was not in my hands. Most days I just tried not to think about the baby and all that lay ahead. I focused on that day, that hour, that moment.

Other times, I obsessed about every moment of the future. I rehearsed a story about a beau who got killed in service to the country. Perhaps in the Sudetenland. A good German man with a good German name. Hans Fischer or Rudi Müller, perhaps. He had answered the Führer's call and had fallen in service to the Fatherland.

No one would care about a lovers' tryst when soldiers were being called to the borders and tensions were mounting as the Führer set his sights on expanding his territories. There were plenty of girls who'd gotten themselves in a similar condition and weren't treated like the pariahs they would have been a generation before. They were treated as respectfully as any other mother in the Reich.

Every baby born was another future soldier or future mother in the service of Germany, and that was all that seemed to matter. If it kept us alive, I wouldn't argue.

Weary, I climbed the stairs to the apartment that had once been my mother's refuge, then Samuel's. Though Mama had sent word that she was safe, and I couldn't be entirely sure Samuel was dead, I could feel the restless bits of their souls trapped within the walls. Captivity was a special kind of torture that had left its mark on both of them, and in turn, a bit of each of them would haunt this space as long as it stood. I wasn't superstitious, but I began to believe that ghosts were well and truly real, and not always remnants of the dead. Sometimes the living left splinters of themselves behind and had to move forward with the fragments that remained.

Even if Samuel were miraculously still alive, he would never be whole again.

Nor would Mama.

Nor would I.

I collapsed into a chair and tried to will myself to make a nourishing dinner. So many nights I made do with bread and a bit of jam or butter, but I knew the baby needed more. I just wasn't equal to the task of doing better. I hated myself for it, but there was no energy left to summon.

I rocked back and forth in Mama's favorite old rocking chair, wishing the motion might somehow lead me somewhere. No matter how long I rocked, I was still in the same place I'd been when I started. I knew I had to do more than I'd done in the four months since Samuel left to plan for the baby and to make a life for us. But that required moving on. It felt like even simple gestures like making a plan for the birth of the baby would mean acknowledging the passing of time. In so many ways I clung to the fantasy that this had all been a dream and that he'd come back through the door and the time we'd been apart would be dismissed as the stuff of nightmares.

But nightmares weren't usually this cruel.

Deep within me, I longed to go to the registry office to ask after Samuel; but I knew that after all the attempts to get travel papers for Mama and my enquiries about the Eisenbergs, I was becoming recognized. If I went in asking after Samuel, I'd surely lose the thin veil of protection that my Aryan appearance bought me. The office was continually staffed by the same few people, so there was no hope of remaining anonymous. I wasn't the only one who'd taken note. The queue of women asking after their lost husbands and sons had grown shorter and shorter. Either they realized the risk was too great, or had been taken off themselves. If it were just me, I would have taken the risk. Knowing Samuel's fate would have been worth attracting attention. But the baby had to be my focus now. I would protect him the way my father never protected me. I would be prudent in a way Samuel hadn't been.

I wrestled with that uncomfortable truth. Samuel had been foolish.

Of course, he'd burned with worry for his parents and sister. He loved them dearly and would have traded his life for theirs. I could not fault him for this.

But they were either gone or beyond our reach.

Giving his life by causing trouble with the authorities served no purpose other than to leave me a widow and to ensure our baby grew up without a father.

It was foolish. It wasn't noble. It was selfish.

And I could not forgive him for it. Perhaps in time I would, but I knew it would be a long way off.

As I rocked, I realized I could no longer pretend that the baby wasn't coming. I had to do something to prepare. Tonight. It didn't have to be big, but it had to be something. I trundled back down to the shop and wandered about the displays, pretending for a moment that I was one of my own clients.

The baby needed clothes. This I could do.

I browsed the sturdy cottons and soft wools that mothers favored, but I found myself among the impractical silks and satins that were seeing far less use these days. One of my favorites was a fine matte white satin. Many brides chose it for their wedding dresses and many mothers for their babies' christening gowns. It seemed like an extravagance, but it was one I could actually manage to provide for the darling child who would be born with so many other disadvantages.

He would be born Jewish in the middle of a country that despised him. He'd be born without the love and protection of a father. He'd be born to a mother who would struggle constantly to give him even the smallest boon beyond his basic necessities. But he could have *this*.

Unless a miracle occurred and I was able to leave Germany, I wouldn't be able to have a proper bris if the baby were a boy, nor an equivalent blessing in the synagogue if she were a girl. But just because we couldn't have a ceremony didn't mean the baby shouldn't feel welcomed into the world. I cut several lengths of some of our softest fabrics along with material for a swaddling cloth like the one Mrs. Eisenberg had wrapped Samuel in for his bris. I added a few patterns for baby gowns and the notions I'd need to complete them. Mama had always insisted on paying back into the till whatever fabric we used, but this once I would defy her meticulous bookkeeping and take what I needed without bothering with the records.

I retreated upstairs where Mama's sewing machine now resided in a windowless interior room. When she was forced to work out of sight, her one joy had been working in the bright sunlight of the parlor window. But now I always did my sewing after shop hours. More and more, I could not trust that any neighbor who spotted me sewing by kerosene lamp at all hours of the night wouldn't find some reason to mention it to a block captain. The block captain might find some reason to question me, which could lead to no good outcome.

I selected one of the patterns and cut the fabric with Mama's best scissors. When I was first learning, I would cut out a dozen or more pieces of fabric under Mama's watchful eye and marvel that the jumble of pieces, if assembled properly, would become an actual dress. Even as the years passed, I never lost that sense of wonder. There was something soothing about looking at the pieces of material and forcing myself to have faith that they would come together, almost miraculously, to create an article of clothing. If I couldn't take joy in reading anymore, at least I could have this.

I spent that night engrossed in the small garment I crafted from a daisy-yellow flannel. Carefully stitching, embellishing it tenderly; even finishing it with my initials hidden in the hem. I didn't know if my baby was going to be a boy or a girl. I didn't know if my child would be drawn to the law as I was, to music like his father, to some combination of both, or to a path uniquely his own. I didn't know how I would care for the child and make a living. I didn't know how to keep either of us safe. But as I clipped the final thread and released the gown from the machine, I knew at least the baby would have one beautiful thing to his name, and it seemed like slightly better than nothing to get started with.

CHAPTER TWENTY-EIGHT

Hanna

October 1939

Hitler finally got the war he'd been hungering for, but for those assembled in the lecture hall, there was nothing more pressing than the results of our latest papers. Professor Bauer was lecturing us on the faults of our latest compositions, and I was allowing myself to hope that none of his critiques applied to my work. I'd provided a clear argument and not tried to embellish my thoughts with overly flowered prose or tirades that could not be supported by the text. I sat fidgeting in my seat, waiting for our papers to be passed back.

It wasn't biology or chemistry, or any of the courses I'd wanted to study, but I found that delving into the depths of German literature proved fascinating. I'd been assigned to write for the university newspaper and found it more fulfilling than I'd imagined it could be. There were fewer women enrolled in the university than I'd hoped, but it wasn't surprising given the government's encouragement of women to stay in the domestic sphere. The men, especially the professors, were generally aloof toward the women, though not overtly hostile. I found I had to be more persistent in class to be heard, but it wasn't anything I hadn't expected. Once my name began to circulate with the newspaper and my articles garnered a favorable response, the men's attitudes warmed slightly and even the professors were more interested in my contributions to class.

Finally, at the end of class Professor Bauer returned our papers, and my marks were better than respectable. I exhaled with relief and gathered my things for the next class.

"Your analysis of Schiller was spot on, Fräulein Rombauer," Professor Bauer said as I walked by his lectern. "I wish the rest of your class had taken the trouble to make such a thoughtful approach to the paper."

Professor Bauer actually looked like a professor should in my imagination. He wore sensible clothes, completely oblivious to and ambivalent about what might be deemed fashionable. He was the antithesis of Klara and Aunt Charlotte. He wore glasses, and his black curly hair was in need of a good cut, but the overall effect was charming. Though he was young, he walked with a pronounced limp, and availed himself of a cane when he had to walk beyond the confines of a classroom. I wondered if he'd suffered an injury at some point or was afflicted with a birth defect. I wasn't bold enough to ask, but I knew his ruined leg was the only thing keeping him from the front.

"The subject matter was fascinating," I said. "Surprisingly so."

"You're surprised to find interesting the greatest work of one of the great German masters? Curious."

"That's not what I mean. I've just never been of a literary bent," I explained.

"Yet you're pursuing advanced studies in literature. Even more curious."

"It had been my intention to study medicine," I said. "But given the circumstances . . ."

"It didn't seem wise to prepare for a career you would not be able to pursue."

"Exactly."

"It's preposterous to me how men can spend their lives surrounded by the love of their mothers, wives, sisters, and daughters but not think them capable of the same tasks as men are. Or worse, know that they are capable of these things, but keep them repressed to satisfy the needs of their own insecurities. What a sad way to live."

"You speak a very unpopular truth, Professor."

"An unfortunate hobby of mine," he said.

"Rather a dangerous one in times like these," I said.

"Wise for one still so young. How sad. You should be exploring your newfound freedoms. A girl your age should be laughing with friends, finding out how many beers are too many, and dating the wrong boy. You shouldn't have to be worried about this crazy government of ours. Needless wars. Mark my words, this generation will lose their youth just like the one before it."

"Professor, I hope you will understand when I say I hope you'll be proved wrong, though in my heart of hearts I know you won't be."

"I understand you perfectly, Fräulein Rombauer. And I look forward to reading more of your work."

"Thank you, sir."

I nodded and trekked out into the bright light of the corridor, surprised to see Friedrich right outside the door in full uniform. His face looked dour, and the students gave him a wide berth as they scuttled on to their next classes. He'd never mentioned his plans to come to campus that day, but he rarely felt the need to convey his plans to me.

"What a pleasant surprise," I said, hoping my face hadn't fallen at the first sight of him. I plastered on a smile that I hoped looked genuine enough and crossed over to him. As he was in uniform and possibly on duty, I didn't offer him a kiss on the cheek or any other such familiar gesture.

"You seemed to be in the midst of a very serious conversation with your professor," he said, glancing over my shoulder into the room where Professor Bauer was still collecting his papers.

"He was complimenting my last assignment," I said.

"That seems quite a long conversation for such a brief matter," he said, his eyes narrowing. He was suspicious of the good professor, and this would not bode well for him if Friedrich could not be pacified.

"Oh, well," I said. "I had a question or two about the work. That sort of thing."

"If you're doing so well, why would you need his help?"

"I'm doing well precisely because I ask for clarification when it's needed," I said. His features grew sharper. I had to deflect. "I won't have your colleagues thinking I'm wasting my time here. If I'm going to attend university, I'm going to be top of my class to make you proud."

This mollified him a bit, but he was still on edge.

"Walk with me, Hanna." It was not a request. He *was* here in an official capacity.

"What do you know of Professor Gerhardt?"

"He teaches composition. A stern man with a reputation for being harsh with his marks, so anyone who can avoid taking his classes usually does. I think he's reasonable once you get to know him, though."

"Nothing surprising in his lectures? Nothing unseemly?"

"Goodness, no. Though I can't imagine how conversations about the proper uses of a semicolon or the benefits of adverbs in prose could turn to anything scandalous," I said.

"You would be surprised," he said. "You never heard any rumblings of him getting students involved in different off-campus organizations?"

"No, not at all." And it was true. I'd been seen on campus with Friedrich often enough that if there were any illicit activities going on, no one would have dared confide in me. Trust was a rare commodity these days, and my stock would have been especially low with anyone who had a word to say against the government. I didn't blame them. Whether I liked it or not, I was dangerous.

"Just be on the lookout," he said. "We fear there are more than a few attempts to subvert our leader and the party from these very halls, and others just like them across the country. They question his actions at every turn and show him no loyalty."

"Well, it is the nature of academics to question things, I suppose."

"Useless eggheads, if you ask me," he replied with such venom I expected him to spit his words on the sidewalk. "We need fewer poets like your professor back there and more men of action. Farmers and fighters. I wonder that he hasn't been called up to service yet. A young man like him should have signed up himself rather than wait for conscription."

"You didn't notice his leg, then?"

"A cripple?"

"Well, not fully. But yes, he can't walk far without a cane."

"A useless eater then," he said. "A drain on resources."

"He's educating future teachers," I said. "It seems to me he's doing the most for the country that he possibly can under the circumstances."

He didn't look satisfied by my answer but could produce no rebuttal. "Just be observant. There are corrupting influences everywhere and we need to stamp them out."

He wanted me to be his informant on campus. Perhaps his decision to let me attend university hadn't been so selfless after all. If I were to discover that a prominent professor was inciting students to stand up to the party and passed the information along to Friedrich, it would be a big boost to his career. A future spent spying for him loomed ominously in my thoughts and I was repulsed at the prospect. I didn't want to be his private investigator, whether he felt his cause was righteous or not.

He left with a perfunctory kiss, and I gave him a smile that didn't go deeper than my lips. My only solace was that he could not hear the workings of my mind or the beating of my heart. If he'd been able to see all that, he would have had me on a train to oblivion that very night.

"A word, Fräulein Rombauer?" Professor Bauer called at the end of the next class. I'd been so distracted on campus since Friedrich's visit to school that I was hardly able to concentrate on the lecture. My notes were sparse and illogical. The next exam would be challenging if I wasn't able to get someone else to help fill in the gaps of what I'd missed.

"Yes, Professor," I said, approaching the table at the front of the large lecture hall.

"You weren't very attentive today," he said. "That's unusual for you."

"That's a remarkable observation in a room with more than a hundred other students," I said.

He cleared his throat and shuffled some papers for a moment. "It's easy to notice when the most attentive student in the room has lost her focus. It's a gift after years in the classroom."

"I suppose you would gain that sixth sense after a while. Yes, I was a bit distracted. My apologies. It won't happen again."

"I was more concerned about you than about the class. Are you well?"

"Quite, thank you."

"I don't suppose this has to do with the uniformed man who paid you a visit after our last class?" he asked.

He was too perceptive for my own good. I wished I could tell him to mind his own business, but I couldn't bring myself to speak that way to a professor. Especially a kind one.

"No," I said. *Let this be the end of the conversation for your own good.*

"I'll just say this. If you're in danger, tell someone. There are those who will help you. *I* can help."

"Thank you," I said, hoping he would take it as a dismissal.

"I don't suppose the visit had anything to do with the disappearance of Professor Gerhardt? We've reason to be alarmed."

Enough. I couldn't know this. I was a liability to him. To everyone.

"That man was my fiancé, Professor," I said, hoping my tone was imperious. If he thought I was one of them, then he wouldn't say anything else that might endanger him.

"I see," he said. "I didn't realize . . ."

"No," I said. "Clearly. Captain Schroeder does enjoy coming to campus to pay me a visit from time to time. As any good fiancé is wont to do."

"Of course," he said. There was the unmistakable shadow of disappointment on his face as he resigned himself to the information I relayed. Whether he was disappointed that I was spoken for or in my apparent political leanings, I couldn't know. "I admit I'm surprised."

"At what? That I'm engaged to be married? I'm not sure that's a compliment, Professor."

"No, well, perhaps it's best if I say nothing."

"By all means, speak your piece," I said.

Anger flashed for a moment, but his features settled into a stern resolve. "You're bright, Hanna. More than that, rarer than that, you know your worth. Why would you make an alliance with a man who represents a party that wants to take women's place in society back a hundred years? I can't imagine you being happy in a voiceless marriage."

"Well, sometimes the decision to marry is a complicated one," I said.

"It should never be," he said. "When I married my Sophie, it wasn't a difficult decision. It was as natural as the next beat of my heart. When she died, it was as though she took half of me with her. I hope you won't settle for less than that. It's what you deserve."

He spoke with a tenderness I hadn't heard before when he mentioned his wife. I had not known he had been married and I wanted too much to ask him about her. But I couldn't engage him any further without betraying myself.

"Choice is an amazing thing, Professor. And a luxury that isn't always afforded even to the most deserving. My apologies again for my behavior in class. It won't happen again."

Tears stung my eyes as I left the classroom. If only I could truly confide in him or anyone else. If only these were like the hurts of my youth that could be soothed by a mother's embrace. But my mother, and anyone who was willing or able to protect me, was gone. This kind professor thought he could help, but if I reached out to him, it would probably lead to my ruin, and certainly his own.

In another life, I might have been able to look up to this man and admire his intellect. To respect how he'd made a glowing career for himself despite the hardship that nature or misfortune had dealt him. But all I could see was a good man whose kind nature was nothing but a liability in this world that had become so terribly cruel. He could probably remember a time when good deeds were rewarded and selflessness was a virtue, but that had all been before my time. And sadly, not all that long ago.

I rushed off to my next class, one with the infamous Professor Gerhardt that Friedrich had been so concerned about. I arrived at the classroom, and instead of everyone sitting in their places attentively waiting for the professor and chatting quietly with their neighbors, there was a panicked buzz with students standing in clusters throughout the room.

"What's going on?" I asked a nearby student—a young man by the name of Klaus from the university paper who had always been friendly.

"Rumor is, Gerhardt's gone missing," he said. His voice was flat. No one who went missing ever came back. "The last time anyone remembers seeing him was Tuesday."

The day Friedrich had come to visit. It wasn't a coincidence.

No one seemed to know how to proceed. It wasn't the first time a professor had gone missing, but it was the first time it had been one of mine. This kindly, silver-haired old man who spent his life teaching grammar and composition hardly seemed like a threat to a regime that boasted such strength.

The girls stood with their arms crossed over their chests as they spoke. Bracing themselves. The boys with their hands on their hips, looking ready to act. But there was nothing they could do.

I had visions of the Nazis hauling the sweet old man off into a truck and wanted to weep on the spot. Instead, I turned on the ball of my foot and went home to Aunt Charlotte and Uncle Otto's. I couldn't ask for their help, for they wouldn't grant it even if they wanted to, but it was a place to think in quiet.

When I arrived, Uncle Otto and Aunt Charlotte were already home, along with Friedrich. I was asked by the butler to join them in the parlor. None of them was surprised to see me home from class so early.

"A new opening in your schedule," Friedrich said by way of greeting as he bent to kiss my cheek. "It must be a little relief to lighten your course load."

"Not especially," I said. "I enjoyed composition rather well."

"I'm sure they'll be able to dig up a new professor before too long," Friedrich said. "But if you wish to keep up your skills in the meantime, you can feel free to write me love letters. I promise to give you a thorough critique."

"Of that I have no doubt," I said, trying to feign some levity.

"We're hoping that now that Gerhardt is no longer an influence on campus, we'll see less trouble," Friedrich said to Uncle Otto, continuing the conversation my arrival had interrupted.

"Cut off the head and the snake dies," Uncle Otto said, nodding his head in approbation.

"In this case I fear we're dealing with a Medusa. More snakes than you would care to count."

"We need more farmers and fewer poets," Uncle Otto said, raising a glass to punctuate his words. "Shut the damn place down and put them all to work in honest jobs."

"If only there were more of those to go around," I interjected. Friedrich arched a brow.

"True enough, darling. That will come. We must trust in our leadership to provide, but without unity, they cannot focus on these important issues. That's why we must get these insurgents in line."

"Has there been a government in the history of all mankind that had universal approval?"

"But this isn't a simple government, darling. It's a new order. A new experiment in the way things are done. When we win the war, and if this new order is allowed to flourish without the menace of impure and foreign influences, it will be glorious."

And it was all too clear what had happened to Professor Gerhardt. He was in a prison or a camp somewhere, unlikely ever to know the taste of freedom again in his lifetime. And I was engaged to his captor.

CHAPTER TWENTY-NINE

Hanna

October 1939

The university newsroom was a delightful hub of activity. Though what we reported was never of great significance to the outside world, there was no convincing us that we weren't breaking stories of such magnitude that the world was daft not to stand up and take notice of our journalistic brilliance. Of course, the world didn't give a fig for the scribblings of college students in Berlin on what were surely some of the most banal topics to ever be set to print due to heavy censorship, but none of that mattered to us as we toiled away in the newsroom fueled by bad coffee and the shared delusion of our own adequacy as reporters.

When I entered that day, a hush fell, and heads drooped down in silent labor.

"What are you working on?" I asked Klaus. He was usually friendly, but he didn't raise his eyes from his paper.

"It's a memorial to Gerhardt," he said. "It turns out he didn't survive his little stay in prison. Hardly a wonder for a man of seventy-four."

"My god, that's awful," I said. "Such a sweet man."

"Don't pretend you didn't have anything to do with it," he spat. "Have your boyfriend lock me up, too, if you want. But he was a good man and a decent professor. He deserved better."

"He did," I said. "And I didn't have a thing to do with it. When I was asked if I'd heard anything suspicious about him, I denied it. And I still do."

Klaus snapped his mouth shut but looked far from mollified. I was still in league with the enemy, and that was enough.

"What about Professor Bauer?"

"What about him?" I asked.

"Do you know anything about his disappearance? He's gone missing, too."

"No," I said. "It can't be true."

"No one has seen him in two days. He's missed a class, and that's the first one in fifteen years."

"I'll get to the bottom of this," I said, tossing the expensive leather bookcase that Aunt Charlotte had given me by Klaus's feet.

I took off in the direction of Professor Bauer's office, running with the abandon of a young child. I arrived gasping for air and sweating despite the autumn chill. I didn't know what I expected to find there. Professor Bauer in fine form, waiting with a reasonable explanation for his absence? Unlikely. But I had to see for myself.

The door was ajar, but there was no cheerful fluttering of pages nor his usual persistent *clack-clack-clacking* of typewriter keys. I heard drawers slamming and books thudding to the floor. I felt the air expel from my lungs as I reached for the doorknob, hoping that my brain hadn't correctly interpreted the malice behind the sounds in that room.

Friedrich was there, sitting at Bauer's desk. His steely blue eyes were locked on the task at hand proving that Professor Bauer was an insurgent and a threat to the Reich.

"Hanna, I thought you were in class," Friedrich said as he registered my presence.

"Not at the moment," I said. "I heard the rumor that Professor Bauer had gone missing. I wanted to see for myself if the rumors were true."

"You're very interested in his welfare," Friedrich retorted, raising his eyes to me. "Should I be concerned?"

"He was—is—my professor, Friedrich. And a good one. Of course I care about his welfare as I do about that of all my fellow men."

"Be careful where you spread your goodwill, my dear. It's a dangerous thing to care about the wrong people."

I'd rather risk my neck than my soul. I yearned to say it but swallowed back the words.

"I take it Professor Bauer has met the same fate as Professor Gerhardt?"

"I cannot discuss an ongoing investigation, but I would not expect his imminent return."

"I can't believe he'd be involved in anything nefarious," I said. "He's not the troublemaking sort."

"You'd be surprised. Treachery comes from unexpected quarters more often than you'd imagine."

"You have all the evidence you need then, don't you?"

"Oh, my sweet girl. You are an innocent."

"How do you mean?"

"I don't need evidence. I just have to make it look like I tried to find some."

"Is one lame professor worth all this trouble?"

"It only takes one spark to ignite a flame, darling. It's time you headed home."

"Very well," I said, feigning compliance.

"I'll see you for dinner," he replied, his eyes diverting back to the page. Of course he'd been invited. He was there more often than not, at my aunt's invitation.

I left the professor's office, but did not return home immediately. I went to the newsroom, where Klaus still pecked at the typewriter.

"Do you want a real scoop?" I asked, picking up my bag and speaking low so no one could overhear.

"Why would you give it to me?" he said.

"Because I'm fairly certain my journalism days are at an end. If you want to cause a sensation, you can write that Gerhardt and Bauer were taken on suspicion of unpatriotic behavior without any real evidence. Mention my name in this and I'll haunt you for the rest of our days—which won't be numerous."

"Yours or mine?"

"Both. I'd advise against a byline, too."

"Prudent," he said. "You're sure this is true?"

"Yes, and we're a school newspaper, not *Le Monde* or *The Times*. All you need to do is raise suspicion."

"You're an evil genius, you know that?"

"In the current scheme of things, I think working on the side of evil may be the right side of history."

"That all depends on who wins, doesn't it?"

"Too right. Now I have to get home. Just remember, if you saw me, I just came to get my bag, and this was nothing more than a quick chat about the weather. Are we clear?"

He nodded and I whisked out of the room for what I knew was the last time.

"WHAT IS THE meaning of this?" Friedrich asked, dropping a copy of the school newspaper on my dinner plate two days later. He pulled out his usual chair and took the cigarette case from his breast pocket, flicked it open, put a cigarette to his lips, and lit it with a series of fluid motions. I'd never known him to smoke before now, but the strain was getting to him.

The headline read WHERE HAVE THEY GONE? STUDENTS DE-MAND ANSWERS ABOUT MISSING PROFESSORS.

The article went on to name the professors who had gone missing—Gerhardt and Bauer being the most recent, but there had been others over the past few years. Klaus gave dates and specific circumstances of their disappearances. There were both men and women on the list, ranging in age from their thirties to their seventies, and they had worked in various specialties from combustion to mathematics.

"What do you mean?" I asked. "I left the paper. I felt that Aunt Charlotte needed me, and I wasn't getting course credits for it anyway."

"You didn't encourage anyone on staff to write the article? I saw how upset you were in Bauer's office."

"I was upset, I admit. He was a good professor. He was generous with grades because he liked me. But I had no idea about these other disappearances. They all happened before I arrived."

"That's true, Friedrich," Aunt Charlotte said, using her sweetest voice. "Hanna knows better than to cause trouble. It's not as though this article will help the professor's cause."

"Quite the opposite," Friedrich said and took another long drag from his cigarette. "He's being questioned about it as we speak. If students were that loyal to him, who knows what he influenced them to do."

I willed my face not to betray the feelings in my gut. Professor Bauer was being tortured now because of the article I'd encouraged Klaus to write.

"Surely the professor left behind instructions for just such an article in case he was taken in," Uncle Otto suggested. "Sounds like the sort of scheme those types engage in."

Friedrich looked thoughtfully at Uncle Otto. "You have a valid point there. I'll make sure the question is brought before him."

At least he was still alive. For how long remained to be seen.

"The whole thing is an unfortunate mess," I said, hoping to convey a distance between myself and the paper. "It does nothing but dampen spirits when we need to be unified."

Friedrich brightened. "Well said, darling. I'm glad you see it that way."

"Our Hanna is as bright as they come. She's always bound to see the right side of things," Aunt Charlotte said.

"Then she'll be bright enough to understand that it's time for her formal studies to change their direction. The universities are all a hotbed of dissension now. I've found a more suitable arrangement.

There's a villa on Schwanenwerder Island where young women of good standing can go to recuperate from the toils of daily life and learn the skills they need to be exemplary wives and mothers. I've enrolled you there to begin next week. It's a lovely villa right on Lake Wannsee, and you're sure to be comfortable there. Once your course is complete, we will marry without delay. I see now that I was foolish to allow our engagement to drag on, but we'll rectify that soon enough."

I blinked for a few moments, not knowing how to respond. "How long will I be at this . . ."

"School," he supplied. "It's one of the Reich's bride schools. The program isn't wholly new, but the Führer has asked us to expand it based on the successes it's already had. This is quite an opportunity for you, my dear. The most elite members of the SS send their brides there and you will be among them."

"How long?" I repeated.

"Six weeks," he said. "It's not onerous. I daresay the women I've met who have studied have enjoyed their experience. It was more of a vacation than a training program. A lot like your BDM was, I expect."

"If you think the BDM was like a vacation, clearly you never went hiking with us," I said, crossing my arms over my chest. The table erupted in laughter. Friedrich's temper had been defused and I'd evaded it once again. But my luck had run out and soon he'd be keeping the leash so short I'd be tethered to him irrevocably.

Later that night, after Mila had helped me into my nightgown and seen me turned in for the evening, Aunt Charlotte appeared with a gentle rapping at the door. I set down my book as she entered.

"You've had a narrow escape, my dear. You were clever enough to calm his fears this time, but he won't be fooled so easily a second time."

"I don't know what you mean, Aunt Charlotte."

"I'm not a man. You needn't play coy with me. I could tell from the very look on your face that the article was your doing. You looked terrified."

"Of course I was terrified. I don't need to have written the article for him to blame me for it."

"Well, at least you know how the game is played, my dear. You cannot afford to even be adjacent to a scandal, given your mother's eccentricities. You have to be above reproach and even then, your position isn't fully secure."

"It sounds like I'll be walking through a minefield instead of down the aisle," I said. "Not an enticing prospect."

"You are observant. I just hope you'll be smarter and avoid such obvious minefields in the future. This one could have cost us all dearly."

"So you don't mind him sending me off to this 'bride school,' whatever it is?"

"No. I hope you'll learn a good deal during your time there and find yourself better able to commit to your husband and future family. What else could an aunt want for her niece?"

"A future of her own choosing?"

"Don't waste your time on childish fantasies, my dear. It will only lead to disappointment."

CHAPTER THIRTY

Tilde

November 1939

My feet felt as though they'd swollen to the size of life rafts as I waddled back from the market with a few staples for my kitchen. I'd looked lovingly over the meat counter, but opted for potatoes and cheese, saving every possible pfennig like Mama instructed. With so many men now out of the country and fighting the war Hitler and his followers had so desperately wanted, there were far fewer orders for suits. And because the men were gone, women didn't take as much trouble to have new dresses. Everyone felt the burden of the war on their already filled days, so ready-made clothes became an attractive alternative to homemade for those who could afford them. Because of the lull in business, I'd had to dip into Mama's hoard of money more often than I'd wanted, so I cut my expenses wherever I could. The only indulgence I allowed myself was the occasional yardage for clothes for the baby, though I chose more practical fabrics than white satin for the rest of his garments.

I found untold peace in piecing together little gowns and rompers when I had an evening free from urgent commissions, which was more and more often these days. It felt like I could do precious little to protect him from the world, but at least I could do this much to prepare for him. He had a rather impressive wardrobe for a child who hadn't even been born yet, which felt like an extravagance in such times, but it was a comfort to know he'd be well clothed for the first year of his life.

He'd be born within the next two weeks, sooner if my instincts were right, and I was finally able to gather up something more than dread at the prospect of bringing him into this world gone topsy-turvy. I'd closed the shop and would have to keep it that way until I'd recovered from the birth. I'd made plans with a private midwife to deliver the baby at home. I couldn't risk registering in a public hospital. I'd made what few plans I could to prepare for his arrival and had to leave the rest to luck.

I was looking forward to my humble lunch, followed by a half hour working on a romper made of soft maroon wool, but a block before I reached the shop, I stopped in the middle of the sidewalk so abruptly that I narrowly escaped being trampled by the people behind me.

The shop door was flung open, and even from this distance, I could see a pile of broken glass where the pane had been broken by the butt of a rifle. There were three uniformed men upending displays in the shop and calling for me to come out of the building. Someone had discovered my lineage, and I was now "too Jewish" to be running a business.

The moment that I'd dreaded had come for me.

I stood frozen to the spot on the pavement, staring unblinkingly at the shop my mother had so lovingly created to provide a living for us. In that moment, I knew I'd never be able to set foot in it again. In that moment, all the plans I'd so carefully made for the baby's arrival were as useless as silk armor.

Move, Tilde. You must move.

My inner voice was right. Soon, someone would notice me staring and I'd be found out.

I'd completely stalled in my quest for a travel visa, too overwhelmed by the prospect of impending motherhood and leaving without knowing Samuel's fate. I realized how foolish I'd been. I'd put myself and the baby at risk, and I was furious with myself for having been so neglectful.

I thought of all the places I could go, but each seemed less likely than the last. My mother's friends, those who remained, would be too frightened and too strained with their own worries to take me on as a burden. My father had made it abundantly clear he would not help. There were a number of kind patrons, but no one I knew well enough to ask for such a momentous favor.

Except Klara.

It was risky. Incredibly so. But I could think of nowhere else to go. She might refuse to help. She might well leave me to my own devices. I didn't believe she was cruel enough to turn me in, but I couldn't much trust her beyond that.

But she *might* be willing to help. And that chance was enough.

I turned around on the crowded sidewalk and willed myself to have the energy to walk all the way to Grunewald. It had been a comfortably long walk before the baby, but now that the little one was on the point of arrival, it seemed he was draining me of all my energy. The wind was biting cold, but as the market was only a block from the house, I hadn't bothered with a hat and gloves, and I was now bitterly regretting that decision. I didn't have the money on hand for a taxi, and even if I had, I wouldn't spend the last money I had to my name. I tried not to think of the hidden fortune in Mama's bedroom as I coaxed each foot forward, and had to fight the urge not to sit on every vacant bench or café seat that I passed. When Klara's house finally loomed in the distance, I felt myself sag with relief.

I couldn't knock on the front door. If the butler saw me, especially in my current state, he'd certainly report my arrival to Klara's parents. In their view, I was an unmarried expectant mother, the very last sort of person they'd want their daughter consorting with. If they knew the truth about me, they'd approve even less of my being on their property. No, my only chance was to find Klara alone and pray she would take pity on me.

Luck was, for once, on my side as I saw a back door left open by a careless maid. It was in the rear part of the house one flight down from Klara's room, and given the time of day, I stood a good chance of not being noticed. Luncheon wasn't too far off, so the staff would be in the kitchen, which was a fair distance from this rarely used staircase.

The door to Klara's room was ajar, and I could see her agonizing over piles of clothes. It appeared as though she were alone, so I knocked softly on the doorjamb.

"Tilde!" she exclaimed, pulling me into her room. "You didn't warn me you'd be coming over for a visit!"

I put my finger to my lips, hoping her outburst hadn't alerted anyone to my presence.

"What's wrong?" Her eyes finally settled on the roundness of my midsection. "Oh."

"No one knows I'm here. I snuck in the back door. I figured it was best."

"Likely. My god, you look ready to fall over. Sit down," she ordered, as she scooped up a mountain of clothes off a side chair that was finer than any piece of furniture my mother had ever owned. She dumped the clothes on the bed with an unceremonious grunt and produced a footstool from under it. She lifted my ankles and placed them atop the tufted surface without waiting for my cooperation. She scooted over her desk chair from across the room and sat close enough that she could take my hand in hers. I felt tears threatening at the sweetness of this simple gesture, of feeling taken care of in some small way, but now wasn't the time to give in to sentiment.

"Tell me the bastard's name and I'll wring his neck for you," she said.

"You're jumping to all the wrong conclusions," I said.

"You haven't come to me for help because some faithless git left you high and dry with a baby?"

"Well, you're not entirely wrong, but he wasn't a faithless cad. He's dead." I hadn't spoken the words aloud before, but they were even more painful than I'd predicted.

"A casualty of the war," she said. "Killed in Poland?"

I could cling to this lie. It was the one I'd rehearsed. A good German soldier cut down in his prime during the war. It would keep me safe and provide a future for the baby. But I couldn't let Klara think Samuel was of that ilk. It felt disloyal to Samuel and unfair to Klara. If she was going to protect me, she had to know what danger she was accepting.

"No. My husband. He was taken to a camp," I said. I didn't have to explain more.

"A casualty of the war," she repeated. "Probably killed in Poland. I don't need to know more."

"It's probably best that you don't."

"So how can I help? What do you need?"

"Well—travel papers, which might as well be asking for the moon. But even before then . . . the baby is coming soon."

"How soon? Do you need to lie down?" She stood, looking around wondering where to start preparing her room.

"Not *that* soon," I said. "A few days at least, I think. But not much more than that. But I have to ask, why does your room look like the aftermath of a typhoon?"

"I'm getting ready to go to the posh school for brides the party has set up on Lake Wannsee. I'm meant to be packing my bags. I'm going to be married in a few months."

"Oh, how wonderful, Klara. And here I've interrupted you. I'm so sorry."

"No, this may be ideal. I've a reason to be away from home and will have an easier time hiding you somewhere else."

"This was a mistake. I shouldn't have come here and brought danger to your doorstep. You're about to be a bride. The last thing you need is this. I just didn't know who else to turn to." I felt a cold bead of sweat at the nape of my neck as I realized I'd been so preoccupied with my own safety and the baby's, that I hadn't considered the risk to Klara in all of this. It was an understandable oversight, but I was still ashamed of it.

"Nonsense," she said. "I'll think of something. I know the island well. We used to spend summers there. I might be able to find a quiet house for you to tuck away in. The trick will be finding someone to help deliver the baby."

"I don't want you getting into trouble for my sake, please," I said.

"Helping a widow in her time of need? Seems like the act of a civic-minded young wife, doesn't it? Don't worry. We'll devise a plan. I leave first thing in the morning. I want you to follow me in a taxi about an hour after the chauffeur takes me. Can you manage that?"

"Certainly," I said. "I just wish I were prepared . . . I had to leave everything behind." I didn't want her to know that the goons her parents endorsed so enthusiastically had smashed in my shop door, but she had to know the danger I represented.

"I see," she said. "And people will have seen you come this way. I hope you were discreet." Her arms were folded over her chest as she thought out her plans.

"Very," I assured her. "I didn't walk a direct route, as much as I wanted to."

"Good. There's enough suspicion in the air these days we don't need any more, else we'll be so deep in conspiracy theories we'll drown," she agreed. "We'll find some things that will work for you and the baby here."

"You're taking on too much," I protested again. "I never wanted to put you in harm's way. I'd made such careful plans. I had money hidden. I had clothes for the baby. I had a plan. I did everything I could not to attract attention."

"What's the old saying? Man plans and God laughs? You were right to come to me. As woefully unequipped as I am to help, I'm probably your safest option. If you'd gone to a hospital, there would have been questions."

She spoke with certainty. She heard things from her family and there had been proof enough that the party had their hand in everything—including every last medical facility in Berlin. I had to accept her charity even if it was putting her at risk.

"Where can I stay tonight that won't cause you trouble?" I asked.

"In my bed," she said, simply. "That way if the baby decides to come, I'll be right here to help."

"But what if someone comes in?" I asked.

"What if the roof caves in? We'll deal with it if it happens. Now I want you to spend the day resting. Feet up or else. If you need to get your blood moving, you can go for a spin about the room. Nothing more strenuous, understood?"

"Fine by me. The walk here was enough exercise for today," I said, rubbing my belly.

Klara put me to work, giving her my opinion on which clothes she should take with her to this bride school she'd been enrolled in. I was able to spend the day conserving my energy, though I wasn't able to relax entirely. The prospect of uniformed men breaking down the door, or even a maid coming to change the sheets, had me in knots.

"I'm sorry I didn't keep in touch much this past year," she said, folding some of her underthings. "I should have been a better friend to you."

"You have your own life to lead. And for a short while, I was very happy. And I'm grateful for you now."

"Please don't say that," she said. "I'm just trying to be a passable human being. If I'm able to help you, I'll have at least made some progress on that front."

"I wish you'd speak more kindly about yourself," I said. "In the four years I've known you, you've been warm and decent even when you had every inducement not to be."

"Well, if there is a God, I hope he takes as charitable a view of me as you have. It may be my only chance for some redemption."

CHAPTER THIRTY-ONE

Hanna

November 1939

As I crossed the threshold of the bride school, I felt just as nervous as the day I descended the train from Teisendorf and entered Uncle Otto and Aunt Charlotte's household. The worn suitcase was long gone and my dresses were far smarter, but my worry stone still weighed down my little handbag as though it were a cannonball instead of a few mere ounces of rose quartz.

I'd tried leaving it tucked in the back of my drawer, but more and more I was compelled to feel the surface, smooth from years of worry, of the stone between my thumb and forefinger. Each time I glided my fingers along the surface, I felt myself chanting a prayer. *Mama, keep me safe. Mama, get me out of this place.* But these were prayers that could not be answered. As the iron gates clicked behind me, it was plain there was no escape for me.

The villa on Schwanenwerder Island was just as luxurious as Friedrich had claimed. It was newly built and designed specifically to teach young women like me to be the perfect German bride, the prefect German wife, the perfect German mother. The building was designed to be light and full of air. To bring in the verdant landscape of the island and the wholesome sounds of the lake. But with light come shadows.

A maid showed me to a foyer and whisked my case away to the depths of the building. She gave me no instructions other than to wait, and I felt dwarfed by the vast empty room. I pulled my green tweed coat close around me.

"I'll show you to your room," an imposing woman said without preamble, gesturing for me to follow her. She was tall and broad-shouldered, dwarfing me in size. She used our time walking to the room to lecture me about how to make the best use of my time at the villa. I was to learn how to be the spiritual leader for my family, but to follow my husband in all things.

I ascended the staircase beside the head matron—Frau Scholtz, as she introduced herself—and watched as our dark figures entwined on the walls as we walked past. The wooden floors gleamed with polish and there wasn't a speck of dust to be found. There was no sign of life beyond the writhing of our shadows on the corridor wall. We stopped at one of the doors and she opened it with a key from a large ring at her waist.

"Here you are, my dear. I trust you'll be comfortable. The captain asked that you have a nice view and some privacy, so I've ensured you have a lovely view of the lake and gardens."

I crossed the room and peered beyond the heavy drapes. The trees were thick around the villa as well as around the rest of the properties on the island. I could make out the rather exotic thatched roof of the adjacent house, but aside from that, it would be easy to think the villa was the only house for miles. Beyond the trees, Lake

Wannsee seemed to stretch on like an ocean, with gentle waves that ushered in a cool breeze all year. I could almost imagine salty sea air, though we were miles from the ocean. If it had been summer, it would have been paradise itself. In winter, it was moody and gray, and hopelessly beautiful.

"It's lovely, thank you," I said, giving her a genuine smile. This might be endurable. The room was small but nicely furnished. I'd expected something more like a dormitory, but this was closer to the feel of a small, quaint hotel. A subtle smell of coffee and toast permeated the air, though it was long past breakfast, mixed with the gentle perfume of cut flowers.

"You take your time settling in. Luncheon won't be for several more hours."

She took her leave, the door clicking behind her as she left. My case had already been placed on the chair by the bed by some efficient maid. I removed my suit jacket and heels, attempting to breathe for a few moments before having to mingle with people at mealtime. I turned my attention to the bouquet of flowers on the desk and noticed a card from Friedrich. *"May your time here prepare you for a life of service to the Fatherland."*

I put the note back next to the cream-colored hothouse roses and gardenias that probably cost a king's ransom. No mention of love or our impending nuptials. It was all about the country, the party, the Führer. There was no room for romance in this.

Perhaps it was just as well that I couldn't be certain of how I felt for Friedrich. It put us on equal footing. He reserved his affections because he was devoted to his cause and I because I was unready to bestow them on anyone.

I lay down on the bed, a million thoughts crossing my mind.

What on earth did this school plan to teach us? Would Aunt Charlotte be able to pull off a wedding to her standard in two months' time or would I get a reprieve? Would Mila find Mama's medical texts in my wardrobe and report them to Aunt Charlotte and Uncle Otto?

If the marriage to Friedrich happened, and it seemed I had little choice in the matter, what would remain of me?

There was a knock at my door and I sat up, wiping the haze from my eyes, and crossed to answer it.

"They told me you'd just arrived!" Klara said, sweeping me into her arms. "I'm so glad you're here. You have no idea, but you're the answer to all my prayers—if I made any, that is."

"I had no idea you were coming, too," I said, melting for a moment at the relief of seeing a familiar face. "How long have you been here?"

"Since yesterday," she said. "And it's dull as a hundred-year-old garden hoe. I've never been happier to see a person in my whole life."

"So you're engaged?" I asked. "No one told me." Much had happened in my short university career, and keeping tabs on Klara hadn't really been possible.

"Well, it was rather sudden. Ernst was a good friend of the man I was dating when you went off to uni. We went on a double date, and it was clear I was better suited for Ernst and Georg was better for Ilse. Ernst met with my father not long ago and things fell into place. I imagine Georg will propose to Ilse any day. It's a shame she won't be here, too. She's lovely, really."

"Your head must be spinning. But are you happy?"

She paused a moment. No one asked these things anymore. "Oh, well, he's nice enough. Not bad to look at. Promising career. He's no Captain Schroeder, mind you, but it's an eligible match."

A few months earlier, I would have asked her if she was certain about this man and if she was ready to make such a momentous decision, but it would serve no purpose to ask the question now. If she was here, the marriage was as good as consecrated. "I just hope he knows what an incredible match he's made and spends enough time thanking his lucky stars that he ever crossed your path."

"Oh yes. He's as devoted as a lapdog. It's much nicer to be venerated than loved."

We collapsed into giggles on my bed. "I missed you, Klara. I laugh a lot less when you're not around."

"We'll have to make sure our husbands are chums so we can raise trouble together. Houses side by side and raising our babies like brothers and sisters. All of that."

That future shone like a glimmer of sunlight on the lake as I pictured it. Companionship. Purpose. A pleasant life. I could survive it. I wouldn't be happy. I could imagine myself drowning the tedium of my daily life in something the way Aunt Charlotte lost herself in jewels, furs, and fancy clothes. What would it be for me? Gardening? Charity work for a cause Friedrich approved of? Surely I could find something.

"So what is it like, this school?" I asked. "I can't get into my head what it is I'm supposed to do here."

"It's not fascinating stuff. Housekeeping, baby rearing, gardening, and such. But the girls are nice enough and the instructors are kind. It's not as prestigious as your university, mind you, but it's not like the BDM where the matrons fancied themselves drill sergeants, either."

"Well, that's something, I guess."

"And given who you're engaged to, you'll be treated like a Hollywood starlet. They'll love you just like everyone else does."

"Do you?" I asked. "After all that happened, I wasn't sure you truly cared to see me again."

"Listen, I'm not proud of the things I said. I was being petty. But I hope you're not given to grudges, and that you'll forgive me."

"I just wish I understood it," I said.

"It seems like everything happens for you. You waltzed into Berlin, charmed everyone, became the darling at BDM, and won Friedrich's heart all before you'd unpacked your suitcase."

"That's never how I intended for any of this to happen. Honestly, I try to look back over the past year and I can hardly recognize my own life."

"Well, I suppose turmoil and war makes all our lives seem a little eerie, but you've come out on top every time. I've been trying my whole life to be the daughter my parents wanted, and I've been one big disappointment after another. Until very recently, at least."

"You're witty and vivacious and everything a person could want in a daughter. If they don't see that, they're fools."

"I wasn't an asset with the party. But now Ernst has taken a liking to me, and I've met with their approval in some estimation at least. Poor Mama acts like I'm going to botch it somehow. As though if I say one wrong word or make one clumsy gesture, he'll forsake me."

"It's exhausting," I agreed. I got enough of the same treatment from Aunt Charlotte, and she was, in her way, a thousand times kinder than Klara's mother seemed to be.

"By God it *is* exhausting," she said, leaning her head on my shoulder. "A good mother would tell me that I'd be well rid of any suitor who scared so easily. But not my mother. She'll peck at me every second until the wedding. Probably during and after, too. 'Stand straight, Klara. Men don't like girls who slouch.' 'Be careful not to spill, Klara. Men don't like sloppy girls.' 'Don't talk too much, Klara. Even if he seems interested. Men don't like chatterboxes, no matter what they might say.' But truly . . . that isn't the type of man he is."

"Well, you'll be able to move out of her house and start your life anew. And it sounds like this Ernst just might prove himself worthy of you. But I truly am sorry if I ever hurt you."

"You really are an angel, aren't you? You never did a single thing designed to hurt me, but you're apologizing to me for my petty behavior."

"Still, if I hadn't come along, you'd have gotten your prize." *God, please,* I thought. *If only they'd married before I came along, I'd have been spared so much, and she'd be happier. He'd probably be happier with a wife like her than one like me, too.*

"Unlikely. He was only interested in me until someone more elegant came along. If it hadn't been you, it would have been someone else. And to be honest, I never wanted Friedrich on his own merit. I only wanted him to please my parents. That isn't fair to him, now, is it?"

"I'm sure your Ernst is a much better match," I said. "And that will count for far more in the long run."

"Let's hope you're right," she said. "Thank you for forgiving me for being such a chit. I promise it won't happen again."

"There's nothing to forgive," I said. "But promise me what you said before. The houses side by side. Babies. All of it."

She held up a pinky and I encircled hers with mine. "It's a deal."

"It's the only way I can imagine surviving this, Klara. Truly."

"We'll get through this together," she said, her tone uncharacteristically serious. "If we can't have the lives we want, we'll carve out the best version of them from the lives we're given."

"I'm so glad," I said, the looming tears now giving up their pretenses and spilling over onto my cheeks.

"Come now, I won't let you languish in the misery of housewifery. We're both too interesting to meet such a fate."

But were we? When I thought of Aunt Charlotte's friends, all so polished and poised, but seemingly vapid and uninterested with anything beyond the tiny sphere of their lives, I wondered if they weren't as vibrant as we were once upon a time. Were they really devoted to the idea of tying their entire identities to their families, or had they dreamed of other things? Were they future doctors and dancers, architects and businesswomen who had been forced to put their dreams aside to meet with the expectations placed on their shoulders like a yoke?

CHAPTER THIRTY-TWO

Tilde

November 1939

I met Klara as instructed at the edge of the property where she was supposed to attend her course. The area was densely forested and abutted the lake. If anyone asked, I'd use the excuse that I was a maid to one of the brides in attendance delivering some missing articles to my mistress. It explained both my presence on the island as well as my small suitcase. Inside the case were a few personal items and nightgowns Klara had lent me to get through the birth. She'd even managed to scrounge up a few small blankets for the baby, though she wasn't able to procure a gown or sleep suit for him. I thought of the little wardrobe I'd made that was tucked in a drawer at home and cursed the men who'd destroyed my carefully laid plans.

Klara came to my side almost immediately as I left the taxi. She'd been watching attentively so that my arrival would be noticed by as few people as we could manage. We quietly walked into the thicket around the edge of the property. A stately villa lorded over the lot.

It was white and soaring against the moody skies and looked large enough to house a hundred people in such spacious quarters that they'd never see one another unless they chose to. It seemed an odd place for a school, but I couldn't pretend to understand the party's ways of thinking.

Finally, we reached the edge of the adjacent property and came to the door of a disused cottage.

"This is the best I could do, I'm sorry," Klara said. "The family that owns the place is friends with mine. I was able to chat with a maid who was out in the courtyard and find out where they were. They're off on vacation for another week, but the main house is lousy with servants. I managed to convince the maid to find me a key to the old caretaker's cottage. She swears no one comes here."

"She won't talk?" I asked, breathing heavily with the exertion from walking across the grounds.

"I paid her off. Handsomely," Klara said, turning the key and swinging open the door to the tiny cottage, and gesturing me inside. "She promised to keep an eye out in case anyone takes a notion to visit out here, but she says no one has bothered with the place in months."

She pulled the sheet off a moth-eaten sofa, and I wondered why anyone had gone to the trouble of protecting the ancient piece of furniture from dust and debris. The cottage was furnished with a bed that was in only slightly better condition than the sofa, a minuscule sitting area, and a rudimentary kitchen. Klara had snuck in as many provisions as she dared so she wouldn't attract too much attention by coming to visit me more than once a day.

"This will be better than fine, I assure you." I opened a cabinet to find a mop, a broom, and a whole host of cleaning supplies. Cleaning the space and making it safe for the baby's arrival would at least give me something to occupy my days. Klara had been thoughtful enough to include a few novels and some writing paper and pens with the nightgowns she'd packed for me. None of the rest of her clothes would fit me before the baby arrived, so I'd be forced to wear the flowing white nightgowns most of the time.

She'd yet to find someone capable of delivering the baby, nor had we addressed what to do if I went into labor and needed help before her daily visit. It was a gaping hole in the plan, but at least I was tucked away from the heart of Berlin. Giving birth was such a daunting prospect, I hadn't the strength to consider the life that lay beyond. I sat down on the dusty sofa and, miraculously, felt myself able to breathe. I'd never visited Schwanenwerder Island, though it wasn't far from the heart of Berlin, and many of the elite Jewish families of Berlin once had homes there. The party confiscated many of them, and I was hiding right in the lion's den, but I was too tired to be afraid. I'd used up my allotment of fear for one lifetime. In that moment, I focused on how the cottage was ensconced by the verdant landscape, and the thick, towering trees. It made me feel hidden and safe. It was hard not to feel at least a little safer nestled among the trees, though in truth I was closer to the heart of the vipers' nest than I should have dared to tread.

"You're sure your friends won't mind if I'm here?" I asked.

"They'll never know. No one has stayed here in years. As long as you keep the blackout curtains on the windows and don't make too much noise, you'll be just fine."

"You're placing a lot of confidence in this. What if the servants have been told to scout the outbuildings for this very thing? Times are hard and people are desperate for places to stay."

"It's the best we can do for now. I only wish there were a phone here," she said, looking around and seeing nothing but deficiencies.

"How many caretakers' cottages do you know that are equipped with phones? I'll be just fine here. Better than giving birth out in the woods alone."

"I suppose I can't argue there," she said. "And damn everyone who has made it so you can't deliver this baby safely in a hospital where you ought to be. And damn those who've made your life more difficult because you're Jewish."

"You knew?" I asked. We'd never broached the subject before. It had been enough that she suspected the father of my child was.

"I had my suspicions. Your father leaving. Your mother never being in the shop. It seemed as good an explanation as any."

"If you figured it out, I'm lucky I wasn't forced out of business or locked up months ago," I said, my hand reflexively going to shield my swollen belly. "The rest of them must have figured it out by now."

"Don't give them that much credit. I was paying more attention to you than they were. They might have found you out eventually, but it would have taken a while. You blend in better than most."

"Thank goodness for that, I suppose," I said, rolling my eyes. "Too Jewish for the Aryans, too Aryan for the Jews. Being without a people is tiresome."

"It never mattered to me, you know," she said, using the sheet to wipe away dust from the kitchen table. "I know that doesn't mean much given all that's happening to your people, but it never mattered to me."

"I believe you," I said.

"So now you understand why I . . . well. It doesn't matter. I just hope you don't hate me."

"No," I said. "I couldn't bring myself to hate you."

"Even though I stand up to be counted with a party that hates your people?"

"Even then. You haven't been given many choices. I can see that clearly."

"It doesn't excuse it," she said.

"No, but the blame isn't yours alone."

"I have to go," she said with a shake of her head. "They're expecting me."

"Go. Learn to be a good German wife. Make your Ernst proud."

"Maybe I'll learn something that will be useful to you," she said. "Wouldn't that be a pleasant surprise?"

"You can come teach me after the others have gone to bed," I said to her. "Go."

She dashed off toward the big house and I was left in the cottage. My fatigue had abated, and I was filled with the urge to scrub every surface of the building until it shone. Mama had mentioned the surge of energy before birth, and I wondered if it meant the baby would soon be on his way. I filled a bucket with warm water from the tap and began scrubbing from the tops of the cabinets down to the floors.

I thought about Klara's confession. She'd known for years that I was Jewish. She remained my friend despite this, knowing it would see her censured and even damage her prospects for marriage. She'd always been one to make bold choices, and I admired her for it. But all the same, she was one of them. My life depended on her being trustworthy. Even more, my child's life did.

I thought of the women converging on the house to the west. I could see them gathered from my little window. They giggled and sipped coffee in the lounge. They were happy and warm. Soon to be wives, and mothers not long after. They would spend six weeks ensconced in luxury, learning from a curriculum I could only imagine. Some practical skills, to be sure. How to feed, clothe, and diaper a baby. I wouldn't have minded sitting in on those courses myself. Sewing, washing, and mending, I expected. But throughout, I knew these women would be instructed that they should teach their children that their babies were superior to my own. My heart ached that their sweet children would be poisoned at such a young age.

But I couldn't worry for their babies. I had to worry about my own. I scrubbed for hours until my back demanded I stop, and I ate some bread and cheese from the stores Klara had procured for me. I wondered that she, who had no obligation to me whatsoever, had extended kindness to me, at great personal risk, when my own father had not. The baby moved, revivified by the food I ate.

"You're being born into a strange world, little one. But I promise I will do all I can to keep you safe."

And I knew that simple promise was a taller order than it should have been.

I sang the lullabies to the baby that my mother had sung to me. She should have been here to help me as I made my own transition to motherhood. Or I should have been in New York with her. But life was anything but fair these days, and the most important task ahead of me would be to ensure that the precious baby inside me didn't learn that lesson too well or too soon.

CHAPTER THIRTY-THREE

Hanna

November 1939

M otherhood is your sacred duty," the head matron of the school proclaimed. "It is not a burden or an unpleasant task, but the very reason for which we were born. We must embrace motherhood with joy and enthusiasm for the good of Germany and our beloved Führer." Klara looked over at me with a wink. She was bored as ever with these lectures about duty and sacrifice. We didn't sit at desks in stuffy classrooms, but rather in a solarium, each ensconced in an oversize woven chair. It was the start of winter, and we watched the gray clouds swirl over the lake as they threatened snow. Flames licked at the logs in the open fireplaces; the gentle roar and snap of the fire was the percussion to our matron's diatribe.

The woman who ran the school, Gertrude Scholtz, was the sort that couldn't be described as handsome or plain. She lived somewhere in between and seemed indifferent to how others perceived her. She was of middling height—shorter than me and taller than

Klara—with light brown hair that she wore in a crown of braids. I imagined she was thin as a girl but had been made softer by childbirth. Rumor had it she had four children already and, despite her heavy involvement in party affairs, was eager to have more. She was the perfect German woman, according to the Führer, and her placement as our leader wasn't a happy accident.

There were twelve women in our "class" and before this morning's lecture, the most strenuous activity had been sipping coffee in the library with the others enrolled in the course.

There was staff to wait on us and the accommodations were as luxurious as those at Uncle Otto's house. The ten women, apart from Klara and me, were all engaged to officers in the SS. Because Friedrich was the highest ranking among our fiancés, they spoke to me with a deference I hadn't expected. The party loved hierarchy and everyone in it loved knowing where they stood in the pecking order.

"This is something we have lost as a people. A reverence for motherhood and an understanding of the sphere where women belong in the world. We see the Bolsheviks and their cries for equal rights for women, but it is degrading to our status as mothers of a nation. We were not born to take the place of men. To toil in a career, to have influence in politics and the outside world, that is the province of our husbands. While you are with us, you will remember what the world seems to have forgotten. That motherhood and the role of woman as the center of her household is not something to be degraded. It is something to be honored."

There was an enthusiastic round of applause and I found myself joining in. Motherhood *should* be revered. It was a noble calling and one that demanded a lot of sacrifice. I just wasn't convinced it should be a woman's only option.

A few of the women were actually moved to tears by the head matron's speech, and she looked at them with a beaming smile as they dried their eyes. They were the ideal women for marrying into the SS. They believed all of Frau Scholtz's impassioned rhetoric.

We were dismissed to the lounge to await luncheon. I suspected we'd be subjected to a practical lesson on diaper changing or bread baking or some such.

"She's an inspiration," one of the other women—Hilde—said. She was a dainty thing in her mid-twenties. Sweet of temperament, but not exciting as a conversationalist. "The way she speaks. Every young girl in Germany should be made to listen to her. We'd see a blessed change in this country, that's for sure."

"Hear, hear. But I'm sure the Führer is working to spread her message throughout Germany. He depends on strong families for a strong Germany," another said—Trina. One of the oldest in the group, and the most outspoken. I could see her becoming a leader in the women's societies if given the chance.

"That sounds like a slogan for a poster," Klara said. "Perhaps that's what we'll be doing this afternoon. Painting posters for the glory of the Reich."

Trina chuckled. "Oh, you're a funny one, aren't you? Every group needs one, don't they?" At least on the face of it, she was taking Klara's sarcasm for flippant humor, and it was probably just as well for Klara's sake.

"That's what I'm here for. What's a school without a class clown?" The rest of the women laughed, though none of it felt genuine.

"I think these weeks together are going to be quite useful," Trina said. "It's one of the best ideas to come from the party, and that's saying quite a lot." I nodded, knowing that anything less than fervent approbation would be noticed.

"My mother never had the chance to teach me much in the kitchen and I've only mastered a few dishes. I'm sure my Hans will be grateful for anything I can learn in the kitchen. One can't live on fried potatoes alone," Hilde said.

"Oh, they could, but they'd weigh as much as an armored lorry. Not much use to the SS in that case." Klara was in full force, and I wanted to scream at her to bite back her jibes. If they fell on the wrong ears, she'd be in serious trouble.

"What about you, Hanna? What skills are you hoping to hone while you're here?" Trina asked, her tone imperious as she drank her coffee.

"Oh, I think I'd benefit from help in a wide variety of ways. It's one thing to help around the house. Quite another to run one." She looked mollified at my sycophantic answer, while Klara failed to conceal the rolling of her eyes.

"Well said," she replied. "We'll all be ascending to the most important role of our lives soon. It's best to enter into that state as well prepared as we can."

"Absolutely right," Hilde agreed. "I never dreamed I'd get to study in such a place. My parents are still speechless that Hans wanted to send me. They've not stopped talking about it for weeks."

"It's lovely here," I said without artifice. "They couldn't have chosen a lovelier or more restful spot."

"They're hoping to give office girls the chance to unburden themselves from the rigors of their outside work and help them transition smoothly into their new lives. To train up young girls who are fresh out of school. That they chose a haven for us was no mistake."

"You'll have to excuse me, I think I ought to lie down for a bit before the afternoon session," Klara said, setting her coffee cup on a side table.

"Are you unwell? Should we ask for help?" Trina asked, setting aside her own cup and looking like she'd enjoy nothing more than to spring into action and save the day.

"I'll be just fine," Klara said. "Don't fret about me."

"I'll come sit with you at least. Make sure you're not in need of a doctor."

"No, no. We don't want to bother the medical staff for this. It's just been such an exhilarating morning I think I need to lie down to process it all. I'll be fit as a fiddle before long. I wouldn't dream of having any of you miss any of the vital information they're sure to pass on this afternoon." Klara eyed me meaningfully. "But if it will make you feel more at ease, Hanna can walk with me to my room so you know I'm settled."

Trina looked like she wanted to object. To take the honor for herself. But, of course, the fact that Klara and I had an established friendship took precedence over her overwrought desire to help.

"Can you believe these women?" Klara asked as soon as we were out of earshot. "Have they all been drugged? I've never seen anything like this."

"They're devoted, that's for sure," I said, putting my hand at the crook of her elbow for good measure in case anyone was looking at us.

"That doesn't begin to describe it. It's a mania," she said, shaking her head.

"Well, such enthusiasm can't last. Even for Hitler, his star has to go into decline at some point."

"I don't want to be within twenty miles of him when it does. Nor any of these kooks. The thought of spending another six weeks here with them makes me want to jump off the roof."

"Klara, you have to be careful with that. I know your humor, but the girls here don't. If they take offense to what you do, you'll be taken from here and sent someplace much worse. Please tread lightly. And don't kid yourself that it's just six weeks. These women are marrying our fiancés' colleagues. We'll be stuck with them for years."

"Perish the thought. What's worse, you sound like a kinder version of my mother. She's been after me my whole life to 'play nice' and I'm afraid I'm not very good at it."

"Strange times give us strange tasks. But regardless of whatever we have to do here, it's only a few weeks. They can't change us that much. We can let them think they have, but we'll know in our hearts who we truly are," I said, though I wasn't convinced of my own words.

"I think you're being foolish in your optimism. This war is going to engulf all of us. They want us equipped to act, but so busy that we don't ask questions."

"You're probably right, but we've got precious little choice. We might as well make the best of this, hadn't we? Give it an honest chance? It's what you always say, isn't it?" I pressed.

"I don't know, Hanna. All of this seems so strange to me. If it weren't for Ernst, I'd run from this place screaming like a banshee. But being able to say his wife trained here was so utterly important to him, I didn't want to disappoint."

"You love him, don't you?" I asked, suddenly feeling my lungs constrict with envy. I hated that I felt this way. I should have celebrated her happiness, but I could honestly say I didn't begrudge her. I just wanted it for myself as well.

"I see that he's a better man than most in the party. My parents wanted me to marry the highest-ranking party member who would have me. They would never have allowed me to marry outside it, no matter his pedigree or my feelings on the matter. I won't let more romantic sentiments cloud my judgment on that score. I've wasted enough time pining after men who would never treat me as well as Ernst does."

"You're a walking contradiction, aren't you? You scorn the idea of this school, but you're here to please a man."

"My life's ambition, don't you know? If you can't beat 'em, confuse the hell out of 'em. That's my motto."

I wrapped my arm around her. "You know you're better off, don't you?"

"Friedrich isn't unkind to you, is he?"

I went silent. I thought back to the fateful Christmas party the year before. "Not usually."

"I swear, if he hurts you, I'll throttle him myself."

"You know you won't," I said. "You'll make a pretty face just like I will and pretend it never happened."

"We ought to get out of here, Hanna. We should. Ernst would come with us. We should escape to Switzerland and make a plan."

"And you're the one who told me to give up on childish dreams. You know I'm stuck. I've tried a dozen times or more to get out of this marriage. To convince Friedrich I wasn't right for him. My course has been set for me since my mother died and I set foot on the train to Berlin. You know it as well as I do. I won't finish university or be a doctor. I'll just be the housewife in the neighborhood who's handy with home remedies. Nothing more."

"It doesn't make it right."

"That has nothing to do with things, I'm afraid. I should have been dealt a better hand of cards, but in the end, it's all that I'm left to play."

I looked at Klara, who appeared ready to shake me by the shoulders to bring back the version of me that had believed in a life beyond what our families prescribed for us. How the tables had turned for us.

CHAPTER THIRTY-FOUR

Tilde

I thumbed through one of the mystery novels Klara had packed and wished I had one of Grandfather's books instead. I had no taste for murder and intrigue even in good times. I tossed the novel aside and reconciled myself to the truth that I wouldn't have been able to focus enough to read no matter what I'd brought along. So I cleaned. There wasn't a surface that wasn't scrubbed with soap, water, and the hard bristle brush I found. Every item was either polished, dusted, or put away in a cupboard. The only chore I didn't tackle was getting down on my hands and knees to give the floor a proper cleaning, but I was afraid I'd not be able to lift myself up again until Klara's return. I had to settle for a make-shift floor mopping with rags attached to the end of the broom handle.

I put my hands on my hips and surveyed the one-room cottage with dismay. There were no more chores I could contrive, and I was alone with my own company. I'd made it bearable since Samuel left by letting work consume me. It was a comfortable habit, and I felt exposed without it.

I crawled into the bed, which had significantly less dust than when I had arrived, and willed myself to sleep, knowing that the sporadic pains would probably start in earnest any day. Possibly even hours. The two weeks I thought I had now seemed beyond unlikely as the baby's movements had slowed as he ran out of room to stretch. He had to be getting uncomfortable, and I could surely empathize with his plight.

Back in the shop, we'd had a steady stream of expectant mothers as clients. They needed dresses that would allow for their changing bodies, and they often seemed keen on imparting the advice they'd been given.

"Rest as much as you can as your time draws near."

"Don't rest too much before the baby is born, or you won't have energy to deliver the baby."

"Sleep when the baby sleeps."

"Use the baby's naps to catch up on housework and cooking. A baby is no excuse to let things backslide at home!"

It was all contradictory and maddening. I wanted my mother there to reassure me about things. Her advice wouldn't be much more reliable than that of the women from the shop, but it would be of more comfort coming from her. I wanted Samuel there, pacing and nervous as he could see my behavior change as my body prepared for birth. I wanted the distraction of calming him so I wouldn't be left to focus on my own discomfort.

But I could have neither. Mama was unreachable. After her initial letter confirming her arrival in New York, I hadn't received a single note. Hitler's men were masterful at discerning secrets from the barest scraps of information in correspondence, so we made the pact not to communicate until the war was over, or I was free from

Germany. Even if there was an emergency, there was nothing she could do for me, nor I for her.

And Samuel was beyond my reach.

I still cried out for him in the night.

I spoke to him, even though he wasn't there.

I still wept for him.

Grief is an odd bird. I would be working in the shop, sorting the patterns or organizing the notions, and would find my face wet with tears I wasn't even aware I'd been shedding. I'd never thought the process was so completely and utterly . . . involuntary. I'd imagined the widows clad in black and sniffling into their hankies had some measure of control over their emotions, but now I knew this largely wasn't true. My body needed to grieve as much as my soul, and I had no choice but to let it.

I felt my abdomen grow rock hard as one of the pains washed over me. I panted the way some women said was helpful, and it released its grip before too long. It was stronger than any of the others, and my hope of waiting to deliver the baby until I had somewhere else to go seemed the height of folly now.

"Couldn't you just stay put for another year?" I asked, glancing down at my belly. "And maybe the size you were three months ago?"

The reply was a kick that would have been rather swift if he'd had the room to take a proper swing.

"Okay, I understand. And I'll get you a soccer ball when you're old enough. Might as well put those skills to use."

The baby seemed to settle down and I was able to take fuller breaths until another surge racked me. I didn't have my watch to check the time, but the last two contractions were certainly closer than any of the previous had been. I felt as helpless to stop this as I did my tears for Samuel, and so I closed my eyes and trusted my body to do what it could to survive. I could do nothing more than try to get out of my own way.

Klara wasn't due for hours, and I might still have hours yet before the baby would make his entrance into the world, so I held the quilt close to my chest and prayed that I was enough to be mother and father to the innocent baby who deserved so much more from the world than what he was getting.

CHAPTER THIRTY-FIVE

Hanna

We gathered in a large room of the villa that had been transformed into a half dozen little kitchen stations, three rows of two tables with two women at each table. I stood next to Klara at our table, no doubt made from heavy German oak and battle-scarred with years of use. It was laden with potatoes, carrots, apples, rye flour, a jar of marmalade, cheese, and a host of other ingredients. Klara gave me a discreet glance that didn't hide her dread. She was lousy in a kitchen, and I wasn't any better.

"What on earth is this?" she asked opening a jar of a thick white paste. She took a sniff and wrinkled her nose. "Cream gone off?"

"Quark," I responded, recognizing the jar from home. "Papa eats a fair amount of it, but Uncle Otto won't allow it in the house."

"I can't say I disagree with him," she replied. "It's, well, it's not exactly foul or anything, but it's just that it can't decide if it wants to be cheese, yogurt, or butter. I like food to be decisive."

"Ah, Fräulein Schmidt, you need to open your horizons." Frau Scholtz began striding down the aisle. Klara's color rose when she realized the head matron had overheard her comment. "For too long we have depended upon butter from Denmark, wheat from Canada, fruit from the tropics. There is no need for such wastefulness when we live in such an abundant land. We can grow what we need here in the Fatherland and reduce our dependence on foreign powers. This is one of the most important duties you will have as wives and mothers in the Reich. Making your kitchens as close to nature as you can and grown here in our own glorious soil."

For the next hour, Frau Scholtz lectured us on the ideal diet. Heavy with potatoes, locally grown fruits and vegetables, whole grains, and fish. We were to reduce or eliminate our consumption of meat, anything imported, and anything that was overprocessed or filled with chemicals. It was one lesson I couldn't find too much fault with, though of course Frau Scholtz's heavy-handed style was grating.

"They can pry my butter and beefsteaks from my cold, dead hands," Klara whispered.

"Don't give them any ideas," I said, wishing my words were closer to hyperbole. She returned a grim nod.

The lesson was the most interesting we'd had to date. Rather than focusing on patriotic dogma, Frau Scholtz discussed the foods grown and cultivated in Germany and how to run a household that didn't rely too much on resources from the outside world. It was the closest thing to one of my university classes and I found myself taking copious notes.

"Some things never change, do they?" Klara whispered with a gentle nudge of her elbow and a wink. "Always teacher's pet."

"What, the content is interesting for once," I replied with a wink in turn, going back to my notes.

"Fräulein Rombauer, since you're so keen on conversing with Fräulein Schmidt, you're clearly well versed in today's topic. Can you tell the class what are three of the foods I mentioned we should eat more of?"

"Fresh vegetables, fish, and cheese," I said, after a quick glance at my notes.

"Name two we should continue to eat at our current levels," she continued, her tone taking on the quality of a low growl. She was disappointed not to have a reason to scold me in public.

"Grains and fowl," I said, not breaking eye contact with her.

"And what are two we should eat in moderation?" she pressed.

"Pork and fats," I said, crossing my arms over my chest.

"And why those in particular?"

"Because they take more resources to produce. And I imagine the government needs them for soldiers and not civilians."

"You'd do better not to imagine, Fräulein Rombauer, and to listen subserviently to those who know better than you. I don't imagine you deigned to question your professors when you were lording about at university with all the men?"

I could have told her that at the university we'd all been encouraged to offer our positions on the topic at hand and defend them with the evidence and logic at our disposal, but that would have served only to infuriate her further. I said nothing.

"If it's fine with you, I'd like to continue our lesson," she said, as though I'd stopped the lecture and not she.

"Yes, Frau Scholtz," I said. She wanted me to look down in submission, but I couldn't give her the satisfaction. She rewarded me with one last glower.

"It is high time you practiced the skills you will use most in your married lives. Remember that little will endear you more to your husbands than a well-cooked meal."

She charged us with making an apple tart, and though I'd watched my mother make pie crust a number of times, I'd never attempted it on my own.

"You really do have a genius for getting on her bad side, don't you?" Klara said in a low voice as we set about the task.

"Everyone has a talent. I guess that's mine. And it's not even fair; you talked out of turn before I did."

"Yes, but I'm marrying a common lieutenant and you're marrying the captain. She holds you to a higher standard." Klara could hardly keep a straight face as she tried to imbue her words with solemnity.

"She envies his clout," I said, perfectly deadpan. It was plain that she was an ambitious woman in a system that did not value her beyond her ability to spread propaganda and keep women under control.

Klara said nothing but turned back to the recipe card Frau Scholtz had passed out to us. It seemed each pair was given a different recipe and that all of the dishes together would compose a hearty meal. The apple tart was the fiddliest recipe of the lot, and I knew she'd not given it to us at random. She had no serious quarrel with Klara, but she was determined to see me humbled before the group.

"She hates us," she muttered, looking at the recipe. We both looked over at the pair of girls who'd been lucky enough to be assigned to the fried potatoes. Trina and Ulla, two of Frau Scholtz's particular favorites, had been selected for that honor. The hardest part of their task was waiting until twenty minutes before the meal was ready to begin their dish so they wouldn't have a platter of cold, soggy potatoes to serve.

We toiled to make a passable apple tart with the ingredients provided, and though Klara and I weren't particularly talented in the kitchen, we produced a result that, at bare minimum, didn't incite ridicule from Frau Scholtz. It was better than we'd feared, and substantially better than the side dish produced by the girls next to us: a plate of white asparagus that more closely resembled long skinny lumps of charcoal than a dish fit for human consumption.

We carried our food to the dining room, and I was silently assessing the work of my classmates. The roasted chicken looked palatable, and the potatoes were hard to mutilate. Some of the other side dishes looked far more suspect. I vowed to eat a massive portion of the tart Klara and I made with a smile on my face, even if it tasted like we'd substituted sawdust for flour.

But when we reached the dining room, a dozen men in uniform were seated in our usual places. Thankfully Friedrich wasn't among them, so I was able to breathe a little easier.

"Now ladies, we will learn the art of how to serve a formal meal," Frau Scholtz said. And for the next half hour we learned the ins and outs of serving from the right and clearing from the left and all manner of etiquette that would befit a footman in Uncle Otto's house. We stood along the wall as the men ate, either praising or deriding the various foods we placed before them. The tart met with a warm reception, to which Frau Scholtz gave a resigned sigh. The men cleared away leaving a wake of dirty dishes, glasses, and cutlery in their wake, with no more thanks than a few courteous nods as they left the room.

It looked as though a plague of locusts had descended on the dining room and devoured our morning's labor, leaving us with nothing, and it seemed all too apt a metaphor for the futures we were all facing.

I AWOKE TO the sensation of a hand covering my mouth. I heard the words "Don't scream," but of course, those very words filled me with the urge to do just that.

I willed myself not to panic as I took stock of the situation.

I am in a villa on a lake outside the city.

I can breathe freely.

I am not in pain.

As those essential truths entered into my consciousness, I was able to process more. I knew the voice.

Klara.

I touched her hand gently to let her know I was calm and would not call out.

Yet.

She removed her hand and whispered, "We must be quiet."

"What on earth is the matter?" I whispered back. "What is so urgent you couldn't have waited until morning?"

"I'll show you, but you need to come with me. Put on your boots and coat."

"I'm not dressed," I protested.

"It won't matter, where we're going. But please hurry."

I wondered if the incessant speeches about our duty and devotion to country and family had finally turned her brain and she'd lost her mind. But even if it were true, it was my duty as her friend to see exactly how far into the abyss she'd fallen.

I followed her from the house and out onto the grounds, suppressing the litany of questions burning in my breast. The whys, whos, and wherefores could wait. Clearly, she needed me, and I'd have to attend to whatever it was she needed.

"Hanna, I know I've no right to ask a favor of you, but I need one tonight. It's quite literally a matter of life and death. And more than anything I need you to keep this secret. Promise me."

"I can't promise before you tell me. I have no idea what you want from me." I began to panic that this was some sort of setup, and that Friedrich was somehow using Klara to test my loyalty. "I have to go back to my room. This is madness."

"Hanna, if you don't come with me, someone may die."

"And if I do, that someone might be me."

"I promise, if anything happens, I'll take the blame." Tears welled in her eyes, and for the first time in a long time I saw something of the friend I'd made soon after I arrived in Berlin.

"Fine," I said. "I'll go."

"And you won't tell a soul?" she pressed.

"I swear," I said. "As long as you meant what you said about taking the blame if anything happens. But tell me what's going on."

"You've got a deal," she said. "I'll tell you on the way."

We absconded into the night and remained mute until we were a safe distance from the villa.

"Your mother delivered babies, right?" she asked.

"Frequently," I said.

"And you helped her?"

"I did," I said. "She was training me as her assistant."

"Well, this may be a day when we're both glad of that. A friend of mine is about to have a baby and she needs your help."

"She should go to a proper doctor," I said, pausing in my tracks. "I've never done this on my own. It's dangerous."

"In more ways than you know, but I'll ask you to hold any questions on that score until later. Just know that if there were any other, safer avenue for her to have her baby, we would have taken it. Please say you'll help."

"Of course I will, not that you've given me much choice."

"Good. We're nearly there."

"I wish to anything I had my mother's kit," I said. "I didn't dare bring it. It's collecting dust in the back of my wardrobe, being of no use to anyone. Just like me."

"You'll be of use tonight," she said. "And I've gathered up some basic supplies. It may not be all you want or need to do the job like you're used to, but it's better than nothing."

"Before I enter the door, tell me you've been careful? No one has seen you coming and going?" I'd landed myself in trouble with Friedrich too many times to hope for his understanding now. Especially when we were in such a public situation, mixing it up with the brides of the party elite. An embarrassment here would be far more costly than one behind closed doors.

"As careful as I can be. If we were spotted at all, we have an explanation at the ready, but of course even the most airtight alibi can be pulled apart with the right questioning. I shouldn't ask this of you, I know. But I am."

"Very well," I said. "I'll do what I can for her."

"Tilde," I said with recognition as we entered the caretaker's cottage on the edge of the adjacent property. "The dressmaker. I know you."

She nodded, unable to speak. She was standing in the corner of the small room, her hands gripping the back of a ratty armchair, breathing through one of her surges. She had to be close.

The old caretaker's cottage was polished clean and glowing with warmth. She'd had the presence of mind to get a good amount of water boiling and was pacing about the room, working with gravity instead of against it. Her instincts were good ones.

I'd only spent a couple of afternoons in the girl's presence but had been impressed with her efficiency and her professional comportment. How she'd come to deliver a baby in such a state, I didn't know. But it wasn't the time to wonder about such matters. The baby was coming, and Tilde would need help.

"Will you be able to help her?" Klara asked. Worry was etched on her face. Tilde mattered to her more than as a dressmaker or tutor. She cared dearly for this woman and was willing to risk everything for her.

"If the birth is uncomplicated and both mother and baby are healthy, then yes. I'm confident I can deliver the baby without a mishap. But I can't make promises. I haven't been involved in her care and I don't know her history."

"That's fair. Just do what you can for them. I trust you."

I helped Tilde to the bed and asked her to lie down.

"I don't want to lie down. I want to move," she protested.

"Good. That's very good. The more you move the easier it will be. I won't make you stay in bed long, but I want to check how things are progressing."

She agreed and lay prostrate on the bed. She had a few moments of calm between her contractions, and I could see the feeling wash over her as she allowed her muscles to relax as she stretched out on the bed. Good. Let her conserve her energy while she was willing.

"How long have you been feeling pains?" I asked.

"Oh, four hours or so. Gradual at first. I thought it was a back-ache. Those are common enough these days."

"I'm sure they are," I said, patting her leg. "But I think you'll be ready to push soon. Four hours isn't too bad for a first-time mother."

"Glibly said by a childless woman," she retorted, not without humor. "We'll see what you say when your turn comes."

"Well and truly warranted," I said. "I want you to guide me. When your body feels ready to push, you tell me. Will that be all right?"

She nodded and I could see from the tension in her face that another contraction was coming.

"Now," she said, "please, now."

CHAPTER THIRTY-SIX

Tilde

November 1939

I don't know how long I pushed, but I remember collapsing into Klara's arms and coming to with the baby swaddled in a blanket being placed on my chest. Klara sat next to me on the bed with one hand on the baby so he wouldn't slip off my chest. I moved my arms to hold him, but they felt heavy and weak.

"Don't try to move too much. You lost a lot of blood," Hanna warned.

"She's so pale. Is she going to be okay?"

"I think so. I've seen worse and we got it stopped. But she has to rest and needs lots of care."

"I'll be fine," I said, mumbling despite myself. I realized each of my movements felt exaggerated, even the subtle movements of my lips and tongue. "How is the baby?"

I looked down at the bundle in my arms trying to assess. He wasn't crying but was taking the deep, even breaths of restful sleep.

"You have a beautiful daughter," Hanna said, smiling for the first time since I'd met her. "Healthy as a horse, and I've never seen such a gorgeous head of dark curly hair on a baby."

A girl? I'd always pictured a boy to replace my Samuel. But now that she was in my arms, I couldn't imagine her otherwise.

"Her father," I said simply by way of explanation of her riotous hair.

"Do you know what you want to call her?" Klara asked, moving a damp tendril of hair from my forehead.

"Simone," I said automatically. The closest I could think of to Samuel. "And Devorah for her father's mother. May her memory be for a blessing."

"Simone Devorah. Beautiful," Hanna pronounced. "Are you hungry?"

I'd barely taken stock of my surroundings apart from the baby, but the reminder of my physical needs sent a rumbling through my stomach. I nodded. Hanna sprang into action, throwing together a meal from the supplies Klara had brought.

"Thank you," I said, trying not to shake from the effort of speaking. "Both of you."

"Don't mention it," Klara said. "I'm just glad the pair of you are all right. Let's focus on getting you some dinner and rest."

"Breakfast," Hanna corrected. "It'll be dawn soon. We'll need to get back before long or we'll be missed."

"And we'll need an excuse for the bags under our eyes and yawns during class," Klara said with a wink. "I guess not much has changed since high school."

"Late-night gab fest between old friends who will soon be too busy with the toils of married life to have much time for friends," Hanna said, sagely. "Surely they won't begrudge us that."

"No, they seem to be rather keen on us having a 'last little bit of fun,' don't they?" Klara said, her face falling. "Feels like we're preparing for our executions instead of our weddings."

"It *is* a new life," I said, summoning the strength to sit up a bit more. "But if you choose well, it's worth the sacrifice."

"I wish I'd met your Samuel," Klara said. "If he was able to convince you of that, he must have been something."

"He was," I said. I'd spent so many months trying not to think of Samuel so that I could function, that once I allowed him back into my thoughts, a painful torrent of memories ensued. My heart broke anew for our sweet daughter, who would never know for herself what a wonderful man her father had been. I could tell her every day for as long as I took breath, but it wouldn't be the same as seeing his small acts of kindness. The way he saved the best of every dish for me. The way he always made little carvings for his sister out of scraps of wood that weren't fit for use in their instruments. The endless patience he had with the unruly small children of wealthy patrons who wanted an instrument worthy of the talent of their "young prodigies." He would have been a father so many orders of magnitude better than my own that I felt the grief wash over me.

I let the tears flow, unafraid of the sensation. I would not, for the sake of the tiny life in my arms, lose myself to this grief. But I was strong enough to let myself feel it.

Klara looked over at Hanna, her expression alarmed.

"This isn't all that unusual. Her body has been through so much tonight that it needs to cleanse itself. Just let it all go, Tilde. You'll be fine."

I would be. I smiled weakly through the tears and placed a kiss on my daughter's forehead.

For her, I would be.

Despite looking as though she too wanted to cry, Klara giggled. "Remember, motherhood is your sacred duty. It is not a burden or an unpleasant task, but the very reason for which we were born."

Hanna chuckled as well, apparently remembering one of the lectures from the school.

"I'm glad you both know there's more to life than that. But right now, in this moment, it *does* feel like quite enough."

They fed me a meal of potatoes and cheese with the promise of smuggling meat and vegetables to me the next day. I ate ravenously, trying to replenish my strength. I finished every morsel of food before me and felt like I could have eaten ten times as much and not satiated my hunger.

"I should stay with her," Klara said as Hanna washed my plate. "She's still so peaked."

"You'll do her more harm if she's caught. We can come back tomorrow night—well, tonight now," Hanna corrected. The first rays of weak sunlight threatened at the horizon, and it wouldn't be long before someone noticed them missing from their beds.

"We'll be back as soon as we can," Klara said, kissing my temple and then the baby's. "Be safe."

I nodded my agreement and watched as they disappeared into the last precious moments of the dark.

It was only a few minutes later that I heard the sounds of men's angry shouts and Hanna's and Klara's terrified screams in response.

CHAPTER THIRTY-SEVEN

Hanna

November 1939

Stop where you are!" a voice demanded. Klara and I put our hands in the air and made no movements. I blinked against the intrusive light from the flashlight and tried to keep the bile down in my throat.

We were only a hundred yards away from the caretaker's cottage at most. Tilde. The baby. They'd be found. The guards would know that she'd have a reason for hiding and would beat it out of her with an efficiency that terrified us all.

"Y-yes, sir," I managed to stutter. Had I not been blinded by the beam of light, I'd have used his rank, for I was certain he was in uniform and would want his status acknowledged. "We're unarmed. We're from the school."

"Very well," he said. "Do you have papers?"

"In our rooms," Klara supplied.

"What are you doing out of the villa at this hour?" he pressed. "And without documentation?"

"We were going for a morning walk. We're not in the habit of taking our papers with us on our morning constitutional on private property."

"You expect me to believe you're going for a morning walk in this frigid weather at this hour? It's not even five in the morning."

It *was* a ludicrous hour to be awake, and our clothes were ill-suited for exercise. I prayed he was the unobservant sort who didn't notice what women wore, but I doubted my luck stretched that far.

My eyes were slowly adjusting to the flashlight, and I was able to make out the rank of his uniform regalia. "When would you have us exercise, then, Lieutenant? You must have noticed our schedule is quite charged. If Fräulein Schmidt and I don't take our walk now, we'll never have the chance. And I personally find the program is far easier to face if I've kept up with a bit of exercise. I wouldn't want to squander my opportunity here because I hadn't the constitution to meet the challenge."

"She's right," Klara interjected. "We're both exhausted by tea-time if we don't get in a jaunt. Neither of us wants to disappoint Frau Scholtz or our future husbands."

Nice touch. Invoking our duty to the school *and* our husbands. Country and family.

"You don't have permission to be out of the villa," he insisted. "I'll have to speak to your head matron."

"Really, Lieutenant. Do you think that's necessary? We weren't under the impression we were restricted to the house. And we never even left the grounds. Is it worth waking her to complain?"

"Perhaps not, but that will be for her to decide," he said. "Follow me."

We walked back to the villa, and I hoped that the pair of guards was the extent of it. The last thing we needed was a patrol happening upon the caretaker's cottage and discovering Tilde and the baby.

Klara shot me a nervous glance but refrained from looking back over her shoulder at the cottage.

We were made to wait in the corridor outside Frau Scholtz's office. She was dressed and ready for her day's work, which I hoped would work in our favor. If she was awake and working, she would perhaps find it admirable that we were as well.

"A couple of early birds, are we?" she said after dismissing the guard, who had issued his brief assessment of the situation.

"Yes, ma'am. I always have been. My mother always told me to take advantage of the morning hours and I took her lessons to heart," I said. Klara's arched brow let me know that perhaps I was laying on the flattery a little too thick.

"We enjoy a good morning walk," Klara said simply. "We're so very sorry that we disturbed the guards. We were unaware that we were expected to keep to the house."

"No, well. We don't make a formal pronouncement of such things. We trust that you're good girls from good families. It's not exactly good weather for a stroll though, do you think?"

"What are we, the French? I don't believe in coddling. It's cold, but there's neither snow nor rain. I've always thought breathing in the cold air was good for the lungs," Klara said. "And one can't be too robust when starting a new family, can one?"

"No, indeed," the head matron agreed. "Exercise is good for the body and soul, you're right. I'll inform the guards that you're welcome to exercise on the grounds."

"Thank you, Frau Scholtz," I said.

"Provided that one accompanies you," she continued. "We've noticed some unusual activities in the area and fear there may be some vagrants about. We don't want to take any risks with your safety. We promised your betrotheds that we would protect you while under our charge, and we take that duty seriously."

"Naturally," I said. "We appreciate your vigilance on our behalf. But we would hate to be a burden on your security staff. I'm sure we'll be fine if we stick close to the villa."

"Nonsense, that's why we've hired them. I'll tell Lieutenant Richter to have someone waiting at the door for you by half past four each morning. I'll see you at breakfast, ladies."

We scurried from her office like chastened schoolgirls and went back in the direction of our rooms. "What are we going to do?" Klara whispered. "Tilde and the baby need us. The guards will be keeping tabs on us now for sure."

"Of course they will be," I said. "They don't buy the morning walk story at all. We're well and truly stuck."

"My god. What will Tilde do once her food runs out? She doesn't have much more. And she needs rest, not worry. We need to take care of her."

"I don't know what we should do," I said honestly. "But the worst thing we could do is bring attention to her."

"Shit," Klara spat. "I was stupid for bringing her here. I just didn't know what else to do."

"Who would under such circumstances. But she's a clever woman. She'll do her best to stay safe. We have to trust her and her good sense."

"I feel so helpless," Klara moaned, leaning against the wall and sliding to the floor. She dropped her head onto her knees in defeat.

"Because we are," I said. "All we can do now is hope."

"I can't," she said. "There has to be something I can do."

"Don't be reckless, Klara. It's not just you who will suffer. Ernst and your family, too."

Klara said nothing, but I saw resolve brimming in her eyes just as I felt dread rising in my gut.

I'D KNOWN IN my bones that we hadn't heard the end of our early-morning stroll about the grounds and wasn't surprised by the summons to the head matron's office after lunchtime. I heard Klara's voice from the hallway speaking confidently as she always did.

"Hanna can corroborate my story," she insisted. "I was the one planning to leave. She talked me out of it."

"Well, Fräulein Rombauer will have to answer for herself, but I think you're a noble friend to cover for her."

"I wish you'd believe that I'm the one to blame here."

"Oh, I have no doubt of your guilt, my dear. It's her innocence I question."

I sucked in a breath despite the protesting of my lungs and knocked on the door.

A uniformed guard opened it and glanced at Frau Scholtz, who nodded. He stepped aside so I could enter.

"Good afternoon, Fräulein Rombauer. I suspect you've deduced the reason for our little meeting here this afternoon."

My heart thumped against my rib cage as I registered that the head matron and Klara were not alone with the guard standing watch. Several other officials were in attendance, including Ernst and Friedrich. I recognized Ernst from his photos. He wasn't much to look at but was dashing in uniform, and did have a kind face, as Klara was wont to say.

Though his expression was neutral, I could see storm clouds in Friedrich's eyes. No matter the outcome today, he was going to be displeased with me and I would have consequences to pay.

Klara looked to me, keeping her countenance calm, but looking insistent. *Just go along with it.*

"I told you, I was the one who wanted to run away. She had nothing to do with it and I didn't want you thinking she did. That's why I came to you."

"That will be quite enough, Fräulein Schmidt. We'd like to hear from Fräulein Rombauer now. Please, we'd love to hear your version of the events of this morning."

"I'm sure Klara has told you the unembroidered truth," I said. "I don't know what more I can add."

"All the same, we'd like to hear the truth from your own lips," Frau Scholtz said. Friedrich sat, impassive, with his hands folded on his lap as though he were watching a mildly entertaining tennis match.

"Klara came to me in the early morning hours. She was distraught," I said. "She wanted to leave the school. I was worried that she'd wake everyone with her tears, so I took her for a walk out of doors to discuss matters. We had no idea we'd be in violation of any regulations, so we didn't know to seek permission."

"And what reason did she give for wanting to leave school?" the head matron asked. "Attending one of the Führer's bride schools, this one in particular, is an honor."

"That is just what I said to convince her. Klara will forgive me for divulging this, but she has a case of cold feet. Not about her fiancé specifically, mind you, but marriage in general. The coursework here has reminded her of the scope of the commitment she's about to make. If it didn't give her some pause, I'd be worried about her. I just did my best to remind her that scary as it may seem sometimes, marriage is our solemn duty. I tried to convince her that she's equal to the task, even when she doubts it."

"How very admirable of you, Fräulein Rombauer," she said, looking a bit more convinced of the narrative. "Fräulein Schmidt says you do not share her misplaced desire to leave our school. Is that correct?"

"That's correct," I said. "I find it all very useful. I've enjoyed my time here."

"You have a college education. This isn't a bit slow and dull for you?"

"I took one semester of courses, Frau Scholtz. It didn't have time to turn my head that much. Have I given you any doubts concerning my enthusiasm?"

"No, I must admit you're an attentive pupil. I have no complaints on that score."

"Then I'm at a loss for why Klara's explanation isn't acceptable. It was a small matter. One that needn't concern you, let alone a room full of busy officers who likely have better things to do than become involved in the private goings-on of two girls."

"We were brought here on another matter," Friedrich clarified.

"Though Frau Scholtz correctly brought us in on this conversation as well, seeing that it concerns our future wives."

"I'm sorry you were troubled for such a trifle," I said. "I'm sure you have more important matters to attend to."

"Quite," the head matron said. "You may go along to your classes, Fräulein Rombauer. I'll see you this evening."

"Klara too, yes?" I asked.

"Fräulein Schmidt will need to have a private session with me." The head matron's face glowed as if she were treasuring a secret. "She'll be back with you all tomorrow."

I looked over at Klara, whose eyes were widened in surprise. She'd not been expecting a special lecture from the head matron, and I was certain it would be a scathing one.

I didn't dare wish her luck, but hoped she knew my best thoughts were with her as I exited to the corridor. I was halfway down the hall when I heard heavy footsteps behind me. Friedrich.

I turned and waited for him. There was no use pretending I didn't know he was there.

"Do you insist on embarrassing me at every turn?" he asked.

"I'm not sure what you would have had me do. She came to my room in the middle of the night in hysterics. I did what I could to calm her so she didn't wake the house and cause a real scene. I had no idea we'd be guarded like prisoners in the Bastille, or I wouldn't have taken her out for a walk without permission. I was just trying to clear her head."

"And you attracted a lot of attention in the process. You're always in the wrong place at the wrong time."

"These days it doesn't seem like there's a right place at *any* time," I countered.

"There is. At home. Minding your business."

"And that's why I'm here, am I not? To learn how to keep the perfect German household for the perfect German husband."

"Why do I feel like you're going to be trouble to mold into the perfect German wife?"

"I never claimed I'd be any good at it. It was you and Aunt Charlotte who insisted on this. I'd be content to be back in a classroom of a very different sort."

"Yes, with one of your radical professors at the helm, no doubt. I won't abide this, Hanna. I can't have talk. There's enough surrounding you as it is, what with your mother and all." It was the first time he'd mentioned her reputation, but Klara had been right that it had been the subject of gossip.

"What brought you here?" I asked. "You said you were already at the villa for another reason."

"There had been some unusual activity on the property and those nearby. We wanted to make sure there wasn't a problem with vagrants living in the outbuildings and such."

Tilde. The baby.

"And did you find anything concerning?"

"Some evidence of a recently vacated building, but we haven't found anyone else. But we will. They can't have gone far. It's an island, after all."

It was all I could do not to run out onto the grounds and search for Tilde and the baby myself in that very moment. They were cold and alone out in the woods with only the barest supplies. They could not endure that way for long.

"I'm sure you'll find what you're after," I said dully.

"I always do," Friedrich said, raising his hand to brush his finger along my jawbone. "Even if she's a bit of a troublesome little thing."

"If I'm so troublesome, why choose me, Friedrich? There are any number of young girls with perfectly suitable mothers who would make you a better wife than I would. You could find someone so much more dutiful than I am."

Friedrich grabbed my arm and shoved me against the wall so hard that the air was expelled from my lungs and pain radiated up and down my spine. "Because you're mine, that's why. Everyone who matters knows we're engaged, and I won't have you embarrass me. I will break you like a goddamned horse to make you a suitable wife if that's what it takes. The decision is yours."

"It never was, Friedrich."

Footsteps sounded in the distance and Friedrich loosened his grip. "Perhaps not, but I suggest you take the path of least resistance. For your own good."

"I'm here, aren't I?" I asked. "I'm late for class."

"Not another toe out of line, Hanna. My patience has its limits."

I stalked off toward class, not giving him the satisfaction of rubbing my arm where he'd gripped it while he was in view. When I inspected it later, there were certain to be traces of his anger left on my skin; and he would sleep soundly in the knowledge that no one would dare to ask how it happened.

CHAPTER THIRTY-EIGHT

Tilde

held Simone to my breast and prayed I could keep her warm enough. We didn't have so much as a diaper for her, let alone warm clothing, so I did the best I could to keep her swaddled in a blanket and tucked inside my coat. I was wearing only a thin nightgown underneath and shivering so hard that my shaking was causing her to fuss. I only prayed that my body heat and the blanket would be enough to protect her. I fought back sobs that I knew would only cost energy and chill my face. I wondered if my struggle to survive at all was in vain. If these thugs wanted us dead, it would take precious little effort for them to ensure that fate. I was ready to curl up and let the cold have me rather than let them snuff the life out of me themselves.

But I wouldn't.

For Simone's sake I had to cling to hope.

I could hear the voices of the guards searching the grounds and was helpless to do anything but hope that the beams of their flashlights wouldn't find us. I'd bundled up Simone and run with her as soon as I'd heard Klara's and Hanna's voices mingled with the rough growls from the guards, and only narrowly missed the patrol that had come to search the cottage. It had been the smoke from the chimney that had given us away, I was certain.

I hoped Klara and Hanna were safe, but I couldn't spare more than an idle thought for their welfare. They had warm beds to return to, even if they'd meet with a lecture for being out-of-bounds.

The night was one of the most bitterly cold I'd ever experienced, and I knew that I wouldn't escape unharmed if I remained out of doors much longer. Simone had even less time before the cold made a victim of her.

I found myself thinking like my lawyer grandfather. What were my choices?

I could stay where I was. But we would both freeze before sunrise. Unacceptable.

I could try to find shelter elsewhere on the island. But it was dark, and I ran the risk of running into guards and making my situation worse. Only marginally better.

I could sneak into the basement of the big house and try to find a corner where no servant would find us. We'd be warm, but it seemed reckless.

I could return to the cottage and hope that the guards would not return a second time. Not a good option, but it seemed the best at my disposal.

We wouldn't be able to light a fire. We wouldn't be able to cook on the stove. We wouldn't be able to even light candles for fear of attracting attention. Simone still might freeze. But it would be better than staying exposed to the elements.

I moved as stealthily as I could back to the cottage, hiding behind every tree or bush I came to to look for guards, who had the training and experience to be even stealthier than I.

The guards hadn't spent long in the house, and the small supply of food had gone unnoticed. The fire had been doused, but it was still markedly warmer than the outdoors. For this I offered silent thanks.

I set Simone in a small crate as near the smoldering fire as I dared and placed a kiss atop her head. She was still warm and breathing evenly, having barely stirred in the time we'd spent out of doors. I wasn't sure if it had been an hour or three, but the sun was rising in earnest, and we'd managed to sneak back in before daylight had betrayed us. If she'd cried, we would have been discovered. I smiled down at her, now sleeping soundly and blissfully unaware of the danger she was in. I stood to assess the cottage and how to keep it secure.

I thought about barring the door, but there was nothing inside that would do any more than slow the guards' entry by a matter of moments. Barring the only door would do more to slow a rapid exit than to protect us from intruders.

I felt myself grow faint and shuffled over to the lone chair. I looked down to find Klara's nightgown splotched red with blood. I should never have been forced to stir from my bed so soon after giving birth. My hours-old daughter and I should not have been driven out into the biting cold just to remain safe. I summoned the strength to change out of the ruined gown and to replace the rags that Hanna had given me to stem the flow of blood. I even managed to eat a good portion of the bread and cheese Klara had left behind. For just a moment or two, I felt closer to human.

I knew I wouldn't find a moment's rest in the cottage, knowing the guards were hunting for the baby and me. I rocked back and forth wondering what I could do to keep the guards from spotting us.

Precious little.

If they suspected the inhabitants might come back, they would surveil the place. I couldn't keep quiet enough or still enough to avoid detection if they were determined to be vigilant in their oversight of the property.

All I could do was defend us. I looked about the cottage and wished the caretaker had been the sort to keep a metal poker by the fire, but apparently he used some other implement to stoke it. The only potential weapon I found was a scrap of wooden planking from the burn pile. It would be useless against a group—even a pair—of guards, but if a lone soldier approached the door, it might buy me some time.

I pulled the board from the pile and stood it up at my side. It seemed like bringing a tugboat to a naval battle, but it was a little better than being completely defenseless.

CHAPTER THIRTY-NINE

Hanna

I spent a restless night, torn in two by worry for Klara, who I had not seen even at dinner, and for Tilde and the baby. I didn't dare go look for them because I was being watched like some insidious traitor. If they didn't stop me at the door, and it seemed almost certain they would, they would tail me. If I were fortunate enough to find Tilde alive, I would only be leading death to her.

It wasn't until I went to breakfast the following morning that I saw Klara. I'd expected to see her looking like she'd spent a difficult night—perhaps with rumpled clothes or dark shadows under the eyes—but she looked flawless. Smooth, clear skin, shiny coiffed hair, a fashionable ensemble that had never seen a wrinkle. She smiled broadly, but rather than being comforted, I was chilled.

"You look well," I said, sitting as a footman placed a plate of sausage and eggs before me.

"Never better," she said.

"I was worried for you," I said. "The head matron seemed ready to swallow you whole."

"You're so funny, Hanna. Frau Scholtz really is a duck once you get to know her."

"I'd never have imagined you describing her like that. She's ruled this place with an iron fist."

"Well, the job she's doing here is an important one and she takes it seriously. I regret not being more serious about my studies here. I've squandered opportunity, but I'm resolved to make the most of the rest of my time here. I hope you'll take my advice and do the same."

She sounded so polished; it was like sitting across from an actress from a radio advertisement. They'd done something to her. I couldn't be sure what, but she wasn't the Klara from the day before.

"Um, yes. Of course. And speaking of which, I ought to freshen up before our first class. Best foot forward and all that. Are you finished?"

Her plastic smile returned. "That's the spirit," she said, standing to join me.

When we got to my bedroom door, I took her by the elbow and pulled her inside.

"What's wrong with you?" I asked.

"Why nothing at all. I've never been better."

"What did they do to you, Klara? You can tell me."

"The head matron just reminded me of my duties. Nothing more. I wonder if you don't need a similar reminder, Hanna. I'd be only too happy to tell her you'd benefit from a chat as well."

"No, thank you," I said. "If you won't tell me what they did to you, at least swear to me you didn't betray Tilde and the baby."

For a split second her face fell, but her composure returned. "We really ought to get to class, Hanna. We have precious little time left here and we must make the most of it."

"Klara, tell me what you told them," I hissed. "Their lives depend on it."

"I'm going to class," she insisted. "And if I don't see you there in ten minutes, I'll assume the head matron needs to know of it."

"I don't know what they did to you, Klara, but I will find out. You're not yourself."

Her expression hardened. "I assure you, I'm more myself than I ever have been. I'll see you in class."

She left the room with a decorous click of the door. I clutched myself around the middle, feeling as though I were breaking in two. I couldn't breathe for worry about Tilde and the baby. For worry about what they'd done to Klara.

I had to get to class. If I betrayed that I knew anything was wrong, appeared withdrawn or apprehensive, I would find out for myself what they had done to my friend.

I fought with every ounce of my conviction to regain mastery of myself, but I wanted nothing more than to scream. I went over to the basin of water kept in my room and splashed some on my face. I clutched my portfolio to my chest, the one Friedrich had embossed with my name for university, like a shield against a world that had left me friendless and walked out of my room. I shook with every step but moved forward.

The head matron was in charge of our morning class. A lecture, this time, on our duty to country and our beloved leader. She was impassioned as she spoke today. Even more than usual. It may have been my overeager imagination, but it felt as though she were looking more often at me than at any other face in the audience.

I had my portfolio open and made the motions of taking notes so I had an excuse not to make eye contact. Of course, I could have copied down her overwrought patriotic diatribe, but instead I wrote down the names that kept churning in my head: Tilde, Simone, Klara . . . over and over again. There had to be a way to save them all, but I felt as helpless as the baby in Tilde's arms against any of it.

We were dismissed to lunch, but the head matron and Klara were waiting for me at the door.

"Fräulein Rombauer, Fräulein Schmidt says you have been worried," Frau Scholtz said.

I froze. A wrong answer to the question would be disastrous, but I wasn't sure there was a right one. "I'm not sure what you're referring to, but I suppose I have been worried about Klara, yes. She's my friend."

"I believe you've been under a lot of strain, Fräulein. There is to be a small party at the villa next door with many of the officers. You and Fräulein Schmidt are to attend with your fiancés. You may have the last session off to rest and prepare. I'll have coffee and *Lebkuchen* sent to your rooms."

Klara beamed and I forced a smile.

"I didn't bring anything suitable to wear," I said to Klara as we walked back to our rooms. "I hadn't prepared for parties."

"Everything will be ready for you," she said. "No details left unnoticed."

"Do you want to get ready together?" I asked. "Like old times?"

"I'm afraid I'll need to take the time to rest. I want to be fresh for Ernst. I'm sure you'll want to do the same."

She walked briskly off to her room and I entered mine with dread mounting in my stomach. It was a party, but sounded as appealing as a hanging.

The events of the past thirty-six hours registered with my body, and I tossed myself on the bed. It took me a few moments to register the smell of the coffee and gingerbread that had already been delivered to my room and the dress that was hanging on the wardrobe door to air out. It was one of the dresses Tilde had made a year ago. Periwinkle blue satin, demure but not girlish. Perfect for an evening of cocktails with the officers. Aunt Charlotte had sent blue satin heels along with my diamond earrings and bracelet and a new aquamarine necklace. Pale pink lip gloss for just a hint of color. A new bottle of scent, too. It smelled clean and crisp like linen and cedar. Nothing overpowering and showy like French perfume, that would never do. No detail unnoticed, indeed.

This had been orchestrated for hours, if not several days. I wanted to leave it all behind and run. Run far away where Friedrich, Aunt Charlotte, and the head matron could never find me.

But I knew they would find me.

I would never be safe.

I curled up on the floor and pulled my knees to my chest. I swallowed the screams I wanted to let loose into the void.

After a while, I found my breath. I found the strength to sit. Then to stand.

Slowly, methodically, I dressed myself and made myself presentable for the soirée. I found no joy in the beautiful clothes made at the hands of a woman who may have already lost the fight to keep herself and her baby safe. As I zipped and fastened my way into my finery, I racked my brain for any plausible way to help Tilde. Every outcome played out her downfall, and my own.

Fifteen minutes before we were meant to leave, there was a knock at my door.

"I just came to see how you were getting along," Klara said, entering the room. She wore a cocktail dress, not unlike my own, in a deep forest green that suited her complexion marvelously. I wondered if Tilde had been the mastermind behind that dress as well. It had to have been tailor-made, the way it contoured to Klara's shape. She was the picture of health and beauty, and I wondered why Friedrich had ever grown cold on her. But there was no sense in trying to puzzle out his feelings in this matter or any other.

She scanned the space as she spoke, and I could tell she was looking for any sign of malfeasance. Her conversion over to their way of thinking was utterly complete now. There was no rescuing Klara, and my heart broke almost as much for her as it did for Tilde.

Almost.

I don't know what they did to her, but it had to have been dire. Whether they tortured her physically or brainwashed her in the span of a night, something in her was broken.

"How very pretty you look," she purred. "But then you always have been. Won't it be nice to have an evening away?"

"Y-yes," I said. My veneer was still thin. I'd have to do better by the time we reached the party.

She didn't comment on any perceived lack of enthusiasm, but there was no doubt that she felt it emanating from me.

When we arrived at the villa next door, a small band was playing a graceful tune for the cocktail hour that mocked the churning of my gut.

The evening went on and, as was the custom, Friedrich paraded me in front of his colleagues, presenting me like I was a trophy he'd won. Champagne, canapés, and deadly dull conversation flowed through the room like a coursing river.

I excused myself to get some air on the veranda and scanned the grounds for as long as I could stand the bitter cold. I didn't see Friedrich when I returned, so I decided to look for Klara, who had probably found a means of taking a short break from the festivities as well. I thought to look for her in one of the rooms adjacent to the ballroom, thinking there might be an obliging study or library for her to hide out in, but heard the sound of booming male voices coming from the room before I turned the handle.

"You understand the Führer will approve the plan and we'll be able to make some real progress soon. I see no other interpretation for his recent actions."

"It's about time we were given the license to rid Germany of the scourge," another disembodied voice said. "Germany should be for Germans."

There was a murmur of approval from the voices in the room, and I heard the sounds of glasses clinking.

"There will be a day, not long from now, when we'll be able to walk down the streets of our cities and know that the people we meet belong there. It will be a glorious day."

I stood and tried not to gasp as I absorbed the meaning of his words. Not only was Tilde in danger, the rest of her people were as well.

I didn't know how long the congregation in the library would last, but I couldn't be found listening at the door. I turned to leave and nearly ran face-first into someone in the corridor. Klara.

"I'm sorry, I didn't——" I said.

She pressed a finger to her lips and passed me an envelope and a small satchel. I peered inside. A change of clothes and a modest sum of money. The meaning was clear: Tilde had to leave, and fast.

"Find her," she mouthed. "Go now."

She turned and left for the party as though she'd never seen me.

I was flooded with questions. Was this a trap? Why couldn't Klara go herself? Was she somehow at greater risk than I was?

I considered Friedrich and doubted this very much. If Ernst had been deemed an acceptable match by Klara's parents, he was likely committed to the cause. But he didn't have Friedrich's rank or clout. Friedrich had more to lose if I shamed him. What's more, I got the feeling that if Ernst's love for Klara ever came into conflict with his duty, he would choose her. I labored under no such delusion that Friedrich's loyalty to me extended that far.

But there wouldn't be another opportunity. I didn't risk going back to the ballroom, nor to the room where they kept our wraps. If I asked for my coat, people would know I'd gone and Friedrich would come looking outside that much sooner.

The frigid air burned my bare skin that so recently had been warmed by the glow of roaring fires in every room of the house. My lungs protested against the intrusion of the biting cold air, but I ran as quickly as I could in the direction of the caretaker's cottage. There was no sign of life coming from the house, but she would have had to keep herself hidden anyway. I didn't know if she'd found shelter elsewhere or not, but I had no other recourse but to look for her there before combing the forest in a cocktail dress and heels.

I entered the cottage, expecting to find nothing, but hoping that for the first time in ages, I'd be in luck.

CHAPTER FORTY

Tilde

I dropped the plank of wood onto the floor and launched myself into Hanna's arms. I barely knew this woman, but at the very least, she wasn't death arriving at my doorstep. She might have brought it hard on her heels, but I had a few minutes' reprieve.

"Shhhh," Hanna whispered, enveloping the baby and me in her arms. "I can't stay more than a few seconds but take this."

She handed me the satchel and envelope. I peered into the leather case to see a fresh dress suitable for travel. The envelope contained money, but no papers. I'd be able to leave the island, but not get much farther. Hanna opened her own handbag and produced a few more bills.

"It's not much, but it may help."

"Thank you," I said, accepting the offering with a shaking hand. I was back where I'd been a few days earlier, but now with a baby to protect.

"Let me help you change," she said. "You're in no condition to be doing this, but you haven't much choice."

"No," I agreed.

I pulled the dress from the bag. It was a solid brown wool affair, four sizes larger than I would normally wear, but necessary to accommodate my swollen form. The name "Trina Udolph" was embroidered on a label at the nape of the neck. Hanna stifled a giggle when she saw the name.

"What's funny?" I asked her, genuinely glad there was something someone could find mirthful in a moment like this.

"Let's just say Klara liberated the dress from someone who would be less than thrilled to know what it was being used for."

"All the better," I said.

"It will fit better than your maternity dress, at any rate. We want you to look recovered from your travails. You'll have an easier time escaping if you don't look like you're trying to escape."

"Good thinking," I said, wishing the plan had been my own. Hanna was shrewd like my dear grandfather, and I couldn't help but admire her for it.

She looked me up and down, approvingly.

"You look fit for travel," she announced. "I don't think it's safe for you to stay long. Leave as soon as I'm out of sight. Be safe and have a happy life. You deserve so much better."

"You too," I said, gripping her tight. "I hope you'll be so very happy."

Her face fell for a fraction of a second. "I assure you, if there was a way, I'd be going with you. But you go ahead and have a good life for both of us, won't you? I have to go, but know I'll be thinking of you. Klara too, I'm sure."

She disappeared into the night as abruptly as she had come.

Simone looked up at me, blinking quizzically.

"I don't know what happens next, darling, but I know there probably is a next."

I had a million decisions to make in the coming hours, but my only concern was staying alive until daybreak.

I gathered up anything in the cottage that could be of use for travel and swaddled Simone as tightly as I could. I would have given anything for a woolen sleeper for her or even a knit cap, but if I held her close, she'd fare well enough. I had to believe it.

I had no idea where to go, but I didn't have long to make a decision.

I tucked the money away, cinched the satchel closed, and lifted Simone to my chest. I'd stick to the shadows and keep out of sight. I'd walk slowly to keep my strength for the twelve-mile trek into the city. If I were at my fittest, I could have made the walk in under four hours; but in my weakened state and carrying the baby, it would likely take closer to six. But I had food and time. I was prepared and would be able to escape with my daughter.

At least part of Samuel would live on.

I donned my coat as well as the hat and gloves that Klara had lent me. *Given* was perhaps a better term, since it was not likely that I'd be able to return them. I fashioned a sling for Simone from a blanket to help ease the burden of carrying her over such a long distance and settled her inside. I took the satchel in my free hand and braced for the long walk ahead.

"I'm so sorry, darling. You deserve to stay bundled up and warm indoors where it's nice and cozy, but I'll get you someplace safe as soon as I can. We'll just keep our heads down and get into the city and we'll be fine."

I kissed the top of Simone's sleeping head. I didn't know what was next for us, but I hoped my apartment would be at least fractionally safer than the cottage. I surveyed the room and saw nothing else that would be of use. I'd have to get papers and leave the country as soon as I could, by means fair or foul. I focused on the moment when we were safely ensconced on a train heading to the port. I pictured the calm spreading over me with every mile that separated us from Berlin. The long, frigid walk to get to safety would be a memory in just a few days, and in time would be a story I could tell Simone when she fell on hard times.

No, I thought. *Berlin will never be part of her story. She need never know about the hell she was born into. We'll tell her she was born in New York, where no one will shame her for her heritage, and she won't have to keep her head down out of fear.*

I opened the door of the cottage and left without a backward glance at the little space that had been my shelter when I brought Simone into the world. I felt no attachment or sentimentality toward it. I should have been free to give birth in the safety of a hospital or in the peace of my own home. I'd been denied both safety and peace, and for this, my soul raged. I pushed myself into the bitter, dark night, one slow pace at a time, willing myself forward despite my exhaustion.

I'll get you to safety, my darling girl. I uttered a silent vow to the sleeping baby at my breast as I walked along the edges of the property. *And you'll never know true fear for as long as I draw breath.*

I stepped lightly and carefully to minimize the noise of my footsteps as I walked along, but despite these efforts, we didn't even reach the perimeter of the property before the guards spotted us.

CHAPTER FORTY-ONE

Hanna

Despite the bitter cold, my skin shone with perspiration as I snuck back in the side door of the villa to rejoin the party. I blessed the presence of the hallway mirror that allowed me to check that I wasn't too disheveled before entering the ballroom. I smoothed a few flyaway hairs and steadied my breathing before returning to the swirling vortex of the dance floor. I danced at least three waltzes before Friedrich spotted me.

"There you are, my dear. I wondered where you'd gotten to." Friedrich's smile was twisted with annoyance. "You went missing a while back. I must have missed seeing you on the dance floor."

"Ladies' room," I said. "I won't bore you with the intricacies of ladies' undergarments."

"I appreciate the courtesy," he said, winking. "Though perhaps later . . ."

I shuddered at the idea of intimacy with this man, but there was no pretending that I'd have any choice but to submit. I ignored the suggestion and took his hand to go back to the dance floor. At least there, I knew the steps I was supposed to take.

We were only a few measures into a waltz when two uniformed guards came to our side.

"We think we've captured the fugitive," one informed Friedrich without preamble. "We have her in the library, sir."

"Her?"

"Yes. A woman and a newborn, sir."

Tilde. The baby.

I felt a hand reflexively rise to wrap around my midsection but forced it to remain at my side. *They must think this means nothing to you.*

"Curiouser and curiouser. I'll come see her."

I fought to regain my composure and hoped I was succeeding in some small measure. I scanned the room for Klara but did not see her.

"Perhaps I should come in case the baby needs looking after," I said. "I learned a bit from my mother."

Friedrich flinched at the mention of my mother, but assented.

When we entered the library, Klara was already waiting, holding the baby and sitting next to Tilde in an armchair as if it were the most natural thing in the world. Ernst and two guards looked wary.

"Fräulein Rombauer, what is your relationship to this woman?" Ernst said upon my entry. Klara's look was remarkably nonchalant, so I endeavored to emulate it.

"This is Mathilde Altman. She's been my dressmaker on many an occasion. She made the very dress I'm wearing."

"Just as I said," Klara chimed in. "She came to make sure we didn't need any last-minute alterations. Though if we'd known she'd just had a baby, my parents wouldn't have bothered the poor dear."

"I wouldn't hear of anyone else touching my creations," Tilde said with mock seriousness. "Though I admit it wasn't ideal to have to bring the little one along. Our nanny has been ill, you see. But I thought with Klara and Hanna being as much friends as clients, they'd understand."

"Understand? Delighted to see the little darling. Though I thought you'd gone home hours ago. What happened?" I asked.

"Oh, I took advantage of your offer to feed the baby and take a nap in your room. By the time I woke up it was dark, and I couldn't find my way."

"Well, thank goodness the men found you before anyone else. There have been reports of vagrants in the area. Can you imagine what might have happened?" I said, giving a shudder for effect.

"Fortunate indeed," Ernst said, his expression changing to one of concern.

Friedrich looked at Tilde and seemed mollified. I seized my opportunity.

"Poor Tilde must be dead on her feet," I said. "Surely someone could phone for a car to give her and the little one a ride back to town, since she was kind enough to taxi in?"

Friedrich nodded and one of the four guards scurried away.

"Rolf will take you where you need to go, Frau Altman. I trust we won't find you wandering in the woods again."

"I wouldn't dream of troubling you again," she said, the jovial spirit in the room rebounding. "And I certainly don't want to trouble your man to drive me all the way back to Berlin. A taxi will do beautifully."

"There's one waiting in the drive, Captain," the underling chimed in. "Dropping off some guests and hoping for a return job."

The young lieutenant looked eager not to miss out on the festivities, and Friedrich's expression softened. Occasions like these were few.

"Very well. See Frau Altman and the child to the taxicab and handle the fare into town," he said. He turned to me. "Let's go back to dancing, shall we?"

Friedrich said nothing as we walked back into the ballroom. He pulled me into his arms in time with the swell of the music. "Morning stroll, eh?" he whispered in my ear.

"I've no idea what you're talking about," I said. "Klara had cold feet and that's the end of it."

"And you weren't missing for twenty minutes just before the girl was found? That's just coincidence?"

"You're acting paranoid, Friedrich. It's not a flattering look for you."

"Oh, I don't think it's paranoid to connect this many dots, my dear."

"Then why let her go?" I replied. "If you don't think I'm telling you the truth."

"Because she doesn't matter. I don't know why you're protecting her or from what, but in the grand scheme of things, she doesn't matter. But I promise you this, if you step one more toe out of line, it will be *your* neck you need to worry about. Not hers. They warned me that you had some of your mother's same proclivities, but I was blinded by my attraction to you. I won't be so foolish in the future."

I stared at him agape, not caring who on the dance floor might be watching us.

"Don't worry. We'll be married in less than two weeks, and

you'll be plenty busy with your new life to worry about getting into any mischief."

"Two weeks?" I asked.

"Time's up, darling. I've waited long enough. And if that woman I've just let walk out of here means anything to you, you won't put up a fuss. I could have her behind bars where she belongs and the brat thrown in the lake with the snap of my fingers."

I felt my stomach curdle at the veracity of his words and the sincerity with which he spoke them.

The evening wasn't yet over, and Friedrich wouldn't allow us to give the appearance of having quarreled. Klara too was on the floor, dancing with officers as though we hadn't just narrowly escaped the wrath of one of the most vindictive men in Germany. I wanted to cross the room to talk to her but didn't dare risk attracting Friedrich's attention. I danced when she danced until I saw her lingering for a moment at the punch table.

I begged off on my partner, claiming to be parched, and walked to the table with all the nonchalance I could feign.

"I'm sorry," Klara whispered. "They were watching me too closely. I thought you had a better chance of warning her away than I did. If they'd found her in the cottage, there would have been no explaining it away."

"All that matters is Tilde and the baby. And it seems like we did what we could for her," I said.

"But what about the others?" Klara asked. "Tilde isn't the only one trapped in Germany."

"I know," I said, looking down into my lemonade cup.

"You have no idea what they have in store," Klara said, the color draining from her face as she looked out onto the dance floor.

"Stoltz told me, and I'm sure she only has the barest idea of what's going on compared to the men in this room."

"That's what she lectured you about? What scared you so much?"

"It's more than enough. Just keep safe, Hanna. Remember that you mean nothing to these people if you get in their way. And everything if they need something from you."

"We have to do something," I said.

"We'll find a way," Klara said. "Women like us find ways to do the right thing in silence and shadows. The trick, as always, is how to stay alive long enough to make a difference."

CHAPTER FORTY-TWO

Tilde

The taxi dropped me off in front of the shop, which still bore the signs of the vandalism from several days earlier. The door was broken, but remained closed. The contents of the shop were in a bit of disarray, but no one had come to pillage. I was sure a few things had gone missing, but it was far better than I expected. This small remnant of civilization shocked me. So many times in the past months I'd pictured my fellow Berliners as hyenas circling a kill, but in this instance, they'd left things alone. They hadn't enough proof that I was one of the "others" to loot, but they also weren't sure enough that I was one of them to leave me alone. But it would all have to stay behind, and that pained me. None of them deserved any part of my labors.

I walked quietly up the stairs, happy to see that the search had been constrained. The contents of a few drawers had been strewn about, but they hadn't shattered windows or smashed the furniture into splinters as they were apt to do. The cradle I'd procured for Simone was untouched, and I nestled her in to sleep. I'd pictured countless nights rocking her in that cradle with my foot as I worked on mending and commissions, but our tenure in the apartment would have to be of short duration. Like so many of my carefully laid plans, this too would have to change. I could not keep Simone in Berlin a moment longer than necessary.

I checked that Mama's money and other important items were still in place. Miraculously, they were. Once I convinced myself nothing had been taken, I paced around the apartment, nearly wearing tracks in the floor. I didn't think about the mess in the shop below. I just bolted the apartment door and blocked it with a chair. I could worry about broken glass and spoiled fabrics tomorrow. Or maybe not at all. Tonight, all I could do was come up with a plan and try to stop shaking.

I had escaped, but only just.

If Klara hadn't been so quick-thinking, or if Hanna hadn't corroborated the story, I'd have been at the mercy of those goons. I thought of sweet Hanna, so bright and capable, married to the brute with the cold eyes, and I shivered for her. But the sensation passed quickly as I remembered how dire my own situation was. As sad as I was for her, she'd have to save herself, just as I would.

I would be safe in the apartment for now—probably—but how long would that last?

It was clear that people in the neighborhood were looking for people to report. They kept vigilant watch over the neighborhoods, eager to root out "undesirables" like me . . . and they were just getting started. I wouldn't let Simone grow up in fear. I watched the menace grow larger and larger as I grew from a child to a woman. I saw my mother's concern grow into persistent worry only to become outright panic. The gurgling of the contented baby rose up from the cradle. She deserved better.

I needed papers. I needed them for both of us.

Not only would I need travel papers, but a birth certificate for Simone and a host of other identity papers.

I didn't think I had months to make my escape. Maybe weeks, if I were lucky.

Days would be better. Hours would be ideal.

I had to make a miracle out of paper, and I had only experience crafting those from taffeta, silk, and lace.

But as Simone began to stir and make her little cooing noises before crying in earnest, I knew failure wasn't an option.

TWO WEEKS LATER, Simone and I waited in the lobby of my father's law firm. I had made dresses for us both especially for the occasion with fabric I'd managed to salvage from the shop. I dressed in a shade of green that brought out the color of my eyes and played off the caramel glints of my hair. I wanted to look like a wealthy Gentile woman. I wanted to look as prosperous and polished as Papa's new wife. Simone was dressed in a white gown with frills and lace. She looked like a baby from a magazine.

A tall secretary with pursed lips waved us in. Papa sat behind his desk. He didn't pretend to look down at his paperwork in mock distraction. He crossed his arms over his chest and looked out the office window. His expression was that of defeat.

"So very kind of you to see me," I said.

"You've got your grandfather's knack for the art of persuasion," he said, his voice ringing hollow. There was no pride lacing his words.

"I've never been paid a nicer compliment in all my life," I said.

He harrumphed and reached for a glass with two inches of amber liquid on his desk. Whiskey before noon wasn't a sign he was faring all that well.

"Do you have them?" I asked. "I don't want to interrupt your busy day."

He tossed a large manila envelope my way.

"Guard those with your life. I don't care what blackmail you come up with, I can't come up with a second set. You have no idea the favors I had to call in to make this happen."

"Understood," I said, opening the envelope, hoping every scrap of paper in it had cost him dearly.

"Passports, visas, a birth certificate for the baby, a death certificate for the father. Everything you'll need," he explained. "All of them flawless. I've checked them myself."

"Made out in the name of Marianne and Sophie Maillet?" Our middle names had been erased entirely.

"French names are safer," he explained. "You've got a head for languages. I'd try to sound as French as you can until you reach New York."

I looked at the rest of the contents of the envelope. He'd included train tickets from Berlin to the port in Hamburg, and passage on a ship to New York. I hadn't expected this. We'd leave the next day. He wanted us gone. That much was *not* a surprise.

Papa saw my expression of amazement and interpreted it correctly.

"I don't believe in half measures. If you don't escape to America, I've no doubt you'll make good on your threat."

"You mean that I'll find your lovely new wife and my half-brother and half-sister and tell them all about how you abandoned your first wife and daughter because they were Jewish?"

"Precisely."

"Which do you think would be worse for your wife—Anja, is it?—you having concealed a family from her, or the fact that the wife and daughter you abandoned are Jewish? Her family is quite well known in the party. She'd be revolted by the truth. Your father-in-law even more so."

Papa blanched at the mention of his wife's name. Good. I wanted him nervous. "You've done your research, haven't you?"

"Like father like daughter. I don't believe in half measures, either. If you were to betray me, I promise you, she'll know about your past if I have to scream it to her on my way to the gallows."

"I believe it of you," he said. "And I can't say I'd deserve better."

"At least on that we can agree," I said.

"I won't insult you by apologizing, but I've often wished things would have turned out differently."

"You made damn sure they didn't," I said, rising with Simone in my arms and clutching the papers in my free hand like the lifeline they were. "But all the same, in this moment, I'm not angry with you. It may have been against your will, but at least my daughter and I have a chance at life now."

"Use it well," he said. "I trust you will."

Part of me longed to embrace my father. To remember all the kindnesses he'd shown me as a young girl. To try to understand why he felt compelled to abandon Mama and me. But the weight of Simone in my arms—and in my heart—was a reminder that what he'd done was unthinkable. The mere idea of forsaking her was anathema to me, just as it should have been to him.

I nodded and left my father's office without another word. We understood the plain truth: we'd discharged our responsibilities to each other, and our relationship had come to its conclusion. He would breathe easier knowing all the proof of his past life was a continent away, and I would have the space and the freedom to begin a new life where, just maybe, the hole he'd left in my life might have the chance to heal.

BACK ON THE pavement outside Papa's office I looked up and took a full breath of cold air. I blinked against the bright sunlight. I'd spent so long keeping my head down that I hardly knew how to look up again. I spent the past two weeks shaking, waiting for the papers that might never come. For months, I'd done everything right. I'd done everything I could think of to avoid drawing attention to myself, and yet they found me out.

They took my parents-in-law.

They took my sister-in-law.

They took my Samuel.

They'd taken enough. I would not let them take Simone. The papers in my hand gave me hope that I could make good on this promise.

And I would not break the promise I'd made to myself not to let my mother's hard-earned money and treasures fall into the hands of Hitler and his goons. I would deliver them back to her myself. But how to get them out of the country safely wasn't a simple task. It was a dilemma I'd been pondering for the two weeks I'd been waiting for papers.

According to the tickets Papa had procured for me, I had to be at the Hauptbahnhof early the next morning. It was already three in the afternoon; I was out of time to find a solution for smuggling the coins and jewels out of Germany.

I adjusted Simone in my arms and noticed a small rent in the hem of her gown. I'd have to fix it before the voyage, or else save the task for a dull moment during the crossing.

Then the solution to my problem became obvious. I was a seamstress and needed to use those skills to get Mama's things back to her.

It was foolish. It was reckless. But I had to try.

Back in the apartment, I went to Mama's dresser—my dresser—discarded the clothes and removed the false bottom. Every coin, every small treasure she'd hidden for me was still there. I hadn't spent a single pfennig, even at time when the shop only brought in a small trickle of income.

I assessed the contents of the drawer. I couldn't just pack the jewels and money loose in a case. I had to appear to be a pauper, or else I ran the risk of losing everything. I'd heard from neighbors that Jews who tried to emigrate were stripped of valuables and left to start their new lives with little more than a few changes of clothes. And they were the lucky ones. My papers did not identify me as Jewish, but I knew the authorities were more and more loath to let any wealth escape the country, no matter who carried it.

If clothes were all I could take, I would do everything in my power to make each garment count. I could leave everything else behind, but I would not sacrifice what was left of my mother's savings or the emeralds she'd given me for my wedding. I spent my last hours in Berlin sewing secret little pockets into every garment the baby and I owned. Just enough to hide a few coins in each. I hid the necklace in the hem of my best dress and the earrings in the hem of another.

Once Mama's things were safe, I was left with my own memento: the simple gold band Samuel had given me on our wedding day. The

Nazis weren't above taking a wedding band, so I chose not to risk one of my few mementos of Samuel and sewed it into the hem of one of Simone's lacy gowns. I would save it for her, so she could have a token of the marriage that had created her—a brief marriage that had been filled with love and terror in almost equal parts.

But he was gone. I'd known it in my bones for a while now. If he were alive, I'd have felt something other than the hollowness in my gut that had plagued me in the months since he'd left. At least now, Simone made that gaping abyss seem a little less vast.

She was sleeping soundly in her cradle, dreaming peacefully if her expression could be trusted to mean anything. I stopped in the middle of my sewing to smile down at her. "I'll tell you about your papa every day as long as I draw breath, my sweet girl. He was the best, kindest man alive. Too good for this world, but we'll find a way to manage on our own." It was a reminder for myself as much as it was a promise for her.

I'd studied the travel papers carefully now that I was in the relative safety of my own home and memorized their contents. I double- and triple-checked the dates and times and all the identifying information. I couldn't believe anything might be out of order, but I knew I'd be shrouded in worry until we reached New York and I was in my mother's arms. But rather than fight the inevitable, I just allowed myself to embrace it.

These papers were more precious than any of the gold or jewels I'd sewn into the garments already, so I created a special pouch to keep them tucked close to my breast throughout the journey.

I'd spent the whole night hiding anything of value in the hems and seams of the garments and gathering anything for the journey that I thought would be of use and would not draw the attention of any punctilious guards. By the time I finished, I was convinced that even the most discerning guard would be hard pressed to discover my subterfuge.

I still had a couple of hours before the train was to depart, but I couldn't abide staying in the apartment longer than I had to. I filled the fashionable satchel Klara had given me with food and essentials that I might need to have readily available, such as a few changes of clothes for Simone, a supply of nappies, and a canvas bag to store the soiled ones in. I wasn't sure what I would do about washing them while aboard the ship, but that was a worry for later. I then turned to Mama's sturdy suitcase and packed it full of our seemingly uninteresting clothes, a few personal effects of no real value, and an extra pair of good shoes. I didn't look wealthy enough to be of interest to the guards, nor so poor I'd raise suspicions about how I was able to fund the voyage.

I'd keep my head down one last time.

I descended the staircase. This time Simone was bundled up properly in a woolen sleeper and bound to my chest. The travel documents and our small hoard of paper money were secure in the pouch between us under the thickness of three dresses and two coats. I had the satchel in my left hand and the suitcase in my right. Every step was a balancing act, but I only had to make it a few blocks to the train station.

"My, we're rather active for the middle of the night, aren't we?" a voice said from behind me as I crossed the shop floor. I stopped frozen in my tracks and turned to see who had spoken.

"I might say the same, Frau Heinrich," I countered, seeing the small woman emerge into the feeble light that streamed in from the streetlamp. "You gave me a fright. Isn't it rather late—or early—

for you to be out and about?" It had to be close to four in the morning, but it didn't seem too early to make our way to the station for our six o'clock departure.

"One can never be too diligent about safety in the neighborhood," she said. "I take great pride in making sure everything is in order here and that rules are followed."

"I'm sure we're all grateful for your vigilance," I said. I cocked my head and changed my tactic. "I don't suppose you know what happened here? You can imagine my surprise coming home to this disarray after giving birth. I'm still quite shaken by it, to tell the truth."

"Oh, a simple search, my dear. I've worried that something wasn't quite right here, and I can see by the little bundle you have strapped to your chest that I was right."

I looked down at Simone. "Her father is in Poland," I said. "I don't speak much of my husband because our marriage was a hasty wartime union and it's painful to think of him in harm's way."

"I had no idea," she said. "He's in service to the Führer? That's quite different."

"Quite," I agreed.

"So where are you off to, then?" she pressed, pointing to my bags. "It's rather peculiar to go cavorting around with an infant before dawn, is it not?"

"I assure you, Frau Heinrich, I would be nestled in my bed at this very moment if the choice were mine. But I'm going to be with family so I might have some help with the baby. It was my husband's dearest wish. He said he wouldn't be able to serve with a clear head and a clear heart if he thought of me toiling here alone." I repeated the lie I'd told Hanna's betrothed and found it became more natural each time I spoke the words. It probably didn't speak well of my ethics, but I'd have to square it with my conscience later.

"But what of the shop? So many in the neighborhood depend upon your services. Myself included."

"I have no doubt that someone with your attention to detail will be able to find someone to fill my shoes," I said. "With a bit of elbow grease, it could be up and running again in a day or two. Perhaps those men you summoned to search will help you put things right. You'll excuse me, but I have a train to catch."

I turned on the ball of my foot and left the shop behind one last time, my head held high. I wasn't followed or harassed. And I would be able to leave Germany knowing who had chased me from my home. There was some satisfaction in that.

We waited in the drafty train station until the first train of the day pulled in. Every mile that took us out of Berlin felt like a blessing. Simone slept peacefully, lulled by the gentle rattle of the cars.

Once we arrived in Hamburg we waited in a throng of people as desperate to leave as we were. I was certain someone would come to haul us out of line or that the tickets would somehow be invalidated. I felt my heart flutter as they inspected my belongings, now convinced that my clever trick of sewing my small treasures into the clothes had been tried a million times before, and I'd be discovered in a trice.

The guard rifled through, grunting with disappointment that there weren't any items of value. He did linger at my spare shoes but decided better of it when he looked into my green eyes and saw my light brown hair. A few shades darker and he might have looked harder, but he passed me over and went on to the next passenger. My hands shook visibly as I latched the case and satchel, and I walked toward the gangplank, trying to control sobs of relief. Even as the ship pulled out of the harbor, I waited for some disaster to strike, but miraculously, it didn't.

The boat left the harbor and I felt myself breathe easier as Germany grew smaller on the horizon.

I was leaving behind the land of my birth.

I was leaving behind my father.

I was leaving behind Samuel and his family all over again.

I stood on the deck of the ship, Simone swaddled in my arms, and hoped that we were headed toward a brighter future.

CHAPTER FORTY-THREE

Hanna

December 1939

A unt Charlotte stood in my room with me, Mila fussing about as I slipped into my white satin gown and prepared for my wedding. The inevitable day had come and there was no going back. I wondered about Tilde and baby Simone and how they were faring. If there was a just and merciful God, they were already in New York and out of harm's reach. I prayed that even if I would be bound to Friedrich forever, at least Tilde and the baby would have a chance to make happy lives for themselves.

Aunt Charlotte looked at me, appraising my expressions as she always did, so I tried to muster a small dose of enthusiasm to placate her. At least she could make some allowances for wedding-day jitters.

"You look so lovely, my dear. I'm so sorry your mother couldn't be here, but in my own selfish way, I'm grateful I get to take her place. I'll never have the chance to do this with my own daughter and I'm honored to be able to do it now."

I took Aunt Charlotte's hand. While Friedrich was certainly more her choice than my own, I knew she truly was doing what she thought was best for me. She'd been kinder than she ever needed to be, and I was ashamed to think of the times I wasn't grateful for her attentions.

"You've done so much for me, Aunt Charlotte. Today is going to be beautiful and you've worked so hard to make it so."

"Only the best for you, darling. I knew from the moment you arrived, you'd make us proud. There were times I doubted that along the way, but in the end, you've been a credit to all of us. I know your father is proud."

"I wish he could be here today. Certainly, his daughter's wedding is a reason to leave the shop in the hands of his assistants for a day or two." I wanted to be shocked at Father's refusal to come to the wedding, but I was not.

"The Rombauer men aren't known for their sentimentality, my dear. You can believe me on that score. Your uncle worked all morning before we were married in the afternoon. He'd have gone back to work, too, if I hadn't put my foot down. I think our honeymoon was the only time he's taken more than two days off work together."

"That sounds like Papa. Mama always begged him to come off with us to ramble in the woods or go fishing, but he could never be spared. Sad, really, don't you think?"

"Well, you must train Friedrich that working is not the sole purpose of life. The man is the head of the household, but the woman is not without her influence. We must simply be more subtle in our attempts to persuade them. Remind him that his health is of paramount importance to his family, and that rest is an essential part of staying fit in mind and body."

"I don't think Friedrich will be easily persuaded in anything, Aunt Charlotte."

"He's rather obdurate, I'll admit. But you'll find a way to make things work. You're a clever girl." She patted my head as if I were a schoolgirl, but I succeeded in not flinching at the gesture.

"I wish I had your confidence," I said.

"You have confidence in spades. I don't know what you're talking about, dear." She turned to the mirror to freshen her lipstick. Red, exactly the shade the Führer loathed, but Aunt Charlotte clung to a few of her liberties.

"Not when it comes to this. Part of me wonders if I'm not making a dreadful mistake. I don't think I can marry him." I spoke the words I'd been longing to say for months. I found my inhibitions slipping away in these final moments of freedom. It was my last chance to appeal to Aunt Charlotte's maternal instincts and hope she'd save me.

Her face turned to stone as she glared at my reflection in the mirror. "You have to put thoughts like that out of your head. If you allow them to take hold, you'll be miserable for the rest of your married life." She turned from the mirror to look at me as she twisted her tube of lipstick, clicked on the cap, and placed it in her handbag.

"Aunt Charlotte, I've tried, but I simply don't love Friedrich. He should be everything that I want, but he isn't."

"Oh, my dear, you may be all the happier for it. I didn't marry your uncle for love. It was hard at first, but we manage just fine nowadays. Friendly. Cordial. Far better than . . . well, less said the better."

"No, finish, Aunt Charlotte. I want to know what you were going to say."

"Your mother and father married for love, and it didn't end well for her." She couldn't make eye contact with me, but rather busied her hands by fussing with my dress, which was already draped as perfectly as could be hoped for.

"What do you mean? What does Mama's death have to do with it?"

"Well, it's better you know the truth now. It will save you pain later on. Your father adored your mother, but when he understood how risky her behavior was, he reported her to your uncle. They kept tabs on her for weeks and it was clear that she was still practicing medicine. And caring for gypsies and other unsavories at that. They had to take care of the problem."

"Take care of the problem? They told me she'd been in a car accident. You mean, they . . ."

"They did what was necessary to save your father's reputation and his business. Not to mention yours and your brothers'. I know you loved your mother, my dear. You're such a good girl at heart, but your mother's actions were dangerous and selfish. It's a blessing that you and the boys weren't tainted by association. If she had been a right-thinking woman, she would have seen what danger she was subjecting you to and done things very differently. It's all very sad."

"I can't believe you're telling me . . . my father is responsible for . . ."

"No, my dear. Your mother was responsible. She acted of her own accord and put you all at risk. No one is to blame but her."

I gripped the back of a chair to steady myself. "I just can't believe . . ."

"I should have told you sooner, perhaps. I just hope you learn something from your mother's story."

"Not to help others? Not to break the rules?"

"More precisely, that anyone, and I mean *anyone*, might be willing to turn you in to save their own necks. And anyone you care about could be taken down with you. Remember that before you act. I see your mother's rash tendencies in you from time to time. They're tempered by your docile nature, but they're there."

"So don't trust anyone?" I said. "Not Friedrich. Not Uncle Otto. Not even you."

"Darling, if it meant advancing my position in the party, I'd turn you in faster than the ink could dry on your warrant. And there isn't a person who wouldn't do the same."

I struggled to catch my breath. It was true, and I knew it down to the tips of my toes. I would never be safe again.

"I'd hoped people were better than that," I said, swallowing hard.

"Well, you're young yet. You have time to grow more and more disappointed in mankind."

"I suppose you're right about that."

"Come now, this is a fine conversation to have on your wedding day. All doom and gloom. I promise you, if you think less about yourself and more about what Friedrich wants, you'll have as good a chance at happiness as anyone. Not that it really matters in the end. It's too late to go back on your word. It's your choice to be happy or not, but you'll be married in either case. But you're the envy of every girl in Germany today. There has to be some comfort in that."

"Yes, Aunt Charlotte," I said, my voice as deadpan as it had been on my first days in Berlin when I hadn't known what to expect at her hand. She hadn't been cruel in the traditional sense, but in the end, she'd embodied everything my mother hadn't wanted for me.

But as Aunt Charlotte pointed out, it was too late to go back now. It was too late the day I arrived in Berlin, but I had no way of knowing that then. Each moment since I boarded the train in Teisendorf—

even before that; since the death of my mother—had led me to this moment. Aunt Charlotte had begun scheming to make me Friedrich's wife as soon as she learned I would be in her charge. If it hadn't been Friedrich, she would have found someone else, but he'd been the prize. Her objective from the very beginning had been to ensure her place in the Reich by delivering me to him. Friedrich would remember that she provided him with a "proper German wife" at the ideal moment and would reward her time and time again for her service.

Her plan was an unqualified success, and she was happy to sacrifice me at the altar of her ambition.

Uncle Otto appeared at my door, standing ramrod stiff in his uniform. There was no air of distinction about him. He more closely resembled a small boy being forced to wear a stiff collar to church on Easter Sunday than a man in service.

"It's time," he said gruffly. "They're all waiting for you."

"I've got to take my place, my dear. You do look radiant, and I truly am proud of you."

I didn't speak, worried that more might escape my lips than words. I simply attempted to turn the corner of my lips up in a smile that likely looked far more like a grimace, and nodded.

Uncle Otto walked me down the aisle of the municipal building. There were four little girls with candles guiding the way. A choir was singing, though the songs weren't the hymns of my youth. He offered me not a single pat of the hand or kindly gesture as he passed me off to Friedrich.

I stood to face the officiant and accepted that my future would never be of my own making. But to protect Tilde, Simone, Klara, my brothers—and other innocent people like Mila who would suffer on my account if I turned back now—I had no choice.

EPILOGUE

Washington, D.C., 1960

Hanna

Michael came up behind me as I sat at the vanity, putting the finishing touches on my makeup.

"Gorgeous as always," he said. "Though I think the occasion calls for a little something special."

He slipped a black box from his breast pocket and placed it in front of me. I opened the lid to see my worry stone—but made into a pendant and hung on a thick gold chain.

"When did you—" I began.

"I snuck the stone from your jewelry box two weeks ago and had it set for you. You don't use the stone nearly as much as you did. I was confident I could get away with it."

Michael clasped the necklace around my throat and rested his hands on my shoulders. The little pink stone, now entirely smooth, was hanging at the perfect length for my blouse. It was an unusual ornament, but it seemed I was allowed a few eccentricities. As a childless pediatrician no one much expected "normal" from me, and I was freed by that knowledge.

"I figured it was good for you to have a token from your mother with you today. A talisman against future worries."

I patted his hand. He was the kindest of men. When I arrived from Germany in 1946, I was a young widow scarred by a war and by a husband who had been every bit as cruel as I'd feared he would be. The biggest mercy of my life was that he was sent to the front soon after we were married. He fought for two years before he was killed, and rarely had leave to come home. I was allowed to escape my social obligations to the party and "grieve" for Friedrich in peace. In truth, I harbored a secret relief, and found new reason to go on with each passing day. I'd worried Aunt Charlotte would sweep in and whisk me back into "good society," but with the war reaching its fever pitch, I was largely forgotten. It was a gift grander than any I'd ever dreamed of. I used my new freedom to funnel what information I could to the other side. It was a risky business, but with Friedrich gone, the only life I was really risking was my own.

I remembered Klara's words at the dance—*"what about the others?"*—too clearly to let my own safety be of too much importance.

When we met, Michael recognized my pain and wasn't scared by my accent. He forgave me a past entwined with evil. He'd fought in the war as well and bore his own demons. He'd attended university on the GI Bill to become a psychiatrist so that he could help his fellow soldiers after the war. We met in medical school, where I was studying to become a pediatrician. He held me through my night terrors, and I held him through his. He understood about the worry stone and never mocked me for it. He asked me to tell stories about my mother and Teisendorf. He wouldn't tell many stories about his time in the war all that often, but would sometimes tell me about his comrades. I learned from the tone of his voice which ones had made it and which hadn't.

He told me more than most soldiers told their wives, though. He had told me it was because I'd lived through the war firsthand, too, and that I knew something of his pain. The women here in the States, those who hadn't served, had been spared the horrors that the women in Germany, France, and elsewhere had not.

My Michael was an angel on earth, and I thanked whatever luck had sent him to me every day.

"I'm happy she found you," Michael said. "I know how important this was to you."

"Thank you for understanding," I said. "You could come with me."

"You should do this alone. I can meet her another time."

He bent down and kissed my cheek. "I'll drive you so I have an excuse to take you out in town tonight."

He let me ride in peace to the restaurant, knowing when I needed silence as well as when I needed to hash things out.

The restaurant was a classic upscale affair downtown just south of Dupont Circle. If you stayed long enough, you'd see every congressman you'd ever hope to see. I still was uneasy with city life, but I did enjoy the political energy of the city. In a way it was comfortable hardly anyone you saw was "from" D.C., they were all transplants like me. But I did long for the peace of the country-side and begged Michael to retire to some remote hamlet once our careers had come to their conclusion. He made lavish promises of a picturesque house with a wraparound porch on a lake, and I believed each and every one of them.

I recognized Tilde immediately. The twenty years since our last meeting hadn't changed her that much. She had a few gray hairs and a few lines around her eyes, but there was no mistaking her.

Her eyes sparkled with recognition, too, perhaps making a similar assessment of me. I felt like I was a different human altogether from the one who had delivered her baby in the caretaker's cottage on Schwanenwerder Island, but perhaps not all that much had changed on the outside. It was all on the inside.

Tilde

I fidgeted in the little waiting area at the front of the posh restaurant where Hanna's husband had made our reservation. I preferred the homey Italian kitchens and lively delicatessens of Brooklyn to this elegant wood-paneled restaurant with the starched white linens, which seemed of another world. Despite the ice-coated butterfly wings in my stomach, I knew Simone was right. It was past time to search for Klara and Hanna. I spoke of them as though they were family and so often speculated about how they were doing. It was easier than talking about Samuel.

I'd been on the point of searching for the pair of them a dozen times in the fifteen years since the war ended. It hadn't taken long to find Hanna. She was a prominent-enough physician; she had connections all along the East Coast. When I saw her walk into the restaurant, I recognized her immediately. She was no longer the scared little rabbit being fitted for clothes for a marriage she didn't want. She was a fully grown version of the girl who had delivered Simone and risked her life to do it. In those moments, she had been strong and capable, despite what the world had told her. We shook hands and allowed the maître d' to take us to our table, secluded toward the back. Hanna's husband, much like her, had efficiently seen to every detail.

"I'm so glad you were able to meet me," I said without much preamble. "I've always wanted to know what happened to you."

"Well, after Friedrich was killed, I stayed for a while. I did what I could to get information to the other side. It was a small effort compared to what Klara did. It was nothing like enough. But it was clear that the Germany my mother loved no longer existed. Maybe it never did. I wanted a fresh start, so I came here."

I'd been able to find out that her first husband—that Nazi who had gazed at me so coldly—had died, and felt no grief at the news. Nor, it sounded like, did she.

She looked distant for a moment, then focused back on me. "I suppose little Simone isn't so little?"

"No, she's studying at Columbia. Hoping to start law school next year. Following in my footsteps." I produced my wallet, which was replete with pictures. My law practice kept me busy, and my mother had warned me that I'd never see my children, but I'd managed to balance my career and the children with more than a little grace. It didn't hurt that my Benjamin was a doting father not only to the son I'd given him but the daughter I brought with me.

"You sound more than a little proud of that. And well you should be," she said. Her expression was wistful.

"I won't deny it. And her little brother, Levi, will be starting at NYU in the fall. It doesn't seem like so much time should have passed." It was trite; all mothers want to cling to their babies, but after what I'd lived through, I knew how precious life was. Hanna's experience had been different, but she'd seen enough to at least understand a fraction of how I felt.

"It sounds like you took my advice to heart. I'm so glad you've found happiness."

"I knew I'd be a lawyer if given half the chance, but I didn't think I'd have a second chance at love. But fate had other things in mind. I'm rather glad of it."

"Me too," she said. "I didn't think I deserved it. For the longest time I was convinced I deserved to live alone. It took a long time for Michael to convince me to forgive myself for not having done more to save innocent lives. The war was hard to live through, but the aftermath was worse. When we saw the pictures from the camps. The number of people killed. Their names. And I was in the thick of it. It wasn't just killing, it was genocide."

"You did the best you could under the circumstances you were given. And you had a hand in saving me and Simone. That must count for something."

"I certainly hope it does."

"Do you know what happened to Klara?" I asked, finally getting to the question that burned under the surface. "I tried to find you both, but my searches for her never yielded much."

"About two years into the war, she went missing. I caught wind that she'd been funneling information to the other side, much like I was doing, but on a much grander scale. Unfortunately, she got caught and Ernst wasn't as loyal as I'd pegged him to be. I don't know much more than that. She came up on the lists as presumed dead. I've no reason to think they were wrong."

"You came up with more than I did, then. I feared that was the case but didn't want it to be true." It didn't seem fair that such a sweet and vivacious creature was taken so early, but in my heart, I'd known it to be the truth.

"So much was destroyed at the end of the war, it would have been much harder to find out what happened after the fact. But if it makes any difference, I know she thought of you. She mentioned you the very last time we spoke. Spring of forty-two. We were at some official dinner hosted by one of Friedrich's horrid friends. She and I were both leaking information to the Allies by then and probably looked as comfortable as mice in a cat's den. Of course, I didn't know why she seemed so out of sorts at the time, but it only makes sense. If I'd known it was the last time I was going to see her, I would have said so much more."

"Isn't that always the case?" It made me once again grateful I'd had so much time with my mother at the end. She'd known enough heartbreak in her life that a peaceful death seemed like the least life could offer her. I'd have preferred another twenty years with her, but that wasn't meant to be. We'd had almost eighteen years together in Brooklyn before the cancer took her, and it was an incredible blessing by itself.

"Simone wants to see the cottage where she was born," I said. "I had planned to keep the whole story from her. I wanted her to grow up American, but she has a beguiling way of ferreting out the truth."

"Will you take her?" I asked.

"I'm not sure I can face it," I said honestly. "I promised myself

I'd never have to go back. But I don't want to deny her the chance to understand her past, either."

"I don't blame you." Clouds passed over Hanna's eyes for a moment, but she snapped back to the conversation. "I never thought I'd go back to that school," she said. "But I suppose it never leaves you."

"'Motherhood is our sacred duty,'" I said, quoting Klara's snippet from her lectures. "'It is not a burden or an unpleasant task, but the very reason for which we were born.'"

"Lord, does that bring back memories. Maybe that's why I've been such a workhorse. I'm making up for failing at my purpose for living, after all."

"Stuff and nonsense," I said, glad there was a glint of sarcasm in Hanna's eye.

"Let's take her," Hanna said, though I now knew we would be facing a past we both desperately wanted to forget. "And remember Klara.

"Klara was a good friend to both of us. It's funny how she knew us both so well, but we never really got a chance to know each other. In a fairer world, she'd be here with us to gossip over lunch," Hanna said. "I wish we'd all been friends before. It seems a shame."

"It does. But I'd like to think she'd be happy to know we're here together," I said. "And to know that Simone is well and healthy."

Hanna reached her hand across the table and placed it on mine. "If it's possible, I know she is. She saved us both."

And so, Hanna and I raised a glass to Klara's memory with a wish that she could somehow know the gift she had given us all.

ACKNOWLEDGMENTS

As always, this is one of the most exciting and humbling parts of writing a book: thanking everyone who helped bring it about. It seems especially important to thank all the wonderful people involved in the creation of this book, as most of us were working under less-than-ideal conditions (you know, locked down in our homes during a global pandemic and all) for the majority of the time that this book was written. All our jobs were made harder, and I feel even more grateful for the support and love I received during the writing of this book.

- Always first on the list, my rock star of an agent, Melissa Jeglinski. She's always willing to boost me up when I need it, read pages at a moment's notice, and advocate for me and my books with the passion her job requires.

- My marvelous editor, Tessa Woodward, for being such a huge cheerleader for this project, and for me at William Morrow. I am honored that you chose to share your vision and expertise with Hanna and Tilde (and me). Looking forward to many more projects together!

- Alivia Lopez and the rest of the William Morrow team who helped bring Hanna and Tilde's story to the readers. You're amazing, and I appreciate all you do.

- The Tall Poppy Writers, as always, for being such a pillar of strength to me as I navigate this crazy business.

- My writerly family: Heather Webb, Andrea Catalano, Rachel McMillan, J'nell Cieselski, Kim Brock, Kate Quinn, Jamie Raintree, Katie Moretti, Jason Evans, Gwen Florio, Orly Konig, Sonja Yoerg, David R. Slayton, Todd Leatherman, and so many others. You make the journey a lot less lonely.

- My dear friends Stephanie, Carol, Todd, Danielle, Katie, and Gil, thank you for being my lifeline this year. Thank heaven for Zoom trivia nights and masked porch visits! (Also, the people in the above category deserve double credit here, too.)

- To all the wonderful online reader groups, Bloom with Tall Poppy Writers, Friends and Fiction, Blue Sky Book Chat, Reader's Coffeehouse, A Novel Bee, Bookworms Anonymous, Great Thoughts Great Readers, The Romance of Reading, My Book Friends, Women Writers Women's Books, Baer Books, Susan's Reading Neighborhood, and the tireless readers and authors who run them, I am so thankful for your support.

- Mom, Dad, Katie, Maggie, and the entire Trumbly-Petersen crew (and all the offshoots) for decades of love and support.

I'm eternally grateful for all you've done and continue to do for me.

- My new family: Maureen, Jay, Molly, Matt, Jonah, Glenda, Charlie, Monica, David, Linda, Gary, and Melissa, and all the rest of the clan for welcoming me so warmly. I'm so glad to be a part of the family.

- Charlie, Glenda, and Jay (again) for the hard work and tremendous skill you put forth in building our home library. A thing of beauty really is a joy forever. I'm so grateful to you!

- Maureen and Jay (again) for all the hospitality while this book was being written. Your loft was the birthplace of many of the scenes from this book, and I so appreciate you sharing your home with me as I raced to meet deadlines. Thank you for making me feel like a daughter.

- JijiCat, for being the most loyal editorial assistant imaginable. I could not have written this without you at my feet or on my desk. Give me back my chair, though. And to Zuri, for being a great source of entertainment for all of us.

- Ciaran and Aria. It's been a challenging couple of years that threw more curve balls at us than I could have ever imagined, and you're emerging out the other side as amazing young people. I admire your resilience and your fortitude and feel privileged to be your mother.

- My darling Jeremy. Our relationship bloomed as this book was crafted, and I can see that love and optimism in these pages. Thank you for believing in me. Thank you for boosting me up when I'm down. Thank you for sharing your research expertise. And, most of all, thank you for teaching me to believe in second chances. I am so proud to be your wife.

- And last, to all the readers who have read, enjoyed, reviewed, and reached out to me with your kind words for my work. You're the reason I get to keep doing the job I love. With all that I am, I thank you.

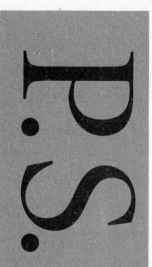

Insights,
Interviews
& More . . .

Meet Aimie K. Runyan

Kaitlyn Hval

AIMIE K. RUNYAN is a multipublished and bestselling author of historical fiction. She has been nominated for a Rocky Mountain Fiction Writer of the Year award and two Colorado Book Awards. She lives in Colorado with her wonderful husband and two (usually) adorable children. ᙗ

Author's Note

The origin of *The School for German Brides* was unique for me in that it's the first of my books that was inspired while researching for another novel. While writing *Across the Winding River*, I came across articles concerning the *Reichsbräuteschule*, the Reich's bride schools, and was appropriately horrified. The idea of a six-week program whose focus was teaching women how to instill Nazi propaganda into the minds of their young children immediately gave me images of an even more sinister version of *The Stepford Wives*, and I couldn't quite wrap my head around what the experience would have been like. I mention the bride schools briefly in *Across the Winding River*, but not in the detail I wanted because, while she was a central figure in the book, sweet Metta was not a main character. In many ways, Hanna's story is a variation of what might have been Metta's story if things had gone differently for her.

Another piece of research that I kept ruminating over was an article about teenagers in Berlin in the early 1940s and their attitudes toward the war. Like Hanna and Klara, they find the political machinations of the adults around them boring and not fully applicable to their daily lives. As Hanna and Klara grow from late adolescence into young ▶

3

Author's Note *(continued)*

womanhood, they learn the hard truth
that no matter how much you might
wish to abstain yourself from them,
politic affects every member of the
society they have influence over. So
many teens in Berlin, especially early
in the war, just longed for normalcy
in their teen years and an end to the
tedium of war talk and the annoyance
of rationing.

But of course as time went on,
these Berlin teens noticed their Jewish
neighbors were disappearing. They
noticed their communist neighbors
were missing. Homosexual, disabled,
immigrant neighbors, taken in a trickle,
then a torrent. It was easy for these
teens to say, "Well, at least it wasn't me
or my family," and move on. But that
attitude, especially as the teens transition
to adulthood, becomes complicity.
Because the Nazis weren't coming for
them, it wasn't their problem. In reading
the shockingly blasé narratives of those
German high school students from
the 1940s, I thought back to my days
as a high school French teacher and
wondered if my students would have
responded much differently. My
conclusion was that while many might
be concerned about the disappearance
of their neighbors and others might be
indifferent, the vast majority would feel
helpless to affect any real change.

But is that an excuse?

It was in the midst of these musings that Hanna emerged. In many ways, she is the victim of tragic circumstances and bullied into bad situations by her callous family, but she comes to recognize her own complicity in the regime she was being swept into. The same goes for Klara, who is just desperately trying to find some measure of acceptance from a family who cares only for brokering for a higher status. My goal was to create two young women who were swept up in the all-encompassing transition from childhood to adulthood under these extraordinary circumstances. Would they do the right thing, or would they be concerned only for themselves?

Of course, not all teens and young adults in the late 1930s in Berlin had the privilege of balking at the tedium of the war and longing for a return to happier times.

Other people their same age were fighting to survive.

Enter Tilde. Given her status as a first-degree *Mischling*, or half-Jew, she was in a precarious state for years before the story begins. She has significantly fewer options than Klara and Hanna but rallies to maintain and use what agency she can. Tilde doesn't have the luxury of a prolonged adolescence or the protection of a powerful family. She is left in a situation that couldn't be much more dire, and little by little, ▶

Author's Note *(continued)*

her layers of protection are taken away. If she is to survive, she may have to seek some help from others, but ultimately, she will have to be the one to liberate herself.

Tilde is a strong woman, forced to be stronger than she ever should have been asked to be. We see her face her own demons time and again, but she refuses to let them win for the sake of her mother, her husband, her daughter— and herself. What I find remarkable is that even in her darkest moment, she never wavers in her devotion to doing the right thing for the people she loves. I've written few characters I admire more.

Hanna and Klara are certainly complicit, despite their efforts to help Tilde and, later, to funnel information to the allies. They aren't intended to be "Good German Saviors," but rather, they're real girls in the first throes of womanhood who have the chance to do some good and manage to make a handful of right decisions even though the selfish ones would have been more expedient. They aren't necessarily great people, but they show the capacity to do some good. And sometimes that can make all the difference in the world.

The bride school on Schwanenwerder Island was a real place. While bride schools were numerous up until 1945, this was the most elite of them, and reserved for brides of the highest rank. The villa where Hanna and Klara attend a dance is the real villa where the Final Solution was agreed upon just over two years later. I chose specifically to set the story a little earlier in the war to give Tilde a more realistic shot of escaping with her life, but I did want to allude to the future evil that would be decided upon in those rooms.

The Jewish owner of the French-language bookshop where Klara gets her illicit fashion magazines is based on a real woman, Françoise Frenkel, who barely escaped Germany with her life.

The rest of the characters are of my own invention, but I like to think their experiences mimic what many would have faced during the war.

Thank you so much for devoting the time to read Hanna and Tilde's story. It was an honor to write it for you.

—Aimie K. Runyan

Reading Group Guide

1. Beyond a tool for soothing anxiety, what do you think Hanna's worry stone represents? Does the fact that it's made of rose quartz have some symbolic value?

2. Maternal relationships play a huge role in the narrative of *The School for German Brides*. They range from mostly healthy to highly toxic. Which mother-child relationship did you find the most intriguing? How do you feel the mothers influenced the way their children react to stress and trauma in their lives?

3. Likewise, many of the fathers and father figures in this story are absent. How does this impact the characters and their growth?

4. Klara is a central figure, but not a main character. She floats between Hanna's and Tilde's worlds, and of course her own. What do you think her purpose was in the narrative? What did you think of her character overall?

5. The two main characters, Hanna and Tilde, spend very little time together throughout the course of

the book. Why do you think the author chose to keep them separated? Is there a deeper meaning at play?

6. Though wildly in love, Samuel and Tilde have a complicated start to their relationship. Do you think he was wrong to try to break things up so she wouldn't stay behind? Was she wrong to press him into marriage?

7. Samuel decides to leave his wife and unborn child to seek out the truth about his family. What do you believe his thinking was in this decision? Do you think he was justified or foolish? Why? How do you feel about Tilde's reaction to his departure and how her feelings about it evolve over the course of the book?

8. Numerous times, characters describe the bride school as luxurious and restful. Does that mesh with the way Hanna sees the building? What ambiance do you feel is evoked in the descriptions shown through Hanna's point of view?

9. How does Tilde manage to pull herself out of her grief and begin to plan for a life without Samuel? What are the signs that she doesn't expect him to come back? ▸

10. Do you think Hanna and Klara ever truly mend their relationship before the end of the story? Why do you think they seem so tightly knit at the bride school after so many months apart?

11. At Hanna's wedding, Aunt Charlotte offers her a dire warning. What were her motives? What do you think of the relationship between Aunt Charlotte and Hanna? How does it evolve over the course of the book?

12. Tilde interacts with her father in two separate scenes in the book. How does the father-daughter dynamic change between the two scenes? How does each character respond differently in the second scene than they did in the first?

13. In the epilogue, it's revealed that both Tilde and Hanna have led full lives. They pursued careers in their chosen fields, remarried, and carved their own paths. Why do you think the author chose to make Hanna barren? What is the deeper meaning? ❧

Discover great authors, exclusive offers, and more at hc.com.